The Travel Bug

Also by Sheila Norton

The Trouble With Ally
Other People's Lives
Body & Soul

The Travel Bug

Sheila Norton

PIATKUS

First published in Great Britain in 2005 by
Piatkus Books Ltd of
5 Windmill Street, London W1T 2JA
email: info@piatkus.co.uk

The moral right of the author has been asserted

A catalogue record for this book is available from the British Library

ISBN 0 7499 0736 3

Typeset by
Phoenix Photosetting, Chatham, Kent

Printed and bound in Great Britain by
William Clowes Ltd, Beccles, Suffolk

With thanks to my lovely daughters for sharing their own travel experiences with me; to the 'Quiz Biz Gang' for the fun in Amsterdam; and to Sue for the Australian info.

For Sue & Dave, Hope & Chris, and Michael

Chapter 1

June 2003: Heathrow Airport

'Don't cry. For God's sake, don't start crying. You'll have us all at it. We'll flood the place.'

Rachel gripped my hand harder, as if she was pressing on an acupuncture point somewhere in the middle of my palm that would freeze the tears before they rolled out of my eyes. Whoops, too late – there goes one, overflowing the dam and running down my cheek. It trickled into the corner of my mouth, and I put out my tongue to catch it, startled by its saltiness.

'Don't cry, Mum!' echoed Sophie, watching me, her face beginning to crumple.

She reached out and gave me another hug. We were supposed to have finished the hugging. We'd hugged at home before we set off for the airport. We'd hugged again while we sat in the departure lounge waiting for the flight to be called. We'd hugged some more when we arrived at the gate. Now, this had to be my very last hug. The last time I'd hold my daughter in my arms until she'd been all the way round the world, seeing things I'd never seen, taking risks I didn't want her to take, and come back a year older. I took a deep breath and held it, closing my eyes and savouring the sweet, clean, *young* scent of her.

Don't go! I wanted to say. *Don't go – don't get on the plane! Stay here with me! It's not too late!*

But you can't do that, can you. What sort of a terrible,

1

selfish mother holds onto her daughter at the departure gate when she's ready to go, upsetting her with overflowing tears and wishing horrible selfish things about flights being cancelled, passports not being in order, or all journeys to Australia being banned for female travellers under the age of twenty-one who are leaving their mothers on their own? No decent mother would be so self-indulgent as to beg her daughter to stay with her just because she was going to miss her.

'Don't go! I'm going to miss you too much!'

Rachel kicked my ankle. She was holding her own daughter Amy's hand loosely, smiling at her, waiting to let her go. Waiting for me to control myself so that we could both let them go.

'Don't make them miss their flight,' she told me gently. 'They have to go now. They *have* to, Maddy.'

Why? It's not fair! Why did they have to grow up? Why couldn't they stay at home, playing with their Lego and their Sindy dolls? Why wasn't that enough for them? *Why wasn't I enough for her?*

'Mum.' Sophie held me at arms' length and regarded me solemnly. 'I'll be back before you know it. Don't make it hard for me, or I won't want to go. I won't want to leave you.'

Then don't!

But I nodded and let my arms drop to my sides. She readjusted her rucksack, stooping slightly to accommodate its weight on her slim back, tucked her arm into Amy's and gave me a last, brave smile as they turned to go through the departure gate. Rachel grasped my hand again and we watched in silence as the two small, dark-haired figures in combat trousers, boots and fleeces disappeared out of sight.

'Bye!' I called out again at the last moment. 'Take care! Write soon!'

They didn't hear. But it didn't really matter. We'd said it all at least a hundred times.

2

We set our faces into expressions of determination – *if we concentrate hard enough, we won't cry* – and went for a coffee together in the airport café. I kept looking round, half expecting Sophie to come running up behind me.

'Surprise! We've decided not to go after all! Much more fun to stay at home!'

But no; they'd gone, really gone. By the time we got home from the airport they'd have taken off, and they'd be on their way.

'They'll be back soon,' said Rachel, swallowing hard as she stirred her coffee.

'I know.' I nodded. I sniffed into a damp tissue.

'And they've promised to phone, and e-mail, and write...'

'I know.'

We chatted about the girls' itineraries to pass the long drive home, reassuring each other all the time about the lovely long e-mails and phone calls we would get from Australia. It was going to be so exciting! We'd hear all about Sydney, and the outback, and the desert, and the Great Barrier Reef. Kangaroos and koala bears and everything! It'd be better, really, than having the girls at home with us, wouldn't it, with all those boring conversations about TV and boyfriends and new clothes...

'No! I *like* those conversations about shopping trips and who's going out with who!'

'I love talking to Amy about what's on telly,' admitted Rachel mournfully.

'I like sitting in the kitchen with Sophie, having a cup of tea when we both get in from work...'

'Going out to the pictures together, just me and her on a Sunday afternoon...'

'Getting a video and a takeaway, or looking at magazines with a bottle of wine and a box of chocolates...'

'Stop it – now you're making *me* cry! I'm trying to bloody drive, here!'

I lit a cigarette and turned to stare out of the window. It was raining. Bloody typical.

3

'Don't smoke in my car,' snapped Rachel.

Bloody typical.

Rachel Hamilton and I had been friends since our daughters started primary school on the same day, fifteen years before. I'd just moved to the area and didn't know anyone. When my Sophie and her Amy came out of the classroom holding hands at the end of that first afternoon, and we found ourselves walking out of the school gates together, it seemed the most natural thing in the world. Rachel had been widowed for just over a year, and was still coming to terms with the struggle of bringing up Amy and her little brother Simon on her own. Me, I'd been on my own since Joe and I split up when Sophie was only two years old – and I, at nineteen, hadn't been much more than a baby either. It wasn't quite so common then as it is now to be a single mum, so we naturally gravitated together and provided each other with help and support, like a new little family.

Of course, a lot of water had gone under the bridge since then. But we'd stayed friends, and so had the girls. When Sophie and Amy both decided not to go to university after their A-levels, bucking the trend, ignoring the fact that most of their friends were applying for degree courses, and instead found themselves jobs in London and started saving up for their Great Adventure, planning to earn enough to go off for a year to see the world, it was a relief and a comfort to us to know they'd be together while they were away. We were supposed to be providing relief and comfort to each other, too: that was the idea. The idea was, supposedly, that it was stopping our daughters from worrying about *us* while they were away.

'You won't miss me really,' Sophie had told me blithely only the day before they left. 'You've got Rachel.'

'Rachel doesn't live with me,' I reminded her, trying to smile. 'Thank God!'

Thing is, you see, Rachel and I might have been best

4

friends but sometimes I didn't think we were particularly compatible.

Take the gym, for instance. To me, the gym was a place of extreme punishment. You only go there because you think it does you good, probably in the same way religious penitents believe in wearing hair shirts, to suffer and feel better for it. To Rachel, the gym was a way of life and, like all obsessive believers, she was determined to convert everyone else to her particular religion. Especially me.

We were at the gym, in fact, a few days after Sophie and Amy left. We were trying to talk about the girls while we were on the bikes, Rachel cycling for England, and me giving the pedals the occasional half-hearted push and leaning heavily on the handlebars. Well, how the hell are you supposed to speak properly at the same time as you're using any of those devil's instruments of torture? I can't even grunt, never mind form any recognisable English words.

I wasn't really *worried* about not having heard from our daughters yet. Impatient, yes; anxious, yes, but not worried. I was reasoning that Australia is, after all, on the other side of the world and if it takes more than a day to get there on the plane, it's unreasonable to expect news to fly home very quickly, even given the amazing technological advances of the internet at our fingertips. On the other hand I was *beginning* to wonder whether maybe we should have heard by now. Maybe something had gone wrong. Maybe they'd missed their connection in Singapore, or lost their tickets, or had their passports stolen, or been arrested on suspicion of carrying drugs in their belly buttons – you hear all sorts of terrible things. Rachel was trying to reassure me. They'll phone tomorrow, she was saying. Or e-mail, yes, they'll definitely e-mail during the next day or so. Or we'll get a text message, just when we're least expecting it. Was my phone switched on now? In my sports bag, in my locker? Who knows, even now as we were speaking, gasping, on these bloody bikes, our phones could be bleeping with messages from the other side of the world. The wonders of modern communication! It might be tomorrow in Australia, but they could be sending messages from their yesterday and we could be receiving them today. Wasn't it amazing?

And as she pedalled faster and faster and waxed lyrical about how amazing it was, I dropped my hands from the handlebars, turned off the machine and staggered to my feet, grabbing my sweaty towel and bottle of water as I made for the door.

'Where are you going?' panted Rachel.

'To have a shower. And a drink. And go home.'

'Wait! Don't . . . I'll come with you. . .'

'No. Don't worry. I don't want to spoil your fun. I'll see you. . .'

She turned off her pedals and looked at me in concern.

'Are you feeling ill?'

'No. I'm just not in the mood.'

I watched her as she climbed up onto the cross-trainer and programmed it for ten minutes. At forty-five, Rachel was eight years older than me, but she'd always looked after herself. Not, you understand, in the way I always had – throwing good money at my body in the hope that it'd thank me for it – expensive clothes I couldn't really afford, creams and make-up designed to take years off my life, regular sessions at the hairdresser's for chemical warfare (auburn curls stop looking cute when you get to about thirteen years old – ever since then, my life has been a constant battle to straighten the curls and tone down the auburn). No, Rachel had always gone in for the healthy natural lifestyle bit. She was small, slim and fit, with shiny straight dark hair, and nothing much ever went into her temple of a body that wasn't organic and hadn't been screened for calories, fat percentages, additives and cruelty to dolphins. She rarely allowed herself to come into contact with any dangerous substances – including men – and what can I say? She looked great on it.

'Are you *sure* you're all right?' she sang out to me as she started the cross-trainer.

'Yeh. I'll phone you later, OK?'

'All right,' she said doubtfully, still looking worried. 'Only I want to do ten minutes on here and then another twenty minutes on the treadmill.'

'Sure. Whatever.'

She sounded like she was actually going to enjoy it. Like I say – best mates, but maybe not very compatible. Not very compatible at all.

'Don't panic,' said Tom later that night. 'It's early days yet. They've only just about got off the plane.'

'I know. I'm not panicking. I'll just feel happier once I've heard something, that's all.'

'Mothers!' he sighed, shaking his head. 'I'll never understand...'

'No!' I snapped, sitting up and switching on the bedside light. 'You *can't* understand so don't even try! You're not a mother, so what do you expect?'

'Hey, hey – calm down, don't bite my head off,' he said mildly, lifting his head slightly to watch me. 'What are you doing?'

'Putting the light on. Reading. I can't sleep.'

'Who said anything about sleeping?' he laughed quietly, snaking an arm across my stomach.

I closed my eyes and tried not to sigh. I thought about saying I wasn't in the mood. Despite all the years on my own, when I dreamed and fantasised about sex all the time and lived on my memories of it, the idea of reading a good book and drifting off to sleep sometimes appealed to me almost as much now as having a rampant session between the sheets. But sex was obviously one of the main reasons for Tom coming round and, even after two years together, I still fancied him like mad. Even if I *wasn't* particularly in the mood, I always changed my mind within a couple of seconds of him starting to kiss me.

However; an hour later I was still lying awake, while he was flat out on his back snoring, and I was still thinking

7

about Sophie and Amy and wondering what they were up to, and what I really wanted to do was to get up and make myself a cup of tea, have a fag, turn on the computer and check my e-mails again; but I knew Tom was right: I shouldn't be panicking yet. Perhaps they were just getting settled into a hostel somewhere. Perhaps they were jet-lagged after their long journey. Perhaps they couldn't find an internet place. Perhaps they'd lost their mobile phones. I picked up the pillow and gave it a good shake, threw myself back down on it and closed my eyes again, willing myself to get off to sleep. It was all very well for Tom – nothing ever stopped him sleeping. He never worried about anything apart from getting enough sex. I used to admire his stamina. I was wildly flattered by the way he wanted me so desperately, so often, so tirelessly, in so many ways and places and positions. I sometimes wondered whether he'd ever reach the stage when *he* wasn't always in the mood for sex . . . but I didn't like wondering that – because it would mean he wouldn't come round any more.

'Maddy?' Rachel's voice sounded anxious on the phone the next morning. 'Are you OK?'

'Hi, Rach. Why shouldn't I be?'

'Well, you *did* walk out of the gym in a strange mood yesterday. And you *did* say you were going to phone me.'

'Sorry. I forgot. Tom came round and by the time I'd cooked him some dinner. . .'

'Oh. I see.'

I could picture Rachel's mouth forming a strong line of disapproval. Rachel disapproved of Tom. She disapproved of the fact that he was married. She disapproved of him cheating on his wife to spend a couple of nights a week with me. She disapproved of the fact that he was supposed to spend those nights, when he was working away from home, in a hotel paid for by his company. Sometimes I thought she just disapproved of him because he was a man, but that was probably unfair.

8

'OK, I know I walked out of the gym but to be honest, Rach, I'm just a bit *bored* with it. Aren't you? Sometimes? Ever?'

There was a stunned silence. I felt like I might do if I'd just farted very loudly in church. *Bored* with the *gym*? Are we allowed to say that, these days? It's almost as daring as saying our favourite food is hamburger and chips or that we never drink water, can't stand the stuff and think it's much nicer to guzzle caffeine all day.

'Bored?' repeated Rachel as if it was a surprising new concept she couldn't quite get to grips with. 'But, Madd! You don't want to give up the fight, do you! If we want to keep a half-decent body we have to *work* at it!'

'I've got enough things to work at, thanks very much. I don't know about you, but I've got my work cut out just getting up in the morning.'

'Yes, well!' she retorted sarcastically, 'if you *will* shag someone half your age...'

'Don't exaggerate,' I replied calmly. I was used to her jibes about Tom's age. He was actually only a couple of years younger than me although sometimes I must admit it felt like he had the energy of a twenty-year-old. He'd never had kids to wear him out – that's what I put it down to.

'Well, I think you need to work out at the gym more than ever, if you're getting these sort of mid-life feelings...'

'Mid-life!' I retorted. 'I'm not anywhere near mid-life, thank you! I'm just pissed off.'

Actually I didn't realise I was pissed off until I said it.

'I'm pissed off, and I miss Sophie!'

I felt ridiculously like crying, now.

'Of course you do,' soothed Rachel. 'I know. I miss Amy, too. Come on, we'll both feel better when we get the first e-mail. Cheer up. Maybe we'll hear from them tomorrow.'

'I've sent text messages. She hasn't replied.'

'Me too.'

'She told me not to phone. Something about it costing her

a huge amount of money if she gets calls on her mobile while she's abroad. I don't understand it.'

'Me neither.'

'I've sent one e-mail already. I think I'll send another one.'

'We don't want them to think we're worried, though.'

'I know.'

I shrugged to myself. I didn't want to be worried. I didn't want to be the kind of mother who whinged on about being careful and not getting into dangerous situations, when obviously half the fun of Sophie and Amy's trip was going to involve facing the unknown, meeting dodgy people with strange accents, and weird animals that hopped along desert roads with their babies in carrier bags on their bellies. But Sophie was my only child. Not that she was really a child any more, of course. She and Amy were twenty years old and had been out at work for two years now. At her age I'd been married, had a baby, and become unmarried again. Even so, this was different – come on, I don't care how small you say the world is nowadays, how new and expensive your mobile phone is and how many tricks it does, Australia's a bastard of a place to get to if there's an emergency. And, of course, when your only child leaves home with just a backpack and the clothes she stands up in, emergencies are all you think about. Even before she left, I'd invented at least a hundred potential emergencies that could occur within the first week, and I needed some reassurance that some of them hadn't already happened.

That day, sitting at my desk at work, I spent far longer than I should have done composing another e-mail to Sophie. The end result was good (although I do say so myself) – bright and perky in its maternal cheerfulness, asking no questions, betraying no desperation, seeking only to hear one word in reply by way of confirmation that the girls had indeed arrived in Australia and that search parties and/or international police force mobilisation were not called for. I felt better already as soon as I hit the 'send' key. It'd only be a matter of time now before I got her reply.

'What are you up to?' asked Hilary, looking over my shoulder.

That's what I hated about working in that open-plan office. Everyone was so bloody nosy. If I wanted to have a quick go at my crossword, or photocopy a recipe out of a magazine, or catch up with my e-mails at work, I got every bugger in the place giving me the Spanish Inquisition about it.

'None of your business,' I said, closing Outlook and reopening the letter I was supposed to be working on.

Hilary's trouble was that she didn't have enough to do. She'd worked there for about half a century and (if you can believe a word she said) *in the old days* she used to practically run the place. As the supplies department of the local council got bigger and busier, and they got more and more managers instead of just the original one boss (supported by – you guessed it – Hilary), they needed more people like me to work for the new bosses, and over the course of time I think she practically became redundant. Either that, or she was so obsessed with watching what everyone else was doing, she'd forgotten what she was there for.

'Busy, are you?' I asked her sweetly without turning away from my screen. In its reflection I saw her scowl and move off to annoy someone else. I put the audio headphones back in my ears and returned to the dulcet tones of my boss, Nicholas P. D. Pleasant, dictating his letters.

Nicholas was OK. None of us actually knew what the P. D. stood for, but we nicknamed him 'Pretty Damn' – as in *Pretty Damn Pleasant*. That kind of summed him up. He wasn't cute. He wasn't sexy or gorgeous or exciting in any way, but he was nice enough. He didn't give me too much of a hard time, even when I forgot to put things in his diary, or when I sent the wrong letter to the wrong department. He didn't go into a testosterone crisis when I spilled coffee over things. Unfortunately, I seemed to be forgetting things,

11

sending things to the wrong people, and spilling things more and more. It was beginning to make me wonder why I ever thought it would be a good idea for me to become a secretary. Couldn't I have come up with anything else? There were quite a few other choices on offer when I left school, for reasonably sensible girls with half a brain in their heads and a handful of O levels. I could have been a librarian and given everyone the wrong books and charged the wrong people fines. I could have been a nurse, and fucked up people's drug regimes or spilt coffee on their bedclothes. The possibilities were endless, but I'd ended up here at the local council offices, making life difficult for poor Nicholas Pretty. Damn, who probably deserved some-one younger, prettier, and not in the grip of premenstrual forgetfulness.

'Heard from Sophie yet?' he asked as he signed the letters later in the afternoon.

'No.'

I'd checked my e-mails eleven times since I sent that one this morning. Nothing. I swallowed back a lump of increasing anxiety.

'I'm sure you will soon,' he said kindly, giving me a smile and handing me back the letters. 'And don't forget about the time difference, will you.'

Of course not. What sort of bloody idiot secretary would forget about the time difference? What sort of prat of a mother would check her e-mail in-box every half hour while her daughter was probably fast asleep in the middle of the night? Come to that, what sort of secretary becomes so obsessive about checking her e-mails every half an hour that her boss notices and feels the need to draw her attention to it? At this rate, I'd not only have a nervous breakdown, I'd probably lose my job too.

I went back to my desk and started sorting out my filing before clearing up to go home. As I picked up papers and sorted them into piles, I caught myself sighing. I actually stopped, mid-sigh, and suddenly it was like I'd risen out of my body (chance would be a fine thing) and I was looking down at myself sitting there in an inelegant slump, elbows on the desk, shoes kicked off underneath it, mouth turned down in an expression of – can that be *boredom*? – as I shuffled through papers that held no interest to me whatsoever beyond earning me the means to pay my bills, to say nothing of my hairdresser and my gym membership. At the thought of the gym membership, my eyes focused on the sports bag stowed under my coat hook next to my desk and for a moment I felt physically sick.

'Rachel?' I told her urgently on the phone two minutes later, 'I'm not coming to the gym.'

'Why?' she retorted immediately. 'Don't you feel well? Shall we go tomorrow instead?'

'No, listen. I'm not coming to the gym again – full stop. I'm stopping my membership.'

'Don't be silly, Maddy. OK, I know you said you were getting a bit bored with it, but you probably just need to change your workout slightly. Set yourself some new targets. Have you thought about increasing the speed on the treadmill?'

Have I fuck. If I'd increased the speed even one fraction of a degree I'd have had to step off the sodding thing completely and just stand there watching it doing its thing without me.

'How about increasing the effort level on the bike? It makes it much more of a challenge!' suggested Rachel enthusiastically.

'No. I don't want to increase anything. I don't want a challenge. I know you're trying to help and I really appreciate your efforts on behalf of my flab, but honestly, I'd rather live with it. I think I quite *like* flabby arms.' (I heard her gasp aloud with shock at this.) 'I don't enjoy the gym,' I went on relentlessly. 'I hate it. I don't know why I've taken so long to admit it. Sorry,' I added a little more quietly, suddenly noticing that Hilary and half the other people in the office were listening to me quite openly and trying to hide their smirks. 'Sorry for letting you down. Can we just go back to having a drink after work, like we used to?'

'We can have a drink on Fridays, if you like,' she said generously, after a pause for thought, 'but I really can't make it more often than that. I need to think about the calories in the alcohol.'

'Sod the calories!' I told her a bit impatiently. 'Have low calorie drinks, then, if it's so bloody important! Put your bike speed and your treadmill gradient up a bit more to work off the calories! Walk home from the pub!' *Get a life!* I felt like adding. But I didn't, because she was still my friend after all, despite her peculiarities.

By the time we met two days later for our one calorie-counted Friday drink, we'd both, finally, had e-mails from the girls. They were in Western Australia – Perth – and seemed to have been spending most of their time since arriving trying to sort out with their mobile phone company why their phones wouldn't work.

'After all that trouble we went to, to get them phones that worked on the Australian and New Zealand networks!' exclaimed Rachel crossly.

I raised my eyebrows and shook my head, having personally never had much faith in the very far-fetched concept of being able to communicate with such tiny phones over such huge distances. If they'd had something the size of a house-brick in their rucksacks I'd have been more prepared to believe it was going to work, but those things they'd taken with them were smaller than matchboxes. If you needed magnifying glasses to use them, how likely was it that they were powerful enough to phone home?

'Anyway, never mind. At least they've found somewhere to e-mail from. And they're having a brilliant time!' I soothed her.

Mostly, by the sound of it, drinking late into the night with other travellers they'd met at the hostel.

'Imagine the state of their livers by the time they're thirty,' commented Rachel predictably.

'Never mind that – what about this bit!' I pointed to a long paragraph in the printout of Sophie's e-mail.

Although it's winter here, the weather's still very warm at the moment so we've been checking out the nearby beaches. The waves are HUGE and there are loads of surfers – it's just like Home and Away! *The lifeguards are all gorgeous hunks in tiny Speedos! Amy and I ventured into the sea the other day and tried to swim, but when this huge monster wave headed straight for us we both panicked and started all this very girly screaming and squealing. A guy on a surfboard was shouting at us 'Dive through it!' but no, we to tried to race it to the shore and got knocked off our feet and half drowned in the process. When we finally surfaced on the beach, coughing and spluttering, my bikini knickers were round my knees and Amy's top was round her neck. How mortifying – especially as the lovely lifeguards were watching us very closely at the time ... In future we'll be staying on the beach.*

We sipped our drinks in silence for a minute.

'They nearly drowned!' I blurted out eventually, spitting white wine over the page.

'They didn't. The lifeguards were there, watching them...'

'Only because of their bikinis! Filthy little Aussie perverts, watching them because their knickers came off in the sea!'

'Maddy, the lifeguards were doing their job, watching them in case they needed help.'

'Yeah, I can guess what sort of help.'

'Look, if you're going to spend the entire time they're away worrying about every predatory male they meet...'

'What about *you*? *You're* worried about their livers!'

She shrugged.

'OK, I admit I don't like the amount they drink. But they're grown up now, Maddy. We have to let them get on with it. They could get kidnapped, raped and murdered just as easily in London as they can in Australia.'

'Well, that's really comforting.'

'Come on then – just this once let's have another drink.' She swallowed the last dregs of her low-calorie tonic and picked up our glasses, clinking them together. 'Same again?'

'Yes. Please. Sorry. I know I'm being pathetic.'

I lit a cigarette and watched her as she headed for the bar, elbowing her way resolutely through the crowds with her toned, non-flabby arms. How did she get to be so strong, so together, so sensible and disciplined and all the things I wasn't?

'You think too much,' said Rachel as she put the glass of wine down in front of me. 'You need to *think* less and *do* more. Get yourself so busy that you don't have time to worry.'

'I'd like to. I'd like to come out for a drink like this every night, to be honest, but you're usually too busy working up a sweat in that torture-chamber.'

'If you're serious about not coming back to the gym...'

'I am.'

'Then perhaps you should find yourself something else,' she added gently.

'What sort of something else?'

'I don't know. It's up to you. You just don't seem very ... well, don't take this the wrong way. But you don't seem very – you know – *fulfilled*, these days.'

Fulfilled. I kept saying the word over and over in my head all the way home, until eventually it began to sound strange and foreign. I opened the fridge door and stared inside, hoping for inspiration. The remains of a cheese and onion quiche stared back at me from its supermarket foil dish. That'd do. I opened a tin of baked beans and tipped them into a saucepan. *Fulfilled. Full and filled.* It was beginning to

16

have sexual connotations. I stirred the baked beans slowly, thinking about Tom, thinking about how fantastic it was when we first met – the electricity building up between us every time he called in at my office, making me shiver and shudder with desire until I became so desperate for him to touch me and kiss me, I could hardly speak. When we first had sex, I thought I was going to die from the pleasure and excitement of it. That was *fulfilment*, all right; I still felt it, too – when I was with him. But not that terrible sick, stomach-churning craving of love and longing I used to feel when we were apart. Now, I had to get on with my life while he was away from me. While he was happily getting on with *his* life with Linda, the wife he never talked about, the wife I never asked about, never worried about – never even felt guilty about. I sometimes wondered if there was actually something wrong with me; a congenital lack of conscience that stopped me caring about things that would have had nicer people tossing and turning in their sleep every night.

Before I knew it, the beans were stuck to the bottom of the pan. Shit. I never was any good at cooking – couldn't even heat baked beans without screwing it up. Perhaps I should join a cookery class, I smiled to myself as I spooned the least burnt beans over the cold quiche and put the saucepan in the sink to soak. Maybe that would give me some *fulfilment*. I took my unappetising dinner into the lounge and sat down to eat it while watching Jamie Oliver on TV. Things could only get better!

Chapter 2

Looking back, I'm mildly shocked at how mixed up I was then. How sad, how bored, how – all right, how *unfulfilled*. I'm not usually like that, you know. You might be surprised to learn that I'm normally quite an upbeat, optimistic type of person. The bottle is definitely half full most of the time, as far as I'm concerned, and what it's half full of is something very delicious and very calorific. I'm actually not the sort of person who cries herself to sleep, for instance, just because she misses her daughter and she's unfulfilled and Jamie Oliver makes her feel inferior with his quick neat knife movements and casual crushing of garlic cloves. I don't make a habit of crying at all, partly because it doesn't do your face any favours and partly because where does it get you anyway? Nobody notices you blubbing away into your pillow when you ought to be quietly getting on with your beauty sleep, and it doesn't change anything, so you might just as well shape up and get over it – whatever it is – without messing up the pillowcase. But that night in June, with Sophie's first e-mail on the bedside table beside me, and her photo smiling at me from its frame on the wall, I tossed and turned and snivelled a bit to myself, and thought a lot about fulfilment or lack of it, and woke up with a feeling of determination. Yes, I thought – looking in the mirror with regret at my red nose and swollen eyes – I was going to *do* something. It might take me a while to decide what it was, but it sure as hell wouldn't have anything to do with calorie counting, flab reduction, or any activity that made my arms and legs ache the next morning.

'Coming to the gym?' asked Rachel sweetly a couple of hours later while I was slobbing out in front of Saturday morning TV eating a bacon sandwich.

'Piss off. I told you. I've left.'

'I bet you haven't. I bet you haven't cancelled your membership yet. It always takes you ages to get round to doing anything.'

'Yeah, well. *Theoretically*, I have. In my mind, I've left.'

'Come just one last time? Please? Keep me company?'

'I know you, Rachel Hamilton. I know your game. You think you can get me back there under false pretences. You think if I come just one last time, that'll be it, I'll keep on coming.'

'Prove me wrong, then.'

How did that happen? I seemed to have lost the argument without even trying.

'Just give it one last try, today, and if you still want to give up, then at least you'll be really, really sure.'

'I'm really, really sure already,' I said, yawning. Even the thought of it made me feel knackered.

So there I was, without really understanding how it happened, back at that bloody punishment establishment again, struggling to maintain some sort of pretence at normal breathing while hanging on for dear life to the handles of a machine that was a cross between a combine harvester and a mediaeval torture device. Why? Why had I let her talk me into coming back here again? I absolutely hated everything about it, hated every minute of it. There was sweat running down my nose, dripping off my fringe into my eyes. I tried to get my towel off the handrail to wipe it away but I couldn't stay upright on the damn thing without holding on. I wobbled, lost my footing, grabbed the rail again and had a quick look around to make sure no one noticed. Luckily they were all too busy watching themselves in the mirrors or

19

looking at Destiny's Child singing their latest song on MTV. Thank God, my time was nearly up and I could get off this thing and never come anywhere near it again.

Press 'Enter' now for extra time.

You must be fucking joking. Extra time? Who in their right minds presses '*Enter*' for extra time, just as they're going into the final minute?

'How're you doing, Maddy?' asked Rachel's voice behind me.

'Bloody awful,' I panted, stumbling off the treadmill and swaying slightly as I waited for the floor to stop its usual trick of pretending to keep moving. 'I feel like I've broken both ankles and had a minor heart attack.'

'Is that all? That's OK, then. Shall we go for a full cardiac emergency and get on the cross-trainers?'

Don't even joke about it. Those things should be licensed for use by suicidals only. There have been moments, three minutes into a stint on the cross-trainer, when I've actually had serious thoughts about ending it all rather than finish the time or summon up the strength to turn it off. Always supposing I could find the right knob to turn it off.

'You go ahead,' I told her casually. 'I might just go and lift a few weights.'

Lifting a few weights was my euphemism for sitting at one of the weight machines having a quiet breather and wiping the sweat off. It looked marginally more acceptable than making a bolt for the bar and downing a couple of swift pints, which is what I really wanted to do. I turned to look at Rachel now, working calmly and tirelessly on the cross-trainer, and shook my head again with disbelief that I'd been talked into coming back here, after everything I'd said. I could be going for a nice leisurely walk in the fresh air instead. Even better, I could be sitting at home with my feet up, enjoying a cup of tea and a couple of chocolate digestives. Well, that was *it*! I'd gone along with Rachel's '*one last try*', and I hated the place more than ever. Never again! I was *definitely* terminating my membership! And I

20

was *not* going to be a pushover for anyone else any more! OK?

That Saturday night, Tom was in a particularly good mood.

'I'll cook,' he said, grabbing the frying pan out of my hand. 'Open the wine, Maddy, and we'll have a glass while the onion's browning.'

He said it with the sort of confidence I might just about have managed to ascribe to 'while the frozen pizza's in the oven'. He was crushing garlic into the pan, *à la* Jamie Oliver, whistling to himself, pouring pasta out of the packet into a saucepan of boiling water as if he knew by instinct how much to allow per person, instead of ending up with enough to feed the entire population of a small town the way I normally did. I poured red wine into two glasses and handed him one.

'Cheers!' he said, smiling at me through the steam from the frying pan. He sipped his wine. 'Here's to us.'

I raised my glass and my eyebrows at him. What was this all about, then?

'I got some good news yesterday.'

He turned back to the pan, shook stuff from a couple of my ancient dusty herb jars into it, gave it a quick stir, turned down the gas and then sat down with me at the kitchen table.

'Yeah?' My mind was working overtime. His wife had finally found out about us and didn't mind? She was quite happy for him to spend as much time with me as he liked, she'd give him a divorce and wouldn't make him pay through the nose?

'Yeah. I've got a promotion.'

'Oh!' I put down my glass and reached over the table to give him a kiss. 'Oh, Tom, that's great. Well done.' He deserved it. He worked hard, put in a lot of hours. He was his company's best salesman. 'So what's the new job?'

'Area manager – northern UK sales.'

'Wow. Sounds good. Sounds...' I met his eyes. For a minute or two, neither of us said anything. There was no

21

noise in the kitchen apart from the spit of the garlic and onions in the olive oil in the pan. 'Sounds very ... northern,' I finished softly.

'Yes,' he said, equally softly but still smiling. 'It is. Very.'

I smiled back at him. The smile was stretching my mouth slightly, making it feel tight and awkward as if it didn't quite belong to me.

'So what will this entail? This ... northern bit?'

'Oh, a lot of travelling, as you can imagine. Manchester one week, Belfast the next, Edinburgh the next ... fantastic opportunity. With luck, I'll be making as much in a week as I sometimes made in a month. I'll have to put in the hours, of course, and I'll be living out of a suitcase a lot of the time.'

I had to think very carefully about this, about how to react, how to express my feelings, my reservations, my sudden doubts and insecurities.

But, 'Where does that leave me?' I asked instead, without having thought carefully enough at all. 'You won't be able to do *this*, will you? You won't be coming round. This won't be part of your area any more. You won't be able to—'

'Hey, hey, hey!' He reached out, touched my cheek, gave me that look, the one that used to have me climbing the walls when I first met him. 'Don't panic. You won't get rid of me that easily. Don't you like the sound of Edinburgh, Maddy-baby? Wouldn't you like some weekends in Scotland, or Ireland? Hm? Eh?'

He was stroking my neck as he said this. It should have felt nice. It's supposed to make you relax, isn't it, and de-stress, and feel sensuous and physical, but it was just annoying me the way I'd feel annoyed by a fly settling on my skin. I brushed him off, crossly, almost knocking him off balance.

'And how's that supposed to work? How am I supposed to come to Scotland and Ireland and everywhere? I suppose I have to drop everything and fly out to stay overnight with you in some hotel, whenever you want me to?'

I didn't mean it to come out like that. I felt a pang of regret as I saw his eyes narrow and his frown deepen while he sipped his wine. He got up and stirred the pan again.

'Would you not *want* to drop everything? To come and see me?' he asked calmly, with his back to me.

Drop everything? How feeble that sounded. What did I have to drop? My gym membership? My calorie-controlled evenings at the pub with Rachel?

'Well, there's my job to consider.'

'Of course. But maybe it wouldn't be too difficult to get time off occasionally? Maybe you could look into it?' He turned to face me again. '*If* you want to, of course.'

I gulped most of my wine in one go before I answered. Of course I wanted to. I was just being awkward, making diffi-culties, because this was all such a surprise, and I was going to miss him, and he didn't seem to have considered the effect this would have on me.

'I'm going to miss you,' I said, at length, getting up. He put his arms round me and rested his chin on the top of my head. 'It won't be the same – I'll miss you coming over like this.'

'I know. But we'll find a way. And this is such a good opportunity...'

Of course it was. I didn't want to ask what his wife thought about the new job. Maybe she'd be getting expenses-paid trips to Edinburgh and Belfast too, and he'd have to ration us to alternate weeks and use different hotels for us both so the staff didn't find it strange and call us by the wrong names. I ate my pasta very slowly and eventually pushed my plate away with the meal only half finished.

'I don't seem to have a lot of appetite,' I apologised.

He didn't comment.

I poured out some more wine and lit a cigarette and watched him as he started the washing-up, giving the occa-sional little cough to remind me that he disapproved of my filthy habit.

Nothing else to do afterwards but go to bed.

*

'You ought to think seriously about giving up,' said Rachel the next day. She'd cooked Sunday lunch for us both and once again, I was skiving off helping with the washing-up while I had a fag.

I shrugged, took another drag and ignored her. She'd been on my case about giving up smoking for half my life. It was just another facet of her healthy keep-fit lifestyle as opposed to my slobby lazy degenerate one.

'I mean it,' she added a bit more severely, turning to frown at me. 'You have *no idea* what it's doing to your lungs.'

'Not as much harm as the cross-trainer was,' I retorted mildly. 'I felt like I was gasping my last breath by the time I got off that bastard.'

We both laughed and she shook her head at me, a despairing sort of shake like she might have done when one of her pupils was failing completely to grasp a concept of elementary physics.

'So what are you going to do?' she asked, changing the subject. 'About Tom?'

I'd just finished telling her about his new job.

I shrugged again and drained my coffee cup. Over its rim I could see Rachel staring back at me. I couldn't read her expression but I suspected it was the Teacher face again and, just for a minute, I felt mean and almost guilty about the way I ignored all her concerns for me. I knew I caused her a lot of anxiety. I knew she disapproved of almost everything I did. I knew my life was given over in fairly large segments to alcohol, cigarettes and illicit sex, a diet of junk food, coffee, and crap cooking, to say nothing of my refusal to walk anywhere. But at least I was happy, wasn't I. I had everything I wanted from life – Sophie... Tom...

'I'm going to miss him,' I admitted, putting my cup down heavily. 'I can't believe he's doing this to me. Especially not now, with Sophie away.'

'He's not doing it to *you*. He's doing it because it's something good for *him*. Him and his wife,' she added pointedly.

There was no need for that, was there? Bitch.

'Sorry, Maddy, but it's true, isn't it? He isn't considering you at all, here. Why should he? He just expects you to fall into line – not to complain, not to make a fuss, and just run after him wherever he goes – whenever he clicks his fingers.'

Well, that was telling me, wasn't it? I couldn't answer. What was going on here? I thought we were best friends. We'd never had a row – not a real row, anyway, only the occasional little bicker about silly things like that time Sophie tore up Amy's homework or the day I borrowed Rachel's black trousers and got a cigarette burn on them. Normal little things like that, nothing to really threaten a friendship. Now she suddenly seemed to feel it was OK to talk to me as if I was a slow pupil in a physics class.

'Maybe I should go,' I said curtly, getting to my feet.

'No need to be like that...'

'Well, yes, I think there is, actually.'

'Just because I've hit a nerve.'

Hit a nerve! What a bloody nerve!

I was shaking as I carried my cup over to the sink. The dregs of cold black coffee slopped over the neutral territory of worktop between us.

'Let's not argue,' she said, grabbing a cloth to mop it up.

'Well, what do you expect? How do you think that makes me feel, all that about Tom clicking his fingers and me running after him? I know you don't like him but he cares about me. He wants me to be with him!'

'Yeah. OK, OK, I'm sorry,' she tried to soothe me. But for some reason it just made me feel worse.

'You think I've got no self-respect! You think I've got no life!'

'Is that what *you* think?' she returned, infuriatingly.

'Well at least I've *got* a man, someone to love me, someone who wants to have sex with me. At least I'm not lonely, bitter and frustrated!'

I felt terrible as soon as I'd said that. Although, to be quite frank, I did think it was true about her being bitter and frustrated.

25

'If you met someone yourself, you wouldn't be like this about Tom,' I added, making it worse.

'You're probably right,' she said, her face completely expressionless. 'Maybe *I* just need a good shag. Maybe *I* should pop up to Manchester or Glasgow and spend the odd night with Tom myself.'

'Oh, very funny. And our relationship is *not* just about sex.'

'No, of course not. The only reason he wants you to drop everything and spend odd nights in hotels with him is so you can discuss world peace and the price of eggs together.'

Drop everything. That phrase again.

'I haven't got much to drop,' I said thoughtfully, my anger evaporating. I picked up the tea towel and started wiping the plates. 'Only my job. But to be honest, I quite like the idea.'

'What idea?'

'Dropping everything. Don't you? Doesn't it appeal to you – giving everything up and just ... going off? A bit like Sophie and Amy have?'

'You'd never manage to carry a backpack.'

'No, all right, I don't suppose I'd like sleeping in a hostel with twenty other people's sweaty bodies either. But just heading off – with no responsibilities. No ties. Nothing to get up for in the morning if you don't want to. No housework to do.' I sighed. 'I wish we'd done all that stuff when *we* were young. Don't you?'

'Maybe. Yeah, I'd like to travel. I've only ever been to Spain and Tenerife. Package holidays. You only see the hotel pool and go on the tourist coach trips. I'd like to see more of the world, yes, explore some more different places before I die!'

We stared at each other wistfully for a moment.

'Maybe we're just missing the girls,' I said.

'Yeah. Maybe we're just jealous of what they're doing.'

'Yeah. And getting old, and silly.'

'Speak for yourself!' she retorted, and we both laughed with relief that the moment had passed – the moment when I

26

felt like walking out on her, and she'd probably have been glad to see me go. After all, who wants a selfish cow of a friend who sits smoking and guzzling caffeine at your kitchen table refusing to help with the washing-up after you've cooked her roast lamb and three veg? But those few angry moments had left me feeling a bit shaky. If I fell out with Rachel, who else did I have?

One thing I *did* have, whether I liked it or not, was my job at Brentwood Council – and its continual supply of dictation tapes full of letters and requisitions for supplies of stationery, toilet paper, filing cabinets and office sundries. I could type those letters with my eyes shut. Picture me, if you will, on this particular sunny Monday morning – the twenty-third of June. I probably had my eyes shut then. I didn't need to look, you see, because I might have been a crap secretary who spilled coffee over things and forgot messages and double-booked meetings, but what I *was,* was a bloody good, highly skilled, word-perfect touch typist. I could prob-ably have won Touch Typist of the Year Award if I could have been bothered to enter for it. And if there was one.

Not like the kids today. They're using computers from about nine months of age. They're still in nappies. They're running around in baby walkers, sitting in high chairs, with keyboards on the tray in front of them, bashing away at the keys before they can even talk. But can they touch-type? Can they fuck as like. I've met smart kids working in the City, working for big banks in their IT departments, who know more about the insides of computers than I know about the inside of my kitchen cupboards, but ask them to type something for you and off they go, two fingers, looking from the keys to the screen and back at the keys again, searching for the J and the C as if someone had moved them since the last time they used them.

And as for speed, I was very proud of my speed, too. I could type faster than Nicholas Pretty Damn could dictate. I'd have his voice plugged into my ears and I'd be waiting for him to catch up with me half the time. I could have just rushed ahead and finished his letters for him. I could have made them up – he'd probably never have noticed. Those letters were so boring, he must have been half asleep while he was dictating them.

'I would be very grateful if you could give this matter your most urgent attention,' was his standard closing line. That day in June, the only things requiring my most urgent attention were my anxieties about Sophie and Amy, who even as I was churning out those letters had now (according to the copy of their itinerary that was Blu-tacked to my kitchen wall) flown from Perth to Alice Springs and should be starting off on a three day tour out into the desert, where people die of thirst, or get murdered by passing weirdos or eaten by wild dogs. And of course, my anxieties about Tom and whether I was going to be dropping everything to rush off to Liverpool and Belfast whenever he asked me to, whether I wanted to or not. And did I want to? Or not?

'I've finished these letters,' I told Nicholas P. D. as he walked past my desk on his way to the coffee machine.

'That's great. Well done,' he said.

That was why I liked him, you see? He always made it sound as if I'd achieved something brilliant, close to miraculous, every time I'd finished typing his letters. If I didn't know him better I'd think he was being sarcastic, but he wasn't. He was genuinely impressed with my speed and my accuracy, and who could blame him? He must have been chuffed with his luck that he got me as his secretary when he started working there.

Strange that just as I was thinking this, he suddenly came out and said it. He'd never said anything like it before. It was a bit spooky. I was in his office, waiting while he signed my perfectly typed letters (no coffee stains that day), and he looked up at me and asked about Sophie again, just being polite really I suppose, asking whether I'd heard from her again and whether she was OK, and while I was mumbling

28

on about getting murdered in the desert or being eaten by dingoes, he suddenly interrupted me:

'You mustn't worry, Madeleine. It won't do her any good, and you'll just make yourself ill.'

'Will I?' I stuttered, taken by surprise. 'I mean … no, I won't. I won't get ill.'

'Good. After all, where would I be without you? Mm?'

Just as I was wondering whether this was some sort of official warning about not taking time off sick, he smiled at me and added, so quietly I had to lean closer over his desk to catch it:

'I'd be lost without you.'

And then I regretted leaning so far over the desk, because I was suddenly aware that my top, which had a fairly modest V-neck when I was in a normal upright position, afforded a view so far down my cleavage when I was leaning over someone sitting opposite me that he could probably see right down to my belly button. I straightened up, quickly, but not before I'd seen his eyes shift down to my V-neck and back again. And not before I'd clocked the expression in his eyes.

This was so shocking, I couldn't think of a single word to say. I mean, Nicholas had never said or done anything remotely sexual in his life! Well, presumably he had, you know, with his wife, in his own time, but certainly not in the office, not even when those young girls from Marketing came along in their short skirts and their tight tops and their fuck-me smiles. He'd always seemed about as sexual as a dead fish.

'Right!' I blustered, grabbing my file of letters off his desk and heading for the door. 'Right, well, yes, thanks!' I stumbled backwards out of the door, shut it, leant on it and took a couple of deep breaths before I noticed Hilary and at least four others watching me curiously.

'Better get on!' I announced to nobody in particular, and walked shakily back to my own desk where I plonked myself heavily down on my chair and typed furiously until everyone had given up and stopped staring at me.

29

a s d f g ; l k j h a s d f g ; l k j h a s d f g ; l k j h a s d f g ; l k j h What was that all about? Was I imagining it? Was he coming on to me? What the. . .

'Who? Was who coming on to you?'

'Piss off, Hilary.' I deleted as fast as I could. 'This is private.'

'Writing private letters in work time, eh?'

'Yes.'

She'd have liked it better if I'd tried to argue but I wasn't in the mood.

'Going for a break,' I told her sharply.

Outside in the car park was the only place where we could smoke. I knew all the other smokers in the council offices by first name. We were a happy, friendly group, bound to each other by our guilty, dirty little habit, but that morning I was out of sync with the others because I was taking my fag break a bit early. I was on my own out there. I leant against the wall and took a few deep drags and turned my face up to the sun. It was hot, very hot, and coming out of our air-conditioned office it felt like stepping into a sauna. I found myself thinking that this must be how hot it was in Australia, but then I remembered it was winter over there. Probably still hot in the middle of the country where the girls were now, though, and then they'd be going on to Melbourne. Would it be warmer in Melbourne than Perth, or colder? I really should have a look at a map. Or look it up on the internet. I'd do that when I went back into the office. Hadn't got much else to do.

The door opened behind me. I looked round and it was Nicholas P. D. He'd followed me out there.

'I just wanted to say. . .' he began, looking uncomfortable.

This was like a bad dream. I couldn't believe it was happening.

'Just that I hope you weren't offended.'

'No, er, no – of course not – I, er. . .' Shit. I stubbed out my cigarette and looked at my watch, tried to look as if I really ought to be getting back to work.

'Not that I didn't mean it – I did. I think you're ... well, you know I think you're the best secretary ... and I would, you know, I do think I'd miss you, if you weren't here I mean, and I consider myself very lucky to have you – well I mean not to have you, not in that sense, not that I wouldn't ... you know! Ha ha! If you know what I mean ... yes, well.'

At the end of this, probably one of the most excruciating things I'd ever had to listen to in my entire life, we both stood there for a few minutes, not looking at each other. I didn't want to make a move for the door in case I accidentally brushed against him. Eventually he gave a little cough, said, 'Yes, well,' again, and, in one sudden movement reminiscent of a snake raising its head to strike, bobbed towards me, pressed a wet, slimy mouth against my lips and tried to push his tongue inside.

Maybe a little strangely, my first thought was that it was a pity I'd stubbed the cigarette out. During the two or three seconds it took me to think this, he'd slid both hands round behind me and was making a grope for my bum.

It's fair to say this wasn't the first time in my life I'd been forcibly French-kissed and groped up against a wall. The time I could remember with the most clarity, I'd been fifteen, and during a youth club disco had gone out the back of the church hall with Billy Sparks, who'd promised me a fag but gave me a bit more than I'd bargained for. But I was more than twenty years older now and, to be honest, it was the lack of dignity that offended me more than anything. I mean to say – for God's sake! – he could at least have chosen somewhere inside, away from the dustbins. Not that it would have made any difference. I would still have pushed him away and told him to fuck off.

'I could take you to court for indecent assault,' I added very coldly. 'Or sexual harassment.'

'I'm sorry – so sorry – I didn't mean...' he gasped, covering his face with his hands. 'It's just that I've always ... liked you.'

It was sad in a way. I thought I liked him, too. I thought he

31

was Pretty Damn Pleasant. Just shows how wrong you can be.

He disappeared quietly back inside, probably to go to the toilets and be sick, while I stayed out there and lit another cigarette. In the circumstances, I don't think anyone, even Rachel, could have blamed me.

I'd probably been away from my desk for about half an hour by the time I felt composed enough to go back inside.

'There's been a phone call for you,' said Hilary smugly as soon as I entered the room. 'A personal call.'

Other people got personal phone calls too. Everybody got personal phone calls. But the way she said personal, the implication was that in my case it was bound to be something disreputable. A call from the police to confirm my imminent arrest for drug smuggling or prostitution at the very least. Surprise surprise, it was only Rachel's mobile number. I phoned her back, hoping she wasn't in class by now, hoping she wanted to have a drink after work so that I could tell her all about Nicholas P. D. before I burst from keeping the shock of it buttoned down inside me. But I didn't even get a chance to ask her. I didn't get a chance to say a word, because as soon as she answered the phone she was screaming, like a mad woman on drugs on a roller coaster with no brakes.

'MADDY! MADDY! We've done it! We've fucking done it, we have, we've done it, we've won, we've won, we've won!'

'What? Calm down, I don't know what you're talking about. Done what? Won what?'

'The numbers! I've only just checked the numbers! For Christ's sake, Maddy, our numbers! We've won, we've won! We've won the FUCKING LOTTERY!'

Chapter 3

The night we found out we'd won the lottery, we went to the pub and celebrated hard. We'd won just over twenty-three thousand pounds; that was eleven and a half thousand pounds each. We hadn't as yet discussed what we wanted to do with it. We'd discussed all sorts of stuff – like whose bank account to pay the cheque into first and who we should tell about it. But all that went out of the window as soon as I downed the first half-dozen drinks and decided to announce the news to the whole pub using a rolled-up copy of the Salvation Army newspaper as a megaphone.

Rachel stayed over at my place that night as I lived nearer the pub, and we had a bit of trouble getting up for work the next morning. Rachel was feeling just slightly delicate – she didn't have a huge amount to drink but she wasn't really used to it, being more in the habit of sipping from a water bottle while running a marathon than knocking back triple Bacardis while singing 'We're in the Money' and falling off bar stools. Me, I was feeling like shit warmed up, having performed my usual trick of not knowing when to stop, when to call it a day, when to listen to the messages being sent from my stomach contents to my vomiting muscles or when to accept that I'd lost the ability to stand up. I didn't remember getting home from the pub but apparently it required the assistance of three strong men and a bicycle. Rachel did a lot of sighing and head-shaking in the morning, and dropped a lot of veiled hints about my lack of restraint during the course of the evening, but all I can say is that I fell asleep with my clothes on and was still wearing my knickers in the morning so things couldn't have been too bad.

'Vacuum cleaner!' I was muttering to myself while I waited for the toast to pop out of the toaster. 'Bloody lounge curtains!'

'What?' asked Rachel mildly without much sign of interest. 'What are you moaning on to yourself about?'

She was leaning against the kitchen worktop, staring at a bowl of cornflakes as if she wasn't sure whether they were going to bite back.

'E-mail from Sophie,' I told her. 'I checked just now, while you were in the shower.'

'Oh!' She looked up in surprise. 'Did you print it out? What did she say? Are they in Melbourne yet? Did they get our e-mails yesterday, about the win?'

'They're still in Alice Springs. They survived their trip into the outback. She says it was absolutely amazing – they climbed Ayers Rock but it's called Uluru now, and they slept out in the desert under the stars...'

'And?'

'And they woke up at five o'clock to watch the sunrise over the Rock, and they're flying on to Melbourne tomorrow...'

'And? What did she say about the money?'

'They're very pleased, and she thinks I should spend my share on a Hoover or some curtains.'

Rachel laughed and looked at me over the top of her glasses.

'Very practical!'

'Is that how people see me, Rach? Am I so bloody boring that even my own daughter can't think of anything else I'd want to do with eleven thousand quid? I mean, for God's sake – a Hoover...'

'It'd have to be a gold-plated one!'

'She says after I've bought the Hoover and the curtains,

34

we should have a nice meal together, and then invest the rest of it!'

'Well, I suppose—'

'Don't you dare! Don't you *dare* say that sounds like a sensible suggestion! I will *not* be sensible with my eleven thousand pounds! You can do what you like with yours – buy a franchise in a health club, buy shares in bottled bloody water – I will *not* do *anything* sensible!' I paused for breath, not looking at Rachel for a minute. 'I want to have fun,' I continued eventually. I wanted to elaborate, but I still felt too sick.

'Fun,' repeated Rachel with her eyes closed. 'Well, there's a limit to how much drinking and smoking you can do with eleven thousand pounds, Maddy Goodchild! Even you.'

How hurtful was that? My best friend, implying that there was nothing else in my life that constituted fun, apart from my fags and my booze?

I mean, what about ... well, there must have been something, let me think. There was Tom – we had fun, and lots of it, but Rachel didn't like hearing about that. I was still struggling to come up with something else when she said, quietly, with her eyes still closed so that I was wondering at first whether she'd actually fallen asleep over her cornflakes:

'What *I've* been thinking is this. Perhaps we should be thinking about the girls. About their travels.'

A pang of guilt made me wince. There was I, too busy being offended by the vacuum cleaner and curtain suggestions to think about helping our daughters out financially. What sort of a mother was I? One sniff of eleven thousand pounds and all my maternal instinct goes out of the window.

'Yes,' I agreed at once, grabbing Rachel's arm and shaking her hard to show how sincerely, how keenly, I agreed. Unfortunately I shook her so hard she dropped her spoon into her cereal bowl and splashed cornflakes and milk all over the worktop.

'What are you playing at, you mad woman?!' she laughed, picking up soggy flakes and throwing them back in the dish.

35

'It's no good, Maddy, I can't eat this. I think I just need another black coffee.'

'Me too.' I put the kettle back on and sat down opposite her. 'But I agree. We'll do what you said. We'll send some of the money out to Australia.'

'Australia?' Rachel looked at me blankly as if she'd never heard of the place. 'Who said anything about that?'

'You did. And you're quite right. It should be our priority. We'll send them both a cheque. How much do you think?'

'Madd, that wasn't what I meant.'

'Wasn't it? Then what?

'Though of course, I agree, we can help the girls out. But wouldn't it be better to wait? Wait till they run out of money, then send them some? Otherwise they might just spend it all straight away – no, I know they're not stupid, but if they have too much in their accounts, and they lose their cards, or get them stolen...'

Rachel, as usual, was right, and sensible, and practical, whereas I was just an empty-headed impulsive fool who was probably going to blow all my money on drink and ciga-rettes.

'What I *meant*,' went on Rachel, sitting up straight and looking at me very seriously, 'Is that we should – *perhaps* – think about what Sophie and Amy are doing. And think about what we were saying, the other week.'

'What we were saying the other week? What other week?' I looked back at her blankly.

'About travelling,' she went on patiently. 'You know. We were saying how we'd like to drop everything and go off to explore the world...'

I stared at her, my mouth open. My heart was beating very fast, thumping away so that I could actually feel it doing its thing, doing it very forcefully and strongly despite all the evil and unhealthy things I'd done to it during the whole of my adult life.

'And were we serious, then?' I said in not much more than a whisper. 'About going off to explore the world?'

'No. But then, we hadn't won over twenty-three thousand pounds between us.'

'And now? Now you think we can be serious about it?'

'Well, maybe not the whole world. Maybe not a whole year of travelling like the girls are doing. Maybe something a bit less ambitious. Like a kind of ... long break. A kind of extended holiday.'

'And you'd really want to do that – drop everything? What about your job?'

'It's OK for me. It's only a few weeks till the summer hols. I could be free for six weeks.' She was smiling despite the hangover. She was excited. She'd been thinking about this – all night, probably, and not saying anything to me. Not that she could have had much of a serious conversation with me while I was dancing on the pub table. 'What about *your* job?' she added, narrowing her eyes at me. She looked almost as though she was holding her breath, like she had her fingers crossed behind her back, waiting for my response. So did this all depend on me, then? On how I felt about my job? On whether I'd be able to take the time off? Whether Nicholas P. D. would let me take extended leave?

'No problem,' I found myself saying with hardly a pause for breath. 'I'm leaving anyway.'

'You're *what*! Since when?'

'Since now. I've just decided.' I felt elated. I wanted to jump up and punch the air, but I was still too hungover to try. Why didn't I think of this before? Why wasn't it the obvious thing to do, the very minute Rachel phoned to tell me about the lottery win? Why, in fact, didn't I march into Nicholas P. D. *Un*-Pleasant's office straight away and tell him to stuff his job, stuff his boring little letters and stuff his pathetic, seedy little sexual advances? 'I didn't tell you last night,' I said, getting up to make the coffee. 'But Nicholas tried it on with me yesterday. Tried to kiss me in the car park.'

'*Nicholas* did?' squealed Rachel, almost dropping her coffee cup. 'You're *joking*!'

'Unfortunately not. It was a bit of a shock, I can tell you.'

37

'God! Was he drunk?'

Well, thanks very much. I may not exactly be a super-model; I may be past my prime and slightly more than my ideal weight, but does it have to be presumed that any man taking more than a passing interest in me needs to have had a skinful?

'No. He wasn't drunk, he was pathetic, and embarrassing, and it was all quite sordid and ridiculous. I won't ever be able to look at him in quite the same light again.'

'God!' she exclaimed again. 'You could do him for sexual harassment, you know.'

'I told him that, too. He's probably crapping himself with fear that I'll actually do it. But to be honest I can't be bothered. He's not worth the hassle. I'm sick of the job anyway.'

'But...' She glanced at the clock and jumped to her feet. 'Shit, I'm going to be late for school, Madd. I'll phone you later, OK? But – don't do anything too hasty, will you?'

'Why not?'

Yeah, why not? Give me one good reason why I shouldn't be as hasty as I damn well like?

'Eleven and a half thousand pounds isn't going to last for ever. Even if we *do* go off travelling, you'll still need a job when we come back.'

Call that a good reason? Huh! Where's your sense of adventure, girl!

I may be many things, but I'm not a ditherer. I'm not one to pussyfoot around once I've made my mind up to something. Nicholas Pretty Damn Odious must have thought the game was up when I marched into his office at a quarter past nine that morning, having taken just ten minutes to compose my resignation letter.

'Maddy,' he said, on a long-drawn-out sigh that sounded like he was drowning, 'Madeleine, can't we at least talk about this? I don't want you to ... you shouldn't have to ... I mean, I know I was absolutely out of order yesterday. I can assure you absolutely – *absolutely* – that it will never, *never* happen again.'

Why did I ever think this guy was pleasant? Watching him grovelling and squirming there, almost wetting his knickers and crying for his mummy, I felt nothing but disgust.

'You're right. It won't ever happen again, because I won't be here.'

It was a shame really. I should have had more pity.

'It's got nothing to do with your ... with what happened yesterday,' I added. 'I'm leaving anyway. I'm going travelling.'

'Travelling?' he repeated shakily as if it was a word he'd never encountered before. 'Travelling where?'

I was about to reply with great sarcasm, to say I was going to the moon and back, circumnavigating Mars, taking a day trip to Venus. But I suddenly realised that I actually had no idea where.

'We haven't decided yet,' I told him with a smile. 'We might just follow our noses.'

'I thought perhaps you might be going to see your daughter. Stay with your daughter in Australia?' he ventured, apparently feeling a little less anxious now that I'd shown no sign of raising the subject of him slobbering over me in the car park.

'Not sure that they'd like us cramping their style. We still have some decisions to make. But one way or another, I'm off.'

'I'll hold your job open for you! There's no need to resign.'

I hesitated. I'd just been about to say that yes, there *was* a need, to get out of that place, away from him and away from this awful, boring job for ever. But somewhere in the back of my mind a little light bulb lit up at the words '*hold your job open*'. Why not? Why shouldn't he? It was the least he could do, really, wasn't it, if I wasn't going to take him to the cleaners for assaulting me by the dustbins. Maybe Rachel was right. If we spent all the money, I'd need a job when we got back, and it might take me a while to find one.

'OK,' I told him calmly. 'If you'll agree to me taking six weeks' extended leave.'

'Certainly, certainly, of course, of course,' he said, nodding his head eagerly as if it was his greatest pleasure in life to agree to any demands I wanted to make. I briefly contemplated asking him to double my wages and make me office manager, but I was worried that he'd think I was accepting rewards for the grope.

'Then I'll take back my resignation for now. And if that's OK, I'll book six weeks' leave as from July the eleventh. I've got two weeks' leave owing anyway. Meanwhile, I'll get on with typing these requisitions – all right?'

He blinked back at me.

'Yes,' he said very quietly. 'Give me your leave form to countersign and I'll send it up to the Directorate. It'll be fine.'

It had better be. Because he and I both knew who was doing the screwing now.

Looking back, I suppose it was a bit odd that I forgot about Tom at first. Put it down to my head being turned by the thought of all that money. Or put it down to the Bacardi Breezer hangover anaesthetising my brain. I'd spent at least half that day on the internet, looking at exciting places in the world that a person with eleven and a half thousand pounds in the bank could reasonably expect to go to, and was compiling a list to show Rachel, when a phone call at about half past four brought me down to earth with a bewildering bump.

'Hi sweetheart. OK if I come round later? Have you got something tasty to heat up for me?'

You may very well mock, but I think it was actually this sort of stuff that kept our relationship alive. Tom never stopped treating me as a desirable sex object, you see – even now we'd been together quite a while and I was heading at breakneck speed towards my forties, and the disintegration of all my faculties that everyone warns you about. Some men might have started taking a woman for granted by this stage, but no, he was still oozing the old charm and blatant sexual innuendo every time he phoned, every time he came round.

I told him (as I always did, no matter what other plans I might have had, no matter what might have been on TV that I was looking forward to seeing or how many times I'd promised Rachel to go to the gym) that of course it was OK for him to come over and that of course I'd rustle up some tasty morsel for him. It was a good thing I knew that he was far more interested in bed than board, otherwise I'd have lost him long ago; tasty morsels of the culinary variety not being exactly my forte.

So we were well into the charred sausages and lumpy mash before I broached the subject.

'Rachel and I are thinking of going away,' I said tentatively, watching his face.

'A holiday? Out of your winnings? Bloody good for you. So you should.'

'You don't mind?'

'Of course not! For God's sake! You haven't had a holiday for – how long?'

Well, let me see, now. Two years, possibly three? I'd certainly never had one with Tom, anyway – he was far too busy paying for his vacations in Florida and California with Linda (who was originally from the States). Not that I was jealous at all, lucky cow, but why didn't she want to go anywhere else in the world other than the one country she already knew better than Mickey Mouse and Michael Jackson put together? Why didn't she want to experiment one year and go to Spain or Italy or even Canada for a change? Still, no one else's business I suppose, and certainly not mine, I was only her husband's secret mistress.

He put down his fork (only so many lumps of mash a person can chew through, with the best will in the world) and reached across the table to touch my hand.

'It's been hard for you, sweetheart,' he said gently, 'having no one to take you away on holidays.'

'I could take myself,' I retorted, feeling patronised, 'if I wanted to! I'm not some pathetic little woman, waiting at home.'

'No, I know you're not,' he agreed hastily. 'But all I'm saying is – now you've got this money – you and Rachel. . .'

He was always nice about Rachel. It was a shame she didn't make any effort to get to know him better, really – they'd probably have got on quite well. They had a few things in common, such as their dislike of my cigarettes and their lack of flab.

'Yes. Well, we thought perhaps – with the girls away travelling. . .'

'Exactly! You won't have them to worry about. So you can go off abroad somewhere, stay in a nice hotel and really enjoy yourselves for a week, or a couple of weeks even.'

'Well, actually, we're thinking—'

'Treat yourselves! Buy yourselves some new clothes too! And what about getting some nice new suitcases?'

Suitcases. If it wasn't bloody vacuum cleaners and curtains, it was suitcases. Couldn't anybody come up with anything *exciting* for me to spend my money on? I looked at him, smiling back at me with the confidence and assurance of someone who knows his faithful, loving mistress is never going to leave him, never going to give up playing second fiddle, never going to jet off around the world with a backpack and not come back for at least six weeks and, ridiculously, I suddenly felt sorry for him. All the cards were in his hands – all the trumps, all the kings, queens, jacks and jokers – and however the game was played, I would always be the loser; yet for some strange reason I felt I had the upper hand.

'When you come back,' he said cheerfully, 'I'll be starting my new job.'

'Oh yes – the new job,' I smiled.

'I'll be at the Manchester office first. You'll be able to come up and see me.'

42

'Yes. Perhaps, yes.'

And perhaps not.

'I've made a list of countries,' I told Rachel excitedly on the phone. 'Listen: Egypt – I've always wanted to go there – and India, and South Africa, and well, perhaps Italy, and the Greek islands...'

'I've made one too. Malta, Austria, Mexico, the Caribbean, the Seychelles...'

'We won't be able to afford those. Not the Caribbean or the Seychelles.'

'Well, we won't be able to afford India, either. Maybe we need to trim our lists a bit.'

'Maybe we should forget it, and just have a normal holiday somewhere.'

'Why? What's the matter with you? I thought you were up for a six-week jaunt?'

I would be, if only I could bring myself to tell my boyfriend, who's got it into his head that we're off for a two-week package to Majorca or Tenerife, that I'm off for six weeks of backpacking. He could be forgiven for thinking the winnings have unhinged me.

'I'm a bit worried about the backpack,' I admitted to Rachel. 'When I tried to lift Sophie's, before she left, I couldn't straighten my back again for three days. It's all very well for *you*.'

The implication was obvious. Hour after hour spent on the triceps press and the shoulder press, to say nothing of all the exercises to strengthen her abdominals and her pectorals, had given her a hefty and well-earned advantage over me in the rucksack-carrying stakes. She could probably carry mine as well, but I didn't think this suggestion would go down terribly well.

'I know it's my own fault,' I added quickly before she could point it out. 'I know I should have worked harder at my abdominal curls and toned my biceps more, but it's too late now, if we're planning on going off in a couple of weeks.'

'Well. I've been thinking about that. We could always take the car.'

Take the car? Had she lost the plot, or had I?

'The car?' I repeated. 'To Mexico? To Malta? To South Africa?'

'We've both just agreed, we need to trim the list. We need to be more realistic. Why don't we just explore Europe? We can travel a long way by road and see a lot of places. We can stay in hotels, or bed and breakfasts, and we can spend as long as we want in each country.'

'France, Italy, Germany!'

'Switzerland, Holland, Denmark! We can go from one country to another, and another, and another, all in the same day, if we want!'

'Yeah!' I was getting hooked on the idea. It was fantastic. Why didn't I think of it first? 'When you think about it, we can see a lot more different places like that than Sophie and Amy are seeing in a year.'

'Absolutely. The world is ... well, maybe not quite our oyster. Our cockle, perhaps!'

Yuck. Always did hate seafood.

'Anyway. Are you coming to the gym tonight?'

'Piss off. How many more times? I've left. I've *really* left, now.'

'Yeah, right. You said that last time.'

'Yes, but you *made* me go again!' I squawked indignantly. '*One last try*, you said! Well, my *one last try* was an absolute disaster. I hated it more than ever. I've left! I'm calling in there tonight, in fact, to terminate my membership.'

'Well, maybe I'll see you there, then, when you call in to terminate it. Maybe we can have a quick drink together?'

I wouldn't have minded if she meant a *drink*. But I knew Rachel. She meant a glass of carrot juice in the Health Bar. And if she thought that meant I'd be nipping back into that purgatory on earth for another quick workout, she had another think coming.

*

I looked around me, gasping, while I used what was left of my will-power to hold onto the step machine without sliding off in a pool of perspiration. Why was I sweating more than anyone else? Was there something wrong with me? The guy on the next machine, when I managed to get a sneaky look at him in the mirror, was pounding away effortlessly as if he was just taking a stroll on a pleasant sunny afternoon with not a drip of sweat anywhere to be seen. He wasn't red in the face and he didn't have the look of desperate death-defying maniac about him that I could see reflected in front of me. Then there were those two on the bikes behind me. They didn't realise I was watching them in the mirror. They came into the gym together, in matching tracksuits, and got on adjacent bikes. He adjusted the saddle height for her – she obviously didn't know the height of her own arse – and now they were pedalling their bikes in synchrony, holding hands and grinning at each other. *Holding hands*! How anyone had the energy for all that carry-on while they were inflicting that torment on themselves was beyond me. I wouldn't have wanted anyone I'd ever been linked with emotionally or sexually to be within a hundred yards of me right at that moment, never mind holding my hand. My hands were so sweaty they'd have slipped out of their grasp anyway and the risk of suffocation by body odour must have been pretty serious.

'You don't look as if you're enjoying this,' said Rachel sadly, watching me as she limbered up beside me prior to moving on to some other form of self-destruction.

I shook my head, the power of speech being a long-forgotten luxury. I struggled with the controls of the machine, trying to take it down at least six notches so that I could breathe again.

'I fucking *told* you!' People looked in my direction and frowned. I smiled apologetically. 'I said I didn't want to do this any more,' I hissed at her. 'I don't know *why* I let you talk me into it!'

I ran out of breath. Drips of sweat flew in all directions.

That was it. I'd had enough. I pressed 'Stop' and practically fell off the machine without waiting for it to give me permission.

'You should cool down,' Rachel told me sternly. 'It's bad for your heart to just stop and get off without—'

'Listen!' I gasped, holding onto her arm as I wiped myself down with the sweaty towel. 'This whole malarkey is bad for my heart. Just *being* here is bad for my heart.'

'I'm only thinking of you,' she told me slightly sulkily. 'You might think I'm being a bully...'

Oh really? Never occurred to me.

'... but I'm just concerned about you, Maddy. If you don't get fit before we go off travelling...'

'What? I'll collapse under the strain of a day on the beach? I'll struggle to down a pint of lager?'

'I was rather hoping,' she retorted sniffily, 'that we might do something just a *little* bit more cultural than that, while we're in Europe.'

'OK, OK, I know,' I said, relenting, as always. 'But face it, Rach. I'm never going to be as fit as you are. I'm a lost cause. We can see all the sights of Europe without me having the body of an athlete, can't we?'

'I suppose so,' she said grudgingly. Then we looked at each other, grinned, and both added together: 'Depends which athlete we're talking about!' – and burst out laughing.

'Come on, let's get changed and go and have a drink,' I said, pulling her away from the rowing machine before she'd had time to give it more than a longing glance.

'We... ell; I suppose we could.'

'The pub over the road? You can buy a grapefruit juice there. Be fair – I can't get a beer at the Health Bar.'

'All right, then!' she agreed, laughing. 'Maybe I could have a glass of white wine, just this once. Get in training for France!'

Bloody hell. Next thing you know, she'll be smoking pot and having sex with strangers.

*

46

I sat at my desk, staring blankly at my computer screen, wondering about our destinations; wondering whether I was really going to come back to work here after the six weeks were over, or whether I'd look for a fantastic new job instead; wondering when Sophie was going to respond to the e-mail I'd sent her, telling her about our plans, and wondering about how I was going to explain things to Tom. Suddenly, I had a lot more important things on my mind than the statements I was typing for Nicholas P. D. Creepy.

'Have you got a minute, Madeleine?' he asked me now, standing by my desk and shifting uncomfortably from foot to foot as if he needed to go to the toilet. He seemed so embarrassed to be with me these days that I had a feeling he'd actually be relieved now when I went away. I got up and followed him into his office.

'It's just a thought,' he said, 'And you can say no, of course, if you're not interested.'

I had a moment of horrible panic that he was going to offer me his body again. Maybe with some special offer attached this time: two for the price of one – buy one shag, get one free – to try to tempt me into it.

'It's all right,' he said a little sadly, seeing the look on my face. 'It's just a house, that's all.'

'A *house*?'

'I've got a house in France. I should have thought ... well, it's just occurred to me really. I thought perhaps you and your friend might be able to make use of it. I do rent it out sometimes, but I haven't got anyone booked in at the moment – not till August.'

'Oh! I ... well, I don't know what to say! I'll have to ask my friend, of course, but – it sounds. . .'

'It's in Carnac, on the south coast of Brittany. It's a nice area, just outside the town, you could use it as a base to explore the whole region.'

'And – how much rent?'

'Oh! I wouldn't charge you!' he responded, looking up at me with a wounded expression as if I'd accused him of fraud and larceny. 'If you want to use it, just take the keys. It's all yours until the ninth of August.'

'Are you sure he won't be expecting something in return?' asked Rachel cautiously that evening. 'You might turn back the bed covers on our first night and find him waiting for you naked in the bed.'

'Oh, God, what a horrible thought! No, I'm sure it's more a case of feeling guilty and wanting to make amends. Fine, no problem – *let* him. It'll be perfect, Rach, just the right distance to make it our first stop. We can stay a few days, or a week, or whatever, and then move on.'

'Yes, you're right – get the keys off him before he changes his mind. Or before he loses the hots for you!'

'I will. Have you heard from Amy, by the way?'

'Yes. I get the impression they're both a bit worried about us.'

'I know. Sophie seems to have gone into a state of shock about the fact that I'm leaving my job to go off travelling. Funny how it was perfectly acceptable for them to do it!'

'Yeah. I think Amy's afraid we might land up in Australia and start following them around from hostel to hostel.'

'As if! We don't want our daughters cramping our style, do we?'

'Absolutely not! This is going to be fantastic, Madd. We're going to have the time of our lives!'

She was right, of course. We were certainly going to have the time of our lives – in more ways than one. Just as well we don't know what's waiting to happen before we set off on life's great adventures, or none of us would ever get out of bed in the morning.

Chapter 4

So perhaps we were trying to copy our daughters. Is that what you're thinking? Well you might be right – maybe we were trying to prove something. That we were as adventurous as them, as bold and daring and willing to take on the world and all its dangers. You know: crocodiles, snakes, forest fires, houses loaned by lecherous bosses. We were up for it all, even if we *were* heading for middle age and beginning to look nothing like our passport photos. Walking away from my secure job at Brentwood Council with only eleven and a half thousand pounds between me and destitution was probably the craziest thing I'd done since I married Joe at the age of seventeen because I was four months pregnant. It felt good to be doing something ridiculous and slightly scary again – and this time at least I wasn't going to wake up to the reality of washing a man's socks and underpants.

I hadn't worked for the council for nearly as long as Hilary, so I wasn't exactly expecting a full-scale leaving party on my last day; but perhaps a couple of drinks at lunchtime might have been nice.

'Anyone fancy going to the pub?' I asked everyone in the office at one o'clock. I'd been about to add that the drinks were on me, but I suddenly became aware that they were all looking at their watches, mumbling about wanting to get on with their work, go shopping for their husband's dinner, get to the bank, eat their egg sandwiches and read their *Daily Mail*, etc etc … and I suddenly thought: What the hell? Why should I offer to buy this crowd of morons a drink, anyway, just because I was the lucky one who was getting out of here? They weren't my friends – they were just other people who happened to share my fate in working in this dump. I'd already bought them all a drink when I heard I'd won the lottery. It should have been *their* turn to treat *me*!

At least Nicholas Pretty Damn came up trumps and handed over the keys to his house in France and a Bon Voyage card that wished me all the best, avoiding any mention of my lack of enthusiasm for snogging him out the back by the dustbins.

'I hope it all goes well,' he told me, watching somewhat ruefully as I packed all my personal bits from my desk into a carrier bag. He guessed, and I knew, that it was unlikely I was actually planning to come back.

'Thanks. We'll look after the house, and I'll send the keys back to you before the ninth of August.'

For a minute I thought he was going to kiss me goodbye, but, possibly put off by the look of dread in my eyes, he just nodded a couple of times, thanked me for my hard work recently (I tried not to think about all the hours I'd spent on the internet) and left me to it.

'No farewell party?' exclaimed Rachel in disgust. 'No present, no cards, no Good Luck banners in the office? Bloody hell, even *I* got loads of Bon Voyage cards – and I'm going back after the holidays!'

'Yes, well. You've got a good career, with nice colleagues, and—'

'And hordes of untrained teenagers who don't want to learn anything – but at least I won't have to see them for a while after next week! Cheer up, Madd – you've got out of that place now for at least six weeks. And you don't have to go back. You can look for a better job.'

Yes. At thirty-seven, with seven ancient O levels and no computer qualifications, people are going to be absolutely falling over themselves to employ me. Still, I guess there's always temping!

Saying goodbye to Tom was more difficult.

'So it's two weeks in France, then?'

The poor guy was a bit confused, and who could blame him? I still hadn't given him the full story. To be fair, I didn't really know the full story yet myself – but I'd been very economical with the details I'd supplied to him.

'Well, we've got the use of this house in Carnac for a couple of weeks. But we probably won't stay there that long. We'll probably move on ... and stay away a little longer.'

That much was true, anyway. But we had very little idea about where we might go between arriving at Nicholas's house and coming home again, and I hadn't even touched on our plan to visit as many countries as we could. I was working on the theory that too much information would be bad for him at this stage.

Mum, are you crazy? exclaimed an e-mail from Sophie a couple of days before our departure. *I can't believe you and Rachel want to go wandering off to explore Europe like a pair of middle-aged hippies.*

Middle-aged, indeed! I quite fancied the idea of being a hippie, though. I might well wear some beads and put flowers in my hair.

We've met people like you, over here. Most of them seem to be New Zealanders. They buy ancient vans and set off with about as much planning for the journey as if they were going to their local shopping centre.

Hey, let me tell you, it takes me several hours to prepare for a trip to Lakeside!

Well, if you MUST get it out of your system, have fun, but please try not to get into any trouble. Amy and I are not there to come and rescue you!

We're having a great time in Melbourne. It's a great city with a lot of lively bars and cafes and we're making loads of new friends. We've just got back from a two-day tour; the first day was on the Great Ocean Road – very impressive famous coastline with fantastic rock formations – and on the second day we visited a koala sanctuary and then we got taken to Phillip Island where lots of little penguins come rushing out of the sea at sunset and waddle up the beach – very cute!

I was smiling as I logged off the computer. In a few days' time, I could be sending e-mails to Sophie with tales of *our* sightseeing, *our* adventures. We might not see koala bears and waddling penguins but I was certainly going to have more to share with her soon than the latest gossip from Brentwood Council offices or how many minutes I'd done on the treadmill.

Sophie wasn't the only one who thought I was crazy. My next-door neighbour Julie was practically beside herself at the thought of six weeks' worth of free papers sticking out of the letter box.

'And what about the garden?' she asked on a note of hysteria. The clematis will get brown spots and the dahlias will never survive!'

'I'll give them my apologies,' I said. 'But it's the survival of the fittest in this life, isn't it?'

I didn't actually have to worry about papers or post sticking out of the door. Rachel's son Simon was going to be at home until he went off to university at the end of September, so he'd offered to keep an eye on my house as well as hers, in return for the use of my ancient Renault. We were going in Rachel's car, as it was bigger than mine, and in better condition. I doubted whether Simon would give much thought to the clematis or the dahlias, though.

'I'll water them for you, if you like?' offered Julie, apparently distraught at my lack of concern.

'Well, if you really don't mind. Thanks!'

I supposed it'd be worth bringing a decent present back from somewhere in Europe, to come home to a living and healthy clematis.

Then there was the fuss from my family. I had two older sisters, who both lived in Dorset and only tended to phone me with regular naggings about my lifestyle. In fact I sometimes thought I might have subconsciously chosen Rachel as a friend because she took over from where Susan and Diana left off.

'What on earth are you thinking of?' nagged Susan. 'Not even booking hotels before you go?

'It's called spontaneity,' I explained. 'It's more fun.'

'It sounds dangerous.' She shuddered down the phone line. 'You could end up anywhere!'

'We're not going anywhere dangerous! We won't stay anywhere we don't like the look of.'

'But you hear all kinds of stories about women who go backpacking...' She tailed off, leaving me to imagine the worst, and seeming to have forgotten that Sophie was backpacking too.

'What about the house? What about your mortgage and all your bills?' cried Diana.

'All paid by direct debit. Nothing to worry about!' I said breezily.

'But anything could happen while you're away. The house could burn down! The pipes could burst!'

'Yeah, and a tornado could flatten the whole of Essex! Di, do me a favour and be pleased for me. This is going to be the greatest adventure of my life! Don't put the mockers on it.'

'Sorry, love, but I can't help being concerned about you. Walking away from that lovely job at the council offices...'

'It wasn't lovely, and my boss was a pervert.'

'What!'

She seemed to be OK after that. Or maybe she was just too

stunned to say any more. I got really nice Bon Voyage cards from them both the next day.

Rachel stayed over at my place again on the night before we set off. I didn't sleep very much that night. My dreams were strange and complicated and featured a lot of wild animals – which I didn't understand at all but didn't think could be a very good omen.

I took Rachel a cup of tea in bed before the alarm even went off.

'What's the matter with you?' she asked ungraciously. 'Too excited to sleep?'

'Yeah.'

That'd be it. Easier to explain than dreams about tigers and elephants.

'Well, I hope you're not going to be like this the whole time we're away, getting up with the bloody lark. I couldn't hack it.'

Nor could I, as it happens.

'That's what I like about you,' I said sulkily, sitting on the end of her bed to cut my toenails. 'The way you positively brim over with good humour first thing in the morning.'

'Piss off,' she retorted mildly, pulling the duvet over her head.

Her mood improved after she'd fed it a bowl of muesli and several more cups of tea; and after one false start to return for my toothbrush, we were finally away. The sun poked its head round the corner of some misty dawn cloud to herald the start of yet another lovely summer day as we turned onto the motorway heading for the coast, and we looked at each other and began to laugh with excitement.

'*En vacances!*' I shouted happily.

'Yeah! And, also, we're off on our hols!'

Getting onto the car ferry was an adventure in itself. Probably for most people this would have been a straight-forward and unremarkable part of the journey, but you have to remember that we'd never done anything like this before. Despite our maturity and our experience of life in general, as far as travelling overseas was concerned we were little more than virgins.

'Oh my God!' exclaimed Rachel, her eyes out on stalks as we drove towards the ramp. 'Which way? Which way? I'm going to go straight off the edge of this fucking thing and straight into the fucking sea – I know it!'

'No you're not,' I soothed her with a lot more confidence than I felt. 'Just go a bit slower. *Rachel*! Christ! *Slower*!'

She hit the brake just in time to avoid hitting the nice little man in the bright fluorescent jerkin who was trying to wave us onto the correct side of the car deck. I actually saw the fear in his eyes just before she swerved and missed him.

'Jesus!' I exclaimed, gripping the dashboard with white knuckles. 'It's not a computer game! You're not supposed to see how many officials you can knock down...'

'All right, all right,' she replied irritably. 'You can bloody well have a turn at driving next, if you're so clever.'

'Oh, that'd be fair, wouldn't it! You do the easy bit, driving down to Portsmouth, and then expect me to take over as soon as we start on the wrong-side-of-the-road stuff.'

We were getting out of the car now. Rachel was locking all the doors and windows carefully and giving it a last loving look as if she wasn't at all convinced it was going to survive the Channel crossing. She stopped and looked up at me with surprise.

'What do you mean?' she said. 'Wrong side of what road?'

Oh, shit. Should I just go home now?

We had a long talk over coffee in the passenger lounge of the *Brittany Queen*. We established that Rachel wasn't bloody stupid, that she had in fact been to both junior and senior school *and* university, had trained as a teacher and knew quite a bit of geography, that she did actually read news-papers and watch television, had been to Spain several times on holiday (albeit travelling by air) and noticed during said holidays that cars were indeed driving on the right-hand side of the road. She was of course quite aware of the fact that driving on the right was a requirement in most countries – did I think she was a fucking idiot or what? – but she hadn't actually had time to sit down and contemplate this fact during the planning stages of our trip. This was, of course, my fault, having left everything to her as usual and having made no effort to find out whether she was aware of all the hazards she, as the nominated car-owner, might have to face, and having selfishly and thoughtlessly presumed she was up to it. Which, given the fact that she hadn't prepared herself mentally, and had already had to endure the strain of getting us onto the ferry in one piece, she wasn't.

'What do you mean, you're not up to it?'

'*You'll* have to do it.'

'But it's your car! Your precious car, your baby...'

'You've driven it before. I trust you. Just be gentle with it. No sudden gear changes. No stamping on the accelerator. No yanking on the handbrake.'

'I haven't driven it backwards round roundabouts before! I haven't driven it in left-hand fucking *fast* lanes before!'

'Stay in the slow lanes, then. You'll soon get the hang of it.'

Oh, will I? Thanks for the vote of confidence.

I smoked two cigarettes on the trot, ignoring her looks of disapproval, bought myself a bar of chocolate and sulked for the rest of the crossing.

What made it worse was, she was absolutely useless at navigating and hardly knew any French, so there was I, driving a strange car on strange roads in mirror-writing, trying to read a map over her arm and translate road signs all at the same time, while her contribution seemed to amount to changing the CDs and offering me soft mints.

'We need to take the next yellow road on the right. No, the left! The left!' she shouted, turning the map upside down.

'Why do you do that? It makes me so fucking nervous when you do that!'

My nerves were in shreds and so far we'd only driven halfway down the 'sticking out bit' as Rachel insisted on calling it. I couldn't see how I was going to survive the rest of the journey without a migraine, and I'd never had one in my life before.

'I need to have the map pointing the same way we're going,' explained Rachel patiently. 'It's all right. I won't get us lost.'

We realised we were lost somewhere between the green bit, and the big area of yellow with a white dot on it.

'It's your fault,' said Rachel as we pulled over to the side of the road. 'You kept telling me to turn the map up the other way. We must have gone left where we should have gone right. Where that black line is.'

'That isn't a road, Rachel. It's one of the squares. The squares of the fucking map.'

'So what's the point of them, then?'

I sighed. Which of us was supposed to be the teacher? Since when had I acquired a geography degree?

'The squares are to help you find places on the map.'

'Oh, that's OK, then, isn't it. So find us!'

There weren't even any soft mints left.

We pulled up at a café in the next little village. Darkly dressed Frenchmen looked up at us from their drinks with looks that could easily have been interpreted as pure hatred. We walked to the bar through a fog of choking smoke and reverberating silence.

'Go on.' Rachel nudged me as the proprietor raised one eyebrow at us while continuing to chew something unsavoury and wipe the counter at the same time. He looked like René in *'Allo 'Allo* but without the sense of humour. 'Ask him.'

I nudged her back. She was getting seriously on my nerves and if she wasn't careful I'd get back in the car and

57

drive off, leaving her at the mercy of this crowd without the benefit of my superior French.

'*Excusez-moi, m'sieur*,' I began.

Heads turned in the smoke-cloud behind us. Someone spat on the floor. I held on to Rachel's arm and struggled on: '*Nous sommes...*' My mouth went dry. What the hell was '*lost*'? I knew it, I knew it ... I fumbled in my bag for the phrase book. Shit. Left it in the sodding car. '*Nous cherchons...*' I tried again, bravely. '*Nous cherchons la route pour Carnac.*'

I beamed at him, feeling triumphant. I'd done it! I'd communicated with a native! Nothing to it! I must be a natural linguist.

'*Carnac*,' repeated M'sieur after a moment of studied concentration, during which he took whatever it was out of his mouth, looked at it doubtfully, rolled it between his thumb and finger and put it back between his teeth again. '*Carnac?*'

'*Oui!*' said Rachel excitedly.

I glared at her. Trust her to think she could get in on the act now it was all going so well. 'Yes' was probably the only word she knew.

'*Carnac*,' I agreed again. '*S'il vous plaît*,' I added for good measure.

There was another split second of silence, and then suddenly the whole place erupted into an orgasm of frenzied speech. M'sieur was waving his arms in this direction and that; bobbing his head towards the road and jerking a thumb the opposite way at the same time. The sour and surly-looking clientele who moments earlier had looked as if they wanted to murder us and bundle our bodies up in sacks had now all jumped to their feet and were vying with each other to shout the loudest string of incomprehensible directions. Words fell upon us in streams, rivers, torrents of French that had never seen the inside of a phrase book, uttered with the sort of speed and urgency that most English-speaking people reserve for major world disasters or horse racing commentary.

'*Je ne comprends pas,*' I whispered nervously, but this only resulted in a doubling of both volume and speed, and an increase of arm waving until it looked as if they were all about to take off in flight.

'Let's go,' muttered Rachel against my ear. 'Pretend you know what they're saying, for Christ's sake. They're all fucking mad.'

'*Merci!*' I shouted into the mêlée, following Rachel's headlong flight towards the door. '*Bonjour!*'

We'd driven halfway to the next village before I realised I'd run away yelling hello instead of goodbye. But by then we were both hysterical with laughter and busy congratulating ourselves on our superb handling of the situation. Trouble was, we still had no idea where we were.

'Here's a sign!' screamed Rachel suddenly as if it was the funniest thing we'd seen yet.

It was. It told us Carnac was sixty-three kilometres away, in the direction we'd just come from.

We sat at the side of the road drinking orange juice we'd bought on the ferry. I'd have preferred a double vodka, but I was having more than enough trouble driving while sober. The map was spread out on the grass in front of us.

'Right,' said Rachel. 'We must be about here.'

I glared at her. How would she know? She didn't have the map upside down.

'And we're heading for ... here.'

'No. That's the wrong coast. Jesus!' I took a long, shuddering drag from my cigarette before continuing, 'You can't be *that* stupid – you're a bloody science teacher! Why do you find this so difficult?'

'I don't know. We can't all be good at everything, Maddy. Maybe you should be asking yourself why you're so stressed out.'

'Stressed out? I'm not stressed out – I'd just like to get onto the right road and get to where we're going.'

'Of course, so would I, but *I'm* not being so bloody

bad-tempered about it, am I? You really ought to practise some breathing exercises, you know, or go to yoga classes.'

'*Yoga* classes? Fucking yoga classes? What about *you* going to some map-reading classes, or come to that, some classes in driving on the right-hand side of the road in your own car!'

'There's no need to be nasty,' she said primly, staring straight ahead. 'Sometimes, Madeleine Goodchild, being with you is almost as bad as being with a man.'

Shit, that really is straight talking. That really is below the belt.

'I'm not *that* bad, am I?' I asked, stubbing out my fag and looking at her anxiously.

She laughed.

'No, not quite, but I can remember having rows with Keith that were almost identical to this.'

'I'm not surprised, if you were always this bad at map-reading!' I smiled. 'OK, let's try again. We've got to get onto this road here, and then we need to come down here and head for. . .' I looked up at her. 'What's the matter?'

'That car. It drove past, now it's turning round and coming back.'

As she spoke, the silver Citroën cruised to a halt behind Rachel's car and the doors opened. Two silver-haired men got out of their silver car and strolled nonchalantly towards us. One was tall and bearded and had a cigar in the corner of his mouth after the style of Clint Eastwood in *A Fistful of Dollars*. The other was smooth and smiling and suave-looking, like he could be a model on the shirts page of a mail-order catalogue.

'Leave this to me,' I told Rachel firmly, getting to my feet and brushing grass and ash off my jeans. I was mentally rehearsing some of my best French phrases. They mostly had to do with ordering wine or booking hotel rooms but there must be something I could come up with to suit the occasion?

'I hope they're not going to ask for directions,' commented Rachel drily.

'*Bonjour!*' I greeted them pleasantly. '*Pouvez-vous nous aimer?*'

There was silence for a moment, then the bearded one laughed softly and said:

'My French isn't too great, but I have a feeling you just asked if we could love you.'

'Oh shit! Not *aimer*! *Aider*! *Pouvez-vous nous aider*! Can you help us!' I shouted, feeling myself go very red. 'And anyway! You're English!' I made it sound like an accusation.

'Sorry.' He smiled.

Rachel sniggered. I ignored her. She certainly couldn't have done any better.

'Don't worry, your French is better than mine,' said the smooth guy, very smoothly. 'We thought you looked like you could do with some help.' His eyes twinkled and he smiled even more broadly. 'We could always work on the *loving* later!'

Best offer we'd had this side of St Malo, anyway.

'So what's the problem?' asked the bearded one. 'Lost your way?'

'Maddy was driving,' said Rachel, as if that explained everything. Great. Sounded for all the world as if I'd been carelessly meandering around the French countryside wilfully getting us lost while she was unconscious.

'And Rachel was *trying* to map-read,' I added very pointedly.

'So where are you headed for, girls?' asked Smoothie, still smiling.

Girls indeed! I glanced at Rachel just in time to see her fluttering her eyelashes at him. This was indeed a turn-up for the books, believe me. Rachel had had one or two brief relationships since Keith had carelessly died prematurely from a bad heart, but to be honest I'd rarely seen her even twitch a muscle of enthusiasm for any man anywhere. I'd always privately believed that even if George Clooney had walked naked into her bedroom on a Saturday night with a bottle of

Amaretto and a box of condoms she'd probably tell him she was planning to do her ironing.

'Carnac,' she said now, making it sound like the name of an erotic French perfume. 'Do you know it?'

'Know it!' They exchanged glances, grinning broadly. 'Whereabouts in Carnac are you staying?'

I read out the address.

'Yes. Know exactly where it is,' said the bearded one. 'Just off the main road through the pines, on the way down to the seafront. Just across the way from where we're staying.'

'*You're* staying...?' gasped Rachel. I watched her eyes light up, with a kind of fascination akin to dread. 'You're staying in Carnac too?'

Oh, well, what an amazing coincidence. Why didn't I see it coming?

'We stay there every year. We're in a campsite – Camping Les Étoiles. We're on our way back there now. Want to follow us, or are you staying here for a picnic?'

'You must have dropped straight out of heaven!' exclaimed Rachel with a nice little giggle. She folded up the map roughly and slung it into the back of the car. 'Lead on!'

'But not too fast round the roundabouts,' I warned them. 'I still have to concentrate on going back-to-front.'

Actually they were both very nice, as we found out when they finally got us safely to Carnac and we invited them to join us for a drink, which seemed the least we could do. We sat at the stripped pine table in Nicholas P. D.'s very pleasant rustic kitchen, pouring cheap red wine down our throats and telling each other our life histories. Well, the bits we wanted to tell. I didn't dwell too much on the subject of Tom, and I noticed that Rachel barely mentioned her late-lamented husband. Made her marriage sound more like a momentary lapse of concentration than a partnership of nearly ten years cut short by a cruel twist of fate. But then again, it was only healthy that she should have moved on by now. I just wished she hadn't chosen the first night of our trip to start the process.

The object of her obvious and increasing interest, Mr Mail Order, otherwise known as Craig, had also been married at one stage and was long since divorced. Max, the bearded one, had apparently been living with someone for the past seven years.

'So where is she now?' asked Rachel, looking around as if she expected this woman to suddenly jump out from behind a chair.

'Living with someone else,' said Max.

'Oh, shit. I'm sorry. . .'

'No problem. She left a couple of months ago. I'm getting over it.'

There was a heavy silence which reinforced everyone's unspoken understanding that in fact he wasn't getting over it at all, didn't want to talk about it, couldn't even bear to think about it and the quicker we changed the subject the better.

'Shit,' said Rachel again, taking another gulp of wine.

I looked at her glazed eyes and thought it was perhaps a good idea to get up and prepare some food.

'Shit,' I echoed, looking in the empty cupboards. 'Forgot to get any shopping.'

'There's a *supermarché* just along the road here,' said Craig. 'We'll show you, if you like. Give you a hand, perhaps?'

'No,' I said at once, before Rachel had a chance to reply. 'Thanks all the same, but I think we need to get ourselves sorted out here – get the shopping, get unpacked, make the beds and stuff. But thanks for everything. . .'

'And maybe we'll see you tomorrow?' added Rachel.

Surprise, surprise.

The combined effects of wild animal dreams the previous night, driving for hours on the wrong side of the road with an incompetent map-reader, and several large glasses of *vin rouge* ensured I slept long and heavily in the surprisingly pretty pink bedroom tucked away under the eaves in Nicholas's holiday home. With the shutters closed, it was still dark when I woke up and I was shocked to see it was actually nearly eleven o'clock.

'Bugger!' Snoring under a duvet for half the day was not the way I'd envisaged spending my six weeks of world travel. I jumped out of bed and flung open the shutters. Brilliant sunshine streamed into the room. I leaned on the windowsill, lit up a cigarette and breathed in the smoke together with the warm summer air, heavily fragranced with the scent of the pine trees. What a glorious day! What a joy to be alive, away from home, away from Brentwood Council and all its tedious supplies of stationery and furniture and fucking toilet rolls! What a joy. . .

'Morning, Maddy!' called Rachel's voice from just below me.

Trust her to be up before me. I leaned a bit further over the windowsill. There she was, sitting at the rickety wooden picnic table just outside the kitchen door. The little flag-stoned courtyard was surrounded on all sides by a privet hedge covered by rampant honeysuckle. Beyond the hedge, the pine forest stretched into the distance. The scent was so sweet and heady, it made me feel almost giddy. On the table in front of Rachel were a pot of coffee and a loaf of French bread. And, on the bench opposite her, looking up at me and giving me a cheerful wave as I leant, practically naked, out of the window, were Batman and bloody Robin.

'Morning Craig, morning Max,' I muttered, diving back into the safety of the room and banging the shutters closed. 'Bloody well come for breakfast, why don't you?'

I showered and pulled on a T-shirt and shorts. The shorts were new but the zip only just about did up, on account of the fact that I'd bought all my new clothes in a size twelve, planning to diet before I started the trip. Now I wished I'd been more realistic and got fourteens.

'Is this a late breakfast or an early lunch?' I asked, plonking myself down on the bench next to Rachel. She, of course, looked neat and trim and lovely in her tiny bum-hugging shorts showing off her toned thighs. Craig was having trouble keeping his eyes off her. Just as well – at least he probably hadn't noticed my boobs hanging over the windowsill like barrage balloons.

'It can be whatever you like!' Max smiled. 'We brought you some fresh croissants and a baguette. They're best eaten straight away.'

'No problem!' I broke off a large hunk of bread and spread it thickly with butter.

'Your shorts are undone,' he pointed out kindly.

I sucked in my breath, tried, and failed to zip the shorts up halfway. At this rate, and with croissants like these, I'd have to go shopping for bigger clothes any day now.

'So what are you girls planning to do today?' asked Craig, pouring coffee and stretching out in the sunshine.

'Well, I guess we'll explore the area,' I said at once, looking at Rachel for confirmation. She, however, was looking back at Craig.

'What do you suggest?' she asked coyly.

'Well,' he responded, 'we'd be happy to go for another swim, if you'd like us to introduce you to the beach?'

'*Another* swim?' I looked at them suspiciously. 'Have you been to the beach already?'

'We like to swim as soon as we get up,' nodded Max. 'Beat the crowds.'

Before the fucking sea warms up? What were these guys – fanatics?

'We swam at about nine o'clock today – it was beautiful,' went on Craig. 'And then we went to the hire shop to get some bikes.'

They were. They were bloody fanatics. I glanced at Rachel nervously, making eye signals at her to indicate that we should perhaps be thinking seriously about getting rid of them fast. But she was simpering at Craig again and I could see it was a lost cause.

'We've got tandems,' he added. 'We thought you might like them. Coming to the beach with us?'

Tandems? Oh, *tandems*! Now you're talking!

65

Rachel and I were laughing aloud with excitement as we threw the breakfast/lunch plates in the sink and hurtled up the open wooden staircase to get our swimming things from our rooms.

'Towels!' I shouted. 'Where are the beach towels? Where's the sunscreen stuff?'

'Have you got snorkels?' called Max from downstairs.

'No!' I retorted, giggling. 'No, I think it's just a heat rash!'

I'd always fancied riding a tandem. By the time we got to the beach I couldn't remember why. I hadn't had so much fun since my last smear test. Why are bicycle saddles *like* that? Who designed them? Why don't they fit women's anatomy?

'You weren't planning on having any sex for the next five years or so, were you?' I whispered to Rachel as we got off the bikes and walked to the beach with the gait of recently delivered mothers.

'I think I could forget a little bit of saddle-soreness if the occasion arose,' she said with a wince, watching Craig, in his nifty denim cut-downs, wheeling his bike ahead of us.

Such commitment. One could only feel humble.

Up till the moment when my genitalia ignited, I'd actually quite enjoyed the tandem ride; certainly more than riding one of those bikes-from-hell in the gym, anyway. Max, at the front of our bike, had been doing most of the work, and there's something to be said for pedalling along with a fixed view of a pair of quite pleasant buttocks moving energetically just in front of you.

'Look at the view!' he'd called out cheerily as we cycled down the tree-lined, café-lined main street through the centre of Carnac-Plage, where tacky souvenir shops to rival those in Southend offering baseball caps, postcards of naked women and Carnac rock cohabited happily alongside smart restaurant-bars where waiters served coffees and cold beers at the tables outside on the shimmering pavement.

Oh, I'm looking at the view. I am, I am! Thanks very much!

We settled ourselves on the beach under a sun umbrella, plastered ourselves with factor twenty, leant back and sipped cold beer we'd bought at the nearest bar. The cries and laughter of strange French children wafted across the beach as we stared up into a clear blue sky.

'Didn't think it got this hot in France,' said Rachel.

'It's even hot in *England* this year,' I reminded her. 'And we're nearer the equator here.'

'Hark at you two,' laughed Craig. 'Supposed to be off to travel round Europe, and you're already talking as if you're in the jungle when you've only just hopped across the Channel.'

'You don't think we're going to do it, do you?' smirked Rachel. '*You* think we're just two silly women who couldn't even manage to get ourselves to Carnac, never mind travel round Europe.'

'Well...'

Shading my eyes against the sun, I watched their faces – Rachel pretending to be indignant, shaking her head and peeping flirtatiously through her eyelashes, Craig looking back at her with undisguised desire as he tipped the last of his beer down his throat – and I tried to ignore the feeling beginning to gnaw inside me that, if we weren't careful, we could end up staying in Carnac far longer than we intended – and Rachel could end up not exploring much further in the world than the inside of Craig's trousers.

But it couldn't have been worrying me too much yet because at that point I closed my eyes, dropped my beer can and fell sound asleep.

Chapter 5

Of course I saw it coming between Rachel and Craig, and part of me wished her well. To put it crudely, I thought a shag might do her good. It might stop her looking so prim and proper about Tom and me, might get her off my case for a while. I just would have preferred that she hadn't met someone on the very first day of our travels, before we'd had the chance to go anywhere or see anything. But as it happened, even on that first day on the beach I found something else to amuse myself with.

I'd only dozed off for about half an hour when I was woken up by Craig and Max standing over us, waving something in our faces.

'Snorkels! We've got you some snorkels. Come on, let's go.'

'Go?' I asked sleepily, rubbing my eyes and blinking into the sun. 'Go where?'

'Snorkelling, Maddy. Have you ever tried it?'

'No,' I said at once, pulling a face. 'I can't...'

'Of course you can' protested Max, pulling me to my feet. 'It's the easiest thing in the world! You'll love it.'

'No, I won't!' I insisted, looking at the mask and tube in his hand with a healthy suspicion. It reminded me of nasty surgical procedures I'd seen on TV hospital dramas.

'Maddy, don't be such a spoilsport!' scoffed Rachel, getting to her feet and brushing the sand off her legs. She stripped down to her bikini with what looked like two easy fluid movements. 'Come on, let's at least give it a go now the boys have bought us the equipment.'

The boys looked at her with undisguised admiration while I, grudgingly and with a lot less fluidity of movement, extricated myself from the tight shorts and T-shirt that were by now sticking nastily to my flesh. They ran ahead of us down the beach carrying *the equipment*, while I plodded unenthusiastically after them.

'It's all very well for you,' I hissed at Rachel. 'You know I can't swim very well.'

'You don't need to,' said Max, slowing down and walking with me. 'You just have to drift along.'

'Well, I don't *drift along* very well, either,' I retorted ungraciously.

'I'll show you,' he offered kindly. 'You won't drown, I promise.'

I wasn't convinced. I was remembering the problems our daughters had encountered in Australia where the waves ripped their bikinis off. To be fair, my own bikini was so tight it would take a tidal wave to even loosen it, and as we waded into the sea I noticed that the waves here were small and friendly looking. The water felt cool after the heat of the beach, but not as freezing as I'd expected, and by the time I was waist-deep I was beginning to relax a little.

'I still don't see the point of it,' I said, watching Craig and Max put the masks over their faces and bite on a horrible piece of rubber. It looked about as pleasurable as a dental extraction.

'It's because of what you can see,' explained Craig before closing his mouth over the thing and sticking his face into the water.

'Well, how difficult can *that* be?' exclaimed Rachel, who'd by now put on her own snorkel and was watching Craig swimming out to sea with his air pipe sticking up out of the water like a shark's fin.

Rachel wasn't a bad swimmer. As with everything that required energy, motivation and some degree of physical fitness, she was streets ahead of me; but like me she'd never been taught properly, she just had more confidence, and more strength.

Wearing her snorkel, she duck-dived under the waves and began to swim after Craig with her own wild version of the front crawl. Within a couple of minutes she'd surfaced, spluttering and coughing. She took off the snorkel, shook the water out of it, stared at it in disbelief and shouted at Craig:

'It leaks! The bloody thing leaks!'

Craig and Max were both laughing out loud.

'You were going under the waves,' explained Craig. 'You can't do that and not expect the tube to fill up with water.'

She tried again, this time flailing her arms even more wildly in her desperation to do it right. Again, she came up gasping, spitting out mouthfuls of seawater.

'Just relax!' called Max. 'Try just floating on the water completely still.'

And then it happened. I know it's always easy to say this when you're watching someone else do something you haven't tried yourself but, watching Rachel spitting and gasping and getting crosser and crosser until finally she stood up and threw the snorkel back at Craig with 'trying to fucking drown me' being the gist of her complaint, I could see quite clearly what she was doing wrong. And I had a sudden, definite, excited conviction that I'd be able to do it right. You see, I had no problems whatsoever with lying on the water completely still. I could float all right. It was my favourite activity in the sea; I could never see the point of thrashing around using up all that energy if you were supposed to be on holiday.

'Can I try?' I asked Max.

'Of course.' He helped me put on the mask. I didn't like the feel of it over my nose at first but I resisted the urge to push it off and shout about suffocating. He adjusted the straps to fit my face, attached the breathing tube and told me to bite on the mouthpiece and close my mouth around it. Well, admittedly I'd been asked to do worse things than that

70

in my time. To my surprise I found myself automatically breathing through the tube. 'OK?' He looked at me a bit anxiously. 'Still nervous?'

I shook my head. If I tried to talk now, I'd forget to breathe.

'Good! Put your face in, and then just float. And remember – keep breathing through your mouth.'

I lowered my face into the water. Wow. This was a revelation to me. I'd never been happy about getting my face wet. My usual version of swimming was a fairly pathetic breaststroke, head held high out of the water. But without the need to hold my breath or struggle and flap around, this was a doddle. I stretched out, floating on my stomach, looking at the wave patterns on the seabed. I could see pebbles and seaweed and ... there was Max, peering at me through his mask, pointing out to sea. Copying him, I kicked my legs gently and used my normal slow breaststroke arm movements to pull myself through the waves after him. Out in the calmer, deeper water we both stopped and floated again. Here, the water was perfectly clear and we could watch the miniature shoals of hundreds of tiny silvery-blue fish swimming in circles beneath us. This was amazing! Why didn't I learn to do this years ago? What was I doing, all those times on seaside holidays as a child? Why did I waste so much time building sandcastles and jumping around rock pools with a stupid little net like a frigging fairy? Why didn't anyone ever show me how to do this before?

By the time we began to get cold and headed back for the shore, I was bursting with pride and excitement.

'I did it! I snorkelled!' I laughed aloud as we ran back up the beach.

'You're a natural,' said Max. 'You took to it really well. I can't believe that was your first time.'

Rachel nodded and smiled at me but I could see she was seething. She threw her snorkel on the sand and stretched out in the sun to dry off.

'I think I prefer to have a swim. A *proper* swim,' she said slightly disdainfully.

71

'Of course. Each to their own,' said Craig. 'Not everyone takes to it.'

'I'm never usually any good at anything like that,' I said in wonderment.

'No, well. Floating around on the surface isn't exactly physically *demanding*, is it,' retorted Rachel.

Not that you're jealous or anything.

I didn't retaliate. I was too chuffed with myself. Before the afternoon was over I'd been in the sea twice more and considered myself a snorkelling expert.

During the next couple of days we went everywhere as a foursome. Although I was tempted to go back to the beach and show off my snorkelling some more, I was conscious of the need to explore as much of the area as we could. It would have been highly embarrassing, when everyone at home asked us to relate our travellers' tales, to say we'd been to the beach every day. We drove down to the Quiberon peninsula and watched the furious waves churning up the sea on the Côte Sauvage – the wild western coast. We visited the pretty yachting harbour at La Trinité sur Mer, where every other restaurant seemed to be a crêperie selling delicious Breton pancakes served with thick whipped cream, and La Baule, where the vast three-mile crescent of perfect sandy beach and the esplanade of luxury hotels made us feel as if we were in a Mediterranean resort. We walked around the famous lines of prehistoric standing stones in Carnac itself, wondering how the ancient people of Brittany had erected so many hundreds of tons' worth of stone.

'Must have worked out a lot at the gym,' I said quite seriously, getting a glare from Rachel in response.

By the end of the first week, Brentwood Council and its supplies department might have been part of another life, or a dream. I was tanned and relaxed and happy. And Rachel was having it off with Craig.

*

I spent my evenings with Max, at the bar on the campsite where the two guys were staying. We wanted to stay out of the way of the others, and besides, the wine was cheap and the atmosphere at the open-air bar was lively and friendly. Max was good company and we found plenty to talk about as we knocked back our drinks in the warm, clear night air.

'I hope you don't think,' he began bravely on the first night we escaped the house, when we noticed the rubbing-in of after-sun lotion working its way towards its logical conclusion between Rachel and Craig, 'that I don't fancy you.'

'It's all right.' I smiled, touching his arm gently. He was a really nice guy, and let's face it, you don't come across that too often in life – especially one who's good-looking and not gay – so I hated to see him squirm. 'It's OK, I wasn't expecting us to have sex just because the other two are at it.'

'I suppose it's just too soon for me. You know, what with Karen walking out on me – I'm OK about it now, but. . .'

'Max, honestly, you don't have to explain. I'm seeing someone, anyway.'

'Oh, yes. Tom, isn't it? Was he . . . OK about you coming away like this with Rachel?'

'Yes, he's fine about it,' I said abruptly.

Bloody well ought to be. He's with his wife after all.

Tom and I phoned each other every couple of days. It felt strange, and strained, as if he, like my job at the council offices, was part of another life I'd left behind. He kept asking if I was missing him. Why would he ask that? We often spent longer than a week or two apart anyway, when he was busy with his own life, his own job, or away on holiday with his wife. Why was this so different? Could it be because I was the one, this time, who was out of reach? Surely he couldn't be feeling insecure, could he?

'So when are you coming back?' he asked, as we went into the second week.

'Um . . . I'm not quite sure yet,' I mumbled. 'We might drive on a little way . . . see some more places. . .'

'Oh. Right.' He laughed. 'Your money's not run out yet, then?'

Well, even I would have had trouble eating, drinking and smoking my way through eleven and a half thousand quid in a week.

'No. We're fine. So we might as well...'

'Yes, sure. Of course. Keep in touch, sweetheart.'

'I will.'

'And who's that? I can hear someone talking.'

'Oh, it's only Max. Just a friend. Yes, of course I'm missing you! Got to go now.'

We went to the internet café every other day to keep in touch with Sophie and Amy. They'd moved on to Sydney now, and had been enjoying seeing all the sights, as well as shocking all the local 'élite' by turning up at a performance at the Opera House dressed in shorts and hiking boots. They hadn't been turned away but they'd had some strange looks from the 'high heels and pearls brigade' as Sophie put it. I'd had a good laugh at this, but the following day after I'd sent her back an e-mail describing how we'd been spending every day with Craig and Max, I had a call on my mobile which made me realise that our own antics were not going to be viewed with such amused tolerance by our daughters. It was nearly midnight by French time. Max and I were strolling back to the house from the campsite bar. I'd had a lot to drink and when my phone started ringing I wasn't even sure what it was.

'It's your phone,' said Max, slurring only slightly.

'Phone? Where's the phone?'

'Your mobile. Is it in your bag? It's ringing – quick; get your phone out of your bag, Maddy! It's ringing!'

I stumbled and nearly fell against him as I struggled to fish it out of my bag.

'Hello? Who's that? Sophie! Oh, Sophie, hello, darling. Max – it's Sophie.'

He smiled and sat down by the roadside to wait for me. I went to sit down on the grass next to him but missed and fell over his legs, dropping the phone in the road.

'Hello! Hello, Sophie? Are you still there?' I was convulsed with the giggles by now.

'Mum?' replied a rather stony voice. 'Are you OK? Are you *drunk*?'

'Only a little bit!' I laughed. 'Don't worry, darling, Max is with me, I won't get arrested or anything.'

'This Max.' She sounded like my mother. 'How well do you know him?'

I snorted with laughter.

'Mum, it's not funny – I'm very concerned about you. There you are, in a foreign country, with these *strange men*, getting drunk...'

'Yes! It's lovely.' I paused, and added, 'And what are you and Amy up to then, darling? Are you having a lovely time, too? Not mixing with any strange men or getting drunk, I hope?'

'That really isn't the point.'

'Sorry. I know. It's lovely to hear from you, Sophie, and I promise I will be good. OK?'

'Well,' she relented, sounding slightly less alarmed. 'As long as you're being *careful*. Only, you and Rachel aren't used to going abroad, are you, and ... where is Rachel, by the way?'

'Back at the house. Asleep. Well, in bed, anyway!' I added with another snort of laughter. Max joined in, laughing loudly and making a few obscene gestures by way of illustrating what Rachel might be up to.

Thousands of miles away in Australia, though, Sophie wasn't laughing. There was a disapproving silence on the other end of the invisible connection between my mobile phone and the booth where she'd apparently paid for a phone card at nine o'clock in the morning because she was so concerned about her mother's behaviour in France.

'You're not *doing drugs*, are you?' she asked suspiciously.

'Don't be silly, darling,' I reproved her. 'Now, just you stop worrying yourself about us, and tell me more about Sydney.'

75

Sophie began to describe the boat tour they'd had of Sydney Harbour, and the lovely beaches that were so close to the city, although it was too cold to go swimming, and by the time she hung up she seemed to have calmed down a bit about the whole problem of her wayward mother.

'But I really think you should watch yourself with those guys, Mum,' she added as we said goodbye. 'And especially Rachel. Amy will *not* be impressed when I tell her what's going on.'

'Just tell Amy her mum's absolutely fine. There's nothing to worry about. I'll send you another e-mail tomorrow and tell you all about where we've been, OK?'

The phone call had sobered me up and we walked most of the way back to the house in silence.

'You still miss your daughter?' said Max eventually.

'Of course I miss her! It's not quite as bad, I suppose, as when I was at home, 'cos I've got other things to see and do here, to take my mind off worrying about her. But I think about her all the time.'

'You could have travelled out to Australia yourselves with the amount of money you won.'

'I know. But we didn't think they'd want us following them around, and besides, they're staying in hostels and moving on every week or so. By the time we got over there, they'd probably be in New Zealand.'

But I still felt unsettled the next day.

'I think we should think about moving on,' I said to Rachel over breakfast.

'Do you?' she replied flatly, biting into a croissant. It was amazing to me that Rachel had acquired the habit, so quickly, of eating croissants and *pains au chocolat* for breakfast. What happened to her healthy eating programme? Why wasn't she nibbling on bits of Ryvita and sucking a melon slice like she normally did?

'Yes,' I said firmly. 'We agreed that we wouldn't stay here too long; we wanted to see other places, didn't we.'

'I know. But it's only been just over a week. There's no hurry, is there? I thought you were enjoying it here.'

I busied myself buttering another croissant. This was going to be difficult. I knew it – Rachel was going to want to stay in Carnac because of Craig. If I pushed her too hard, too soon, about leaving, she'd probably dig her heels in and refuse to budge until he did. And then – even worse – would she want to follow him back to England and cut short our travels altogether?

'As long as we leave before Friday,' she added.

'Friday?' I echoed, looking up at her in surprise. 'What – *this* Friday?'

'Of course,' she replied calmly. 'You won't want to be here when *he* turns up, will you?'

'He? Who?'

'Oh! Sorry!' Rachel dropped her croissant back onto her plate and wiped the flaky crumbs off her mouth with the back of her hand, laughing out loud. 'I forgot to tell you. He phoned last night while you were out.'

'Who are we talking about, Rachel? Who phoned?'

'Nicholas Pretty Dodgy! He's coming out on Friday, to stay here for a week before his next tenant arrives the following weekend.'

'You're *joking*!'

'No. And if I was, I don't suppose you'd be laughing, anyway.'

'You're damn right I wouldn't. I can't believe he's coming over while we're still here. Shit, Rach, we need to be *well* out of here before he arrives.'

'I guessed you'd say that.'

'He isn't expecting to pick up the keys from us, is he? Shit, I hope not!'

'No. He said not to worry if we were out at the beach or whatever as he had another set of keys.'

'I don't want to be out at the beach. I want to leave his bloody keys in his bloody kitchen and be a hundred miles away.'

77

'So we'll be off on Thursday, then, I suppose?'

'You don't mind?'

'Course I don't. I just didn't want to rush off, like now, before I'd had breakfast – the way you were talking...'

'No. I'll be honest – I was nervous of asking you about moving on. Because of Craig.'

'Craig? What about him?'

Had I stepped into a parallel universe or something? Or had she forgotten who she was sleeping with last night, since he left this morning to get a change of clothes?

'Well, you know, you have been *seeing* each other, so to speak, and I thought perhaps...'

This time she laughed so loud, her last mouthful of croissant crumbs sprayed out all over the table.

'Maddy, we're not exactly *in LURVE* or anything. Do I *look* like I'm going to be crying my eyes out? Plenty more where he came from, I hope.'

To say this took me aback would be an understatement. Rachel was the *good* girl, the *nice* girl, the one who didn't have casual sex (or any sort of sex at all, come to that, for as long as I could remember). This all seemed so unlike her, I was left wondering whether she was suddenly going to light up a cigarette, knock back a bottle of brandy and slob out in front of the TV all day.

'I think it's about time I had a bit of fun,' she said quietly, catching the look on my face, 'don't you?'

'Absolutely,' I nodded. 'Croissants for breakfast, sex for dinner. Good for you, Rachel. Not a problem. Go for it.'

'Not as if I'm hurting anyone,' she added pointedly.

As in – not sleeping with a married man.

Point taken. So maybe I'm still the bad girl, after all.

The plan, such as it was, was to head towards Paris and then east in the direction of Belgium and Germany. But first, I had to get Rachel over her fear of driving on the right.

'I'm not doing all the driving. We're either taking turns, or we're going straight back to England,' I told her. This needed a no-nonsense, take-it-or-leave-it approach. She had to know I meant business.

'OK, OK. No need to be so aggressive about it,' she said moodily.

Craig looked up lazily from pretending to read a French newspaper.

'I'll take you out for some practice if you like.'

'Great!' I answered for her. 'And teach her how to map-read while you're at it!'

'You're not so bloody wonderful yourself,' retorted Rachel. 'You said how terrified you were of going round the roundabouts.'

'OK, girls, don't argue. We'll take you *both* out for some practice,' suggested Max. 'We could do with a laugh, couldn't we, Craig?'

By the day we left Carnac, the two guys had certainly had their fair share of laughs at our expense. But both Rachel and I were driving competently, and almost confidently, on the correct side of the road, and Rachel had learnt what the squares on the map were for, and knew which roads we were supposed to be taking towards Paris. It was a major step forward.

'Can't thank you enough,' I told Max as we hugged them goodbye.

I looked round at Rachel. She was doing her best to thank Craig, in the few minutes we had left, in the way he'd appreciate the most.

'Come on, come on, that's enough,' I snapped. 'Time to get going, Rach, and you're first in the driving seat!'

Slowly, and with great concentration, she carried us forth out of Carnac and along the main road towards Vannes.

'Are you sure you're OK?' I asked eventually, as neither of us had spoken for about fifteen minutes. 'About leaving Craig?'

'I'm fine,' she replied, smiling to herself but not taking her eyes off the road for a moment. 'Absolutely fine. Never look

79

back, Maddy – that's the trick. Never look back and you'll be OK.'

Jesus. I wish someone had taught me that lesson a long, long time ago.

En route to Paris, we stayed overnight in a little stone-built pension just outside Le Mans. Madame was large and dark and intimidating, gesticulating perilously with a huge bunch of keys like a very butch jailer from *Prisoner: Cell Block Nine*.

'Your room!' she barked aggressively, thrusting open the door of a small, musty but pleasantly furnished bedroom at the top of three flights of stairs. Despite her great girth she still had enough breath after striding up these to march to the window, fling back the shutters and hoist open the sash window with an almighty grunt of effort that reminded me of the last stages of labour. Fortunately it was a very warm night, as I had serious doubts whether it would ever close again.

'Thanks,' I said timidly. 'Very nice. *Très jolie.*'

She nodded her head at me, pointed to a notice on the wall listing the fire instructions and rules of the house, and left us to it, slamming the door after her.

'*Très aimable!*' I muttered, at which the door was flung open again and Madame, giving us a suspicious and disgusted look as if she'd caught us in an act of extreme indecency, announced in ringing tones, but fortunately slowly enough for me to translate, that breakfast would be served at eight o'clock *précisément*. The implication of her tone was that any latecomers would probably be slaughtered and served up with the cold cuts. We both attempted to look suitably impressed. The door was duly slammed again and Madame's footsteps thundered all the way down the three flights of stairs.

We held our breath, waiting, listening, in case she came back again with another forewarning of doom. Eventually Rachel sniggered; I felt a giggle rising from deep down in my throat; we looked at each other and that was it. We both exploded. We howled, we moaned, we cried with laughter. We fell on the bed, rolled around, and laughed until we ached.

'This is great!' she said at length, wiping the tears from her eyes with a corner of the purple bedspread. 'This is absolutely great, Maddy! I'll never forget it!'

She didn't need to say, because we both knew: she wasn't just talking about Madame. She didn't just mean tonight, or this guest house, or the sheer pleasure of laughing until we nearly wet ourselves. She meant – everything. Being away, being together, being on our own, with no immediate worries, no immediate responsibilities, and nothing to get up for in the morning other than the eight o'clock breakfast deadline.

'It's great,' I agreed, giving her a quick hug. 'But let's get showered and changed and go out for a meal before she locks us in for the night. I've got a sneaky feeling we'll never see the light of day again.'

And we entertained each other, over dinner in the little restaurant next door, with silly stories about how Madame probably murdered all her 'guests' and hid their bodies under the floorboards, until we'd scared the shit out of each other so much that we had to take it in turns to sleep all night and were so knackered in the morning we didn't make it down to breakfast until five past eight.

There was no jam left for our croissants.

Chapter 6

Rachel, having changed the habits of a lifetime by having some fun with Craig in Carnac, was true to her word and didn't once look back. Instead, she looked around, and she looked forward. In Paris she fastened her eyes upon a pretty young student called Philippe who was staying in the city to further his education, and she duly looked forward to teaching him a thing or two. By the time we'd climbed to the top of the Eiffel Tower with Philippe trailing behind us like a lovesick puppy, the conclusion was inevitable. Fortunately as well as being (according to Rachel) a fantastic lover, young Philippe was also pretty good as a tour guide. I, at least, learnt a lot of Parisian history as we roamed the city for four full days. I don't think Rachel took a lot of it in. She looked too tired.

Not having to conserve my limited energy for love-making, I fell in love with Paris instead. We took a boat tour on the Seine on the first day. It was a hot, intense morning with a denim-blue sky reflected in the swirling water of the busy river. I leant on the side of the boat, listening to the commentary in French, English, German and Italian and gazing in awe as we glided past famous landmarks like Notre-Dame and the Louvre, and under famous bridges such as the Pont Neuf, which even I knew meant New Bridge, and which was apparently the oldest bridge in Paris. I immediately liked it for its contrariness.

The second day was mostly taken up by our trip to the

Eiffel Tower, and up the Eiffel Tower, and down again, and the recovery period spent by Rachel in Philippe's arms in the Parc du Champs de Mars, and by me strolling, alone and fascinated, around the base of the Tower, marvelling at the lovely tackiness of the souvenirs on sale.

On the third day, we ambled down the Champs-Elysées from the grandeur of the Arc de Triomphe, pausing far more often than was strictly necessary at the dozens of shops and pavement cafés that took our fancy. We wandered, mouths open in awe like the best of tourists, around the vast Place de la Concorde, hearing about all of its bloody past in one eloquent lesson from Philippe, who was studying European history and wanted to become a teacher.

And on our last day we strolled through Montmartre. Apparently the most famous artists in French history – Renoir, Van Gogh, Gauguin and Picasso – all lived and worked here. I could understand it. I felt like knocking out a few quick pictures myself, but I'd left my felt-tips at home so I made do with the camera. We ended up at the Sacré Coeur and climbed up to the dome, having just about recovered the strength in our legs from the Eiffel Tower jaunt, to get another great view over the whole of Paris.

'I love it here, don't you?' I said to Rachel as we stared out over the rooftops and traffic below. 'I think I could live here.'

'Fuck that,' she whispered back. 'They don't speak English, Madd. And they want sex non-stop!'

Can't have everything, I suppose.

'What did Sophie say?' she asked me as we hit the road again. We'd stopped off at an internet café as usual before leaving Paris.

'Oh, not a lot. Just talking about Brisbane, how beautiful the city and the river and everything are, and how they're enjoying the weather 'cos it's a bit warmer than in Melbourne and Sydney. How about Amy? Any goss?'

'Well.' Rachel gave me a sideways look and hesitated. 'Not really.'

'What's that supposed to mean? Come on, what did she say? Are they all right? Have they lost anything? Are they in trouble? Is one of them ill, or something?'

'Calm down, calm down!' she laughed. 'No, there's nothing wrong. I just wondered if Sophie mentioned anyone else, at all?'

'Anyone else? Like who? What sort of anyone else?'

'A guy. Someone called Ryan.'

'Ryan? No. Who is he?'

'I don't know. Maddy, don't keep looking at me like that – keep your eyes on the road! I don't know who he is, just that Amy sort-of implied that Sophie was going out with him.'

'Going out with him?' I squawked, aware that I was repeating everything Rachel was saying, like a parrot. But I was so shocked. I mean, Sophie had always told me everything. I'd always had all the rundown on every boy she'd ever dated. That was one of the things I was missing – the cosy mum and daughter chats about the latest boyfriend, what she thought of him, whether he was worth seeing again, whether she was thinking of sleeping with him – no, there wasn't a lot she didn't tell me. We'd always had some good laughs about some of the rubbish ones she finished with after only one or two dates. And now, there she was on the other side of the world, going out with some – some Aussie Ryan – and she couldn't even be bothered to mention him, couldn't even spare the time to drop his name into an e-mail to her mother. I had to find out about it from Rachel via Amy.

'I expect he's just some guy they've met at one of the hostels,' I said. 'Probably they've both had a drink with him once or twice, you know, more of a friend, more of an acquaintance, than an actual boyfriend as such...'

'That's not the impression I get from Amy. She says Sophie's been seeing a lot of him. She says they started seeing each other in Sydney.'

'In Sydney?' I squeaked. 'And he's turned up again in Brisbane?'

'Yes. It doesn't sound like a coincidence, does it?'

I drove in silence for a while. My mind was whirling with possibilities. Maybe, despite what Rachel obviously thought, it was just a coincidence. The girls had already told us how they sometimes made friends with other back-packers, moved on, and then came across the same people again later in another place. A lot of travellers seemed to follow the same routes around Australia and as they all sought out the cheapest hostels it wasn't too surprising if they did occasionally cross paths with people more than once. If this Ryan guy was someone important, Sophie would have mentioned him: no two ways about it. I started to relax.

'I'm sure there's nothing in it,' I insisted stubbornly. 'She'd have told me if there was.'

'Yes, I expect you're right,' said Rachel lightly.

I wanted to look at her again to try to gauge whether she really meant it, but I was coming up to a junction and needed to concentrate.

'Which way?' I shouted as I slowed down and looked around hopelessly for road signs.

'Right! No, left!' She tried to turn the map round without me noticing. 'Definitely right!'

Some things never change.

Our next stop was Lille, just on the French side of the Belgian border. In Paris, we'd been too scared to drive into the city so we stayed at a hotel in the outskirts and did our sightseeing by Métro, which was an experience in itself but was made a lot easier by having Philippe with us. We decided to follow the same plan in Lille. I took over the navi-gating, got us to a suburb where it was only a short train ride into the town centre, and where, according to our guidebook, there was a reasonably priced small hotel just along the road from the station.

'We're getting good at this,' I commented proudly as we turned off the main road following signs for the hotel.

Then we pulled into a petrol station and filled the car up with diesel instead of petrol.

'I told you: *Gasoil* is diesel – we've been over this before. Why didn't you let me do it?'

'Oh, stop being so bloody bossy. If your French is so wonderful, you should have been watching what I was doing. I thought all the pumps were the same.'

'What? Don't be stupid – how can they all be the same? Are they all the same in England? Do you fill up from the diesel pumps at home?'

'All right, don't keep nagging. What are we going to do now?'

I ran my hands through my hair and stared at the car. It'd stalled as soon as we tried to pull away from the petrol station and there were now three cars waiting, not very patiently, behind us. One driver leant out of his window and fired a string of staccato French exclamations at us, accompanied by some gesticulations that looked like threats of hanging, drawing and quartering. Another leant heavily on the horn and glared at us through the windscreen.

'I think we're in the shit,' said Rachel prosaically.

'I think we're going to have to push it,' I told her. 'Come on. One on each side.'

'Where to?' she shouted over the top of the car at me as we began heaving it forwards.

'Just out of here,' I gasped, 'onto the side of the road. Then we'll have to think.'

Fortunately we didn't have to think for too long. By the time we'd got the car out of the petrol station entrance and onto the roadside, we'd attracted quite a lot of attention – not least because it was very hot and we were both wearing cut-down jeans and fairly skimpy strappy tops. Like a pack of hungry scavenging mongrels hoping for scraps, about half a dozen unsavoury looking local yobs were soon hanging around us at a not-very discreet distance, leering and muttering ugly French phrases that sounded as obscene as they no doubt were, while tugging at their own clothing in a way that reminded me of boys of infant-school age needing to go for a pee.

'Do we make a run for it and abandon the car?' I whispered to Rachel.

'No! My car!' she wailed, stroking its bonnet. 'We can't just leave it here – with all these foreigners around...'

'Oh, all right, Rach, we'll wait around until a group of middle-class Englishmen come along, shall we?'

'Very funny.' She was almost in tears. 'Anyone would think I'd done this on purpose.'

'Excuse me, ladies,' said a voice behind us with an unmistakable public-school accent, 'but I couldn't help noticing you seem to be in a little bit of a fix.'

'Can we be of any assistance?' added another voice, even posher.

'We can speak the lingo, if you need a bit of help,' joined in a third. 'Or perhaps a tow to a garage?'

A group of middle-class Englishmen! We whirled round to face them.

'Where did you lot spring from?' I asked, feeling quite faint at the thought that I'd somehow conjured them up.

'Boulogne actually,' said the first guy smoothly. 'Just driving by...'

'Noticed you having a little bit of trouble here...'

'Don't like to see two damsels in distress. Especially with all these damned foreigners hanging around!'

The pack of wolves had melted back into the shadows as soon as they appeared.

'If you could just help us to get to a garage,' said Rachel, almost breathless in her relief and gratitude, 'we'd be eternally grateful.'

'Steady on! No need for all that,' laughed the most posh of the three. 'Come on, then, Charles – tow rope in the boot. Want one of us to steer for you, ladies? Bit tricky if you're not used to it.'

By the time we'd deposited the car at the nearest garage,

and listened in silent awe as Charles, Stuart and Winston gave fluent instructions in French about what was needed (a complete washout of the car's stomach and bowels by the sound of it), we were ready for a meal and more than ready to repay our rescuers by inviting them to join us.

Our Three Musketeers, we discovered over dinner, were on a business trip, staying only for three nights in Lille before heading back to London. Winston was the only one of the three who wasn't married so I guessed Rachel would have her eye on him before the evening was over. She continued to amaze me. I couldn't believe that this was the same Rachel I'd known all this time. In the space of two and a half weeks in France, to my certain knowledge, she'd had more sex than in the whole of the last fifteen years.

As for me, I had no difficulty in gently rebuffing a some-what surprising, but terribly polite, invitation from Charles (over the coffee and liqueurs), to go back to their hotel with him and have 'a bit of hanky panky'. He took my refusal on the chin, like the gentleman he obviously was, and kissed my hand very chivalrously when we said goodnight at our hotel later on.

This was just as well, really, because the following day when we came down for breakfast, Tom was sitting there waiting for me.

I suppose the way I said, 'What the hell are you doing here?' didn't get things off to a good start.

'I came to see you,' he said, holding out his arms to me. 'Surprised?'

Bloody flabbergasted.

'Why?' I demanded, aware that I was making it worse. 'You never said!'

We'd talked on the phone the previous evening. I hadn't even twigged anything was strange about the fact that he'd asked the name of the hotel we were staying in. I just thought he was taking an interest. Should have known it was unlikely that a man would take that much interest!

'I wanted to surprise you!' he repeated, letting his arms drop to his sides and the smile drop from his face. 'You don't look very pleased to see me.'

'Well. Yes.' I sat down on one of the sofas in the hotel reception area and he plonked himself down next to me, looking hurt. Rachel, eyes wide with surprise, raised a hand to him in a half-hearted greeting and made a quick exit in the direction of breakfast.

'It's just – a bit unexpected,' I said lamely. 'Not that I'm not pleased to see you ...' I turned to look at him. At thirty-five, Tom was still one of the most attractive men I'd ever met. Women watched him across rooms, across streets, and I couldn't blame them. His hair was brown and tousled, in that careless way that made him look as though he'd just got out of bed. His eyes were dark and passionate. He was slim, he was fit, and his smile would turn your heart upside down. He wasn't smiling now, though. He looked like a little boy who'd just been told he couldn't stay up late.

'I'm sorry,' I said more gently. 'It's sweet of you to come.'

'I missed you,' he said, putting an arm round me, taking hold of my hand. 'I've got a couple of days off. I thought we could spend a long weekend together.'

Was it nearly the weekend again already? I realised with a jolt that I was barely even aware what month it was, I'd been so relaxed, so carefree.

'That'd be nice,' I said. My mind was doing acrobatics of adjustment. Ten minutes ago I'd been laughing and joking with Rachel about silly things: the way the shower in our room turned on so fiercely it had made her yelp with surprise; the possibility of hot or cold croissants for breakfast; the disaster the previous day with the car; the adventure ahead, of the train journey into the city centre. I'd been a free spirit, a traveller, a person with nothing to consider beyond where to buy her next cup of coffee. Now, suddenly, Tom had appeared, like a memory of another life. He wouldn't have laughed at those same stupid things we were laughing about. He didn't belong here – it didn't feel right. He didn't fit.

'I'll show you and Rachel the sights,' he was saying. 'I've been to Lille before. It's beautiful. You'll love it. And then,' he added, squeezing my hand and smiling at me, 'after the weekend, we could go back home together. You've been away for nearly three weeks now. You must be ready to come back, aren't you, sweetheart?'

I pulled my hand away. Ready to go back? No, I wasn't! I'd hardly got started! I was just getting used to this life, just beginning to relax and enjoy it. I'd barely made inroads yet into my lottery winnings. If Rachel and I carried on as we were, spending fairly carefully, we could make it last much longer. So far we'd only been in France. What about Belgium, Germany and Switzerland? What about all the rest of Europe?

I looked at the expression on Tom's face; the look of pained surprise that I wasn't, already, jumping up and down with excitement at the thought of packing my bags and going home with him almost immediately. And I realised I'd been lying. I wasn't even, if I was honest, particularly pleased to see him. I was annoyed. He was intruding. OK, so I hadn't been absolutely straight about how long I intended to be away. It was probably mean to leave him with the idea that I might be back after two or three weeks. But I had warned him that I equally might not be. Why couldn't he accept that? Why couldn't he, for once, be the one to stay at home and wait for me? I'd spent the last two years waiting around for him.

'Did you come to check up on me?' I asked him abruptly.

'Of course not!' he looked even more pained. 'Maddy, I just wanted to see you! I thought—'

'That I might be enjoying myself? Having a good time without you? Seeing other men, even, God forbid?'

'What's got into you?' He was beginning to look annoyed now, and I suppose I couldn't blame him. 'I've come all this way to see you.'

To bring me home.

'Nobody asked you to,' I retorted childishly.

He stood up, picked up his jacket, turned away from me.

'Well, then. You've made your point,' he said coolly. 'I'd better not hang around. I wouldn't want to spoil your enjoyment.'

What is it with us women? We never know what we want. We think we want a plain pink carpet and then we scream about the dirt on it. We think we want a puppy and then moan about the mess it makes and what it costs to feed it. We think we want a man and then we spend the rest of our life complaining about him. We think he's a pain in the neck, he's annoying, he's difficult, we'd be better off without him and we want him to go. Then at that moment when he turns round and starts to walk away. . .

'Wait!' I shouted. 'Don't go. Don't be like that. I'm sorry, Tom. Come back.'

He hesitated, halfway across the hotel foyer, his back still turned to me, his jacket half on. Two elderly ladies on their way to breakfast stopped and stared at us: the mad English woman shouting after the handsome English man. Was there going to be a barney? Should they stay and watch?

Tom turned slowly and walked back to me.

'Maybe I shouldn't have come,' he acknowledged. 'Or I should have told you I was coming.'

'Yes. That would have been better.'

'Do you want me to stay? Or not?'

'Yes. I do. I'm sorry. Let's have a few nice days together. But I'm not coming home yet, Tom.'

'OK.' He shrugged. I wondered if, even now, he anticipated talking me into changing my mind.

'Let's go and have breakfast, then,' I said. 'Before Rachel hogs all the croissants.'

'Croissants? Rachel?' he said in surprise, finally smiling again.

'Oh yes! Wait till you see the change in her. Fattening food, wine, men – I'm expecting her any day now to nick one of my fags or roll herself a joint.'

91

The mention of men was a mistake. Tom's smile faltered slightly as we headed for the breakfast room. Insecure. That was it. He really was afraid that I was going to meet someone else. The sheer cheek of it astounded me – he had a wife waiting for him at home!

'Hi, Tom. This is a surprise,' said Rachel, looking up from her coffee. Neither her tone nor her expression made it sound like it was a pleasure.

'Nice to see you, Rachel,' he replied, appearing not to notice.

And it was only when he reached across and kissed her lightly on the cheek that I realised something. We hadn't even kissed each other since he'd arrived.

It wasn't a problem Tom being with us. In fact, it worked out quite well, as Rachel promptly announced her intention to spend the day with Winston. I suspected she'd probably agreed to this to allow Tom and me some time together – or, perhaps, to avoid spending any time with Tom herself. She treated him with a coolness that might have spilled over into open hostility if she'd been less concerned about our friendship.

So instead of catching the train into Lille town centre with Rachel, I ended up catching it with Tom. Instead of sightseeing with Rachel, sighing together over the romantic old Flemish buildings around the central square, while also managing the odd sigh over the local policemen, and the contents of the shop windows, I spent the morning on a very efficient and very informative sightseeing tour with Tom, probably learning a lot more about the chequered history of the town but having a lot fewer giggles. And at lunchtime, instead of finding a funky little café-bar with Rachel, where we could have a cold beer and sandwich sitting outside on the pavement and make up funny stories for each other about the passers-by, Tom took me to an expensive restaurant where we went inside, out of the sun, into a dark room with dark wood tables and chairs and silent service from unsmiling waitresses who brought us heavy leather-bound menus.

'The onion soup looks good,' said Tom, translating for me. 'And we must have the *moules marinière* for the main course. Mussels are the speciality here. And then perhaps. . .'

'Tom,' I said, closing my menu and laying it down firmly on the tablecloth, 'it's nearly thirty degrees outside. I'm in a beautiful foreign city for one of the very few times of my whole life. I'm sorry, I don't want to be ungrateful, but I don't want soup. And I don't want mussels.'

'What, then?' he asked, looking at me with startled eyes over the top of the wine menu.

'A salad. And a pint of beer.'

He frowned slightly, with puzzlement rather than annoyance, but he called the waitress and ordered my salad and his mussels without further comment. And it occurred to me, as we waited for the meal, that he didn't really know me at all. I'd never liked onion soup. And I hated bloody mussels with a vengeance.

'I start my first stint in Manchester on Monday,' he told me as we strolled back through the old part of town later in the afternoon. 'I'll be working in the area office up there for a couple of weeks. I went up for a day last week to meet the sales team. Had a very useful meeting. They're good guys – all terrifically hungry.'

Hungry? A vision of Tom's plateful of *moules marinière* came unbidden into my mind, along with a horrible picture of a crowd of drooling young men, napkins tucked into their shirt collars, sauce dripping from their fingers and their chins as they sucked out mussels and tossed the shells aside, mopping their plates with hunks of bread and smacking their cheeks with pleasure.

'Hungry for what?' I asked.

He looked at me as if I was slightly stupid.

'Work! New accounts! Success!' he said with what I thought to be a most unnatural gleam in his eyes.

93

Oh, OK. I suppose there are many different types of hunger.

We spent two more days together, during which the type of hunger afflicting Tom was amply demonstrated in the hotel bedroom – morning, noon and night. It was a good thing that Rachel was being kept occupied by Winston. Call me perverse, but I was beginning to feel just a tad used. For the price of a return Eurostar ticket to Lille, he was certainly getting his money's worth in the rumpy-pumpy stakes. Was that all he wanted? Was that, as Rachel had hinted, all this was about?

He was travelling back on the Saturday night, as he had to be in Manchester ready to start work on the Monday morning. On the last evening, we had dinner together and then sat in the bar arguing about the fact that I didn't want to go back with him. He started off by trying to bribe me with the offer of a weekend in Manchester, but before he even saw the look of disbelief on my face – how did he think a weekend in a hotel in Manchester was supposed to compare with another couple of weeks touring Europe? – he suddenly stopped, frowned, and shook his head, saying no, no, he'd forgotten, I'd better not go to Manchester next weekend – sorry – not then. . .

'I suppose Linda's going?' I said flatly, stubbing out my cigarette.

He looked at me in alarm. I never usually mentioned her. He probably thought I was going to fly into a jealous rage; but, obviously, if I'd been going to do that I'd have done it long ago.

'It doesn't matter,' I said. 'I didn't want to come, anyway. I'm staying with Rachel. We're going on to Germany.'

'Why?'

'Why? Because we want to!' I exclaimed, exasperated. 'Because we can! Because we're enjoying ourselves!'

'And that's all that matters?'

'Yes, Tom, it bloody is all that matters! Sophie's in

Australia, Simon's looking after my house, I've got a bit of money and I've probably made myself unemployed. What the hell else have I got to worry about?'

'Me?' he replied quietly, looking down at his cup of coffee. 'Doesn't it matter what I think? That I might miss you?'

I wanted to hit him.

'That's bollocks!' I retorted. Fortunately, no one around us in the bar seemed to speak English. 'Why would you miss me? You just get on with your own life – you always have. Your job, your wife...'

'It's never bothered you before.'

'No! And it doesn't now. But I don't see...' I sighed crossly, screwing up my hands into fists in my frustration. 'I don't see how the fuck you can expect me to come running home because you miss me!'

'Well, then. That kind of says it all, doesn't it,' he said stonily.

'Tom, we've never had that kind of relationship. It's never been possible. For obvious reasons.'

'And what about if it was possible? Supposing things were different?'

'In what way? I don't know what you mean. How different?'

He suddenly reached for my hands across the table, took hold of them and uncurled them from their tight, angry fists and held them, tight, squeezing my fingers until I flinched.

'I've been doing some thinking while you've been away,' he began, so quietly that I had to lean across the table to hear him. 'I've been thinking about Us. I know I've always taken you for granted. To be honest, I don't know why you've put up with it. I've been a bit of a bastard, haven't I.'

'I knew the score. I had a choice. Rachel would say I've been a bitch myself – carrying on with a married man. She's probably right.' I shrugged. 'I've never had much of a conscience. Linda's the only one not doing anything wrong, but I've never let myself stop and think about her, so yes, I must be a bitch, and you must be a bastard.' I smiled weakly, my anger evaporating.

'Maybe. But supposing I told you it wasn't going to be like that any more?'

'In what way?' My fingers were hurting. I wanted to pull them out of his grasp, but he was staring at me so seriously, looking so solemn, I didn't like to. I'd probably have pins and needles in my hands for the rest of the day.

'Don't you know what I'm trying to say, Maddy?' he persisted. 'I'm trying to tell you: I've decided to leave Linda. I'm going to tell her next weekend that I want a divorce, and then we can be together. We can live together, sweetheart – properly, all the time, and now you've left your job you've got nothing to keep you in Brentwood, nothing to keep you down South. We can move to Manchester, or Edinburgh, or Liverpool – wherever you like!'

He paused for breath and finally let go of my hands. My fingers had gone stiff and white like a corpse's.

'Now do you want to come back with me?'

Chapter 7

After Tom left to go back to England that Saturday night, I stayed in our hotel room on my own. It wasn't an interesting hotel room, sadly, or even an interesting hotel. It was one of those chain-motels you get on the outskirts of big towns everywhere in the world, so that once you've gone through the door you could be in America, England or China and not even the food being served would give you a great deal of a clue about where you were. With nothing much to do other than try for the third time to translate the fire notice, I gave up and lay on the bed with my eyes closed, until Rachel came back later from her last day with Winston.

'Are you asleep?' she whispered, taking off her shoes and throwing them across the room.

'Yes. I'm having nightmares about shoes flying past my right ear.' I sat up and watched her getting undressed. 'Did you have a nice day?'

'Yes. You?'

'Not really. Have you had dinner?'

'Yes!' She looked at her watch. 'I thought you'd gone to bed. I was just going to have a shower and—'

'Don't! Don't let's go to bed yet. I want to go out for a drink.'

'Are you all right?' She stood in her bra and knickers, looking at me, perplexed. 'Didn't you go out for dinner?'

'Yes. Ages ago. I just want to talk, though. And maybe get drunk.'

'You look like you've had a couple already.'

'Minibar.' I smiled at her, indicating it with my thumb. 'Empty now.'

She looked from the bottles on the floor by the bed, to the empty cigarette packet on the bedside table, with growing concern on her face.

'Something's happened,' she said, sitting down on the bed beside me.

'Yes. Tom's going to divorce Linda. He's asked me to marry him.'

'Shit.' She hung her head, looking like she was going to faint from the shock. 'What are you going to do?'

Do? What was there to do?

'Like I said. Get drunk.'

We went down to the hotel bar and I got stuck into the vodka and tonic. What was I trying to do? Forget about it? Block it out, pretend he'd never said all that stuff to me, promising me he was going to tell Linda their marriage was over, that he'd be free to live with me, that he'd marry me, take care of me, make up for all the time he'd taken me for granted...

'I'm still not coming back to England,' I'd told him stubbornly.

He'd sighed and said fair enough, if I'd made up my mind, maybe he could understand me wanting a last fling before we settled down.

'Settle down!' I repeated crossly to Rachel, knocking back another drink. 'Who says I want to settle down?'

'But you might do afterwards,' she said, surprisingly, staring into her glass with a kind of faraway look, 'after this trip is over. After all the money's been spent. Don't you think about that, Madd? Don't you wonder how you're going to feel?'

'No!' I retorted vehemently. 'And I don't *want* to think about it. I thought we were just going to enjoy ourselves! Enjoy ourselves without *worrying* about anything else – the future, what happens when we go home – all that crap. I thought we weren't going to think about all that!'

I lit a cigarette and purposely blew the smoke towards her, feeling cross and somehow betrayed. I didn't want her sitting there staring into her drink and getting all maudlin about going home. I wanted her to cheer me up.

She waved the smoke away, pulling a face.

'Sometimes, Maddy, I just don't understand you.'

Oh. Oh, I see! That's great, that is. I'm looking to my best friend for a bit of sympathy and commiseration, and what do I get? *I don't understand you.*

'What don't you understand?'

'Well, for a start, this thing about Tom. Sorry, I know you're upset, and I'm trying, I'm really trying to understand, but I don't. Anyone else, *anyone*, who'd been seeing someone for two years, and playing second fiddle to his wife, would be *ecstatic* if the guy suddenly flew out to see them and said he was getting a divorce and wanted to marry them! What's the matter with you? Why's it so terrible? Why aren't you pleased?'

'Because he expects me to just ... suddenly ... just because *he's* decided now ... he wants me to just go running, as soon as he clicks his fingers ... and go and live in Manchester, or Glasgow, and...'

'What have you got to lose? What's stopping you?' She gave me a very direct look through the haze of smoke I was trying to put between us. 'Anyone would think you didn't love him.'

'Love? "What's love got to do with it?"' I quoted flippantly. I laughed and shook my head. 'It's just bollocks, isn't it. Fucking bollocks.'

'Is it? I don't know. I've purposely stayed clear of it. Since Keith ... I didn't want to risk it.'

'I know,' I said, still laughing. 'Pure as the driven snow, you were, till we came on this trip.' I was very drunk by now. Swaying in my chair. You know how you get to that stage where you think you're being very, very funny but nobody except you is actually laughing? 'Like a vestal fucking virgin!'

'But you don't know *why*, do you. Why do you think I never wanted to risk it?'

'What? A relationship? The whole *lurve* thing?' I frowned, trying to think sober thoughts. 'I dunno. I suppose because you were so much in *lurve* with Keith, and after he died, you couldn't...'

'Wrong.'

'Eh?'

'I didn't really love Keith. Don't look at me like that, Madd – it's bad enough saying it out loud, without you looking at me like I've just sworn in church. I know it's a shocking thing to say. It's a shocking thing to feel, too. I've never told anyone before.'

And you choose to tell me now I'm so pissed I can hardly concentrate?

'When did you realise, then? How long had you been married before you decided you didn't love him?'

'I realised it before we even got married.'

I put down my drink with a shaky hand.

'Jesus! Why? I mean ... you and Keith ... well, you met while you were still at school, didn't you.' I knew this much at least. She'd never told me very much about Keith, but I'd heard this story several times, about how they went to different universities and only saw each other during the holidays. I always thought how romantic it was. 'And you stayed together, all the time you were at university, even though you were miles apart from each other,' I prompted. Something about this pleased me, at a level I couldn't quite explain even to myself. It was kind of reassuring that even back then, when Rachel was the same sort of age I was when my marriage collapsed in an ugly heap, there were young couples devoted enough to each other to turn their backs on the temptations of the 'free love' society of the 1970s and stay true to each other through thick and thin.

100

'Yes. What a fucking waste,' she said. 'What a stupid fucking waste.'

I don't think I could have been more shocked if she told me she'd been arrested for drug smuggling and prostitution.

'A waste? How do you mean? How can you say that?'

She turned to me, slowly, a sad smile on her face.

'You didn't go to university. You should have done, Madd. It's the best experience of your life. I wanted Amy to go but she was determined to get a job as soon as she'd finished her A levels. This thing about travelling the world – that's what they all want to do now. It's all very well, but it's probably wasted on youngsters of their age, and I suppose you could say the same about university. I wasted my time at Bristol.'

'Of course you didn't. That's a ridiculous thing to say! You got a good degree, and you became a science teacher. I wish *I'd* got a career like that. . .'

'I don't mean *that*. I know: compared with a lot of students, I got on OK. I worked hard; I did well in my exams. They were all going to parties and pubs every night of the week – having a good time, forgetting to do their assignments, not bothering to turn up for lectures. . . I never did any of that.'

'Because of Keith?'

'No. It wasn't anything to do with Keith,' she said quietly. 'It was because I was totally in love with a medical student called David.'

'You had an affair?'

The shocks were piling on. I was almost sobering up.

'I wasn't actually unfaithful to Keith. . .'

'Well, then! What are you beating yourself up about?'

'But only because I never got around to it. I met him at the folk music society. He borrowed my plectrum, and that was it.'

'Plectrum?'

'We both played guitar, Maddy. Everybody wanted to play guitar in those days. It was the coolest thing you could do.'

101

'I know. I had a go myself, but my fingers started bleeding...'

She gave a tut of exasperation.

'That's normal. Everyone's fingers bleed. You have to get through that, for God's sake.'

She hadn't changed. She was apparently just the same when she was learning the guitar at nineteen as she was now about the gym. No gain without pain – the more pain the better.

'I don't believe in bleeding,' I told her evenly, 'unless it's medically necessary.'

'Yes, well.' She gave me a rueful grin. 'We took ourselves terribly seriously in the seventies, didn't we. I think everyone at our university wanted to bleed for one reason or another. We used to write songs and poetry about love and peace and harmony. We wore beads and flowers and did a lot of protesting about wars and the voice of youth. We were complete prats. We didn't have a clue what the fuck we were talking about.'

'Every generation's the same, though, isn't it – more or less. If young people weren't idealistic, there'd be no hope left in the world.'

'Well, if the whole generation was a bunch of idealistic knobbers, David and I were probably the worst. We thought we were Bob Dylan and Joan Baez. We spent all our time practising chords and making up horrendous lyrics about the colour of the sun and the unity of mankind. I wouldn't mind, but neither of us was any good. It must have been excruciating for anyone to listen to.'

'But you ... liked each other? You were attracted to each other, obviously?'

'Yeah. I'd never felt quite like that about Keith. It was... wonderful, and terrible. Like continually smelling gorgeous home-baked bread and not being allowed to eat it. We never made love. But only because David was so *honourable*. He wanted me to call off my engagement.'

'So why *didn't* you?'

She sighed.

'Because I was too scared and too stupid to tell anyone I'd changed my mind. Keith and I always said we'd get married as soon as we finished university. Our families had planned it for so long – the bridesmaids' dresses were chosen, the invitations were printed – you know what I mean? It wasn't an option to back down.'

'So you got married, and had Amy, and Simon.'

'Yes. It was fine. We were OK. It wasn't as if he was mean, or nasty, and it wasn't as if we argued, or anything, but...'

'But he wasn't David.'

'I know it sounds pathetic, but I never stopped thinking about him. We kept in touch. Occasionally we met up – just as friends, you know, just for a drink and a chat about old times. And that feeling was still there. It never went away.'

'Christ. Rach, I had no idea...'

'Why would you? I never told anyone. I don't know why I'm telling you now. The thing is, you see, I've felt guilty ever since.'

'Why?'

'Every time I saw David, I'd make up my mind to go home and tell Keith I wanted a divorce. But I never had the guts. I took the easy way. I stayed in a marriage that was a complete sham, with a husband I didn't love, and I kept the man I really loved hanging on for me, wasting his time. I let them both down.'

A solitary tear ran down her cheek and she wiped it away quickly with the back of her hand.

'I betrayed them both,' she whispered. 'I was a coward.'

I got up and tried to perch on the arm of the chair where she was sitting, but I was still too pissed to do it without falling off. I put my arms round her.

'No, you weren't. You didn't betray anyone. You were a mother. You were trying to maintain ... the status quo.'

'I wanted it both ways. I wanted to be with David, but I was scared to leave Keith. So I let things run on like that, and

103

you know what the result was? *No one* was happy, Maddy! That's what I did – I made *all* of us miserable. I never had the guts to tell Keith I didn't love him, but he knew. He died unhappy, and it was my fault.'

'You didn't do *anything* wrong!' I told her. 'You've blamed yourself because Keith died so young and you didn't love him!'

'They said he must have had a heart condition all his life, without knowing it. Imagine that: no symptoms, no illness, no idea whatsoever that anything's wrong with you and then suddenly, just...' she snapped her fingers in the air, 'just dead. Gone. Over and out.'

'Some people would say that's a good way to go.'

'Not for the people left behind. Not for a wife who might have been secretly wishing her husband could just disappear off the face of the earth, and make it easier for her to get together with someone else.'

Oh yes. They say you should be careful what you wish for, don't they.

'And after that,' she said, looking up at me with a ghost of a smile, 'we never *could* get together. We were doomed, David and I. I couldn't have lived with the thought that I'd got what I wanted because of Keith dying. I never saw David again.'

But she'd felt guilty ever since. I wondered if that was why she punished herself with so much exercise and so little fun in her life. But it was hardly the time to ask.

'Are you OK... now?'

I put another drink in front of her. She'd still only had a couple of glasses of wine.

I couldn't understand how she did it, all that emotional stress with hardly any alcohol to take the pain away.

'I've accepted my life the way it is,' she replied briskly. 'I've got my job. I enjoy my lifestyle – keeping fit, eating healthy food, looking after myself. This trip was always going to be a one-off. We're stepping outside of our real lives, Madd, we both know that. We're doing things we don't normally do.'

'You are! Croissants and sex!'

'Absolutely! But when we go back...' She shook her head. 'We're not like Sophie and Amy, are we. We're not twenty years old, just starting out, ready to share a flat, try a job, change it, find a boyfriend, dump him ... You're going to be forty in a few years' time. If you don't want to settle down with Tom, what do you want?'

I want to live in a house made of chocolate shortbread. I want to grow wings and fly up through the clouds and find the magic land in the sky. I want to meet fairies in the woods and dance with them in the moonlight. I want to fall in love and I want it to last forever.

But there you go. I don't believe in fairy stories, do you?

I had a terrible hangover the next day. Rachel had to drive. I sat with both hands braced against the dashboard, groaning every time I opened my eyes.

'You're not exactly helping,' she grumbled as we crossed the Belgian border. 'I might need you to translate something.'

'I can't speak Belgish anyway.'

'Maddy, honestly – everyone knows there's no such thing as Belgish.'

'What is it, then?' I whispered. It hurt my head too much to speak any louder. 'Belge? Belgique?'

'I thought you were the linguist! I'm surprised at you! It's Belch, isn't it!'

'Oh, I can do that all right,' I muttered, demonstrating.

'Oh, please. Your breath smells like a pig farm. You're not going to be sick, are you?'

'Not if you don't talk about it. Why does it feel like we're going downhill all the time?'

'I don't know. Must be something to do with your stomach contents. No! No, don't be sick in the car! I'm pulling over! Hold on – don't be—'

Too late. I felt a lot better afterwards, though.

*

105

She didn't talk to me for most of the rest of the way through Belgium. Not in Belch, not in Belgish, not even in English. I thought she was being a bit unreasonable. I wasn't actually sick in the car – I managed to get most of it down the outside. It washed off all right. I even used some of the new perfume I'd bought in Paris, to spray the inside of the car to take the smell away. It was like driving a mobile tarts' boudoir. All the rest of the way, she kept pulling faces and giving this little dry cough as if breathing it in had damaged her lungs.

'Come on,' I said as we sat down with coffee and sandwiches at a motorway services. Why do these places look the same all over the world? We could have been on the M25 apart from the signs being in French (not Belch) and the prices being in euros. 'Come on; let's not fall out. I'm sorry, OK? I didn't mean to be sick.'

'When are you going to stop drinking yourself into oblivion?' retorted Rachel primly. 'Don't you think you're getting a bit old for it?'

Old?

'No, I don't, actually. I like it. It takes the edge off things. I know you can't understand how I feel – about the Tom thing,' I added, 'but I don't really want to talk about it any more at the minute.'

'Fine.'

'So let's just forget it, shall we? And go back to enjoying our trip? Please?'

'All right, Maddy,' she said with a sigh. 'I just feel a bit sorry for Tom, to be honest, that's all.'

I nearly choked on my coffee. Sorry for Tom? Christ, that was a first. Up till now she'd seemed to rate him only slightly more deserving of sympathy than Adolf Hitler.

'He'll get over it,' I said lightly. 'I'll spend a weekend in Glasgow or wherever with him when we go back. Now then – are we venturing forth to Deutschland, or what? Their beer's supposed to be excellent.'

'OK, *gehen wir! Komm mit!*'

106

'Bloody hell! You speak German!' I looked at her with a new respect. 'You never said!'

'Well,' she replied smugly, 'you're always going on and on about being the linguist, just 'cos I don't speak French.'

'Did you learn it at school?'

'No,' she admitted with a grin. 'Keith used to watch a lot of war films. I just picked up a few phrases. If we need to say anything about the Luftwaffe or prisoner of war camps, I'm your man.'

'Excellent. I'm sure that'll come in handy when we're booking into a B & B.'

We were laughing together again as we got back into the car and headed for Aachen.

It wasn't only the thing about Tom that I was pushing to the back of my mind. I was worried about Sophie again. Since Rachel told me about this Ryan person, it had been niggling away at me, causing me to wake up at night with a start, wondering why I was upset, and then remembering – there's something she's not telling me. OK, I know, she was twenty years old and perfectly entitled to have a relationship with some guy in Australia, even if his name was Ryan, without telling her mum about it. I'm not that type of mother who insists on being told every last detail of her daughter's life, right down to what colour knickers she's wearing and how often she goes to the toilet. It's sad and pathetic when mothers can't get a life of their own and live through their kids instead. I was not like that – was I? It's just that it was out of character for Sophie to keep quiet about something like this. I'd sent her an e-mail about it, of course, trying, in the limited time allocated on the computer in the internet café, to convey maternal interest and concern rather than prying and interfering. Difficult when what I really wanted to do was to pry and interfere.

Amy mentioned in her last e-mail to Rachel that you've been spending a lot of time with someone called Ryan. Who's he – another backpacker you've met in one of the

107

hostels? Just a friend? Or a 'romantic interest'?!? Spill the beans!

That was OK, wasn't it? Light, bantering, just a touch of the girls-together-gossip feel about it. So why hadn't she replied? Twice I'd checked my Hotmail in-box since I'd sent it. Nothing. She was obviously offended, or annoyed by my nosiness ... or she just didn't want to tell me. Every time I thought about it, I had to have another cigarette. The anxiety was eating away at me. I didn't like Ryan, already, without knowing anything about him, for giving me all this grief and costing me a fortune in fags.

And then, as if I didn't have enough to worry about, Rachel nearly got us arrested.

To be honest I did think she was driving a bit fast, especially for someone who only a few short weeks ago didn't even know which side of the road she was supposed to be on. But we'd both gained so much confidence since we'd left Carnac; now that we were used to the road signs and everything, the roads through France, and now Belgium, were a sheer pleasure compared with the congested British motorways with all their frustrating roadworks and contraflows. My hangover had left me feeling sleepy and I'd closed my eyes for a few minutes, lulled by the smoothness and straightness of the road, the quiet hum of the engine and the warmth of the sun through the car window.

'Shit! What's he doing?' muttered Rachel suddenly.

I opened my eyes just in time to see a police car pulling in in front of us.

'What's that for?' she asked me sharply. 'What does it mean?'

An illuminated sign, SUIVEZ NOUS, had appeared in the back windscreen of the police car.

'Follow us,' I said, suddenly wide awake. I sat up straight in my seat and glanced at her. 'You must have been speeding.'

'That's crap! I wasn't! I was only doing...' She hesitated,

obviously having absolutely no idea what speed she was doing.

'You must have been. Either that or there's something wrong with your car. Something broken, or hanging off or whatever.'

'Hanging off!' she retorted in disgust. 'I do not have things hanging off my car!'

'All right, all right, just concentrate on staying behind the cops, for God's sake, Rach, or we'll both end up in prison.'

'Don't be ridiculous, Madd. They don't do things like that in civilised countries. You've been watching too much crap TV as usual.'

'They do. Believe me, they— Rach, watch out! He's indicating to turn off at this slip road. We have to follow him.'

'Are you sure he means us?' She looked in the mirror. 'Maybe he's telling someone else to suivez. That lorry behind? It looks a bit overloaded. I bet it's nothing to do with us. Shall I just carry straight on?'

'No!' Panic made me screech like a strangled cat. 'For fuck's sake Rachel, just turn off! Now! I do not want to spend the night in a Belgian jail. Turn off! Rachel! Will you just please— thank you.' I mopped the sweat from my brow as she swerved off onto the slip road at the last minute, without indicating, our departure accompanied by a fanfare of hooting horns from the drivers behind us on the motorway.

We followed the police car down the slip road, round a roundabout and into a lay-by, where Rachel pulled up behind them.

'What are we supposed to do now?' she asked me in an aggrieved tone. 'I really think this is all a bit unnecessary, don't you? We weren't doing anything wrong.'

'They're getting out,' I hissed. 'And coming over. Don't argue with them – all right? Look at the size of their weapons!'

'Mmm!' she grinned.

'And don't flirt with them, either!' I told her fiercely.

'They'd probably arrest you for that, too. Just leave the talking to me, all right?'

She wound her window down and I leant across her and said with what I hoped was a charming smile and a perfect accent:

'Bonjour, messieurs. Comment allez-vous?'

'Good afternoon, ladies,' replied one of the policemen in such perfect English he might well have just stepped out of Kensington High Street. Unsmilingly, he flashed his ID at us, then took a pen out of his pocket and began writing down the registration number of the car. I felt Rachel flinch with annoyance and gave her a warning nudge.

'I would like to see your driving licence please,' he said.

Rachel passed it to him and he proceeded to copy down the details before handing it back to her. By now she was bristling with offence as if she'd been personally insulted.

'Do you know why we have asked you to stop?' asked Big Gun, fixing Rachel with a solemn stare.

'She was going a little bit fast,' I said, and smiled at him again, an apologetic little smile to indicate that OK, we knew we'd been naughty girls but hey, no damage done, we'd just be on our way now and wouldn't do it again.

He completely ignored me, continuing to stare at Rachel.

'Do you know what speed you were driving at, madam?'

'Not exactly,' she admitted. 'But it wasn't very fast. To be honest I could have gone a lot faster if I'd really wanted to. I was being careful, you know, because I've only just got used to driving on the wrong side of the road.'

I closed my eyes and sighed, images of Belgian prison cells coming unbidden to my mind.

'Madam, when we overtook you, you were driving at one hundred and seventy kilometres per hour. That is very much too fast.' He glared at her again. She raised her eyebrows, looking impressed. I kept my fingers crossed and prayed she wouldn't say it was a personal best speed record.

'For this,' he went on, writing in his book again, 'You must pay.'

110

The other cop, standing behind him, pursed his lips and put his hand on his gun. I had a fleeting but very scary vision of the next day's newspaper headlines back home:

ENGLISH WOMEN SHOT DEAD BY BELGIAN TRAFFIC POLICE
'They were driving very much too fast,' said a spokesman from the Brussels police headquarters. 'And their French was crap too.'

'It's because of your roads, you see,' Rachel was saying. I couldn't believe it. Why did she never seem to understand when to shut up and say nothing? I nudged her so hard I hurt my elbow, but she just carried on: 'Your roads are so much better than ours at home. We're just not used to being able to zip along like that, with no cones or diversions or anything. I got kind of carried away. I expect it's different for you, Constable, you know – being used to it.'

Constable! I cringed. I hung my head and closed my eyes, waiting for the first shot to ring out.

'You must pay,' he went on, as if she hadn't spoken. 'You must pay us now.' He tore a page out of his book and handed it to her.

Rachel and I both stared at the figure on the form. Fucking hell. It was just as well we'd won the lottery or we'd be going without food for the rest of our trip. The policeman folded his arms and stood there, waiting, eyeing us warily as if he suspected we'd try to do a runner. His mate, standing behind him, coughed twice and kicked the ground like a restless pony wanting to get going. I started to reach for my handbag but Rachel stopped me with a hand on my arm.

'Wait. This is ridiculous. I'm not going along with this!'

'We haven't got any option,' I warned her in a sharp whisper against her ear. 'We've got to pay them now.'

'They can't make us,' she retorted childishly. I felt my heart sink. I'd seen Rachel in this mood before. I think it came from teaching teenagers – she had no fear of

111

confrontation and would argue the toss till the bitter end … even if the end was very bitter, like a Belgian prison for example. She looked up at the traffic cop again now and said in an imperious voice like a duchess deigning to address her gardener:

'Are you sure you're within your rights to demand this sort of money from people without any sort of written warning? It's a very large amount.'

'Madam,' he replied calmly, 'this very large amount reflects the very high speed at which you were driving. This very high speed is against our law. You have broken our law and we are very much within our rights to demand this money.'

'And if we haven't got it?' she replied, putting her hand back on my arm as if to stop me protesting.

She looked smugly back at the cop, thinking she'd got him now, but again he replied without an ounce of expression in his voice:

'Then you must follow us to a cashpoint where you will withdraw the money. We are also within our rights to insist that you do this.'

He touched his gun very briefly, just a sort of reflex action like he was checking it was still there, but it was enough to make me shiver with anxiety.

'Come on, let's just pay him and get it over with,' I whispered.

'But what if we haven't got any money to withdraw?' countered Rachel triumphantly.

See what I mean? She's like a dog with a bone, just won't let it go. Sometimes I wonder if she's really bloody stupid. Most people just don't pick arguments with two cops wielding guns, in a foreign country, do they?

The officer sighed deeply, looked behind him at his mate, shook his head and said in the same flat tone as if it was of no consequence to him whatsoever:

'Then I regret, madam, that we would be forced to ask you to come with us to the police station, where we would invite you to remain as our guests until such time as the money became available to you.'

At this, finally, he managed a thin smile. The bastard.

Rachel, the light of battle having finally faded from her eyes at the mention of the police station, pouted and tutted as she got out her purse. Having topped up our supply of euros from a cashpoint that morning, we were fortunately able to rake together enough cash to pay the fine, leaving us barely enough to buy our next coffee.

'Kindly complete the form,' said Lethal Weapon One, passing the paperwork and a pen to Rachel. 'My colleague will give you a receipt for the money.'

With which he turned on his heel and retired to his car, leaving Number Two Cop, obviously a junior, to fulfil his part in the proceedings, which he did with great deliberation, completing and handing over the receipt and waiting in silence for Rachel to finish filling in her name and address and signing her name to the effect that she was now a convicted criminal.

'Can we go now?' she asked sulkily as she handed back the completed form.

Junior Cop, who maybe didn't speak such good English, or perhaps wasn't allowed to speak to convicts until he'd passed his final exams, waved his hand haughtily in the direction of the slip road back onto the motorway and turned away, following his boss back to the police car, where they both sat watching us while Rachel started up the engine and pulled away.

'Slowly,' I warned her shakily, looking at them in the mirror. 'They've probably got their fucking guns trained on us.'

'Fucking Belgians,' she muttered as we headed back to the motorway. 'No sense of humour, that's their trouble.'

'The thing is, though,' I said, starting to giggle now I knew we'd got away from them without getting locked up for the night and were out of gunfire range, 'they just don't realise, do they? They think we're upset, but are we?'

'We are not!' agreed Rachel with a laugh.

'Are we bothered by their pathetic little games?'

'We are not!'

'Do we care about their stupid little fines?'

'We do not!'

'And why don't we care?'

'Because we've won the fucking lottery!' we sang out together.

Anybody would think we didn't have a care in the world, wouldn't they.

Chapter 8

'Any news from Amy?' I asked Rachel anxiously as I logged off Hotmail with a frustrated click of the mouse button.

It was our first evening in Germany. We'd managed, without any mention of the war on Rachel's part, to book into a small hotel near the centre of Aachen, just over the border. At seven o'clock it was still hot as we strolled around the historic town centre, and people seemed to be thronging to the town squares to hang around by the fountains, laughing and joking and going from bar to bar. There was a kind of gaiety in the air that probably came from the combination of a huge student population and the warm summer night. In the Market Square, in front of the town hall, an enthusiastic local rock group was playing old Beatles numbers. We sang along as we mingled with the crowd with a kind of swagger, feeling great about ourselves, imagining ourselves to be famous already: Maddy and Rachel, popular heroes, survivors of a Belgian police swoop. *Money?! Pah! What do we care about money? Take it – we don't need it – what we care about is freedom! The freedom of innocent tourists to zap up and down the motorway at whatever speed they like!*

But then we came across the internet place and decided to check on the girls' progress before settling down at a pavement table outside one of the bars for our pre-dinner drinks. My exuberance had soon faded when I saw the empty in-box staring at me from the screen. *No New Messages.* Shit. No need to rub it in.

'Yes, I've got another e-mail from Amy,' said Rachel a little snappily.

I glanced at her in surprise, but she was logging off in a hurry, almost as if she didn't want me to read it. Not that I would have done anyway, of course, but her attitude made my alarm bells ring louder than ever.

'What's the matter?'

'Nothing.'

'Rachel, what is it? If it's something to do with Sophie, tell me – I'm already worried.'

'Yes, it's something to do with Sophie. But I don't know why *you're* worried. It's Amy I'm worried about. Sophie's leaving her on her own all the time, apparently, to go off with this Ryan.'

'Oh, come on, Rach – Sophie would never do that! You know she wouldn't! She and Amy are like sisters, like twins – they'd never let someone come between them.'

'I thought that, too. But it seems some guy has come along and changed all that.'

'I can't believe it. Perhaps Amy's just feeling a bit ... left out? A bit miffed because she's not seeing anyone at the moment? You know how it is...'

I tailed off unhappily under Rachel's direct gaze.

'No, Madd. I don't know how it is. We expected them to stay together, didn't we. We wouldn't have been happy about them going away like this if we thought one or the other of them was going to just go off and—'

'She hasn't,' I insisted. 'No way. I don't believe it. There's some misunderstanding. Sophie will probably e-mail me tomorrow and there'll be some explanation for all this and we'll be laughing about it in a couple of days' time.'

Rachel gave me a ghost of a smile in response and we went back out to the street to sit in the evening sunshine with our German beers. But the pleasure had gone out of the day. I didn't even feel like getting pissed.

*

116

'I miss the sea,' I said a bit moodily a couple of days later after breakfast. We'd spent two very hot days exploring Aachen, taking in the cathedral, the City Hall and all the museums. We'd done the guided tour and heard all about the history of the town as an important meeting point of Germany, Belgium and the Netherlands. We'd even visited the famous thermal baths, used ever since Roman times to ease aching limbs and cure all manner of ills.

'I don't feel any healthier,' I'd commented to Rachel afterwards.

'It'd take more than a thermal spa,' she'd retorted.

Thanks, friend!

And now we'd checked out of our hotel and were having a last stroll through the town to buy some souvenirs before moving on. The heat of the sun reflecting off the stone walls of the old buildings was already intense, and we were looking longingly at all the fountains gushing cool refreshing water.

'I know what you mean about the sea,' agreed Rachel. 'Maybe this is the wrong sort of weather to be doing cities. Maybe we should have stayed near the coast.'

'No. It's been fun, and I wouldn't have missed Paris for the world – or Lille. But maybe, after Cologne, if it's still as hot as this we should think again. I feel claustrophobic just at the thought of going further into central Europe. I don't think I've ever been so far from the coast in my life. Even in Brentwood we can get on a train to Southend if we're desperate.'

Rachel laughed.

'We don't have to go to Cologne. We can change our minds, can't we? We always said we wouldn't make too many plans.'

'Are you sure you don't mind?'

'No. I'm easy, as they say. Where do you want to go?'

'Well, I was looking at the map last night, actually. We could get to Holland from here, in no time.'

'Could we? Cool! Could we go to Amsterdam?'

'Yeah, easily. Probably only take a couple of hours. Then after Amsterdam we could explore the coast...'

My spirits were lifting at the thought. The sea, the sea!

'I thought we weren't going to make plans,' Rachel reminded me.

'OK, then. Just Amsterdam, for now – yeah?'

As we drove out of Aachen I was singing '*Tulips from Amsterdam*' lustily, if somewhat out of tune, and Rachel was reading to me from a Dutch guidebook. Just as well we didn't know then that, over in Australia, events were building up to a crisis. A dirty great rock had been dropped in the pool of our carefree happiness and so far only the very first ripples had reached us here on the other side of the world. The tidal wave was on its way.

En route to Amsterdam, we stopped at another roadside 'rest' for lunch.

'There's internet facilities here,' I pointed out, putting the tray down on the table. I'd been anxious ever since that e-mail from Amy, and nothing was going to make me feel better until I'd got one from Sophie. 'Shall we check up on the girls before we go?'

'Yes, why not.'

I sipped my coffee, nibbled my sandwich. Neither of us really wanted to discuss the situation in Australia between our daughters and some unknown *Ryan*, which was weighing heavily on our minds. Maybe I'd have a message now, full of happy chat about how Sophie had been out a couple of times with this guy, how Amy had sulked because she'd felt left out, how they'd argued a bit but now it was all sorted out, everyone was friends again, and Ryan? No, that was nothing, just a couple of dates, nothing to get excited about, she'd forgotten about him already ... and we could go on with our trip without any more worries or undercurrents. If only!

*

Hi Mum!

Well at least there *was* an e-mail today. I sighed with relief. Nothing too terrible could have happened. I read on eagerly.

Sorry I haven't replied to your last couple of messages. Have been pretty busy. Stayed in Brisbane for a few days and from there, we've been travelling up the coast. First stop was Noosa – not much there apart from tourists and surfers but very pretty. The weather started to pick up, which was good because the next stop was Hervey Bay, from where we did the three-day trip to Fraser Island (the biggest sand island in the world – you have to go there with a 4 × 4 truck.) A group of us from our hostel went on the trip together – taking loads of food and alcohol supplies because we had to camp out for two nights. There was me, Amy, Ryan – and the rest of the group were Americans, who couldn't drive the truck because they only knew how to drive automatics! It was really odd driving on sand through a rain forest! Then we got to this 75-mile long beach!! I had a turn at driving the truck on the beach – it was excellent! At night we sat outside the tents cooking dinner over the fire ... lovely, until the morning when we found half of our food had been carried off in the night by dingoes!

After our return to the mainland we made the 13-hour bus journey to Airlie Beach. It's getting noticeably warmer the further north we go, even though it's winter – we're in the tropics now! We're staying here for a while, in a really nice hostel with a huge bar! And we've arranged what we hope will be one of the highlights – a sailing trip around the Whitsunday Islands. Will let you know how it goes!

Hope you and Rachel are behaving yourselves. Don't let any strange men buy you drinks – OK? And take care driving! You're still not really used to the roads. Are you still in Germany? Where are you going next?

Look forward to hearing from you again. Lots of love!

119

My heart felt light with relief. I knew it! Everything was fine. What was Rachel so upset about? OK, so this Ryan person was obviously still travelling with them, but he was just mentioned as part of the group. Privately, I felt more certain than ever that Amy was just feeling disgruntled because, perhaps, he'd taken a fancy to Sophie. Maybe she wanted him herself. Men! They always caused trouble, even when they weren't aware of it.

'Nice e-mail from Sophie!' I sang out happily to Rachel.

There were only two computers, and she'd been using the other one. I looked round at her. She'd logged off, and was sitting with her head resting on her hand, looking like she was going to cry.

'What?' My voice wobbled with alarm. 'What's the matter? Didn't you get one from Amy?'

'Yes,' she said, shortly, without looking up at me. 'I did.'

'Is something wrong?' I wondered whether to voice my thoughts about Amy being jealous, but decided against it. 'She's not ill, is she?'

'No. She's not ill.'

'And they're having a great time, by the sound of it. Sophie's telling me all about the trip to Fraser Island, and driving the truck on the beach, and the dingoes ate their food, and—'

'And Sophie spent the whole trip with Ryan, and Amy felt completely miserable.'

There was a silence.

I was, to be honest, torn between sympathy for Rachel's distress on behalf of her daughter, and irritation that she was taking it so seriously. I had to remind myself that if the boot was on the other foot and Sophie was feeling upset because Amy had a possible boyfriend (I still only thought of him as a *possible* boyfriend), then yes, I guess I'd be worried too. After all, they were a long way away and we couldn't do anything to help. But for God's sake: wasn't she being just a tad melodramatic? Even when the girls had their inevitable disagreements when they were little kids, we always used to

120

try to let them sort it out on their own. This was all beginning to sound a bit like playground stuff, wasn't it? *I'm not being her best friend any more because she went off with someone else.* I couldn't believe Amy was so petty, to be honest – or that she'd come crying to her mother about it instead of sorting it out with Sophie herself.

'Amy shouldn't be worrying you,' I said with some annoyance. 'Writing to you about stuff like this.'

'Of course she should, if it's making her miserable and ruining her trip!' snapped Rachel.

I stared at her in surprise.

'Rach, *we're* not going to fall out over this, are we? Come on, they're not children, they can sort it out. Perhaps you should tell Amy to talk to Sophie about how she feels, because, to be quite honest, from Sophie's e-mail I don't think she's got any idea. She seems to think they're having a wonderful time…'

'Yes, I'm sure she does,' retorted Rachel drily. She stood up, sighing, shaking her head. 'Come on, then. Are we going?'

'I want to send a quick reply to Sophie.'

'OK. I'll wait for you in the car.'

Shocked by her abruptness, I reread Sophie's e-mail, my pleasure in it spoilt now that I was forced to ask myself whether my daughter was really selfish enough to be ignoring her friend's feelings. I typed a few quick lines telling her about Aachen and about our decision to go to Amsterdam, and added a final paragraph:

Rachel's worried about Amy. She seems to imply in her e-mails that she's not very happy at the moment. Is everything OK?
PS You still haven't told me who Ryan is, by the way!

Rachel was OK, but quiet, for the rest of the journey. I tried to tell her that everything would be fine, that the next e-mail from Amy would probably be full of excitement about their sailing trip and about how she and Sophie were getting on

121

fine now. I tried to suggest that any two friends would find it hard to manage a trip around the world without having their occasional spats – look how we carried on, and we were only away for six weeks together! I even suggested that their hormones could be to blame; but as soon as I'd said this I regretted it, getting a glare and raised eyebrows from Rachel in reply. Rachel didn't believe in hormones. Her philosophy was that if you ate a good diet of nuts and berries, got some fresh air every day and exercised regularly, such things would never trouble you. Personally I preferred to hedge my bets by taking a cocktail of vitamin pills to supplement my junk food diet – and God help anyone who got in my way a few days before my period.

Our guidebook had warned us against trying to drive in Amsterdam, and luckily we managed to find a room in a little hotel in the outskirts. It was, as all the local buildings seemed to be, very tall and narrow. The lift took us up to the fourth floor but our rooms were on the fifth, and approached by a very steep staircase that would never have passed building regulations in the UK. Once we got to the little landing at the top of the staircase we had to climb up three more steps to our own door. We thought we'd made it then, but no such luck. The other side of the door, the steps went on up, finally bringing us out in the middle of the room.

'Jesus!' exclaimed Rachel. 'This is bloody dangerous, isn't it. If you get out of bed in the night to have a pee, you could fall straight down those stairs.'

'Obviously not the room they reserve for disabled guests,' I agreed. 'But look at it!'

It was worth the climb, and the hazards. It was obviously the highest room in the hotel, and stretched from the front to the back, with windows at both ends giving views over the city and the surrounding countryside. Rachel leant on the windowsill and stared out, while I inspected the room.

'Two double beds! And armchairs! And a fridge!'

'And a BIG TV!' noticed Rachel as she turned away from the window. 'Mm, good choice of hotel.'

We'd got a bit lost on the approach to the city, ending up in an industrial area, and what with the effort of making pleasant conversation and keeping off the subject of Sophie and Amy as much as possible, we'd both been feeling edgy and tired by the time we finally got checked into this place, and we'd both been blaming each other for the fact that it hadn't looked too good from the outside.

'Much better than it looked,' I agreed.

'I don't feel like doing anything much now,' said Rachel, throwing herself down on her bed.

'No.' I put on the TV and tried to tune into an English language news station. 'Let's just chill out for a few hours, then we can go out to eat.'

Within ten minutes, with a particularly inane game show still playing on the TV, we were both sound asleep.

When I woke up it was nearly eight o'clock. I rubbed my eyes and shook my head, annoyed at having slept for so long at such a ridiculous time of day. But when I looked over at Rachel, I saw she was still out for the count, snoring gently, her arms stretched out above her head as if in a gesture of surrender. If we were going to go out to eat, we really needed to get ready and get going, but I didn't like to wake her up. I tiptoed past her into the bathroom, closed the door quietly and had a shower, taking my time, imagining that the gentle hum of the shower and splash of the water would probably rouse Rachel slowly from her sleep. No such luck; when I went back into the bedroom she was still in exactly the same position, snoring a little louder. I got dressed and did my hair. It always took me longer to get ready than her, anyway – I wore more make-up and spent more time trying to make my hair go straight. It was OK for Rachel with her natural look – easy to achieve, I suppose, if you fed yourself all those nuts and fresh air. At least I wouldn't have to rush tonight, and have her watching me with that air of disguised impatience: *It's all right, don't worry, take your time. I know you need to work harder than me to look good – what do you expect if you treat your body like a dustbin?*

But even when the dustbin was suitably arrayed with a couple of layers of various skin-enhancing potions and decked out in its best clothes, the Perfect Body was still sprawled on its bed, dead to the world.

'Rachel?' I called softly. I sat down next to her on the bed and touched her arm gently. 'Rach, are we going out, or what? Time's getting on.'

'Ow!' she moaned, rubbing the place where I'd touched her arm as if I'd thumped her one with a hammer at the very least. 'Leave me alone!'

'Come on, Rach. It's quarter to nine. We've got to find somewhere to eat.'

'Don' wanna eat,' she mumbled, turning over with her back to me. 'Wanna sleep.'

'It's not night-time yet.' I was beginning to get annoyed now. I tugged at the duvet, pulling it half off her before she yanked it back, groaning.

'Go 'way! Go back to sleep. 'S the middle of the night.'

Honestly. For someone who didn't believe in hormones, she was the grumpiest person I ever met when she woke up. Well, the time for niceties was over.

'WAKE UP!' I shouted next to her ear. 'We're GOING OUT!'

She howled in distress and put the pillow over her head.

'Don't want to go out,' whispered a pathetic little voice from beneath the pillow. 'Don't feel well.'

'What's wrong?' I didn't feel very sympathetic. She was fine before she fell asleep.

'Got a headache. Got a tummy ache. Got a sore throat. Got a—'

'Yeah, all right, all right. No need to go right through the medical dictionary.'

Bugger. I'd just spent nearly an hour getting ready to go out. And not only that – I was starving. I stared ruefully at the bit of her head showing underneath the pillow.

'What about if I found us a takeaway and brought you something back?'

'Oh, oh, I don't know. I don't know if I could eat anything ... well, maybe just a tiny morsel might make me feel better.'

She lifted the pillow off her face and blinked up at me.

'But you'd better not go out on your own. You don't even know where we are.'

'I'll ask at reception.'

'You don't speak any Dutch.'

'Everyone around here speaks perfect English.'

'No. No, Madd, I can't let you do that. I'll have to ... come with you.'

She heaved herself, groaning, to the edge of the bed and with an almighty effort, as if her tiny slim body was a huge cumbersome weight, struggled manfully to her feet, swaying slightly, rubbing first her head and then her stomach. Holding onto the bed with one hand, she stepped gingerly into her jeans as if it was a feat of great agility and pulled a T-shirt over her head.

I watched this performance with increasing irritation from the other side of the bed. She was no more ill than I was. She just didn't feel like going out.

I can't begin to guess what we looked like that evening, heading out of the hotel – two crazy English women, one dressed up and made up to the nines for a night out, the other in jeans, T-shirt and trainers with her hair unbrushed, staggering and protesting every few minutes about her head, her throat or her stomach hurting.

'Oh, oh, I can't go much further,' she moaned, leaning against a car. We'd only progressed halfway down the street and I'd already decided we'd better go to the first place we found that sold food of any description; she was making too much fuss to walk very far.

'Rachel!' I warned her. 'Get off! They're trying to back the car out!'

Too late. With a throaty chug of diesel, the big sleek German car began to reverse out of its parking space. Rachel stumbled and sat down surprisingly neatly on the ground. If it wasn't for the fact that she looked like she was going to cry, I'd have had a good laugh.

'Come on,' I held out my hand to pull her up.

The car had stopped and the driver lowered the window.

'Iss your frendt OK?'

'Yeah, she's fine, thanks,' I nodded. 'Sorry about that – leaning on the car. She felt a bit funny.'

'Funny? Thiss is *funny*?' said the woman in the passenger seat, leaning across her husband, staring at us.

'No, not *funny*. Not funny as in *ha ha, joke*, kind of funny.' I shrugged. This was impossible. 'Don't worry about it.' I smiled. 'Thanks anyway.'

I pulled Rachel to her feet and waited for them to drive off, but still they sat there, watching us.

'Why do you say not to worry?' said the woman. 'What do you mean? Worry about what?'

'*Piss off*,' muttered Rachel under her breath.

'What did you say?'

'We're off!' I said loudly, pushing Rachel in front of me along the street. 'She said *we're off* – Bye!'

'I think you are *trunk*!' exclaimed Mr Nose-ache, very rudely I thought, as he raised his window again and drove smoothly off along the narrow street.

'And *I* think *you* are a prat,' Rachel told their departing rear view calmly.

We both sniggered.

'Looks like another nation that doesn't appreciate our sense of humour,' I said. 'Are you feeling any better?'

'A bit,' she admitted in a brave little voice. 'I think I might be coming down with a cold.'

Oh. Nothing too serious, then. And there was I imagining she had the bubonic plague at the very least.

'Probably,' she said with considered wisdom as we stopped and looked thoughtfully in the window of the first little restaurant we came to, 'it's because I haven't been eating as much fresh fruit and vegetables as I do at home.'

126

Probably. That and the booze, and the sex. But then who was I to talk? It was pretty much my standard diet after all.

'This is a vegetarian restaurant,' I pointed out. 'We could eat healthy for a change, if you like?'

'Oh. Well, OK, I suppose I *might* be able to force down a *little* bit of a meal, as long as it's something really kind of *light*,' she said in her weak invalid's voice.

Before I'd had time to answer she was through the door and asking for a table.

'That was fabulous, wasn't it,' I said, two hours later, licking the last of my dessert off my spoon and pushing the dish away. 'Best meal I've had since we left France.'

All of four days ago.

'Mm.' Rachel was scraping the bottom of her own bowl. She looked up at me anxiously, remembering that she was supposed to be ill. 'I think that probably did me good.'

We'd worked our way through three courses of very filling, very hearty vegan food, having discovered mid-meal that we'd stumbled on one of the trendiest little restaurants in Amsterdam and were lucky to have got a table without booking.

'Not as much good as half a grapefruit and a tomato salad, though,' I reminded her a little cruelly.

We went back to bed early. Apart from the meal, it had hardly been worth getting up. At least I'd had the pleasure of putting on my make-up and taking it off again. And surprisingly, considering that we'd only been awake for a couple of hours and hadn't even had much to drink, we both went straight back to sleep. Must have been the Dutch air.

The next day, having both topped up our sleep requirement to the point of overkill, we were awake early and raring to go. Well, maybe that's a slight exaggeration. I bounded out of bed with my usual enthusiasm (wanting a coffee and the first fag of the day) while Rachel, declaring herself slightly better but 'still feeling a little fragile', swallowed a couple of paracetamol and took her time.

'We've got a whole new city to explore,' I tried to encourage her over breakfast – a rather meagre affair of two choices of cereal and two choices of bread, with slices of cheese and ham so thin you could see the plate through them. 'New sights, new smells, new experiences. New men,' I added in the hope of getting some reaction. 'Dutchmen. You know. They're famous for... Dutch courage. And Dutch uncles. And well... going Dutch!'

'And Dutch caps!' she retorted with the beginnings of a smile.

'Yes!' I agreed. 'And don't forget Double Dutch – twice as much for your money. Just look at the size of them!'

It was true; they all seemed to be at least six feet tall. Where were all the small Dutch people? Hiding away at home, too embarrassed to come out?

We got a tram into the city centre, and wandered for a while along the canals, over the bridges, looking at the tall old buildings that all seemed to lean inwards towards the water.

'They had to build them like that,' supposed Rachel, 'because of the tall people.'

'But they're so *thin*, too!'

I meant the buildings, but Rachel nodded seriously and said yes, that was because of all the cycling.

There were bikes everywhere. I'd never seen so many bikes in my life. You took your life in your hands crossing the road. They flew at you from all directions. They were parked everywhere, too: chained to railings, bridges, street signs, houses; hanging from lamp-posts, shackled to house-boats. Wheels were left hanging where bikes had been stolen; bikes without wheels were left dangling from their chains. In places it was hard to know which part of the road was for trams, which was for cars, which for bikes and whether any of it was for pedestrians or whether you just had to breathe in and squeeze between them all.

'I'm worn out with this,' I told Rachel after a while. 'Let's get on a boat.'

The canals. This was the way you were supposed to see Amsterdam, wasn't it. Like Venice, if you hadn't been round it on the canals you couldn't even say you'd been there. We queued for tickets and waited with a motley crowd of tourists for the boat to come in. It was packed. We jostled our way on board (no nice orderly British queuing here of course) and threw ourselves into two available seats.

'I wanted a window seat,' Rachel hissed to me from across the aisle and three places back.

'Tough!' I hissed back. 'At least you've got a seat. Someone might get off in a minute.'

'On the left,' crackled a disembodied voice over the speakers at the front of the boat, 'is the house of Anne Frank.' People got to their feet and took photographs over the heads of their neighbours of the uninspiring building and its attendant half-mile queue of dispirited tourists waiting for admission. Other people began jostling each other to get off the boat.

'Should we go and see it?' asked Rachel anxiously, moving into a vacant seat directly behind me. 'It's one of the top ten things in the guidebook.'

'No, bollocks to it – look at the queue. I'd rather stay on the boat.'

We drifted on along the canal, staring with fascination at the variety of houseboats moored along the banks, some with their own roof gardens and patios, complete with flower tubs, tables and chairs.

'Nice life,' I commented over my shoulder to Rachel. 'Everything you could want in one little boat. Look at all the pot plants in the window of that one.'

'They're probably cannabis,' she said.

Oh yes. I'd forgotten about that. It gave me something to think about for the rest of the boat trip, and planted an idea in my head. Why not? This was Amsterdam, after all. I watched from the boat as a group of young girls, probably a hen party in the grip of a hangover from the night before, swung along the canalside arm in arm with each other, laughing loudly and proudly displaying, to the amusement of passers-by, the logos on their matching T-shirts: GOOD GIRLS GO TO HEAVEN — BAD GIRLS GO TO AMSTERDAM.

Bad girls? They were probably cute little pussycats compared with me. I was the prototype, the bad girl to beat all bad girls. I could show them all a thing or two about being bad. I'd probably screwed up more lives than they'd had hot dinners.

So I might as well have a little more fun while I had the chance.

Chapter 9

When we'd had enough of floating around Amsterdam listening to the tour commentary, Rachel and I got off the boat and found a restaurant with tables outside in the sunshine where we spent a pleasant hour enjoying our lunch.

'So what else do you want to do?' asked Rachel, leaning back in her chair, her coffee in front of her on the table.

'You feel OK now, then?' I asked cautiously.

'Well – you know. Better than I was last night, but maybe not *completely* better...'

'Shall we have a walk, then? See a bit more of the city? Find a coffee shop, perhaps?'

She sat up and looked at me in surprise.

'You've got a coffee there. Do you want another one?'

'No. That's not what I meant. I meant a *coffee shop.*'

Rachel stared back at me.

'Yes. I heard you the first time. Don't you like the coffee here? What's the matter with it?'

'Rachel, it's not *coffee* I'm talking about.'

'Maddy, I think you've had too much sun. You're not making any sense. Do you want a coffee or don't you?'

'I thought you'd read the bloody guidebook? What's the matter with you? The coffee shops here aren't famous for their *coffee* for Christ's sake! I thought we might have a try of ... something a bit more interesting.'

She blinked, leant back in her chair again, exhaling with a

gasp of surprise, looked up at the sky, sat forward again, opened her mouth, shut it, shook her head and said finally:

'Fucking hell, Maddy. Drugs? I don't believe you.'

'Only *cannabis*. It's not really a drug.'

'You *what*?'

'Well, you know. Not a serious one. No worse than this,' I indicated my packet of fags.

'Yes, well. Some of us have got more respect for our bodies.'

'Oh, sorry, yes, I forgot about your body being a temple. Shit, sorry, some of us like to *live* a little while we've got the chance...'

'For God's sake. You're not a bloody teenager. You're not some bloody *student*, only over here for the drugs – didn't you get all that out of your system when you were at uni?'

We were both silent for a moment.

'I didn't go,' I said. 'Remember? I was the one who got pregnant at seventeen and ruined her life.'

'No you didn't,' said Rachel a little more softly. 'You didn't ruin it. You've got Sophie.'

'I know. I know that. But I didn't do... all those things. I had to grow up. I didn't get the bit in between.'

'Nor did I, really. Even at uni I didn't get very involved in all the partying.'

'So now's your chance. Come on – it's legal here! We might never get another chance to find out what it's all about.'

'I don't smoke,' she said huffily. 'I gave up when I was pregnant with Amy. I'm not going to start again now.'

'Well, try the cake, then. Space cake. That's hardly likely to kill you.'

'Maddy,' she said, fixing me with a look that suddenly reminded me of my mother when I was a teenager and first started having a few drinks. 'I'm not interested. But I'm not going to try and stop you. In fact, if you want to try these things, I'd rather you did it while you're with me so I can look after you.'

132

'Well, thank *you*, Miss Maturity!' I snapped crossly. Then we caught each other's eye and suddenly both began to laugh.

'All right,' she said, putting down her cup. 'Let's have a bit more of a walk, then, as we haven't seen this side of the town yet – and we'll see if we can find a coffee shop later on.'

'OK. You sure you feel all right?'

'Yeah, I'll survive.' She gave a little cough and shrugged it off bravely. 'It's only a small city. It'd be a shame not to see as much of it as we can.'

It would be easy to get lost in Amsterdam, I decided a few minutes later as we strolled over yet another bridge over a canal. I was holding the map – no point giving it to Rachel as she'd spend most of her time with it upside down – and knew roughly where we were supposed to be but, to be honest, each of these bridges looked much like another. Hadn't we been down this street before? And wasn't that the building we were looking at this morning, or was it just somewhere very similar?

'Do you know where we are?' asked Rachel.

'Oh, absolutely.'

Well, I had a pretty good idea. It was either this street just *here* on the map, or maybe we were now coming into this street just *there*.

'There's another bridge up ahead, if that helps.'

In a city of more than a thousand bridges, this probably wasn't the most helpful landmark she could have pointed out but I nodded and pretended to find it enlightening. She'd only panic if she thought I'd got her lost.

We crossed the bridge, followed the road a little further and took a right turn.

'This looks a bit of a sleazy area,' commented Rachel. Then, 'Christ! Look at *this*!'

She'd paused to look in a shop window. I stopped behind her and looked up from the map to be confronted by a display of leather and rubber gear that would have made an Ann Summers catalogue look like a children's picture book.

'Bloody hell! What's *that* for?' I pointed at a very nasty looking instrument displayed beside some fairly standard vibrators.

'No idea.' She turned her head on one side to consider it from a different angle. 'Would you *wear* it, or *do* things with it, do you think... and look at *that*...'

'Well, don't stand there gawping like Alice in Wonderland. There's a live sex show next door if you fancy going in?'

'Maddy!' she exclaimed, shocked. 'No, I *don't* fancy it, thank you very much. Honestly! How absolutely revolting! I really don't think they should have things like that, you know, actually on display in a public street, for everyone to see.'

'Well, it goes on everywhere, after all,' I shrugged as we walked on. 'I suppose they're just a bit more open about it here than we are in England.'

'No, Maddy,' retorted Rachel, obviously now well onto her high horse and enjoying the ride, 'it does *not* go on everywhere. Have you seen live sex shows at home in Brentwood? Do you see *things* like that in shop windows in our town centres?'

'No, obviously not, but—'

'Exactly. I really think they should clean up their act. I mean, it's a very nice city and everything, I like their bridges, and I realise it must have been very hard work having to dam the river and dig all the canals and all that.' Rachel had been reading the history of Amsterdam while I was getting ready to go out that morning. 'But I don't think that's any excuse for this sort of vulgarity – well, worse than vulgarity! *Depravity* might not be too strong a word.'

We'd turned another corner by now and Rachel was so carried away with her own righteous indignation that she hadn't looked around her until suddenly, forced by the crowd of people in the very narrow street, she found herself right up against a window, her nose practically against the glass.

134

'Jesus fucking *Christ*!' she shrieked, jumping back from the window as if she'd been burned. 'For fuck's *sake*!'

She'd come nose to nose with a prostitute who, dressed only in a tiny white thong and skimpy matching bra, was smiling and beckoning to a group of tittering young men standing just at Rachel's shoulder. She pushed her way back through the crowd, gasping as if she was drowning.

'This is *horrible*! Look at them!'

In every window, on both sides of the street, smiling girls wearing not much more than their lipstick were showing off their assets to the throngs of tourists.

'They're just trying to make a living,' I told Rachel quietly, 'just like you and I.'

'Are you mad?' she retorted. 'This is *not* how *we* make a living, Maddy Goodchild, you know that very well!'

'They're probably very hard up. It's probably the only way...'

'Oh, don't give me that. Have they tried waitressing? Or helping out in a shop, or even working behind a bar like you used to do.'

'No need to bring me into it.' I was beginning to get annoyed now with her narrow-minded attitude. 'Maybe they can earn more money like this than by doing a bit of waitressing or working in a sweet shop, and bloody good luck to them.'

'Well, I think it's outrageous. Young children could be innocently walking down this street and be scarred for life!'

'You wouldn't bring young children to the red light district, Rachel. Stop being so boring.'

'Well, *I* didn't want to be brought to the red light district, actually; you didn't bloody *tell* me you were bringing me here!'

'I didn't know I was bringing you here for fuck's sake; the map doesn't actually have red crosses on the map for every prostitute's window! Can we just keep walking? We're kind of in the way here.'

The crowd, good-natured and mainly out for a curious gawp at the girls, jostled us from side to side as we made our way along the street, Rachel keeping her eyes fixed on the horizon.

'The curtain's closed on that one,' I chuckled, pointing out a window to our left. Rachel forced a glance and looked away again.

'So? What, she's packed up and gone home?'

'No! I can't believe you're so naïve. She's obviously got a customer in with her.'

Rachel stopped dead and stared at me. She glanced at the curtained window again, looked back at me, and shook her head slowly.

'You're joking,' she said. 'It's only three o'clock in the afternoon!'

'Well I'm buggered,' I said sarcastically. 'I bet she even works on Sundays!'

We walked the rest of the way out of the red light district in silence. Rachel was obviously too stunned to speak. Brentwood High Street was going to be a bit tame by comparison.

By mutual consent the next stop was going to be the coffee shop. As if to make up for her lack of sophistication in the brothel department, Rachel decided to take charge of this venture.

'The drug culture,' she told me with an air of authority, 'is nothing new to me. Sometimes when we were students the parties went on for several days at a time. Everyone was so stoned they didn't realise it was night-time or daytime.'

'I thought you said you didn't get too involved in all the partying at uni?'

'No. *I* didn't, no, but well, you know, my housemates used to come home *completely* stoned and tell me all about it.'

'But you did experiment yourself, a little bit?'

'Oh, yes. Of course. Everyone did,' she replied airily.

'What? Coke? Or just dope? Not heroin, surely?'

136

'Oh, no, nothing like that. Never did anything too *heavy*. Not *that* stupid!'

'So you just smoked dope?' I persisted. 'What was it like?'

'Hard to remember now,' she said vaguely. 'I didn't do it regularly.'

OK. I think I get the picture.

'This place looks all right,' said Rachel as we passed a nice little teashop next to a bridge.

'I don't think so! You'd probably have as much chance of getting a joint in there as you would in a Wimpy Bar. You have to look for the green sign in the windows. They're the ones that sell the stuff.'

'I knew that really.'

'What about here, then?' I paused at the door of a place with a very dark interior. It didn't even need the green sign in the window – the smell of the stuff being smoked inside was enough to knock your socks off.

'Don't fancy that one,' said Rachel, wrinkling her nose. 'There's a horrible smell.'

Laughing, I persuaded her inside and we found a table near the door where the 'horrible smell' wasn't so strong.

'Maybe the cannabis you used to smoke when you were a student had a different smell,' I told her, trying to save her face.

'Well, I think this Dutch stuff,' she replied, regaining her superior stance, 'is probably quite a bit stronger. You need to be careful with it, Maddy – especially your first time. I've seen some terrible things happen with people overdoing it on their first try.'

'Really? What sort of terrible things?'

'You know.' She lowered her voice. 'The usual. People thinking they can fly, jumping out of windows.'

'Did that happen to any of your friends, then?'

'Jesus, yes, all the time. It was a regular thing. Lucky they survived. Lucky they had me to look after them, to be quite honest.'

'I can imagine,' I said drily. 'Rachel, I don't think this place is waitress service. Shall I go up to the bar? What do you want?'

'No!' She got to her feet immediately. 'I'd better do it – you won't understand what to buy. What are you going to do – have a smoke?'

'No, it feels a bit antisocial smoking it on my own. I'll have a black coffee, please, and a piece of the cake. Why don't you share a bit with me?'

'No, thank you, not for me,' she replied primly. 'I'll just have a glass of wine.'

'They don't serve alcohol in here,' I pointed out.

'Don't they?' She looked at the bar in surprise. 'Well, how ridiculous is that? On the one hand they're encouraging the use of illegal substances, and on the other hand they won't even sell you a glass of bloody wine.'

'They're probably not licensed to sell alcohol. They *are* called coffee shops, not pubs, after all. Anyway, apparently it's not a good idea to drink and use cannabis at the same time if you're not used to it, is it? You're more likely to get sick that way.'

She fumbled about in her bag for her purse.

'I knew that really.'

Yeah, right.

Through the pleasant fug of smoke I watched Rachel coming back from the bar balancing two cups of coffee and a plate of cake in her hands.

'Sorry. I should have come and helped you.'

'No, no, that's fine. I can manage, you just sit and relax – this is your treat,' she said in her superior-but-tolerant voice. She put the plate down in front of me and sat watching me, her chin propped on her hand. I picked up the slice of cake and broke it in half. It looked just like a piece of a child's birthday cake, with icing and hundreds and thousands on the top.

'I don't think I'd better eat the whole lot,' I said. 'Come on, have some with me.'

'No, really, I'm fine.' She took a sip of her coffee and smiled at me like an indulgent aunt. 'You go ahead. I'll just watch you.'

She made it sound as if I was going to climb to the very top of the climbing frame and whiz down the slide.

'Well, I don't suppose there'll be much to watch. I'm hardly likely to start dancing a jig as soon as I've eaten it. Doesn't it take about an hour to have any effect?'

'Does it? I mean, er, yes, of course, I know it does, but I want to keep an eye on you, just in case. In a strange city, you know – there's no knowing what might happen to you if you're *under the influence.*'

'Heaven forbid. I might end up in one of those windows!'

'Maddy!' She shuddered. 'Don't even joke about it.'

I bit off a corner of the cake and chewed it thoughtfully. It tasted just like carrot cake. Quite nice really. I took another mouthful.

'Steady,' warned Rachel. 'Don't rush it.'

'Why?'

'Well, er . . . you know. Better to take your time and enjoy it,' she said vaguely.

'It tastes so completely innocuous.' I took another bite and finished off the first half-slice. 'I can't really believe there's anything in it.'

'That's the trouble. That's what everyone thinks.' She nodded wisely.

'Well, maybe I'd better not eat the other half. Fair enough, I don't really want to be ill. Are you sure you don't want the rest?'

'Quite sure, thank you. Why don't you wrap it up and take it back to the hotel? You can have it later.'

'Yeh, right – and probably get arrested! You're still not supposed to have anything in your *possession*, you know, even here.'

'I know. I knew that really.'

It was beginning to sound like her theme tune.

We sat in silence, finishing our coffees. The place was

really quite comfortable. The background music was of the dull-thump-base-beat variety, but fairly low volume. Leather sofas flanked low tables, giving the feeling of relaxing in someone's lounge. Through the pervasive sweet-smelling smoke I could see people smiling happily and murmuring in soft conversation. How different from the noisy aggressive atmosphere of so many pubs! How much nicer this stuff must be than alcohol! What a civilised country this was.

'I really like this,' I told Rachel. 'I think I could get used to it.'

'That's how people become addicted,' she responded sharply.

'Oh, don't be bloody silly; I've only had a couple of mouthfuls of bloody carrot-cake. It'd take a lot more than that ... I bet if I ate the whole bloody cake off the shelf I wouldn't even experience a *fraction* of what I feel when I've had a night down the pub!'

'I wouldn't be too sure about that.'

'Well, I actually don't think there was anything *in* that half a slice. I've heard that can happen. Sometimes the way the cake is mixed, it's a bit uneven, so you might not even get anything in your bit.' I picked up the other half-slice and looked at it for a minute before stuffing it decisively into my mouth. 'Might as well go the whole hog.'

'Shit, Maddy; I really don't think that was a good idea. You're going to feel *so bad*.'

'Good. Better than not feeling anything! Come on – have you finished your coffee?'

'Don't you want another cup? Don't you think you should sit here for a little while – just in case you start—'

'What? Jumping up and down and throwing my knickers in the air? I don't think it's very likely, but if I'm going to feel strange maybe I'd be better off feeling strange back at the hotel.' I led her out into the sunshine of the street, where we both blinked and rubbed our eyes as if we'd just woken up. 'This way, I think!' I proclaimed with more confidence than I felt. 'From the map, it looks like we can get a tram just round this corner.'

Rachel was very quiet on the tram. I sat next to the window, staring out at the city streets and wondering when I was going to start hallucinating, seeing bright lights or singing happy little songs about peace and love. By the time we got back to the hotel I was beginning to feel totally let down and disappointed. If this was what being a junkie was all about, it was amazing anyone ever bothered to waste their money on a second fix. I'd felt less sober at a wake. We went up to our room and I decided to take a shower straight away. When I came out of the bathroom, Rachel was lying on the bed with her hand over her eyes.

'Are you all right?' I asked her. 'Tired?'

'No. I feel a bit rough. Probably that cold coming over me again.'

Great. Just in time for another whingey evening out. I bent down and looked at her more closely.

'Blimey, you do look a bit pale, actually. Have you taken any paracetamol?'

'No. I . . . I think I might just have a glass of water.'

She started to sit up, but the colour drained completely from her face and she swayed alarmingly on the edge of the bed.

'I . . . think I'd better go . . . to the bathroom,' she slurred. 'Don't feel . . . very well. . .'

I grabbed her arm and helped her totter into the bathroom, where she collapsed beside the toilet and proceeded to throw up violently, groaning and crying to herself that she wanted to die.

'Shit, Rach – what the hell have you had to drink?' I asked her when she eventually sat back against the bath, panting, exhausted, with a wild look in her eyes.

'Nothing! What do you mean – drink?' she replied weakly. 'I've been with you all day – you know I haven't had anything to drink.'

'Well, you're acting just like—' I looked at her in sudden shock. 'You didn't sneak some of that cake without telling me, did you?'

'No, I fucking didn't! Even if I'd wanted to, I don't think I could have eaten anything in that place. The smoke was so bloody awful, it was making me feel sick just sitting there.'

She looked up at me, realisation dawning in her eyes.

'I've been drugged, haven't I,' she said in an outraged tone of disbelief. 'I've tried to keep myself pure and clean, and what happens? I get drugged by the fucking *smoke*! I'm a fucking passive dope-smoker!'

In the circumstances, I probably shouldn't have laughed. But can you blame me? If it hadn't been for Rachel's passive smoking, the whole coffee-shop experience would have been a bit of a non-event. As it was, at least one of us got to get stoned in Amsterdam. Despite being the bad girl abroad, I'd had a lovely slice of carrot cake and no ill effects whatsoever, whereas Rachel *Body-Is-My-Temple* Hamilton passed out on the bed in a drug-induced stupor and didn't even get any pleasure from it.

Yes, I was laughing then.

But not for long.

I'd told Rachel before about her choice of ring tone. It's fine to have 'Bat Out of Hell' screaming from your mobile phone if you're a Hell's Angel or a rock chick, but really, when you're a forty-five year old science teacher who doesn't even believe in hormones, I wasn't sure that it was terribly appropriate. Especially not when it woke me up at four o'clock in the morning in a strange hotel room in Amsterdam.

'Shit!' I shouted, swinging my legs off the bed before I was properly awake. 'What the fuck?'

'Hello?' Rachel was saying in a sleepy voice. 'Hello, who's that?'

'Shit!' I repeated, sitting back down and rubbing the back

of my neck. 'Your *fucking* phone! What's the time? Who the hell is it?'

'Amy!' I heard Rachel saying. Suddenly we were both wide awake. 'What's the matter?'

There was a long period of silence at our end, during which Rachel nodded, and shook her head, and occasionally just muttered, 'I see,' and 'Right,' and 'Oh, no.' I watched her, growing increasingly uneasy. Of course, it wasn't the middle of the night in eastern Australia; it was probably early afternoon. But Amy must have been feeling pretty distraught to phone her mum when she knew she'd be asleep.

I got up, still watching Rachel's face, and put the kettle on, busying myself with the little packets of instant coffee and long-life milk to stop myself from panicking. It wasn't until Rachel gasped:

'Coming *home*?' that I ceased all pretence, dropped the cups back on the tray, and . . . panicked.

'Let me speak to her!' I shouted, holding my hand out for the phone.

'No!' said Rachel, glaring at me. 'Sorry, Amy – it's just Maddy. Yes, of course she's upset. No, of course she doesn't think it's your fault. Amy, don't cry. Come on, it's all right, don't cry, everything's going to be all right.'

'Of course it's all right. Let me speak to her! Let me speak to Sophie! Tell her to put Sophie on the phone!'

I was dancing on the spot, trying to take the phone out of Rachel's hand, gabbling like an idiot. This was ridiculous. They couldn't talk about coming home, just because of some silly squabble over a boyfriend. This was meant to be a trip of a lifetime. They'd been saving for it ever since they left school. They'd never get another opportunity. If they wasted it, they'd never forgive themselves.

'Of course you can come home. Don't be silly. Of course nobody's cross with you. You haven't done anything wrong,' Rachel was saying in a soothing voice.

'Don't tell her that!' I almost screamed in frustration.

'Rachel, don't tell her they can come home! They can't! It's stupid! Let me *speak* to her!'

'Hold on a minute, darling,' said Rachel. She covered the mouthpiece with her hand. 'Maddy, just shut up, will you? I'm trying to talk to my daughter and she's *very* upset.'

Her voice was like ice, like steel. I almost took a step back. The timid sorry little invalid of the previous night had vanished and been replaced by a drama queen.

'Yes, but listen. She's upset now, but don't let her think they should come home! For Christ's sake, they mustn't—'

'Mind your own business. Nobody said anything about *Sophie* coming home.'

From that moment, even though I sat on the bed shaking my head and making pleading eyes at her as Rachel continued to say soothing things to her daughter, I knew in my heart that it was all over. For the girls, and for us too.

Chapter 10

Rachel and I were both subdued on the journey home. It was a bitter contrast from our outward journey, when our spirits had been so high and we felt as if we had the whole world at our feet.

'Slow down,' I warned Rachel several times during the short drive to the Hook of Holland, where we were getting a ferry back to Harwich. 'Remember the Belgian Robocop.'

It didn't even raise a smile. We'd come dangerously close to having a row, back at the hotel. Not about going home – that was a fait accompli; there hadn't been any point arguing about it – but about who was driving. She'd insisted that she should take the wheel because I'd 'done drugs' the previous day.

'But I felt completely normal! I might as well have had a buttered bun for all the effect it had.'

'That's not the point. Would you drive a car if you'd drunk a bottle of wine, even if you thought you felt perfectly OK?'

'No, but that's different.'

'Maddy, I'm not going to argue about this. I want to get home in one piece. *I'm* driving.'

'But *you* were the one who felt ill!'

'I've just got a cold, that's all. I *told* you I had a cold coming.'

'Right. And that was why you looked completely spaced out, your pupils were the size of the Atlantic Ocean and you were as sick as a dog?'

'Probably the smoke in that place didn't *help* my cold, but the fact remains that *I* didn't indulge in any experimental practices.'

In the end I gave up arguing. Now the effects of the smoke had worn off she was never going to admit it, and anyway, she was a woman with a mission: get home, meet Amy at Heathrow. Everything else was unimportant. It was as if the last few weeks of carefree travelling had just been a dream.

'You don't have to come back with me,' she'd told me in the early hours, after Amy's phone call. 'You can carry on, on your own.'

'Don't be stupid. Of course I'm coming back with you.'

'You could go on and explore the coast. Lots of women travel on their own – you'll probably meet people.'

'Rachel, for the last time: I don't want to go on without you. It wouldn't be any fun. It doesn't matter. If you're absolutely insistent on going back...'

'I am.'

'I'm sure Amy doesn't expect you to...'

'I want to.'

Subject closed. I felt, although it was never said, that Rachel held me partly to blame; as if, by refusing to believe that this was all my daughter's fault, I was almost as bad.

And she certainly did blame Sophie.

Sophie hadn't phoned me until a couple of hours after Amy's early morning call. Rachel and I were just packing up to leave.

'Sophie, what's going on?' I asked her urgently. 'What's the matter with Amy? Is it true she's coming home?'

'Yes, Mum. Jesus, this is such a disaster. I've spent the whole afternoon trying to talk her out of it. Is Rachel upset?'

'Upset? Of course she is! She's going back to England – we both are.'

'Oh, *fuck*. Sorry, Mum, but – why? There's no need for you two to cut your trip short. It's Amy's decision. If she can't hack it, it's up to her.'

146

'Can't hack it? That sounds a bit harsh, Sophe.'

'Mum, I'm sick of trying to persuade her to stick it out. She's been like this for ages now. She was OK for the first couple of weeks we were away, but since then she's been gradually getting worse. To be honest it's becoming a drag.'

'What is? What exactly is the problem?'

I saw Rachel, across the room, raising her eyebrows and shaking her head. From her point of view, the problem was obvious. Why was I wasting my time asking? The problem was Sophie.

'She's homesick. She's miserable – spends half her time saying she wishes she'd never come. I can't understand it – I never thought she'd be like this.'

'Do you think it's because you're spending time with ... this Ryan?'

There was a silence. I could hear Sophie sighing. Then –

'Is that what she told Rachel?'

'I think so. Yes.'

She laughed.

'Well, all I can say is it's a good job I did meet Ryan or I'd be going out on my own most of the time. Amy just wants to mope around in the hostel feeling sorry for herself.'

'Tell me straight. Is she going home because you two have fallen out?'

'No, Mum. She's going home because she's miserable and she won't make any effort. I guess I sound like I'm being a bitch, but I'm just so exasperated. I'm sure we'll sort things out between us when I get back.'

'Are *you* all right?'

'I'm having a great time! Not that I don't miss you, of course,' she added anxiously, making me smile, 'But I've got no intention of cutting *my* trip short. What about you? How have you enjoyed Amsterdam? I hope you haven't been trying any of that bloody space cake – it's a lot stronger than you might think. What? Mum? What are you laughing at?'

'Nothing, love. No, of course we haven't been doing any drugs – what do you take us for?' I caught Rachel's eye and grinned, but she looked away quickly, glancing at her watch, letting me know that she was anxious for us to get on with our packing and get going.

I wanted to ask Sophie a lot more. About Ryan especially. But it was difficult in the circumstances; it'd have to wait.

'I think,' I told Rachel gently after I'd hung up, being as tactful as I could, 'that half the problem is, Amy's been terribly homesick.'

'That's bollocks,' she retorted. 'She's never been homesick, even when she was a little girl.' She looked at me and shrugged. 'But I guess it makes Sophie feel better to say that.'

Neither of us mentioned it again. We had a long journey home ahead of us, and arguing about the girls wasn't an option.

It was a long, tedious ferry crossing from the Hook of Holland. Too long to sit in silence reading English papers and magazines, however hard we tried.

'I bought us one of those T-shirts each,' I told Rachel, coming back from the shop and throwing a bag down on the seat next to her. 'They were reduced.'

'What T-shirts?' She picked up the bag and peeked inside. 'Oh, Maddy, honestly! Why?'

I shrugged.

'Just thought it was appropriate.' I pulled one out of the bag and held it up in front of me. GOOD GIRLS GO TO HEAVEN – BAD GIRLS GO TO AMSTERDAM.

'Appropriate for you, maybe!'

'Hang on. Who's the junkie around here?'

'Very funny. Thanks, but I can't see me wearing it at home.'

'Go on. Wear it to school. Give the kids a laugh.'

'So where are you going to wear yours?' She gave me a sly look. 'In bed with Tom? Or does he already know you're a Bad Girl?'

'Yes,' I said, putting the T-shirt back in the bag in a

scrunched up bundle and throwing it down on the seat. 'Yes, he does. But there you go – it's true, isn't it.'

'Sorry, I forgot you wanted to stay off the subject of Tom.'

'Oh, don't worry. I know I'll have to sort it out when I get home. One way or another.' I lit up a cigarette, took a drag and blew smoke crossly towards Rachel, who coughed pointedly and turned away. 'See?' I snapped. 'Bad girls smoke, and drink, and fucking swear, and—'

'Why are you so hard on yourself?' she returned abruptly.

'Me? That's good, coming from you, punishing yourself on the treadmill every night and putting yourself on all those lettuce leaf diets.'

'And you punish yourself by disliking yourself.'

'I don't.'

'You do!'

'Maybe that's because I don't deserve to be liked. Even by myself.'

'You do talk some crap,' she said mildly. 'What did you ever do that was so bad?'

Well, now. That's a question and a half, isn't it?

I was interested in sport and fitness once, you know. Or, to be honest, I wasn't so much interested in doing it as in watching it. And to be totally honest, it wasn't so much the sport itself I liked watching as the boys who were taking part. I'm talking about a long time ago, now – back when I was at school.

'I was actually really keen on competitive swimming.'

'Were you?' Rachel looked surprised. 'You've always said how much you hate anything remotely physical.'

'Yeah. I suppose sometimes you react against things. You know, like if you eat too much chocolate, and it makes you sick, you don't fancy it any more. Or if you drink too much vodka...'

She laughed.

'Maddy, I've known you for a long time, and I've lost count of the number of times I've seen you eat too much

149

chocolate and drink too much vodka, but you've never stopped wanting them both again the next day!'

'Well, all right, all right.'

You can stop laughing now; it wasn't that funny for Christ's sake. Anyone would think I was the only person in the world who ever ate chocolate or drank vodka.

'And you're saying that's what you did with sport?' she carried on, still laughing, almost reduced to tears now by the hilarity of this whole theme. 'You had so much of it you made yourself sick, and it put you off trying it again?'

'It wasn't quite like that. But if you're just going to snort with laughter,' I retorted, offended, taking another drag of my cigarette, 'I won't tell you.'

'Oh, come on. I'm sorry. Tell me, Madd. Please. I promise I won't laugh.'

It was quite funny really. I used to follow the local swimming squad. I thought they were wonderful. It all started when I was going out with a lad in my class called Ian, who was a fantastic swimmer. He asked me along to watch them training at the pool and before I knew it, I was hooked. The excitement, the adrenalin, the warm, wet atmosphere, the smell of chlorine and sweat and pent-up testosterone. Poor Ian didn't last long; I took up with another swimmer called Phil within a week or so of going to the pool, and poor Phil, it was only a matter of days before I'd moved onto Graham. I went to every training session and watched every race. I thought of myself as the club mascot. I wouldn't like to say what they thought of me, but nowadays there are pretty derogatory terms for girls who sleep their way through sports teams, aren't there.

Joe was probably about the sixth or seventh. It started off just the same. Come on: we were sixteen; our hormones were screaming – there weren't any niceties about it. A quick shag behind the bike sheds, another one the next week in his bedroom while his mum and dad were out – and I found out I was pregnant a few weeks before my seventeenth birthday.

Madeleine Goodchild, pregnant groupie of the swimming

club. A lot of the boys weren't even sure who the father was. They whispered and sniggered as my belly grew bigger and more obvious, and eventually I stayed away from the pool, and Joe did the honourable thing and married me. Madeleine Appleby, seventeen-year-old bride, seventeen-year-old mother, nineteen-year-old divorcée. But I reverted to my maiden name as soon as Joe and I were divorced. Goodchild by name, bad child by nature.

'You make it sound as if it was all your fault that you split up. But probably you were just too young – and getting married because you're pregnant never works,' protested Rachel.

But it was all my fault. We were ridiculously young – just children – but if I'd waited my whole life I probably wouldn't have met anyone else half as good as Joe. There he was, a father at only seventeen. You hear about other boys this happens to, and do they stick around and support the girl? No, they bugger off, don't they, scared shitless of the responsibility. People shake their heads and say you can't blame them. Why can't you? It takes two to tango. The girl can't run away from her baby so why should he?

Joe wasn't like that. He was kind, and gentle, and I think he really loved me. Of course, I was too young and stupid to appreciate that. When the novelty of having the baby began fairly quickly to wear off I was bored and cross, and I took it out on him. He went off to work every day – he was training to be a car mechanic – and came back every night – while all his mates went out drinking – to our one room in my parents' house, where all we could do was watch the TV quietly so that the baby didn't wake up, and all I could do, out of sheer frustration and regret at how my life had turned out, was pick on him, constantly goading him to provoke a row, until eventually he'd sigh and say, 'Give it a rest, Madd.' Just that – give it a rest. Most lads would have walked out, but he just used to shrug and say he knew it was tough for me, stuck at home with the baby, while he at least was going out to work and learning a trade.

151

'Why don't you go out with your mates some evenings?' Joe suggested eventually.

And partly because I was afraid, myself, of the black mood I'd sunk into and how it was choking the life out of me, I agreed. I don't know who he thought I was meeting every Tuesday night, because I sure as hell didn't have any mates left who wanted to go out with me. So while he looked after Sophie, I got on the bus and went into town to the only place I could think of – the pub next to the swimming pool where everyone from the swimming club went – and slipped gradually back into my old ways. Joe had left the squad but there were plenty of other fit, available, attractive young men falling over themselves for a bit of attention from a young woman at the end of a gruelling training session. The guy I picked was called Ben. I didn't particularly like him. I can't even remember his other name. The first time we had sex, I cried afterwards and promised myself it wouldn't happen again. But it did. And after a while I stopped worrying about it. It was just something to do.

'You weren't enjoying it?' Rachel asked me quietly.

'I don't think I ever asked myself that. It was – a sort of release. Some girls go out and get drunk; I went out and had sex. I think I'd kind of abandoned my self-esteem.'

'Don't you think it might have been post-natal depression?'

'Maybe. But Rach, other women go to see their doctors and get medication. Me, I just hung around with swimmers and got laid a lot.'

'So what happened? Joe found out?'

Oh yes, he found out all right. He turned up at the pub one evening having left Sophie with my parents. I think he'd been getting suspicious. I always tried to shower the smell of chlorine off me but it clings to your skin, especially when it's come from someone else's sweaty body. I'd got bored with Ben by now, but I made the mistake of starting something with another lad, Paul, while Ben was still smarting with the humiliation of being dumped. I was with Paul in his car in the pub car park when I heard Joe's voice outside, asking if anyone had seen me.

'Your wife,' Ben told him spitefully, 'is in there, having it off with her latest conquest.'

It was to Joe's credit that he didn't actually believe it until Ben wrenched the car door open and showed him.

He walked out of my parents' house that same night and never came back. I never heard from him or knew where he'd gone. The only contact I had from him was a maintenance payment for Sophie, paid into my bank account once a month by a firm of solicitors in London acting on Joe's behalf. I never went anywhere near the swimming squad again.

'It's a bit much, though,' said Rachel thoughtfully, 'to blame sport for that.'

'I needed a scapegoat.'

'Fair enough.'

By the time we'd driven home from Harwich it was the middle of the evening and we were both shattered.

'Thanks,' I said, heaving my baggage out of the car and struggling to my front door. After putting the bags down on the doorstep, I walked back to the car. Rachel wound the window down. 'D'you want to come in? For a coffee or anything?'

'No. I'll get straight home. Simon'll be waiting up.'

'OK. Rach – I know it hasn't ended how we wanted it to, but...'

'I know.' She reached out of the open window and gave me a kiss on the cheek. 'It's been great, Madd. We've had some fun, haven't we? And at least we didn't spend all the money.'

'That's true!' I was smiling as she drove off. So the girls might have had a falling-out, and I suppose it was only natural for Rachel to be protective about Amy – but at least *we* were still friends.

*

'It feels kind of weird. Twenty-four hours ago, we were still in Amsterdam, having a great time. It all happened so quickly.'

Tom had got the text message I sent him when we were on the way back, and phoned me just as I was about to go to bed.

'Ah, well. I expect you would have been coming home soon anyway.'

How irritating was that! And how typical!

'No! Actually, we wouldn't. We were planning to go on up the coast. Maybe get as far as Denmark. It's really disappointing.'

'Well, in some ways, I suppose. But at least you're home now. You could come up to Manchester for the weekend.'

Oh, deep joy.

'I've only just got back, Tom. I'm knackered. I don't feel like coming to Manchester. Nothing personal, but I really don't.'

'Sweetheart, I've got so much to tell you. I just can't wait to see you.'

'Well – you know where I am, don't you.'

'OK,' he said after only a moment's hesitation. 'I'll come down for the weekend, then, shall I?'

I'll be completely honest with you now. The only time I'd had sex in the past four weeks was during those few days when Tom was with me in Lille – and that was all a bit fraught. I think he'd made up his mind that if he shagged me senseless I'd change my mind and go rushing back to England with him. No offence intended but you know, once you're out of your twenties, one good session is worth several desperate needy ones. By the time he was trying, heroically but without much success, to get it up for the third time, I'd completely lost interest and was thinking seriously about suggesting I turned the telly on and he gave me a shout when he was ready.

But now I was home, well, it was different. I was pissed off. The six weeks of travelling during which I'd anticipated seeing most, if not all, of Europe, had been cut short after three weeks, five days, and only four countries – including Belgium, which with due respect to Rachel's new criminal record, it's only fair to say we went through so quickly, if I'd blinked I'd have missed it.

That first morning I was home I looked around the house, which I'd thought was quite a nice little house before I went away – nothing special, a bit drab in places, but it had been home to me and Sophie for many years and was kind of comfortable in its familiarity – and decided I didn't like it any more. I didn't like the wallpaper in my bedroom. I didn't like the 1970s look of the bathroom with its old-fashioned tiles and its pale blue bath. I hated the stupid tiny kitchen and the little square lounge with its worn-out carpet and faded curtains. Why hadn't I ever saved up and done anything about it, redecorated it, smartened it up? Why didn't I do that with my lottery winnings, instead of gallivanting off around Europe? I sulked to myself as I tipped the dirty clothes out of my bags and loaded them into the washing machine. This was real life again, and I didn't like it. I wanted something to look forward to. It might as well be sex with Tom. At least it'd take my mind off the wallpaper and curtains.

He arrived on the Friday night, bringing flowers, wine and chocolates.

'It's not Valentine's Day,' I said, pleased nevertheless.

We kissed, passionately, and he held me tight to his chest for a long time as if he was frightened I might go away again.

'I suppose I should say I'm sorry about your trip – the way it ended,' he muttered against my hair. 'But I'm not. I'm glad you're home.'

'It's only been a week since we were together in Lille!' I reminded him, laughing. I held him at arm's length and studied him. 'Are you OK? You look ... kind of troubled.'

'*Troubled*.' He repeated, raising his eyebrows. 'You're very perceptive, sweetheart.'

We went through to the lounge where he collapsed on the

sofa, took his shoes off and held out his arms for me to join
him.

'I've had a pretty rough week.'

'New job?' I asked sympathetically. 'Are the guys not …
as *hungry* as you thought?'

'The job's fine,' he responded. He hesitated for a minute
and then went on, in a rush, 'It's Linda. She didn't take it
very well.'

'Take it?' I puzzled over this briefly. What didn't she take?
Her medicine? Her drink? Her punishment?

'The news, Maddy! I knew it was going to come as a bit
of a shock, but you know, I really thought she'd be all right
about it. After all, it's not as though things have been particularly *good* between us for a long while.'

I stared at him. OK, I know it doesn't say a lot for me that
I'd forgotten, completely forgotten, what he said in Lille
about asking Linda for a divorce. True, I'd had other traumas
to worry about, but even so you would have expected the
fact that my lover was planning to get a divorce and marry
me to have made just a *teeny* bit more of an impact on my
mind. In my defence, I could only say:

'Fucking hell. You really meant it, then?'

Now it was his turn to stare in surprise.

'Of course I meant it. What – did you think I was joking
or something? I promised I was going to talk to her as soon
as I got back from Lille.'

'Oh, yes.' I suddenly remembered. 'This was supposed to
be the weekend she was going up to Manchester, wasn't it.'

'She changed her mind after I spoke to her.'

Understandable, I suppose.

'So you did it *over the phone*?'

Twelve years of marriage, twelve years of sharing a bed, a
cat, a house with a joint mortgage – all shrugged off with a
phone call?

He nodded.

'I couldn't wait. I want to be free. Free to marry *you*,
sweetheart!'

156

Privately, I thought it stunk. I could understand why she took it badly: who wouldn't? But, after having it off regularly with her husband for the past two years, it was a bit late in the day for me to start taking Linda's side now. That didn't stop me from taking my *own* side, though.

'Tom – I told you, in Lille. I don't think I want to get married.'

He sighed patiently, like I was just being a little bit awkward, making difficulties, but it would only be a matter of time before I came to my senses.

'There's no hurry,' he said. 'By the time she agrees to a divorce . . . we'll be living together, at least. Honestly, sweetheart, I think you'll like Manchester. Houses are cheaper than down here. We could—'

'No!' I put my hand over his mouth. 'I don't want to talk about it.'

'But, Maddy.' He struggled with my hand. 'I want you to come up to Manchester and see—'

'Please, Tom. Can we discuss this another time? Can we just have dinner? The chicken'll be dried up and the potatoes are probably burnt. Can't we just eat, and go to bed?'

His eyes lit up at the mention of bed.

'I'm not too worried about the dinner,' he said, pulling me to my feet.

'Me neither,' I laughed.

Threw the chicken and potatoes in the bin later on.

Of course, I was only delaying the inevitable. The subject came up again, as I knew it would, the next morning. Again, I distracted him in the way that worked best. By the time he left on the Sunday afternoon, I'd initiated sex so many times he was grinning from ear to ear and I was worn out. But I'd got away with it. He left without seeming to realise I still hadn't agreed to move in with him at all – let alone marry him.

Maybe you think I was just being perverse. But you know, all the time Tom and I had been seeing each other, it had never crossed my mind that he'd do this; I always presumed he'd stay with Linda, that I'd never be anything apart from the Other Woman. I'd got used to it now. I quite liked it. It suited me.

And let's be honest; I'd never forgotten that I made a hash of one marriage. What was the point of a repeat performance?

Besides, I had other things to think about now; other decisions to make now that my Great Travel Adventure had been brought to an abrupt conclusion. If I wasn't going back to work for Nicholas Pretty Dreadful Pervert (and I was more certain now about this than I'd ever been), and if I wasn't going to devote the rest of my life, until the lottery money ran out, to washing, ironing and making lousy dinners, I'd have to start looking for a new job. I looked in the local paper. Plenty of adverts in there. There was sure to be an employer somewhere who'd want someone with my fantastic touch-typing skills and my old O levels. Maybe I could work in a bank, or an insurance office, or an estate agent's – nice one, get a chance to have a nose at everyone's houses. I supposed I should send off some applications or at the very least, in the meantime, register with a temp agency.

I had a friend once who worked as a temp in the big London banks. She earned loads of money and if anyone pissed her off, was rude to her or tried it on out the back by the dustbins (just for instance), she could simply turn round and walk out. The idea of that appealed to me. But, on the other hand, the idea of rushing to get on a crowded commuter train every morning, standing squashed up against other people's chests with their sweaty armpits in your face, didn't do a lot for me. To be honest, I didn't want to do anything. I didn't want to go back to work yet. There wasn't any rush. I still had plenty of money. I sighed, and put down the paper, and picked up the phone to perhaps call a temp agency, and put it down again, and walked aimlessly

158

around the house, looking at the horrible wallpaper and the worn-out carpet, and I thought to myself: It's happening again. I'm *unfulfilled* again. I was OK while we were away – fine then, in fact, full of fulfilment. That's all very well, Maddy, I hear you say, but nobody can stay away travelling for the rest of their lives. The absolute truth of this hit me like a brick in the face that Monday morning in the middle of August when Tom had gone, and I was home again on my own. If I felt unfulfilled before I went away, I felt even worse now. At least I had a job then. At least I had a gym membership, and a friend who wanted to have an occasional low-calorie drink with me.

On the spur of the moment I picked up the phone again and dialled Rachel's number. We hadn't spoken since we got back on Thursday night.

'Hi!' she trilled happily. She sounded almost breathless with excitement. For a moment I felt resentful – what did she have to be so happy about, when I was in the doldrums? Then I remembered: her daughter was home.

'I met Amy at Heathrow yesterday evening,' she told me. 'She couldn't get on a flight from Brisbane till late Saturday night.'

Of course, she would have had to get an internal flight back to Brisbane first.

'Is she OK? How did she feel, flying all that way on her own?'

Why did I feel guilty? The situation wasn't of my making.

'She's fine. Just pleased to be home, I think.' I could hear the pleasure and relief in Rachel's voice. 'D'you want to come over, Madd? Have some lunch with us? Amy's got some photos.'

'Yeah. Sure, that'll be nice.' I tried to sound enthusiastic. It wouldn't do to show that I was jealous, that *I* wanted *my* daughter to be home with *me*. After all, at the end of the day, I was glad she was still out there, still enjoying herself, and hadn't had to give in to homesickness and fly back after only a couple of months of their trip.

Amy looked well; a bit thinner perhaps, a bit sunburnt where she hadn't quite put enough sun block on her shoulders and her nose. She seemed excited at being home so I thought it best not to refer to what she might have missed out on.

'Sophie's face is one mass of freckles,' she told me, laughing.

I looked at her speculatively. Was it wise to discuss Sophie? Was it going to cause any recriminations?

'It's OK,' she told me, seeing my expression. 'Me and Sophe are cool about this. We're being, you know, mature about it. We don't want to jeopardise our friendship.'

Blimey. Cool indeed.

'I just wish she hadn't met him, to be honest,' she continued with a shadow of a sigh, passing me a stack of photos and pointing to the one on top.

I picked up the photo and studied it. My Sophie, my precious little girl, freckled and sun-streaked, smiled back at me from a vast Australian beach, leaning against a jeep, her hand resting casually on the arm of a tall blond young man with a wide smile and wide blue eyes. The hand on the arm looked like a gesture of friendship, of mateyness, rather than love or passion, and despite everything I quite liked the look of him.

'That was taken on the Fraser Island trip,' said Amy, sitting down next to me on the arm of my chair. 'The others are the Americans we travelled with.'

I hadn't really noticed the others. Grouped together round the door of the jeep, all wearing cut-down jeans and T-shirts, they looked like they were jostling each other and laughing as Amy took the photograph.

'They look a nice group,' I commented.

'They kind of stuck together, though. And Sophie and Ryan were like *that* the whole time.' She made a gesture with her fingers. Glued together. Then she shrugged as if it was all water under the bridge now and she wasn't going to keep on about it. Cool. Mature. Fine by me.

I flicked through the rest of the photographs while Amy gave me a running commentary. Sophie outside the first hostel in Perth. Sophie and Amy on the beach – taken by one of the lifeguards. Views of Melbourne, of Sydney, of Ayers Rock. Pictures of sunsets, of cities, of sunshine and rain. And more pictures of Sophie with Ryan. Arm in arm, or sitting close together, laughing, smiling, obviously very happy together.

'What's he like?' Maybe it was a sore point but I couldn't resist asking. He was spending a lot of time with my Sophie and she hadn't told me anything about him. Why not? You can see why I was curious.

'He's OK,' said Amy with a forced casualness. She shrugged again and carried on telling me about the Brisbane River and Surfer's Paradise.

Better drop the subject then. Even I know when enough is enough.

'What's happened with Tom?' Rachel asked me quietly after lunch.

I sighed and shook my head.

'He's told his wife he wants a divorce.'

'And what have *you* said to *him*?'

'I kind of ... kept avoiding the subject.'

'Is that very fair?'

'No!' I retorted hotly, stung as much by my own unease as by her interference. 'It isn't fair, but then to be honest I don't think he's being fair to me, either – forcing this situation on me! I didn't *ask* for everything to change. I didn't ask for him to get a new job up North, or to leave his wife, or to ask me to marry him. I was happy with things the way they were.'

'No you weren't,' she responded calmly. 'You were fed up. You were fed up before we went away, and you're fed up now we're back. You can't blame it all on Tom. He can't seem to win, if you ask me.'

I wasn't asking you actually, but fair enough. I guess

161

that's what best friends are for: to slag you off and tell you a few home truths.

'Maybe you need to look at what else is missing from your life,' she went on relentlessly, 'Before you decide what to do about Tom.'

Well, that told me, didn't it? Back to the *fulfilment* thing again.

She was right, anyway. Enough slobbing around indoors complaining to myself about being bored. I had to get a job. Winning some money on the lottery hadn't given me the right to retire from life. I'd get straight home and get on the phone to the temp agencies. That'd be a start. I could be in work by next Monday, maybe even sooner.

I did it, too. By the end of that afternoon I'd phoned three different agencies, had driven into town and had an interview with two of them already. They'd both assured me they could find me a job in a matter of days. Great. Unfulfilled, me? I'll be the chairman of an international corporation before you know it.

The following day at five past nine, the first agency phoned me back.

'We've got a lovely job for you!' trilled the sixteen-year-old *employment consultant,* in the compassionate tone she probably reserved for unemployed secretaries nearing forty with out-of-date computer skills. 'Secretarial, town centre, nine to five, an hour for lunch, salary AAE.'

'Salary what?'

'According to age and experience,' she said loftily, obviously enjoying her superior knowledge of initials. Salary should be high, then, as my age and my experience were both comparatively immense.

'Sounds good,' I said. 'Where is it?'

'Brentwood Council. Supplies department. Report to a Mr Nicholas Pleasant.' She paused, waiting for me to gasp in excitement at this amazing prospect. 'Shall I put you forward for this temp position, then, Maddy?'

Chapter 11

Quite possibly, Deanna the enthusiastic young employment consultant at Jobs 4 U had never been told to stuff a job up her arse before. She gasped with a kind of theatrical shock, partly bristling with offence at being spoken to like that, but partly (I suspect) with the delicious anticipation of the moment when she'd tell all her friends down the pub about it.

'*What* did you say?' she asked very primly.

'I said tough. Tough you should ask me to work at the council offices. It just happens to be where I used to work before, and I think it's probably best that I don't go back there.'

'Is there any particular reason for that?'

'Yes. But I'm not going to tell you what it is.'

'Only it doesn't look very good, you see, if you turn down the first job we offer you, for no particular reason.'

'Fine. I'll use one of the other agencies.'

'Oh. Well. I suppose there might be something else,' she said very begrudgingly. I heard her tapping away at her computer. 'I could try Barclays Bank for you, if you think you could cope with that type of environment.' Presumably if I could be trusted not to shout 'Stuff it up your arse' at the very important and posey people at the bank. 'Or there's a vacancy at Woolworth's. Might be more suitable.'

'Fine,' I said again, refusing to rise to her insinuations about my lack of social polish.

'Leave it with me, then,' she continued imperiously. 'I'll call you back.'

I can't wait.

As it happened, she called me back later the same day and offered me three weeks' work at a solicitor's office 'specialising in matrimonial and family law'.

'Do you have any experience in the field?' she asked me haughtily.

'Yeah. I've been married, and I've got a family.'

'I mean legal experience. It's specialised work, you know.'

'In that case, no. You'd better look for a specialist.'

'Well, it's OK – they say legal experience preferred but not essential. So shall I put you forward for this position then, Maddy?'

I wondered briefly what would happen if I told her to stick this one up her arse too, but it was almost too much effort and not enough fun.

'All right, then,' I said with a sigh.

'Nice little job,' she said in clipped tones, making me wonder if she was jealous and wanted it herself. 'Nine till five, an hour for lunch, start next week and report to a Mr Johnson. OK, Maddy?'

'OK, Deanna.'

'We'll call you to see how you're getting on.'

'Nice of you. Thanks.'

I hung up the phone and wondered why I didn't feel pleased. Most people would feel pleased, wouldn't they? New job, new start – maybe make some new friends – three weeks was quite good for a temp job after all, and who knows, they might think I was wonderful and offer me something permanent. Wouldn't that be great?

I wandered, not feeling great, into the kitchen to get myself a cup of coffee and a cigarette, and from there back to the end of my lounge where I kept the computer. I logged on and checked my e-mail account, my heart leaping when I saw there was one from Sophie. I hadn't heard from her

164

since we'd been back in England, and I'd been worrying about how she was feeling about Amy coming home.

Hi Mum! she'd written.

Hope you and Rachel got back safely from Holland. I was gutted about you cutting your trip short. You shouldn't have done that. Amy was so desperate to go home in the end I don't think she'd have cared if Rachel was still away, as long as she was at home herself. Have you seen her since she got back? Hope she's OK and doesn't have any regrets. I just can't imagine wanting to miss out on the rest of our trip but there you go – no point in her carrying on, she really wasn't happy.

Ryan and I have just done the sailing trip around the Whitsunday Islands. The weather wasn't great – it was windy and rainy so the sea was pretty rough and we had to hang onto the sides of the boat. We stopped at several of the islands for snorkelling and swimming with the fish, and slept overnight on the boat in tiny bunks – woke up feeling really claustrophobic but the wind and rain soon put paid to that! We're moving on tomorrow, to Townsville, where we can get a ferry to Magnetic Island. I'll try to mail you again from there.

Mum, you sounded so pissed off in your e-mail. It's such a shame you didn't get to finish your trip. Do you really have to go back to work yet? If you've still got enough money left from the lottery win, why don't you think about coming out here for a couple of weeks? You could join up with us in Cairns – we're planning on staying there for a while. Think about it!

I smiled ruefully to myself as I logged off the computer again and looked around the house for something useful to do. Yes, it was nice to think about it, but at the end of the day spur-of-the-minute solo trips to Australia weren't the sort of thing you did in real life, however tempting it was. I had other things to think about, such as a job in matrimonial and family law starting next week, and ... well, Tom, apart from anything else.

Almost as I thought this, the phone rang.

'You kind of spooked me out there,' I told Tom when I heard his voice. 'I was just thinking about you.'

'Really?' He sounded pleased. 'Thinking something nice? How much you'd like my naked body rubbing up against you?'

Never far from their thoughts, is it?

'Mm. Possibly.'

'So when are you coming up to see me, sweetheart? I'll be in Edinburgh next week. I could book us a nice hotel room for the weekend, somewhere in the city centre – we'll do all the sights, have a romantic dinner at a little place I know near the castle—'

'OK, then.'

He stopped, mid-sentence, obviously completely surprised by the fact that I hadn't needed any persuasion.

'That's great!' he said. I felt quite touched by the excitement in his voice. What was the matter with me? Here was a man who apparently loved me, who was desperate to have sex with me whenever possible, who brought me flowers and took me out for expensive meals – what more could I ask for? Why did I sulk around my house feeling sorry for myself, hating my wallpaper and wishing I had more fun in my life?

'I'll get the hotel sorted out right now!' he was saying. 'And your flights – leave it to me, sweetheart, I'll book them. Will you come up on Friday night and stay till Monday as it's the Bank Holiday? Shall I book you from Gatwick or Stansted? Do you want—'

'No, Tom, it's OK – I'll get my own flights. You can organise the hotel if you like – I've never been to Edinburgh so I don't know the best places. I'll fly up on Friday night but I'll come back Sunday. I'm starting a new temp job on Tuesday so I'd like Monday at home. My last day of freedom,' I joked half-heartedly.

166

'OK,' he agreed at once, obviously realising it was better not to argue. 'I'll make it a weekend to remember, baby!'

I didn't have any doubt about that.

'So what's the plan?' asked Rachel.

She was watching me with a critical eye as I packed my overnight bag for Edinburgh, a few hours before I was due to leave.

'What do you mean, plan?'

'What have you got in mind?'

I stopped, mid-contemplation of the merits of a little black strappy evening top as opposed to a silky ivory-coloured blouse, and stared up at her.

'What are you getting at?'

'Are you going to agree to move in with him?'

I laid the blouse down carefully on the bed so it wouldn't crease.

'Or are you going to finish with him?' she persisted as I hadn't answered.

I still didn't answer. You can see where I was on this, can't you. I was prevaricating. And I wanted to be left alone to prevaricate, without having an inquisition into my motives and intentions.

'You're not just keeping him hanging on, are you?'

'Why the hell not?' I snapped. 'He's kept me hanging on for long enough!'

'That doesn't make it right.'

'No, well. I'm not exactly an expert in doing the right thing, am I. You know me, Scarlet Woman Extraordinaire, Bad Child supreme. Anyway,' I added, looking away from the Teacher expression in Rachel's eyes that always made me feel so uncomfortable, 'since when did you care so much about Tom's feelings?'

She ignored this.

'You've got a chance here, Maddy, that's all. If you throw it away, that's up to you. As long as you know what you're doing.'

167

'I know what I'm doing, thank you very much. I'm going up to Edinburgh for a weekend in a good hotel, some nice meals and plenty of great sex.'

'And that's it?'

'What else is there?'

She shrugged.

'Fine, if that's what you really want, great – have a good time.'

I shrugged back. I felt rattled, like she'd taken the edge off the pleasure of my anticipation.

'I think the blouse is probably better than the black top,' she added gently. 'It looks good with those trousers.'

'Thanks.' I picked it up again and folded it onto the top of the bag. 'Come on then – that'll do. Shall we go back downstairs and have a drink? I've got a bottle of red wine open.'

'Have you got any slimline tonic?'

'Gallons of the stuff. You're the only one who drinks it.'

'I'll have it with ice and lemon, then – lovely.'

Can't think of anything more depressing myself, but there you go. All the more wine for me!

Tom met me at Edinburgh airport. He'd driven up from Manchester and hadn't even had time to check into the hotel yet; so I was surprised, when we finally got there, to find that not only was it probably the best hotel in the city, bang smack in the middle of the main tourist area, a stone's throw from the castle and looking much like a castle itself with its high grey stone walls, like something out of a fairy story – but there were champagne and flowers in the room already.

'Ordered them when I booked the hotel,' he smiled, seeing my face.

He put our bags down and kicked the door shut, taking me in his arms.

'God, I've missed you so much.'

'It was only last weekend...' I began automatically.

'I don't just mean this week. I mean always. I've always

missed you when we've been apart. I always wanted more, but it just wasn't possible ... till now.'

He began to kiss me and, as always, everything else went out of the window – the fact that I was starving and it didn't look like I'd be going out for dinner now for quite a while, but most of all the alarm bells that had started to ring like the clappers of hell in my mind at the mention of those words 'till now'. We staggered backwards to the huge bed in the middle of the room, leaving a trail of discarded clothes across the floor like a pair of desperate young lovers on their first night together.

'I love you, Maddy!' muttered Tom against my ear at the height of his passion.

It ruined it for me. It was probably the first time I'd had sex with Tom and hadn't been satisfied.

I know I sound ungrateful. But it wasn't something we'd been in the habit of saying. Is that odd? I suppose it is. We'd been seeing each other for two years and the sex was absolutely fantastic. We'd said a lot of things to each other – many of them pretty cringe-making in the cold light of day – but we hadn't, actually, really got around to discussing the whole Love thing. If anyone had asked me (and now I come to think of it, Rachel had, several times) whether I was in love with Tom, I'd probably hung my head and mumbled in embarrassment. Come on, let's be honest: LURVE – what's it all about anyway? He was probably only saying it now because it seemed right at the time.

'Did I say something wrong?' he asked as we were getting dressed afterwards. 'You seem a bit quiet. Didn't you enjoy it?'

'Don't be silly!' I laughed.

'That's all right then' he said with palpable relief. 'Wouldn't like to think I was losing my touch!'

We went out to dinner, and he talked about his new job, and the people in the Manchester office, and how he was looking forward to meeting the Edinburgh guys, and how he was going to show me all the sights the next day, and we had quite a bit to drink and walked back to the hotel as all the pubs expelled their quota of drunks onto the streets, and it wasn't until we were back in our room that he said it again.

'You look lovely tonight, sweetheart. I love you so much.'

He was unbuttoning my blouse at the time. I stiffened, and he paused and looked up from kissing my neck.

'What's wrong?'

'It's just...' Out with it, Maddy. In for a penny, in for a pound. 'It's just that you've never said that before.'

'That I love you? Well, I should have done. If I haven't, I've been an idiot. A total stupid, selfish, idiot. I can't believe you've stayed with me all this time, the way I've taken you for granted. You must have loved me so much, to put up with it!'

Shit.

He was looking at me with his head on one side, his eyes like a puppy dog's, wide and trusting and ... waiting for an answer.

'Mm,' I said.

As a declaration of undying devotion, it lacked a certain amount of vocabulary; but amazingly, he seemed delighted with this response and proceeded to rip off the rest of my clothes with even greater enthusiasm. I guess he presumed I was too carried away with passion to manage more than an 'mm'. Normally, yes, I would have been. But on that Friday evening in Edinburgh, I made personal history by a repeat performance of orgasm-free sex, finding out at a comparatively late stage in my life how easy it is to fake it and keep a man happy.

But was I happy? I lay awake most of the night, staring into the darkness and wondering why I hadn't taken more notice of Rachel. She was right. Sooner or later I was going to have to make a decision about all this – and I sensed the time was getting near.

If I'd known just how near, I might have got a taxi straight back to the airport the next morning after breakfast. Don't get me wrong: we had a lovely day in Edinburgh, starting off with a visit to the castle, posing for photographs sitting on the famous cannons, looking out over the ramparts at the city below and finishing up with shopping in Princes Street. Kilted pipers serenaded us as we strolled around the city streets, and the old grey buildings that probably looked stark and drab on a typical Scottish rainy day stood out darkly proud against the bright blue summer sky.

'It's beautiful here,' I admitted. 'I had no idea.'

'I keep telling you. Britain doesn't begin at Southend and end at Westminster.'

'OK,' I laughed. 'When I've finished seeing Europe, maybe I'll venture further into the deepest darkest corners of the UK as well.'

'If you like it here, we could always relocate here instead of Manchester. It's just as easy for me.'

I'd been looking in a shop window and hadn't really been prepared for it. In the window, beyond the display of Scottish shortbread, Celtic jewellery, tartan rugs and all the other touristy things, I could see Tom's reflection. He was watching the back of my head, waiting for me to turn round, waiting for me to smile and say yes, that would be lovely, let's buy a house here, I'd love it, I'd be happy for the rest of my life. How long can you look in a shop window as if you're so completely fascinated by a box of shortbread that you can't tear your eyes away from it, even to respond to a life-changing suggestion from your lover?

'I don't think—' I began, without even turning round.

'Please don't say you're still not sure,' he interrupted before I'd even had a chance to decide what to say. His voice was low and urgent. He sounded almost desperate. How had this happened? And when? When had he changed from Tom the happy-go-lucky cheating husband to Tom the frantic suitor? I didn't notice it happening. I didn't like it. I wanted things back the way they were.

'I'm still thinking about it,' I muttered ungraciously, finally turning to face him. 'I need more time, Tom. It's not that easy. When Sophie comes back...'

'She'll be twenty-one! She isn't going to live with you for ever!'

'Maybe not, but I'm not moving out and selling her home while she's away travelling. I can't let her come home and have nowhere to go. Be reasonable!'

He pulled a face, reminding me again of a little boy who couldn't get his own way.

'Let's see how things go over the next few months,' I said, trying for a compromise. 'When Sophie comes home, once she's decided what she wants to do, where she wants to live...'

He shrugged.

'If you say so. But I hope you'll change your mind.'

We walked on in silence for a while until I managed to distract him by talking about the play we were going to see that evening. But I felt uneasy, like there was a big shadow hanging over the nice sunny day. And it was going to get bigger.

After the play we went to a lovely restaurant and over the wine and the food I began to relax and forget my earlier worries. What the hell had I been feeling so anxious about, I asked myself as I downed another glass of wine. After all, this was Tom, good old Tom whose passions in life were good food and good sex and plenty of them. He wasn't about to turn into some sort of possessive bunny-boiler for Christ's sake! He and I had always been on the same wavelength. We worked from the same agenda. No ties, no commitments, no promises – just enjoying each other's company whenever possible. I turned my attention from my dessert and smiled up at him a little drunkenly. He was smiling back at me, and the very last thought I had before everything came crashing down around me was that I'd like to shag him there and then, over the table with its fancy white cloth and tartan serviettes, with the bagpipe music playing and all the waiters watching.

'What are you thinking?' he asked me softly, taking hold of my hand across the table.

'Oh,' I smirked, 'just a few nice thoughts.'

'Me too.'

So shall we clear the table now, then?

Still holding my one free hand (the other one was spooning up the last remnants of my pudding), without taking his eyes from mine he pulled a little box out of his jacket pocket and laid it on the table between us.

A little box. The kind of little box that comes from expensive jewellers' shops and usually holds something small and gold.

'What's that?' I asked in a croak, dropping my spoon on the table.

'Take a look.'

The box sat on the table, midway between his plate and my dropped spoon, like the last pawn in a game of chess. My move? Check, I think. I picked it up very slowly and opened it, even more slowly, holding my breath. Inside, a diamond and sapphire engagement ring twinkled up at me provocatively.

Checkmate.

'I hope you like it,' he said, all in a rush of exhaled breath.

I could feel him watching me. I closed the box and put it back on the table. I couldn't look at him; I was too afraid I'd start crying. This was all my fault. Why did I let it happen?

'It's beautiful,' I told the tablecloth. 'But I don't want it, Tom.'

There was a long silence. Then:

'Please,' he said. 'I want you to have it. I understand what you were saying, earlier, about Sophie, and wanting more time to think. It doesn't matter. I can wait. I still want you to have it.'

'No!' He jumped at the sudden force of my voice. So did the people on the next three tables. 'No, Tom. I'm sorry. I've been trying to tell you, but you wouldn't listen. I can't accept this. It's an engagement ring, and we're not getting engaged. You're still married, and—'

'But not for long!' he countered urgently. 'Linda doesn't want to fight the divorce. It could all be through in a matter of months.'

'But I don't want to be married. I should have told you more definitely. I've been ... prevaricating. But I'm telling you now: I don't want to get married. Not now, not next year, not ... ever.'

'That sounds pretty final,' he said, hanging his head.

'I'm sorry.'

'I thought – all this time – it would be what you wanted. It's why I left Linda.'

'I know. But I'd never said ... you just assumed...' I tailed off, miserably, playing with my discarded spoon. I'd never eat Scotch pancakes again.

'Don't you love me?' he asked in a barely audible whisper.

I put down the spoon and wiped my eyes with the back of my hand. Don't ask me this. Please let's just drop it.

'Not at all?' came another whisper.

'In my way,' I said. 'In my way, Tom, I do. I'm just not very good at this kind of stuff.'

He paid the bill and we left without any coffee. Or any further conversation.

That was partly what did it. A big part of the reason, but not the only part.

Despite the unhappy silent walk back to the hotel and the cold lonely night on the edge of the bed, the polite stilted conversation over breakfast the next morning and the dreadful moment of parting at the airport, when I wasn't sure which of us most wanted to cry – despite all this, Tom still sent me a text message the next day to say he wanted to go on seeing me, even if only as a friend, and I still felt like shit: confused and guilty and not even sure whether I'd ever loved him or even wanted to.

But the other part of the reason was the phone call I had, on that Bank Holiday Monday as I was in the middle of

174

ironing my half-decent clothes ready to wear for my first working week in the world of matrimonial and family law. The call was from Nicholas P. D. Pleasant, telling me he'd been surprised to hear from Deanna at Jobs 4 U that I'd turned down an opportunity to work for him again, and how disappointed he was, and how much he'd like to have me back as his secretary again, and wouldn't I consider it even if he offered me half as much money again as the agency would have paid me?

'No,' I said calmly. 'I wouldn't.'

'Oh, dear. I was so hoping...'

'Well, don't. I'm not coming back to work for you, Nicholas – and even if I wanted to, I couldn't.'

'Oh, dear. Why's that?'

'Because I'm going away again. As soon as possible. Probably tomorrow. I'm going to Australia.'

And the way I feel at the moment, I might not ever come back!

'Two months?' Tom sounded like he was choking.

'Well, I've booked the return flight for two months' time. But I can change it, if I want to.'

I'd made the decision to go to Australia in a split second (the split second that Nicholas Pretty Dire phoned although, to be fair, hearing his voice was just kind of the last straw), and although I'd said very flippantly that I was hoping to go the next day, I didn't really expect it to be as soon as it turned out. I knew it was a lot quicker and easier to get visas these days, on the internet, because I'd seen Sophie doing it. And I knew it was easy to book flights the same way – but I was expecting to have trouble getting one at such short notice. Maybe it wasn't the time of year when most people were going on holiday to Australia; after all, we were still in the middle of a record-breaking heat wave in England, and it was winter out there. Before I'd really had time to think about it, I'd booked myself on a flight to Cairns via Hong Kong that Thursday – three days later. I could have gone the

175

next day but I needed to e-mail Sophie and wait for her reply; which, of course, was so enthusiastic I started packing straight away.

'But what ... what will you do? Out *there*, for two months?'

Tom made it sound like I was going to the depths of the jungle at the very least, or even outer space. 'Sophie and this ... boyfriend of hers – they probably won't stay around for that long just because you're out there!'

'I know that. I'm not just going because of Sophie. That's only part of it. I want to see her, of course I do, but...'

I hesitated. How could I tell Tom that the other part of it had something to do with him? That he, with his leaving of his wife by a telephone call, and his engagement ring over the dinner table, and his talk of house-hunting in Manchester or Edinburgh, had unnerved me to such an extent that I just wanted to put some distance between us – a lot of distance – while I waited for my head to stop spinning and the confusion in my mind to settle down; for as long as it took, lottery money permitting.

'You're running away, aren't you,' he said quietly.

'Yes.'

'From me?'

The silence seemed to bounce and echo along the phone line.

'From me,' he repeated.

'Not just you. Everything. It's not your fault. I need to sort my head out, Tom! I don't know what I want any more. I don't like my house – the wallpaper and curtains are horrible. I don't want to go back to the gym – I hate the treadmill and the bikes make me feel like I'm dying. I don't want to work at the matrimonial and family law place, and I'd like to tell Deanna from Jobs 4 U to go and screw herself, but I *really* don't want Nicholas P. D. phoning me up and badgering me to go back to the council offices.' I stopped, and added thoughtfully, 'Maybe winning the lottery has turned my head.'

176

'I don't think so,' he laughed gently. 'But maybe going off to Europe like that with Rachel has unsettled you.'

'Maybe.'

'And maybe going off again, to Australia, will unsettle you even more.' He paused. 'Maybe you won't want to come back.'

'I will. I will, because of Sophie.'

I said it without thinking. Of course I'd come back because of Sophie! She'd be coming back eventually, after she'd gone on to New Zealand, and South America, and Canada and the USA, and done all the things she'd always planned to do, so of course I wouldn't be staying in Australia; that was obvious. But it wasn't until Tom said, in the same quiet, gentle tone: 'Not because of me?' that I replied, even more quietly:

'No. I think that's what I'm saying. Not because of you.'

'So it's definitely over. Is that what you're saying?'

'I think that would be fairer. Fairer on you. I can't expect you to wait for me to... sort myself out.'

'Well; that's it, then, I suppose.' His voice had become brusque. I wanted to say something nice to him, to soften the blow, and make me feel less like a bitch, but I knew it would only make it worse in the long run. 'Send me a postcard!' he added before he hung up.

Shit. Bet he wished he hadn't left his wife now.

Chapter 12

It was almost as bad telling Rachel.

'I don't understand you,' she said for about the fortieth time, shaking her head and staring at me as she sipped her slimline tonic.

We were having lunch together in the pub garden, the day before I was due to leave. I felt twitchy with a mixture of nerves and excitement, and didn't have a lot of patience with her failure to understand me.

'You never have,' I retorted. 'You never do.'

'What's that supposed to mean? I have *so* tried to understand you.'

'You might have tried, OK, but all I ever hear you saying is that you don't. You don't understand why I don't enjoy torturing myself in the gym. You don't understand why I enjoy wine and vodka and chocolates better than low-fat cottage cheese and –' (I pointed contemptuously at her drink) – 'bloody slimline bloody tonic. You never understood my relationship with Tom...'

'Oh, I understood *that* all right!' she snorted.

'And now you don't understand why I don't want to marry him!'

'No,' she agreed, twisting her glass round and round and staring into it as if its contents were as much of a mystery to her as I was. 'No, I don't understand that. If I were you...'

'Yes?'

She sighed and shook her head.

'Doesn't matter. I'm not, am I. I'm sorry, Madd, I know I should be saying I'm pleased for you, and I'm excited for you, and what a great idea to go flitting off to Australia at the drop of a hat, but ... well, I just don't think you've given it enough thought.'

'Why the hell should I? Look how excited we were at the prospect of going off travelling together when we first found out about the money. Half the fun of it was the spontaneity; not having to give it too much thought!'

'Yes, but then we were going together: the two of us.'

My ham salad sandwich had been lying on the plate in front of me, hardly started. I picked it up and took a bite, chewing thoughtfully for a while before I answered.

'Do you wish you were coming? Is that it?'

'No. Well, yes – of course I'd have liked to come, but now that Amy's home there's no question of it. And anyway, I go back to school next week. That isn't *it*, as you put it.'

'What, then? You're obviously not happy about me going. I can't believe it's just that you're going to miss my scintillating conversations in the pub.'

'Of course I'll miss you, you daft bat,' she said, finally laughing. 'Who else is going to nag me into coming out for a drink?'

'You've got other friends. All those teachers at the school, and what about that girl you go to the gym with now?'

'I don't go with her. I just see her down there sometimes. She's someone to chat to – now that you don't go any more.'

'Well, I'm sorry.' I took another bite of my sandwich. 'I'd have *liked* you to come; it would be a lot more fun. I'm not really looking forward to doing that long flight on my own.'

'You'll be fine. That's the least of your worries.'

I frowned at her.

'So come on, then, tell me. What do you think are the worst of my worries, then?'

'The spiders,' she said flippantly, showing me with her hands how big she thought they were going to be. 'And the snakes. You know you can't stand snakes.'

179

'I'm staying in a hotel, Rach, not a tent pitched on the grass in the middle of the outback.'

'And the fact that you might not want to come back,' she finished abruptly, looking down at her plate. 'That's the worst of your worries.'

Funny. Everyone seemed to think I wouldn't come back. Maybe it was wishful thinking.

One of the most pleasurable experiences of that week had been my phone call on the Tuesday morning to Deanna of Jobs 4 U.

'You can't let a matrimonial and family law firm down just like that, at the last minute!' she squawked in anguish.

Presumably it'd be OK to let down Woolworth's or Tesco's.

'Sorry,' I lied, 'but I haven't got any choice. I'm flying out to Australia on Thursday. Sudden emergency.'

'Well, it really doesn't look very good! I doubt whether they'll want to take a chance on employing you again, if another occasion arises in the future. You have to look at it from the point of view of the legal profession, Maddy.'

'Of course. Absolutely. I quite understand.'

Blacklisted by the legal profession before I've even begun my career as a temp. Must be some sort of record.

'Well, I'll pass on your apology,' she continued grudgingly, 'and I suppose I'll just have to try and find someone else *at the last minute.*'

She gave a huge sigh to indicate the enormity of the task ahead of her.

'I'm sure you won't have any difficulty filling the position,' I said smoothly. 'It sounded such a good job, I expect people are falling over themselves to work there.'

'Yes, I expect so,' she said, sounding like she suspected I was taking the piss but wasn't quite sure. 'Have a good trip then, Maddy, and I hope your ... emergency ... gets sorted out. Give me a ring when you get back. How long did you say you'd be away?'

180

'Not sure, I'm afraid.'

I tried to make it sound like someone might be seriously ill at the very least.

'Oh, dear. Well, good luck, then, and thank you for phoning Jobs 4 U,' she said in her Automated Answering voice.

Amazing. She'd lost her commission and ended up thanking me.

In the few days I had to prepare for the trip, I did a bit of research. I looked at maps and found out exactly where I was going, and realised to my surprise how far north Cairns was in Australia. I looked on the internet and found out what to expect in the way of climate. This was another surprise; my schooldays geography was so basic and deeply ingrained that I'd simply believed the whole of Australia was hot during our winter months and cooler during our summer – whereas in fact, in the tropical north-east of Australia where I was going, it was warm all year round, and even now at the end of their winter the temperature would probably be about eighty degrees. I hastily took all the warm jumpers and jeans out of my suitcase and replaced them with T-shirts and shorts, which took up a lot less space.

I'd never flown on my own before. On the few occasions I'd had holidays abroad, I'd always had Sophie with me. I felt sick with nerves as I got out of the taxi at Heathrow, early that Thursday evening, for my flight at ten past nine. I checked in straight away and wandered around the shops, looking at my watch every five or ten minutes and wondering why the time was going so slowly. Eventually I sat myself down in a restaurant and ordered a meal, with a glass of wine, not so much because I was hungry but because I needed something to do with my hands to stop me continually checking my bag for my boarding pass and passport. By the time I'd finished eating, and done another round of the shops, it was time to go to the boarding gate.

One of my main worries was who I was going to sit next to. Well, you can't blame me, can you? We were going to be flying for twenty-two hours, and it'd be just my luck to get lumbered with someone who fell asleep and snored loudly in my ear or, even worse, someone who didn't sleep at all, and wanted to talk to me all the time when I was trying to sleep. Or someone with a horrible little kid who screamed and bounced on the seat and spat out his dinner. Every possibility was worse than the one before, so you can imagine my relief when I found myself sitting next to a young couple who didn't look a lot older than Sophie and who told me they were celebrating their first wedding anniversary by having a holiday of a lifetime in Australia.

'We both love scuba diving,' said the girl. 'Last year for our honeymoon we went to the Red Sea – that was fantastic. But the Great Barrier Reef has to be the ultimate!'

Having holidays in Egypt and Australia when you were only in your twenties and married for one year seemed such an alien concept to me that I hardly knew how to respond. I spent the first few hours of the flight idly wondering what they both did for a living. Fortunately they spent their time reading quietly, leaving me alone with my thoughts, and it wasn't until the first meal was served that they chatted a little more and revealed that they both worked for a legal practice.

'Specialising in matrimonial and family law?' I asked, stifling a giggle.

'How did you guess?'

The flight was fine except for the fact that the in-flight entertainment wasn't working. I wasn't too bothered about this but I suppose it was distressing for families with kids who'd been looking forward to the scheduled films. To make up for our disappointment, we were all issued with a kind of party-bag, containing playing cards, colouring books and a toy. I put my red plastic kangaroo on my tray next to my bottle of water and pulled faces at him.

'OK, Kangy,' I mouthed silently to him, 'this is it, boy: the adventure of our lives. If you're lucky you might get to meet some of your relatives.'

I carried Kangy the Kangaroo with me in my bag when we landed at Hong Kong. Having him with me made me feel a bit less alone. I had conversations with him inside my head.

'Let's have a look around the shops, shall we, Kangy? See if we can buy something for Sophie? What d'you think she'd like?'

After so long in the air, it was a pleasure to make use of the washroom facilities to freshen up and change into the clean set of clothes I'd packed in my flight bag. I had a cup of tea but couldn't face any more to eat – it seemed like I'd been woken up every couple of hours on the flight and given strange meals at inappropriate times. Not that, by now, I had any idea what the time really was – I'd lost all sense of reality as far as that was concerned, as soon as we started zooming through time zones as if we were in some sort of science fiction.

'OK, Kangy – time to check in again. Ready? Let's hope we sit next to the anniversary couple again.'

No such luck; for this second leg of the journey I had two Australian brothers for company. They spent the first hour or so telling each other jokes and laughing uproariously, fuelled by several pints of Foster's. Fortunately, by the time they were beginning to get so seriously on my tits that I was having fantasies about knocking their stupid heads together and chucking them out of the window, they both fell sound asleep at exactly the same moment, leaving me to settle down myself and grab a few hours of shut-eye while I could.

It was half past four on the Saturday morning when we finally landed at Cairns. The fact that I'd set out on Thursday evening, had been sitting on a plane, doing nothing other than eating, sleeping, and talking to a toy kangaroo and now it was Saturday, seemed too ridiculous even to contemplate. Continental breakfast (which continent?) had been served at three o'clock in the morning and I'd forced myself to eat it because someone had told me your digestive system survived the whole jet lag problem best if you ate little and often. My stomach was beginning to feel like an over-inflated balloon, and despite doing all the leg-gymnastics we'd been shown by the airline along with the safety video, my feet and ankles were swollen to twice their normal size. It took a while to get through Immigration Control because a young Chinese guy in front of us in the queue appeared to be telling a very interesting story about his life. At least, it seemed that way judging by the amount of questioning he was getting and the number of officials who crowded round him. I was relieved, when it was eventually my turn, to be waved through with little more than a cursory glance at my passport. Maybe I wasn't very interesting by comparison.

'Thank God for that, Kangy!' I muttered into my bag as I passed through.

'Excuse me, madam. Who's Kangy?'

'Sorry. I was talking to my kangaroo.' I pulled him out of the bag and held him up to show them. 'He's only a toy.'

'Glad you explained that, madam. Thought for a minute he was a real one,' responded the guy with a dry smile.

And they say the Aussies haven't got a sense of humour.

'Mum!'

At least fifty mothers looked around, but I'd have known that voice anywhere.

'Sophie!'

We ran to each other and hugged so hard, for so long, I was afraid I might be going to break her in half but still couldn't stop. It was a while before I realised we were both crying, too. Silly cows.

'What on earth have you got in your bag?' she laughed when she finally stepped back from me. 'Something hard was digging into me.'

'Oh. Must be Kangy's tail.'

'Kangy?'

184

'My kangaroo. Come on, now. You wouldn't have wanted me to fly halfway across the world all on my own, would you?'

'You're mad!' she laughed happily and, linking her arm through mine and pushing my luggage trolley with the other hand, she led me out of the air-conditioned terminal building into the sudden warmth of the tropical morning.

'Probably,' I agreed. 'Probably this is one of the maddest things I've ever done.'

'Bloody good for you, Mum,' said Sophie stoutly. 'If you can't do something a bit mad at your age, you might never get another chance.'

'I'm only thirty-seven, Sophe, not eighty-seven! I think I've got a few years of madness left in me yet!'

I looked her up and down as we waited in a queue for a taxi outside the airport.

'You're looking well. The trip must be doing you good.'

She was, as Amy had warned me, covered in freckles. She had the same pale skin as me, and didn't tan easily; we both always had to use the highest factor sun protection. But instead of inheriting my auburn curls she had smooth glossy brown hair shot through with natural copper highlights, which glinted in the sunshine. She smiled up at me and I wondered how I'd managed, with a little bit of help from her father, to produce someone so beautiful.

'And when am I going to meet this ... Ryan?' I only just stopped myself from saying 'this young man of yours' and making myself sound like a Victorian grandmother.

'Mum, Ryan is only a friend, OK?' She shot me an anxious look. 'We're not in a relationship or anything.'

'But you're travelling together.'

'Yes. We get on well, and it's kind of convenient, now that Amy's gone home.'

'Well, I have to say I'm glad you're not on your own.'

'Me too. And now I've got you as well, for a while!' she added, squeezing my arm. 'Here's our taxi. Come on, I'll take you to your hotel and you can have a shower and change or whatever. Then Ryan and I will take you out for breakfast.'

Breakfast? I looked at my watch in confusion.

'I think I had breakfast on the plane in the middle of the night,' I told her, 'although to be honest, my stomach feels so uncomfortable I'm not sure that I'll ever be able to eat anything, ever again!'

'Nice cheap trip, then!' she laughed.

'Welcome to Cairns,' said our taxi driver, shoving my suitcase unceremoniously in the boot. 'First time here?'

Is it that obvious?

'Yes,' I smiled. 'First time in Australia.'

'Well, I'm sure you'll have a wonderful time. Most beautiful country in the world. I've never been outside of it,' he said without a trace of irony.

'Thank you. I'm sure I will.'

I sank into the back of the taxi as if I'd been on my feet for hours, and watched the passing scenery through half-closed eyes until Sophie nudged me ten minutes later and laughed:

'Are you awake? We're at the hotel!'

We've made it, Kangy. We've arrived. Fair dinkum, cobber.

Ryan was tall and slim and looked very young – even younger than Sophie. I told him this, without stopping to think that he might be offended, but they exchanged a quick smile and he admitted that he was only nineteen. He reminded me instantly of Joe. He had the same easygoing charm and ready grin, and I felt a lump in my throat at the thought that my daughter might have found a boyfriend so similar to the father she'd never really known.

Except, of course, that they were apparently just good friends. Within minutes of being in their company I had to admit I could see why Amy might have felt excluded. They were a bit like an old married couple: teasing and joking with each other, finishing each other's sentences and acting as if they'd known each other all their lives; but there wasn't

186

anything sexual between them. OK, I know they probably wouldn't have been climbing all over each other and snogging each other's faces off in front of me, even if they were in the most passionate relationship since Romeo and Juliet; but no, it just wasn't there. Believe me, I still know passion when I see it, and I could say without a shadow of a doubt that my daughter and her new friend seemed to have a great friendship going – but they just didn't fancy each other.

'He seems a lovely guy,' I told her when Ryan had settled us at a table in a café and gone off to get our breakfasts.

'He is,' she agreed. 'He's probably the perfect travelling companion. Male without being macho.'

Yes, I suppose I was a bit slow there, wasn't I.

'He's gay?'

She nodded.

'But he's not, you know, *in your face* about it. Hasn't got a boyfriend at the minute, though. He finished with the last guy at Christmas time because he was so possessive. Ryan says it was getting so he could hardly even see his own family without this Jim going off his head. Poor Ryan. He's just too sweet; he deserves a lot better than that.'

I smiled. I got the impression my feisty daughter would have knocked Jim's lights out if she'd met him.

Ryan came back to the table, carrying a tray bearing plates of steak and egg.

'Steak? For *breakfast*?' I touched my stomach gingerly, wondering if there was any chance the fifteen meals I'd consumed during the journey from London were beginning to settle down.

'This is Australia,' laughed Ryan. 'We like our meat, any time of day!'

He sat down next to Sophie and hacked a huge mouthful off the corner of his steak.

'Ryan tells a good story,' said Sophie, smiling at him, 'about a vegetarian pen pal of his cousin's, who came out to stay from England.'

'Yeah.' Ryan chewed his mouthful quickly and started

cutting another. 'This girl arrives straight off the plane from London, and we take her out for a good dinner, as you do, right? So we're sitting at the table, and the bloke comes round for our orders. And it was you know, steak here, and lamb chop here, and steak there, and so on, and lastly he comes to the English girl. And she says, "Excuse me, but I'm a vegetarian." And the bloke says, "Vegetarian, right? So how do you like your steak done?"'

'Without the blood, I suppose!' I said, laughing. I cut into my steak and it spurted red into the middle of the fried egg. 'Whoops! Good job I'm not a vegetarian!'

'Don't eat it if you don't want it, Mum,' said Sophie, watching my face.

'I might not manage it all,' I admitted, chewing valiantly. 'Only we had quite a few meals on the plane.'

It already seemed like a lifetime away.

In the heat of the day, we walked, in what shade we could find, into the centre of the town and down to the seafront, where we sat with a beer at a boardwalk bar overlooking the ocean. I'd barely got used to being on the ground again, never mind taking on board the fact that I was really here in Australia. To travel for such a relatively short period of time and end up on the other side of the world still seemed too much of a miracle to contemplate. It was very hot, and the first beer slid down without any difficulty at all.

'Want another one?' asked Ryan.

'Yes. Here; I'll get them.' I scrabbled around in my purse. 'What the hell are all these coins? It was easy in Europe, with everyone using the same currency now.'

'Kind of difficult to expect Australia to go over to the euro,' pointed out Sophie.

'Don't see why!' I gave Sophie my purse. 'Go and buy the drinks, love – I'm too tired to get my head round this today. I'll study it tomorrow.'

'She may not come back, now,' teased Ryan as Sophie walked away with my all my worldly wealth in her hand.

At least, it may have been all my worldly wealth or it may just have been the price of three pints of beer, for all I knew.

The second beer slid down almost as fast as the first.

'Blimey, Mum. We'll have to carry you back to your hotel at this rate!' said Sophie.

'It's the heat. I'm not used to it. I'll need to drink more while I'm acclimatising, otherwise I'll dehydrate.'

'That's a good one. Don't want to spoil your illusions, but I think it's water you're supposed to drink.'

'Water? Never heard of the stuff!' I retorted, draining my glass. 'Come on; be fair, I'm on my holidays!'

I suppose, thinking about it, my holidays had gone on for quite a few weeks by now. Maybe the excuse was wearing a bit thin, but what the hell. By the time we'd stopped drinking, late that afternoon, having gone straight through without lunch because I couldn't face the thought of any more food, I was practically comatose. Sophie and Ryan didn't *quite* have to carry me back to the hotel, but it was a close thing.

'It's the heat,' I kept protesting as they helped me stagger out to the street, where they poured me into a taxi. 'I'm not used to the heat.'

'It's probably the jet lag,' Sophie corrected me. 'You look knackered.'

'But it's best to stay awake for as long as possible,' Ryan was saying as I collapsed onto the back seat of the taxi and closed my eyes. 'It's really best if you can hold out till a normal sort of time to go to bed. Then you'll be fine tomorrow.'

Normal sort of bedtime be buggered. I was sound asleep in the back of the cab when we arrived back at my hotel, and by half past six, when it was pitch dark anyway as it apparently always is in the tropics all year round, I was tucked up in bed and snoring for England. Tomorrow could take care of itself.

*

189

That first night, I slept right round till ten o'clock in the morning and woke up feeling fine, and from then on I adapted to life in north-eastern Australia as if I'd been born to it – at least, I liked to think so. It was hot and sultry, but often cloudy and it rained more than I expected, although Ryan told me that this was the dry season. When it did rain, it rained suddenly and heavily, and then stopped and dried up almost instantly.

Ryan had been to Cairns a couple of times before. His family was from Brisbane, but when he met Sophie he was living in Sydney, where he'd been sharing a flat with the boyfriend he'd just broken up with.

'I figured it was as good a time as any to go travelling,' he said casually, not mentioning the fact that, according to Sophie, he'd been terribly hurt and traumatised by the relationship and its breakdown, and probably wanted to get as far away as possible for a while. 'I'd moved out of Jim's flat into a hostel while I saved up some money for the trip, and that was where I met Sophie and Amy,' he explained, 'so we've kind of carried on together. I'm like a lot of Aussies – never been out of my own country. I've always wanted to visit New Zealand so Sophe said I could tag along with her, as long as I didn't mind spending the first few weeks finishing off her Australian tour with her. It suits me fine. Haven't been up to Cairns since I was a kid and it's great to be here again.'

'Well, I'm glad,' I said warmly. 'Now Amy's gone home, I'd have been worried about her travelling on her own.'

'Too right. You hear all sorts of stories. No worries, Maddy; I'll be looking out for her. Well,' he amended with a grin, 'we'll be looking out for each other, I guess.'

Sophie and Ryan had booked some tours for their time in Cairns and had managed to get me tickets for the same trips. The first was a ride up the Skyrail, a cable car ride which took us from sea level up over the top of the rain forest to the village of Kuranda where we browsed around the souvenir

190

shops before returning by train – a fantastic journey through tunnels in the rock face and across bridges over great waterfalls.

The next trip was a long coach journey further up the coast as far as Cape Tribulation, stopping at lots of interesting places and being entertained – and educated – en route by Andrew, our driver/tour guide, who told us so much interesting stuff I could hardly take it all in, never mind remember it.

'You fancy him, don't you,' Sophie accused me with disbelief in her voice, seeing me staring at Andrew in admiration as he was telling us all about the native birds of the area.

'Of course I do!' I laughed. 'Why wouldn't I? He's gorgeous, isn't he.'

'But...' She gave me a curious look. 'What about Tom?'

'Oh, well.' I shrugged, trying not to frown or look rattled. I'd managed not to give too much thought to Tom since arriving in Cairns and I didn't particularly want to talk about him. 'I think that's over.'

'Really?'

For some reason it annoyed me that she looked so shocked. Like most people in my life, Sophie hadn't made any secret of the fact that she disapproved of my relationship with Tom.

'Yes, really. I thought you'd be pleased about it, to be honest.'

'It's not for me to be pleased or not, is it, Mum. I'm just a bit surprised, because you haven't mentioned it. And you never said you were having any problems or anything.'

'We weren't. Not at all, until he decided he wanted to marry me.'

'Mum!' Her eyes were huge with surprise now. 'I can't believe you haven't told me any of this. Has he left his wife? Is he getting a divorce, then? When did he...?' She stopped suddenly, seeing the look on my face. 'You don't want to talk about it?'

'Let's put it this way. I'd far rather talk about that young Andrew at the moment, thanks very much. Nice arse, hasn't he?'

'Mum!' laughed Sophie, pretending to be shocked, and then added confidentially, craning her neck to get a better look, 'Yes, he has.'

'Mm,' agreed Ryan with a grin. 'Sure has!'

The nice-arsed Andrew drove us to Port Douglas, a little town forty miles or so north of Cairns, where we investigated the gorgeous Four Mile Beach and took note of the warning signs about the killer box jellyfish. During the hottest summer months it's very dangerous to go in the sea unless there's a stinger net, enclosing a safe area for swimming.

'If you get stung by one of those babies,' explained Andrew, 'you've got about ten minutes to get first aid, otherwise you're dead.'

The first aid required is an immediate dousing with vinegar. Bottles of it were stored on the beach beneath the danger notices.

'Jesus! I'd rather not swim at all,' shuddered Sophie.

'It's safe enough in the winter months. The jellies go back up the rivers and creeks and don't come back till the sea warms up again.'

'I'd rather not risk it,' I agreed.

Makes you realise how lucky we are in England. Only things you're likely to get stung by at our seaside are wasps, and the prices of the ice creams.

I learnt about some more of the minor inconveniences of Australian life at our next stop, Daintree, where we had a boat cruise on the river, and Andrew pointed out the crocodiles lurking near the river bank.

'OK, all I need now is snakes and that's it, I'm off home!' I said, with which he promptly took me by the shoulders, turned me towards a particularly overgrown bank and pointed out a huge snake sunning itself by the river edge.

192

Still, it was worth it to have him holding my shoulders like that.

'Absolutely gorgeous tour guide,' I told Rachel on the phone that night. 'I could give him one, any day of the week.'

I'd decided to give her a call from the hotel, to let her know I was OK and tell her a bit about Cairns.

'Trust you! Five minutes in Australia and you're already lusting after the natives.'

'What? That's a bit thick, coming from you, isn't it? I seem to remember you worked your way through the nationalities when we were in Europe, while I ... behaved myself with complete decorum.'

'Decorum, my arse! Only because of Tom.' There was an uncomfortable silence. 'So I presume you're over him now, then,' she added.

'I suppose I must be, if I'm lusting after the natives, as you so sweetly put it.'

'Have you heard from him?'

'No, I haven't. We agreed it'd be better not to get in touch while I'm out here. A clean break, you know.'

All right, it was selfishness on my part. I didn't want to have to think about him. I didn't want my trip spoilt by his unhappiness, or by my conscience.

'Anyway, he's got such a cute bum, and he's *so* knowledgeable...'

'Who, Tom?'

'No, you fool. Andrew, the tour guide!'

'Yeh, but I'd be careful if I were you. You can imagine how he probably puts it around, in a job like that. Frustrated middle-aged English tourists gagging for it, every minute of the day...'

'Rachel! I'm *not* frustrated and I'm *not* middle-aged! I'll admit I'm gagging for it, but it's difficult really, being with Sophie. She'd be horrified if I suddenly disappeared into the bush with the tour guide. And anyway, Ryan fancies him even more than we do.'

193

'Ryan's *gay*?'

'Yes. It was obvious really. Even in Amy's photos, you could see he and Sophie weren't a *couple*.' I hesitated, wondering if I'd ventured into dodgy territory here, opening up the whole situation of Amy versus Sophie and Ryan again. But Rachel didn't seem perturbed.

'They're obviously good friends, though,' she said. 'Maybe that's what we all need, Madd: a gay man as a friend.'

She sounded so wistful and, to be honest, hearing her voice, I missed her and wished she was with me, to laugh about the tour guide together.

'We've got each other as friends, though, haven't we,' I reminded her.

'Daft cow. I know that. Have a good time, and don't get too pissed too often. Oh, and Maddy?'

'What?'

'That Andrew. Give him one for me!'

Unfortunately I didn't get the chance. I only saw Andrew one more time, and that was a few days later when we were booked for our final trip with his company: to the Atherton Tablelands, the area to the west of Cairns where we drove through rich, fertile countryside and walked through rain forest to see lakes and waterfalls and the famous Curtain Fig. By the time we were walking back to our coach for the journey back to Cairns in the afternoon, my mind was racing with all the things we'd seen and all the stuff Andrew had told us about the plants and wildlife. Sophie and Ryan were walking way ahead of me with some other young people in the party, and I found myself falling into step with Andrew, bringing up the rear of the group.

'Tired?' he asked me with a smile.

'No, not really. I think my brain's just reached saturation point, though.'

He laughed.

'I guess there's a danger in giving people too much

information. But look at it this way – you come all the way to Australia, spend a few days in this area and move on again; it'd be a terrible shame not to learn as much as you can while you're here.'

'Of course. And it's so fascinating ... the wildlife, and everything you've told us about the Aborigine history and culture ... you're so knowledgeable!'

Needless to say I was flirting with him, although it was all true, and I did mean it.

'It's my job,' he shrugged, 'but I wouldn't be doing it if I didn't agree with you that it's fascinating.'

We walked on in silence for a while. I was looking down, watching his legs as he strode beside me in his khaki shorts, at the same time as watching the ground in case I tripped on a root or trod on a snake or giant spider, when he suddenly asked:

'Sophie's your daughter? Is your husband at home in England?'

'Haven't got a husband,' I said, smiling at him hopefully. 'I'm a free woman.'

'That's a shame,' he said.

A shame? This wasn't what I was hoping to hear! I'd rather counted on him being encouraged by the fact, possibly to the point of offering to meet me for a few drinks that night and a guided tour of my hotel room.

'Why d'you say that?'

'Well, I guess it's horses for courses, you know. Not everyone's the same, but I've been married to my lovely wife for ten years now. We met at school and we've been together ever since, and we've got two great kids. I guess I'm just a very lucky guy.'

He smiled at me, and there was pity in that smile. Pity for me, because I hadn't had the same beautiful relationship since I was still at school, pity for me because I was a free woman, a sexual predator coming on to every good-looking tour guide and getting rebuffed because they were married to lovely wives with lovely kids and didn't want to go looking for extra-marital romps in hotel bedrooms. Well, fuck you, Andrew; I didn't really fancy you anyway.

'Actually, I'm just recovering from the break-up of a long-term relationship,' I told him, rearranging my face into what I hoped was an expression of barely concealed grief and pain, 'so I'm certainly not ready to take the plunge into any new experiences just yet.'

So stick that up your didgeridoo, Mr Perfect Marriage, and stop looking at me as if I'm the Wife of Bath on a day trip to Cairns.

'Mum!' called Sophie, looking back at us from the front of the tour group, 'Come and walk with us and stop monopolising poor Andrew!'

A whisper of laughter rippled through the group as several heads turned to look at us.

'It's OK, ladies, nothing to get jealous about, I'm a married man!' quipped Andrew.

I think I could cheerfully have strangled him with one of his mangrove roots.

That evening, after I'd had dinner with Sophie and Ryan, I went back to my hotel room, leaving them to go out clubbing with some of the other young travellers they'd met at their hostel. I poured myself a drink from the minibar, lit a fag and sat down to watch TV, but after switching channels seven times gave up and turned it off. I stood up, walked around the room, sat down again and started reading my book, but it was no good – I still couldn't settle.

'What the hell's the matter with me?' I muttered to Kangy the Kangaroo, who stared back at me morosely. Surely I wasn't rattled just because someone I'd have liked to screw preferred to give me a lecture on happy marriages?

Was I missing England? Was I missing Rachel? Or was it. . .

I'd picked up the phone twice and put it down again before I realised what I was doing. I'd been about to ring Tom.

*

I'd come halfway across the world to escape my confusion about Tom, but it hadn't worked. I'd left Tom behind, but the confusion had sneaked on board the plane and come with me. How unfair was that?

Chapter 13

There was one other thing left on the agenda, one thing that everybody has to do while they're in Cairns.

'We need at *least* one trip to the Barrier Reef,' proclaimed Ryan. 'The first time you go out there, you're so completely gobsmacked, you just can't really take it in.'

Ryan, of course, had been out to the Reef many times in the past. He and Sophie had also had a trip when they were staying at Airlie Beach.

'But I want to go again,' insisted Sophie. 'Like Ryan says, once just isn't enough.'

'We're even nearer to the Reef here in Cairns than we were further down the coast. It's huge – two thousand kilometres of it! And it's actually a group of about two and a half thousand reefs; the largest living thing in the world!' explained Ryan.

'You sound like Andrew,' I told him a bit moodily, having gone off Andrew in a big way when I realised he wasn't up for a fling of his boomerang.

'Thank you! I've seriously considered training as a tour guide, as it happens!'

'You could do worse. Rachel reckons there must be loads of frustrated tourists...'

'Mum!' Sophie looked at me with disdain. 'Honestly! Ryan isn't interested in becoming a tour guide just so he can get laid.'

He winked at me.

'It certainly helps, though! There were a couple of guys on that last trip I could have really fancied. . .'

'Ryan, honestly, you're as bad as Mum,' said Sophie sniffily.

Well, thanks, dear. I'll take that as a compliment.

So there we were, the three of us, on the second Wednesday of my stay, boarding a boat from Cairns harbour. I was a bit perturbed when we were handed out travel sickness pills as we boarded.

'Take them,' advised Ryan, swallowing his own tablet, 'even if you never normally get seasick. This crossing isn't usually as bad as the one we did further down the coast, though.'

'Thank God for that,' said Sophie. 'I was sick on the return trip, Mum; it was so rough, nearly everyone was sick, even those of us who *did* take the tablets.'

Hmm. . .I *was* looking forward to it. I swallowed the pill and resolved to stay on deck in the fresh air. The crossing was a bit bumpy and, although *we* all felt OK, it was noticeable that all the Japanese tourists were very sick.

'It's always the same,' whispered Ryan. 'Most of them seem to have a problem with travel sickness.'

Not much fun for the crew of the boats – no wonder they handed out pills like sweeties. They also came round with 'morning tea' and blueberry muffins, but it was kind of difficult enjoying it when so many people were throwing up around us.

'Have you ever done any snorkelling?' Ryan asked me when we arrived at the reef.

'Have I! I'm a superb snorkeller,' I told him proudly.

Sophie looked at me in surprise.

'I learnt in France,' I told her. 'It was fantastic! I never thought I'd be able to do it.'

'Well, this is the place for the snorkelling opportunity of a lifetime! Come on; let's go straight in. Have you got your camera?'

Before we'd left Cairns that morning, Sophie and Ryan had made sure I'd bought a cheap underwater camera.

'If you don't take photos, you'll kick yourself afterwards,' Ryan had warned me.

The boat was moored at a pontoon, where we queued up to be given our snorkelling equipment – including flotation jackets for those who wanted them.

'That's cool,' commented Sophie, zipping herself into one. 'On our last trip, we had wetsuits – we needed them more down there 'cos the sea's not so warm. But these are good. Put one of these on, Mum, and you won't need to swim at all – just float!'

'I know how to do it,' I retorted. 'I know how to float, Sophe. I don't need one of those. I told you, I'm a super snorkeller.'

Famous last words, as they say.

The snorkelling area was marked out by orange buoys.

'You have to stay inside those limits,' Ryan warned me, 'and if you get tired, there are a couple of floating platforms – see? You can rest on one of those.'

I didn't like his patronising tone.

'I'll be OK.'

I put my flippers and mask on and gave him a 'thumbs-up'. Sophie was looking at me very strangely, through her own mask, as if she couldn't quite believe what she was seeing. This was extremely annoying. She and Ryan were both acting as if it was the most surprising thing in the world that I was going snorkelling at all. Anyone would think I was a novice.

I swam off from the pontoon, put my face into the water and, within seconds, I was confronted by a couple of the biggest fish I'd ever seen in my life. I don't know what I was expecting – after all, I'm sure I'd seen plenty of documentaries about the Great Barrier Reef during the course of my life, and what's the main thing everyone goes there to see? Big fish, right? So I can't quite explain why, when two big

200

yellow angel fish swam straight towards me, looked at me with disdain and carried on swimming past me, I was so surprised I started to open my mouth and shout something out to Sophie, who was swimming just behind me. Of course, it's not a good idea to open your mouth when you're snorkelling. The mouthful of sea water was even more of a surprise than the yellow fish, but fortunately I wasn't too shocked to follow my instincts up to the surface, where I found out for the first time in my life what the expression 'treading water' meant, while spluttering around a bit and shaking all the water out of my snorkel and mask.

Sophie and Ryan were watching me, making 'you OK?' signals at me and looking worried. For God's sake – such a minor technical problem could happen to anyone. I gave them the thumbs-up again, laughing to myself and shaking my head at my own silliness, ducked back down under the water and we were on our way again.

There were ropes floating in the snorkelling area to help you follow a kind of 'trail' if you wanted to. I *didn't* want to. Ryan, just ahead of me, pointed to the rope and held onto it for a moment, as if to show me what it was for. I shook my head disdainfully, and to prove my point turned off in a different direction from him and Sophie, kicked my flippers, pulled hard through the water with my arms and before I knew it, I was alone ... just me and the coral and the fish. Everything Ryan had said about it, everything the guides on the boat had said about it and everything I'd read in guide-books about it was just an understatement. No description of the Great Barrier Reef could do it justice. The coral was pink, and red, and orange, and green, and blue. The fish ranged from great shoals of tiny bright golden creatures flitting past me at the speed of light to beautiful pink damselfish. Big stripy ones, spotty ones, bright coloured ones, little black ones that lurked shyly in the crevices of the coral. Starfish, sponges, creatures that looked like vegetables but moved just when you least expected it. The sky above me was a perfect blue and the sun beat down on my back making me grateful I'd plastered myself with a high factor sun protection. It was hard to believe I wasn't even underwater but just floating on the surface looking down through the clearest sea you could imagine. I was lost, dreaming, suspended in a world that seemed to have no connection to reality. This was wonderful, this was amazing! I could stay here for the rest of my life, just floating, watching the fish, feeling the warmth of the sun...

With my ears half in and half out of the water, it took a while for the strange high-pitched noise to register in my brain. When it finally did, the intrusion to my peace was horrible.

'What the fuck...?' I muttered, bringing my face out of the water and bobbing around a bit as I struggled to locate the source of the noise. It was coming from ... that direction. No, no, hang on a minute ... maybe *that* direction. I took off my mask, hoping everything would suddenly become clearer; that I'd be able to see better; that, in fact, I'd be able to see *anything*. Anything other than the vast expanse of ocean that stretched out in front of me ... and behind me. And to the left, and ... Thank God for that! Far off to the right was the pontoon, with the boat moored to the side of it. How had I managed to drift this far? I hadn't been out here very long, had I? Or had I? It was hard to tell; it was difficult enough to keep track of direction, never mind time. Oh well, probably better start swimming back. Shame – I'd been having such a lovely time.

I put my snorkel and mask back on and began swimming slowly and laboriously back towards the pontoon. The high-pitched whistling sound was getting louder but it took me a long time to realise it was coming from a watchtower on the pontoon. It seemed to be a long, long time, and the muscles in my arms and legs were beginning to scream with pain, before I was close enough to see someone in the watchtower. He was blowing on the whistle and waving. Bloody good for him, I thought irritably, enjoying himself whistling and waving up there. Suppose he thought he was being funny. I stopped swimming for a minute and waved back, but because I was so tired now I began to sink under the water and gave it up as a bad job. This was ridiculous. I seemed to have been swimming for ages and I still had a way to go. Where was the raft Ryan told me about, for resting? Where were the ropes for guiding you around? I suddenly wished I'd listened more carefully before I set off. I didn't appreciate that the ocean was this big. I passed an orange buoy, and realised with my first moment of real anxiety that I'd strayed far outside of the safety-markered area for snorkelling. Well, no point in panicking: I was too tired to swim any more for now, so I'd just have to stop for a bit. I turned onto my back and allowed myself to float for a while. That was better. Be OK in a minute; just give my legs a rest. I closed my eyes and let the hot sun caress me. Yes, this was lovely. I could almost doze off here, if it wasn't for that bloody whistle constantly tooting away. What was his problem anyway?

If you've never been rescued by lifeguards, you probably can't imagine it. The shock, the fear, the relief, the gratitude, the humiliation, the embarrassment. The feeling that you really shouldn't, in these circumstances, be in any fit state to look lustfully at your rescuer's huge biceps or his tiny muscular arse in his little trunks, nor should you be worrying about him seeing your flabby thighs poking out of your swimming costume like great dollops of lard. So many conflicting emotions in one quick rescue: it left me feeling quite weak. To say nothing of the telling-off I got, back at the pontoon. First from the lifeguards, then from Sophie and Ryan.

'I didn't *know* about currents,' I said miserably, wishing the audience of open-mouthed tourists who'd witnessed my rescue would all just piss off now the show was over.

'You should have read the warning notices and not gone beyond the orange buoys, lady,' said my hunky lifesaver with an ever-so-slight shake of the head to show how little he could be arsed to argue about it. He'd done his job, and got a standing ovation for it from the crowd of wannabe snorkellers on the pontoon who'd come all this way to the Great Barrier Reef and never even got their feet wet. Huh! What did they know?

'Just a little bit of *shark* trouble,' I said loudly as I elbowed my way through the crowd to get to the changing room. 'Nothing I couldn't handle.'

They made way for me, watching me, I presumed, with a mixture of admiration and envy.

'People like you make me sick,' said one guy quite calmly as I passed. 'Ignore all the safety procedures and expect someone to risk their life for you when you get into trouble.'

'I didn't expect!' I began, my voice coming out trembly with surprise. 'I didn't know he was coming to rescue me... he just turned up... I'm sure he didn't risk his life!'

'Leave it, Mum,' advised Sophie, suddenly appearing at my side and steering me towards the changing room. 'Come on, don't take any notice. You're safe, that's the main thing. You'll know better next time.'

Alone in the changing cubicle, naked and suddenly cold with only my towel around me as I tried blindly to step into my knickers, I fought back tears of disappointment and humiliation. I'd wanted to be a good snorkeller so much that I'd just convinced myself I actually was. What a sad, stupid, arrogant twat I'd been. Well, they say pride comes before a fall and I'd certainly had my fall. It was going to be a long time before I got back in the water again, with or without a snorkel.

I didn't feel too well on the boat going home. I don't think it was actually seasickness: I think I just felt so stupid and gutted with myself it was making me feel sick.

'Cheer up,' said Ryan quietly. 'Don't let it spoil your day.'

'Sorry, but it has done. And worse than that, it's probably spoilt yours, too.'

'No, it hasn't,' said Sophie. 'We *were* worried about you, but once the lifeguard brought you back, we both had a good laugh.'

Well, great. Thanks very much. Nice to know I've provided the entertainment for the day.

'Mum, you have to laugh about it. No point getting upset. It was really funny, seeing you all embarrassed and bedraggled with that super hunk of a lifeguard giving you a telling-off. We took photos!'

So my humiliation will live on for the benefit of posterity. Fantastic!

When we got back to Cairns I could hardly walk, my legs felt so wobbly. This just seemed to provide Sophie and Ryan with even more amusement.

'I feel like I'm still on the boat,' I complained miserably, holding onto Sophie's arm. 'The ground feels like it's going up and down.'

'You look like the drunken sailor,' sniggered Ryan.

'It's not funny. I feel really strange.'

'Sorry.' Ryan took my other arm. 'Sorry we laughed – come on, you'll be fine. It's pretty normal after a rough crossing. At least you didn't throw up like all those other poor people.'

There had been even more sickness on the trip back; Ryan thought it was because everyone had too much to eat and drink at the lunch buffet on the pontoon. Me? I didn't have anything to eat. I missed lunch completely while I was busy drifting halfway out to New Zealand.

And then, just when I felt so miserable I didn't think it could get any worse, when I got back to the hotel I had a phone call from Tom.

Does that make me sound like a bitch? I suppose it does. But well, when you refuse to marry someone, and decide that the relationship is over, and travel halfway across the world to put some time and space between you, it's not exactly on the agenda to get phone calls from them. Whenever I thought about him, my head swam with a mixture of guilt and confusion, so I'd been trying my best *not* to think about him. I

205

hadn't even told him which hotel I was staying at, so almost my first words to him were:

'How did you get this number?'

'Nice to speak to you, too,' he replied sarcastically.

'Sorry, but it's a bit of a surprise. I wasn't expecting...'

'You didn't think I might still want to keep in touch with you? Not even just to see if you're enjoying your trip?'

'Well, I thought we agreed not to...'

'I got the number from Rachel. She said she didn't think you'd mind me calling.'

'No. No, of course I don't *mind*.'

Damn Rachel. She should have asked me first. There was an uncomfortable silence.

'So how are you enjoying Australia?' he asked with a false brightness.

'It's great, thanks,' I replied.

Great. How inadequate was that, to describe my experiences here? The amazing beaches, the beautiful sea, the rain forests, the birds, the trees and plants. I'd gone on and on to Rachel on the phone a couple of nights ago for about half an hour, probably boring her to tears, just about the rain forests – and that was nothing to the amount of time I'd be talking to her about today's little escapade. But to Tom, all I could find to say was, *'It's great.'* I didn't want to talk to him. It wasn't going to help. It wasn't a good idea.

'Look, it's nice of you to phone, but I ... the others are waiting for me ... we're going out for dinner.'

'OK. Just as long as you're having a good time.'

'Yes. Yes, I am. Thanks.'

'Say hello to Sophie, then.'

'I will.'

'Bye, then.'

'Bye.'

It didn't occur to me until after I'd hung up that I hadn't even asked how *he* was. I felt really bad for a while. But only until after I'd downed the first couple of drinks.

'Mum,' said Sophie, watching me closely as I poured

206

more wine into my glass. We were still only on the starter. 'Do you really think you should?'

'Should? Should what?'

'You're drinking more than you normally do.'

There was an unspoken sense of '*and that's certainly saying something*' in her voice. Ryan looked at her and frowned slightly as if he was trying to warn her off.

'Well, I'm so sorry!' I said somewhat aggressively. 'I'm *so* sorry if I'm embarrassing you and offending you.'

'You're not. That's not what I said. I just—'

'Am I embarrassing *you*, Ryan? Do you find me offensive? Would you prefer me to stay in my hotel room and drink on my own from the minibar like the raging alcoholic my daughter obviously thinks I am?'

Ryan shook his head and looked down at his plate.

'Mum,' said Sophie quietly, 'I'm only trying to tell you I'm worried about you.'

'Well, don't be. It's not your job. I'm supposed to worry about *you*. I'm your mother, I have to do it, it's what I'm here for. I should be telling *you* what to drink and what not to drink.' I took another gulp of my wine. 'Not the other way round.'

'Let's just drop it, shall we? I'm sorry I mentioned it.'

'I get enough of it from Rachel. Don't drink, don't smoke, don't swear, don't eat chocolate, don't slob out in front of the TV, don't fucking breathe...'

'Mum...'

'Well, I *like* drinking and smoking and being a slob so please don't worry about me, darling, because if I die, at least I'll die happy.'

'*Mum!*'

I stopped and looked up at her. There was a glint of tears in her eyes and Ryan's arm had slid subtly round her shoulders to comfort her. They'd both stopped eating and were toying miserably with their cutlery.

I'd done this. I'd hurt my daughter, ranted at her in public and spoilt her evening. Maybe spoilt her whole trip. She probably wished I'd never come to Australia. She was happy, enjoying herself with her new friend before I turned up, and now look at her – sitting in a restaurant, pale and sad and fighting back tears, being stared at by all the other diners, being shown up and shouted at by a drunken slob of a mother.

I suddenly felt completely sober. I pushed away my glass and the bottle of wine, pushed back my chair.

'I think I'll give dinner a miss. I ... think I'd rather have an early night. You two have a nice evening on your own for once. I'll see you tomorrow.'

'No, Mum ... please stay. It's all right.'

'No. No, it's not all right.' I stood up, picked up my bag and turned to go. Neither of them said any more, but I looked back as I left the restaurant and saw they were both still watching me.

'Sorry,' I mouthed.

I carried the picture of Sophie's stricken unhappy face with me all the way back to the hotel. Probably a good thing they were moving on to New Zealand soon. They'd be glad to see the back of me.

I spent most of the time after the Great Barrier Reef Humiliation Day feeling sorry for myself. I slopped around next to my hotel swimming pool, drinking Coke, sunbathing and pretending to be asleep. I was drinking Coke because I'd decided to give up alcohol, and I was pretending to be asleep so that when Sophie and Ryan came round to the hotel to see if I wanted to go out somewhere with them, they'd go away again without waking me up.

It worked twice. The third time, they sat down, one on either side of my sun lounger, and shouted 'Boo!' so loudly I nearly shat myself.

'Jesus fucking Christ almighty!' I swore, louder than I'd have liked to do really in the sunny silent ambience of the poolside, where more elegant and better-behaved people really *were* lying asleep in the sun enjoying the peace and quiet. Well, they were up till then.

208

At least, the looks we got made all three of us laugh together like naughty schoolchildren and it kind of broke the ice.

'Why are you doing this, Mum?' asked Sophie when we'd stopped giggling.

'What? Lying on a sun lounger by the pool? Because I'm on holiday, Sophe. It's the kind of thing people do.'

'I mean why are you *ignoring* us like this, pretending to be asleep – we know you were pretending, we looked round after you thought we'd gone, and saw your eyes open.'

Shit. Never was much good at pretending.

'And why are you drinking Coke?' she added without waiting for an answer to the first question.

'I like Coke,' I lied.

'Liar. You hate it.'

'All right, I hate it, but what else do you drink when you've given up alcohol?'

Even Ryan spluttered slightly at this. Cheeky sod.

'Don't be silly, Mum,' said Sophie. 'You haven't given it up. I'll give it a week at the very most before you're back boozing again.'

I sighed, feeling like a child who's been caught out lying about something rather stupid. It wasn't even worth arguing.

'Look,' she went on calmly, 'don't keep beating yourself up about the other night. It doesn't matter. Let's just forget about it. OK?'

'I showed you up. I was drunk, and embarrassing, and you probably don't want me to come out with you any more.'

'Don't be daft. Look, we've only got a few more days left together before Ryan and I go to New Zealand. Don't let's waste them. Please, Mum, don't let's spoil it.'

'You're not the only person in the world to get pissed now and then. Sophie does it all the time,' Ryan told me with a grin.

'Not *all* the time!' she retorted, digging him in the ribs with her elbow.

'*And* she shows me up and gets embarrassing,' he added cheerfully.

'All right,' I conceded, laughing. 'All right, I'm sorry. It's just that it was such an awful day, with the lifeguard and everything, and then Tom phoning...'

'Poor Mum,' Sophie sympathised. 'Rachel shouldn't really have given him the number. It's definitely over, then?'

'Ye...es. I think so. No – yes, it is. Definitely, I think.'

'Well, that sounds pretty positive!' she said with heavy sarcasm.

'Look, I told him I wouldn't marry him, and that I thought we should call it off, and then I flew off to Australia. I'd have thought it was a pretty broad hint!'

'But it was still unsettling getting the phone call. That's understandable.'

'Especially after your day at sea,' said Ryan with a smile.

'Don't! I'm still cringing about that.'

He laughed. 'You just need to put it behind you, book another trip to the Reef and get back into the water again. Only this time, stay inside the safety zone. Preferably holding onto the ropes!'

'No. Never. I'm never going bloody snorkelling again. I can't believe I actually thought I was good at it. What a prat! Serves me right.'

'But you probably *are* good at it. You haven't given yourself a chance yet! Everyone makes mistakes!'

'Yes, Mum. What did you used to tell me when I was a kid? Remember? That making mistakes wasn't bad – the only bad thing was not learning from them.'

'Yes, well. We all tell our kids a lot of fairy stories, Sophe.'

She looked at me sadly. 'I just think it would be a real shame if you let a bit of *embarrassment* put you off doing something you enjoy. If you don't go back to the Reef again, your only memory of it, when you go home, is going to be of how you felt humiliated and silly – instead of remembering it for all the right reasons: the coral, the fish, the beautiful colours...'

'Sophie's right,' said Ryan. 'She always is. She must take after her mother.'

So of course, with a bit more prompting and persuading, I got off my sun lounger and lived to drink another day. And swim another day. Sophie and Ryan actually came with me to the Reef cruise booking office to make sure I booked another trip, which I purposely arranged for the day after they left for New Zealand. It would give me one more day before I had to decide what to do with myself once they'd gone.

'What are you going to do with yourself,' asked Sophie as if she'd read my mind and twigged my motives, 'after Ryan and I leave?'

'I don't know,' I said morosely, 'and I don't want to think about it.'

'But we want to know,' she insisted. We need to be sure that you'll be all right, otherwise we won't feel like going.'

It's a terrible thing, having children. It makes you lie so much. From the moment they start having lives of their own, as soon as they step outside the front door without holding your hand for the first time, you lie to them. *Of course I want you to go and play with your friends instead of staying at home with me – off you go, have a good time, I'll be far too busy doing the boring old housework to miss you ... Go on, go and enjoy yourself at the disco, take the car, of course I'm not worried about you driving it, that's fine if you stay out late, of course I won't be worried, I'll only be staying awake till two o'clock because I've got a really good book I want to read ...* and:

'Don't be silly. Don't you dare even consider missing out on seeing the rest of the world, just because I've come out to Australia for a while. How ridiculous is that! I knew I was only going to see you for a couple of weeks. It's been a bonus – a fantastic treat. Up till a few weeks ago I didn't think I'd see you for a whole year.'

'But I don't like the thought of you being on your own.'

211

'I'm a big girl!' I laughed gaily, not liking the thought of it myself very much either. Maybe I'd just change my flight and go straight home after they'd gone.

'Are you thinking of moving on and seeing some different parts of Australia?' asked Ryan.

Sophie gave him a quick look. I couldn't quite interpret it, but he gave her the same sort of look back and then they both turned to me as if my answer would provide the key to something earth-shatteringly important.

'I...er...hadn't really made up my mind.' Didn't want to think about it. 'I suppose I might do.'

'It'd be a shame to come all this way and only see Cairns,' said Sophie, 'wouldn't it?'

'Yes,' chimed in Ryan at once. 'There are so many fantastic places to see in Australia, Maddy. It's the most beautiful country in the world, and you've only seen the tiniest corner of it.'

'You Aussies are so patriotic. It's really weird. You never hear us Brits talking like that about our country. Shame, really. It has a few good points.'

'I guess there are other beautiful countries in the world too,' he agreed, 'but to be fair, I haven't seen them yet. Britain's a lot smaller, isn't it, so I guess you guys need to get out of it and go abroad.'

'Yeah. Otherwise we get claustrophobia. So what do you think are the most important places for me to see in Australia?'

Again, a look flashed between them. I wasn't imagining it. There was something up, a secret of some sort, something they weren't telling me.

'What?' I asked Ryan.

'Nothing. Just thinking where you should visit. How about Brisbane? It's the logical next place down the coast, it's a lovely city, and from there you can decide whether to go on to Sydney, or Melbourne, or—'

'You're not working for the Brisbane Tourism Department or anything, are you?' I joked.

'No.' Further secret sneaky smiles between him and Sophie. 'No, but it's my home town, and I think it's beautiful, and I'd like you to see it.'

'OK, you're doing a good job on the PR. But I still don't really want to think about where I'm going or what I'm doing yet.'

'And my parents live there,' he added suddenly, with a rush of urgency that made me start with surprise. 'And they have a big house. And they'd love you to stay with them. They would, really, they're not kidding. They've already offered, and they love having folk to stay, they'd enjoy your company, they really mean it, and I said I'd try and persuade you, so please think about it because they'll be really upset if they think you've gone back to England without meeting you, they've met Sophie and they really loved her and would love to meet you too, honestly they keep telling me how much they want to meet you, and—'

'Blimey!' I interrupted him, before he ran out of breath from the length of his sentence and the desperation of his speech. 'I think I'd better say yes, hadn't I, or we're going to be here all night and I'll probably lose the will to live!'

'That's good!' Sophie smiled.

'Great! I'll give my parents a ring. They'll be well pleased,' said Ryan.

They were both grinning like Cheshire cats. Amazing how easy it was to please them. And once I'd settled down to the idea, and Ryan had phoned his folks and proceeded to go on at me for another ten minutes about how excited they were about meeting me (I was beginning to wonder whether I was really some sort of film star, suffering from amnesia), I had to admit it really was a great idea. Instead of feeling miserable and despondent at the thought of Sophie and Ryan leaving, and wondering whether I'd be happier going home rather than staying in Australia and travelling aimlessly around on my own, I now had a plan; somewhere to go, someone to stay with. I could start to feel excited once more. I might even give myself permission to feel happy again.

Chapter 14

I didn't go to the airport with Sophie and Ryan when they set off for New Zealand a couple of days later. I'd already had one tearful send-off, at Heathrow back in June, and we all agreed there was no point putting ourselves through another one. Remembering the conversation I'd had with Rachel when we first found out about the lottery win, I forced some money on Sophie to help her with the rest of her travels, and we said our goodbyes at my hotel the night before they left; they were being picked up from their hostel by an airport bus in the early hours of the morning. It was strange saying goodbye to Ryan. I'd only known him for two weeks but I'd got very fond of him and I didn't know whether I'd ever see him again.

'Sophe and me will stay friends for ever, whatever,' he assured me with youthful optimism.

And the sky will always be blue. And the sun will always shine. And friends will never fall out, or lose touch, or hurt each other, or forget each other. And the world is a wonderful place.

Yeah, right.

I went out to the Great Barrier Reef again the next day. To say I was nervous would be an understatement. I sat quietly in the boat, looking out at the ocean, trying to persuade myself I didn't feel sick. A couple of women sitting opposite me started up a conversation.

'Are you on your own? Oh, you're so *brave*! We could never travel on our own, could we, Mary?'

They were about fifty and had come from Wales to tour Australia together without their husbands. To be honest I admired them for this far more than they seemed to admire me.

'We've left them at home!' laughed Mary as if it had been a bit of an oversight. I had this vision of two middle-aged husbands slumped in front of their TVs, suddenly waking up with a start to discover that their wives had buggered off to Australia without them. 'You know what men are like,' she added darkly with a raising of her eyebrows.

'Always in the way,' agreed her friend Carol, shaking her head sadly. 'And always causing *trouble*.'

Well, that one was certainly true, anyway.

'We're going in the glass-bottomed boat,' said Mary as we stepped out onto the pontoon a little later. 'It's supposed to be fantastic – you can see all the fish and the coral, through the floor of the boat.'

'It's even better if you snorkel,' I replied before I could stop myself.

'Snorkel?' exclaimed Carol. 'No way!'

'Carol can't swim,' explained Mary, 'and I'm not much better. I can only do a width of our local pool. I'd be much too nervous to go out into the ocean like that.'

'We'll watch *you,* if you're going to do it. You're *so* brave, aren't you!' said Carol.

I was beginning to feel like Christopher Columbus or Scott of the Antarctic at the very least. Shit. The last thing I'd planned on doing was to have an audience again this time.

'I'm not brave at all – far from it. But I've done it before; this is my second trip to the Reef.' I hesitated. There didn't seem a lot to be gained by telling these two about my life rescue episode. 'I'm still pretty nervous, but to be honest there's not much to it,' I added truthfully. 'You don't even have to be able to swim very well. You can wear a flotation jacket and just ... float.'

215

Carol shuddered and shook her head vigorously. The glass-bottomed boat was definitely more up her street, she insisted. But I thought Mary looked tempted.

'Tell you what,' I offered on a sudden impulse. 'If you want to come in with me, I'll show you the ropes.' Literally. Having someone less confident with me would make sure I behaved myself this time and kept to the safe area. 'You can hold onto the guide ropes all the way, and I'll stay near you in case you get worried.'

'Would you really?' Her eyes were wide with excitement. She glanced at her friend. 'What do you think, Carol?'

'Go ahead, go on – you can tell me all about it afterwards,' encouraged Carol.

The strange thing was that, this time, I enjoyed it even more. Without the temptation to get carried away and drift off into the distance, I concentrated on studying the marine life properly. I remembered to use my underwater camera and took my time getting some good shots. And the best bit was that I came out of the sea of my own accord, without being the centre of sarcastic attention. Mary was absolutely over the moon.

'I'm so grateful,' she said, giving me a spontaneous hug as we walked, dripping, to the changing room. 'I'd never have dared do that on my own – and it's been one of the most fantastic experiences of my life.'

Mine too. Now I'd put the humiliation of the previous time behind me, I couldn't wait to try it again. And not only that. I had other plans now, as well.

I got a flight from Cairns to Brisbane two days later. Ryan's mother had called me at my hotel the morning after he and Sophie left, to make all the arrangements, and she was there to meet me at Brisbane airport.

'I'll probably be able to pick you out,' she'd said, 'because Sophie said you look just like her. She said you could pass for her older sister. Lucky you!'

I laughed, although I felt a bit embarrassed by this and wished Sophie hadn't said it.

'Well, we do look a bit alike,' I conceded, 'but I think she was probably being sarcastic. I look like an ancient, over-weight version of my daughter, to be fair, Mrs Cook.'

'Aw, call me Bren, for God's sake, Maddy! And we're really looking forward to meeting you. Ryan's told us all about you.'

That's a worry for a start.

'Looking forward to meeting you too, Bren. Will you hold up a card with your name on in case we miss each other, at the airport? Or should I do something to draw attention to myself? Wear my knickers on my head or something?'

I have this problem, you see. If I'm a bit nervous of some-body, I tend to say the most outrageous things, without meaning to. I don't know why I do it, but it's got me into trouble in the past. Like when I got sent to my headmaster at school for some minor misdemeanour and started telling him a dirty joke. Or when I went into hospital to give birth at the tender age of seventeen, scared shitless, and tried to show off to the midwife that it was my third child and I probably knew more about it all than she did. It's almost a death wish. Although I couldn't explain why, I was a bit unsure about this Bren. But how was it going to help to present myself in a good light by offering to wear my knickers on my head? I mean, you just don't *say* that kind of thing to people you don't know, do you.

There was a brief silence, and then she said without a flicker of amusement:

'I don't think *that* will be necessary.'

Made a hit there, then, by the sound of it.

And as it happened, it appeared she was right. Not that I had any knickers handy anyway as I came through the Arrivals gate at Brisbane, but the likeness to my daughter must have been even more striking than I realised, because Brenda Cook was upon me like an avalanche almost as soon as I'd cleared the barriers.

'Maddy! It's Maddy, isn't it! My God, Ryan was right –

217

you're *so* like Sophie it's just untrue! *Wonderful* to meet you! How was Cairns? Hot? Humid? How about the Aboriginals? Did you get any trouble from them? Last time I was there, they were descending on the city centre every night, drunk out of their skulls. Did you go up the Skyrail? And how was your Reef trip? Did you see Sophie and Ryan off to Christchurch? Isn't it marvellous for the young people these days, the opportunities they have? Don't you wish we'd been able to do those things when we were their age?'

I was opening and shutting my mouth like a fish, trying desperately to answer at least one of her questions before she ploughed on regardless with the next. I think she only stopped in the end because she'd run out of breath.

'Yes,' I said finally, following her meekly out of the airport, pulling my suitcase on wheels behind me. 'Yes, I suppose so, but on the other hand...'

'This is your first time in Australia, Ryan was telling me? And you did some travelling in Europe earlier this year? You won some money on the British lottery? And you're spending it all on touring the world?'

'Well, not quite, no, it wasn't exactly—'

'That's just marvellous. You'll love Brisbane.'

This was such a comparatively short sentence that I realised I was finally expected to respond.

'I'm sure I will. And it's very kind of you ... I really appreciate the offer to stay at your place.'

'It's absolutely no trouble.' She waved this aside as if it was the most ridiculous thing she'd ever heard. 'We have a *huge* house and *plenty* of room, and you won't bother us in the least. Sophie and Ryan stayed with us, you know, when they were here last month. I wish he hadn't left home, of course, but you know what young people are like. Did your Sophie leave home too young? I suppose they all do it. I suppose they have to try out their wings. I try to understand, but it's difficult, isn't it – I think it's always difficult, being a mother – such a trial, especially with an only child. Your Sophie's the only child too, isn't she? I expect you were like me, couldn't face going through all that again – once is bad enough, isn't it.'

'No, actually I—'

'And his father's no help. Men never are, are they? Never been any help from day one, far too busy with his own life, but that's the way they are, isn't it – selfish to the core, the lot of them. But then you did the sensible thing, didn't you? Got divorced and stayed divorced? Wish I'd had the courage to do it myself, but couldn't bear to give up the house and the lifestyle – you know how it is? I expect you had to make some pretty tough decisions yourself...'

'Not at all, it wasn't—'

'But it hasn't been easy. To be honest I'd be better off on my own but there you go, he's Ryan's father after all, not that it seems to have made any difference.'

During the course of this conversation, or perhaps I should say monologue, we'd reached Brenda's car in the airport car park and were heading out on the freeway into the city suburbs. I felt uncomfortable, to say the least, about being subjected to this tirade of family confession having only met her twenty minutes ago.

'I'm sure it's better than having no father at all,' I said lightly, hoping she'd take the hint and change the subject or, even better, shut up completely, preferably forever.

'That's a very interesting point,' she responded at once, to my dismay. 'Very interesting and very debatable. We were only discussing this at our meeting last week. Did I tell you I'm the President of the Woolabong District Women's Group? We were debating the issue of the influence of a father within the family unit? Tell you what? You'd be very welcome to come and talk at one of our meetings? Maybe next week? We've got a guest speaker on the subject of women's empowerment, and maybe you could follow on from that? About bringing up a child without the interference of the male influence?'

The Australian inflection, turning every sentence into a question, had become desperately pronounced in her

219

excitement. I could feel my heart sinking into the very soles of my shoes. How the fucking hell had I got myself into this one? I felt like chasing after Ryan, tracking him down to whatever backpackers' hostel in New Zealand he and Sophie were hanging out in and giving him a bloody good hiding for not telling me his mother was a raving nutcase.

'I ... er ... I don't know ... I'm ... not sure whether I'm the right person,' I floundered unhappily, staring out of the car window at the views of the Brisbane River rushing past.

'Nonsense,' retorted Brenda, condemning me with that one word to a state of dread and trepidation I hadn't known since I'd been picked to read aloud at the Christmas concert at school.

We headed further out of the city into the sunny stillness of the outer Brisbane suburbs. She slowed down and lowered the windows. Strange bright birds called out with strange noises from strange trees. Strange bright flowers drew attention to themselves from strange bushes in strangely familiar front gardens. We could have been in Loughton or Richmond or Ongar except for the foreignness of the flora and fauna.

'This is us!' she sang out cheerfully, swinging the car into a wide driveway at the end of a long, winding cul-de-sac of large, imposing, single-storey houses. The house we pulled up outside was the largest and most imposing of them all, but somehow by now I wasn't in the least surprised about this. 'Chez nous!' she added with a silly, very un-Australian affectation.

The house was, as Ryan had promised, huge. One branch of the driveway swept round to the side of the house and out of sight into the distance, no doubt leading to the paddocks or the swimming pool. We had stopped outside the main entrance, where almost immediately an elderly woman, either a housekeeper or Brenda's mother – at that point it was hard to tell – appeared at the threshold, smiling a greeting and holding her arms out for my baggage. I stumbled, awkward from the time spent sitting tensely in the car and the uncertainty of the social situation ahead of me, into the hallway, and stepped almost head-on into the arms of the most striking-looking man I'd ever seen in my life.

'Patrick!' called out Brenda, following me into the house, her high heels clipping neatly on the polished wooden flooring, 'this is Maddy, Sophie's mother. Maddy, this is Patrick. Ryan's father. My *husband*,' she added in deeply disparaging tones, 'as I was telling you earlier.'

'Pleased to meet you,' said Patrick. He took hold of my hand, and looked deeply into my eyes. 'Welcome to Brisbane. We're absolutely delighted to have you stay with us, Maddy.'

Maybe I was tired from the journey. Or maybe I was bewildered from listening to Brenda's prattle in the car and shocked by being invited to talk at the next meeting of the Woolabong District Women's Group. Perhaps I was just taken aback at the presence of a good-looking man so long after I'd had the use or the means to know what to do with one. Whatever. I looked back into the eyes of Ryan's father, Brenda's husband, Mr Patrick Anthony Cook, and saw the smile softening the lines around his mouth and flickering at the corners of his hazel green eyes, and only one, very inappropriate thought flashed into my mind: *Hm. Wouldn't kick him out of bed.*

Patrick Cook was utterly different from his wife; it was hard to imagine how they'd stayed married for so many years without killing each other. He was quiet, easygoing, casual and friendly. He didn't seem to have a bad word to say about anybody or anything – whereas Brenda talked non-stop, mostly about other people and their problems or what she perceived to be wrong with them. She was a crashing snob and an incurable gossip, and was so house-proud it was uncomfortable to be around her. The house was beautiful. The carpets were about six inches thick and were all plain pastel colours that wouldn't have lasted five minutes in any normal family's house. The kitchen was about the size of my

221

whole house, and looked as though it was equipped for cooking canteen meals for a moderately large factory workforce. The oven frightened me; its doors were big enough to walk into, and shone like mirrors even while she was actually using it. She must have kept a cloth and a bottle of cleaning stuff in one hand while she was basting the meat. There were four sofas and several armchairs in the lounge and it still looked half-empty. And as for the bedrooms – I didn't even get around to counting them.

Keeping the house in pristine condition was Brenda's only hobby, other than nagging Patrick – she moaned at him every time she looked at him. He didn't seem to be able to do a thing right. He was in trouble whether he left his shoes on in the house or took them off, whether he left things lying around or put them away, whether he left everything to her or whether he tried to help – because nothing was ever put away, cleared up or cleaned up to her own standards. If he put something down, she automatically sighed, tutted, and moved it two inches to the right or left. If the slightest crumb fell from his plate or his lips, she'd be behind him with the Hoover, muttering about the carpet. If I offered to help her, she'd retort that I was the guest and should 'absolutely not' be expected to lift a hand to do anything, and she'd then take the opportunity to have another pop at her poor husband for being untidy and bone idle. It was hard not to take sides but I knew it would have been more than my life was worth; I had to listen to Brenda slagging off too many of her 'friends' and neighbours to have any doubts about the forgiving and kindly side of her nature.

I'd only been with them for a couple of days when the conversation over dinner turned to their son.

'It was such a pleasure to meet him,' I told them warmly. 'I couldn't wish for a nicer travelling companion for Sophie.'

'Because he's ... the way he is, you mean,' said Brenda at once, huffily.

'Because Ryan's a genuinely nice lad,' I replied at once.

'At least you know your daughter's safe with him,' she persisted, stabbing crossly at a piece of potato on her plate.

'Bren...' warned Patrick, 'I'm sure Maddy didn't mean...'

'It'd be of no concern to me,' I said firmly, 'if he was straight, gay, black, white, British, Australian or a bloody Martian, as long as he and Sophie got on well together. He's her friend, and I really liked him.'

'That's how most people see it,' put in Patrick, giving me a quick smile and raising his eyebrows at his wife.

Didn't take a degree in psychology to realise that was not how Brenda saw it.

'Oh, stay out of this, Patrick, for God's sake – you and your woolly-minded liberal nonsense. No wonder he turned out—'

She broke off, obviously aware that this was a step too far for even her to go, in the washing of her laundry in public. I was seething on behalf of Ryan. It was hard to believe this silly, bigoted, small-minded little woman was really his mother.

'You shouldn't have let him leave home,' she added, with a venomous glare at Patrick. 'He was much too young. I knew he'd land up in trouble – he was always much too easily led.'

'What sort of trouble did he land up in?' I asked.

'Taken in by that awful... person he lived with in Sydney. My God, the hell he put us through! It was unbearable.'

'It wasn't very pleasant for Ryan, either,' commented Patrick quietly, looking down at his plate.

'... turning up here, at our house, looking for Ryan at all hours of the night,' went on Brenda, ignoring him, 'in an old white truck!' She shook her head, her eyes closing at the painful memory of this terrible social indignity. Whatever must the neighbours have thought!

'Ryan came back here to Brisbane once or twice, when things got a bit nasty with Jim,' explained Patrick. 'Stayed with us just till things calmed down. It was... a bit of a difficult relationship.'

223

'So I heard,' I said sympathetically. 'Poor Ryan.'

'Difficult relationship!' scoffed Brenda. 'There should never have been any relationship, as you put it. If I had my way, that person should have been arrested and put in prison, for inciting... for, for...' She stumbled, obviously very ill at ease about it.

'For daring to love your son?' Patrick finished for her with another smile. I was beginning to understand his smiles. They were powerful. They robbed Brenda of any means of response.

'Love!' she spat angrily. She got to her feet and gathered up our plates. I hadn't actually quite finished, but I put my fork down quickly rather than risk her sitting back down again to wait for me in an ugly and uncomfortable silence. 'What does someone like that know about love?'

'Possibly more than you do,' said Patrick very quietly after she'd left the room.

It was said with such rueful sadness that I glanced at him with a jolt of surprise and pity... but he immediately shook himself and apologised:

'Sorry about that, Maddy. Scrapping about family matters over the meal table with a guest here – bloody rude. My wife gets very worked up about Ryan. She doesn't mean anything by it.'

Don't try to defend her. She's a narrow-minded fuckwit who doesn't deserve such a lovely son!

'She's taken it very hard – Ryan coming out as a gay,' he added very quietly. 'She ... wasn't brought up to understand things like this.'

You mean she's stupid?

'Her family weren't big on ... accepting social minorities.'

You mean all her family are narrow-minded fuckwits too?

'I think she's kind of ... in mourning, if you get my meaning. Mourning for the wedding and the grandchildren that aren't going to happen.'

'I think you're being very tolerant,' I whispered back, so indignantly that I was almost spitting in his face. 'And she's

224

being very unfair. Sorry, I know it's not my place, but I just have to say—'

But maybe it was just as well that I didn't get a chance to say what I just had to say, as at that moment Brenda came back in, with a homemade cheesecake and a face like thunder, and the rest of the meal was eaten in an uneasy atmosphere punctuated by the occasional remark about the weather. It may have been hot outside – but, believe me, there was a distinct and nasty chill in the air in that room.

OK, so let's be quite honest here about Patrick. I certainly fancied the trousers off him but, looking back, I suppose it's easy to see what my problem was. I was still subconsciously looking for someone to take my mind off Tom. If Brenda hadn't been such a cow, or if Patrick hadn't been so patient and uncomplaining about her, I might have just enjoyed looking at him and appreciating the view. That's what good girls do, isn't it? Good girls. Not me.

I didn't want any emotional mess. I'd come all the way to Australia to save myself from it. I'd ended up drinking too much, chatting up totally resistant happily married tour guides and talking to a toy kangaroo alone in my bedroom at night – trust me, I wasn't over my confusion about the break-up with Tom enough yet, to get emotionally entwined with another man. Especially not another married man.

But this would be OK. I was in control. I didn't want anything complicated from Patrick. I just intended to fanta-sise about shagging him. Shagging him would have done me a power of good, and certainly wouldn't have done him any harm. Brenda would never even have known – she was far too busy tidying her house to notice. But I was a guest in their home, they were Ryan's parents, and I was going to have to try and keep my hands off him. Fantasies would have to do.

I discussed the whole situation with Kangy, who fortu-nately had no alternative but to listen patiently night after night and didn't try to offer me any advice. If he had, I know what it would have been. Get out of that house, fast, and stay in a hotel. Preferably in another town. Another state would be good. Another country would be even better. But like I say, unfortunately he was only a toy kangaroo and couldn't give me any advice. So I stayed. And I fantasised.

Brenda didn't go out to work. She didn't have to; she was well provided for by her husband and, as she also had someone to do her housework, her garden, and her laundry, she made a career out of straightening curtains and moving ornaments from one shelf to another. In my more charitable moments, I thought that maybe if she had a job she wouldn't be bored and she'd be less of a cow. But I didn't feel charitable towards her very often.

My début at the Woolabong District Women's Group was an unmitigated disaster. I should, of course, have had the sense to refuse to go, but Brenda kind of swept me along with her. Within a couple of days of my arrival she'd told her Committee that I'd volunteered to do this stupid talk about bringing up a child without a father, and apparently they were all pissing themselves with excitement at the prospect. Obviously hadn't ever heard me speak. I should have had the guts to tell her I wasn't up for it, but it was really difficult when she was already printing off programmes on her PC listing me as one of the guest speakers. And apparently there was going to be cheese and wine at the end of the evening, so what the hell.

I didn't realise I was going to feel nervous. The meeting started at seven o'clock and I didn't feel like eating before we went out. I sat at the back of the hall, listening to the first guest speaker, a local author with the unlikely name of Millicent Milton who'd written a book about women's empowerment, going on about taking control of your life and not needing a man, and as I shakily fingered the folded-up notes of my badly prepared speech I looked around the hall and thought: But all these women are married and most of them don't work! There they sat, well dressed and well fed, free to spend their days however the hell they liked while their husbands earned their pocket money for them, nodding and clapping as this Millie Millie person expounded the tired and unoriginal theories that had got her into print.

'Thank you, Millicent, thank you so much!' gushed Brenda as the applause died down at the end of her little diatribe. 'And now, ladies, we have another very special treat tonight!' My palms were sweating so much I could hardly hold the crumpled up sheets of my notes. 'All the way from England...' Pause for effect. Eyes turned in my direction, hands raised ready to give me encouraging applause at the right signal. 'All the way from England, my very own house guest, Maddy Goodchild, would like to talk to you about Child Raising the Single Parent Way.' She beamed and nodded at me and I got hesitantly to my feet. 'Maddy Goodchild, ladies!' She led the clapping and I stumbled unhappily to the front of the hall as everyone joined in, tapping their fingers politely against their palms, watching me with mild curiosity: Is this going to be boring or not? How soon can we get stuck into the cheese and wine?

I stood in front of them all and cleared my throat. God, this was absolutely fucking awful. I must have been out of my tiny mind.

'So,' I said, my voice shaking as I tried desperately to un-crumple my notes. 'So, I'm here tonight to... er... to talk to you about being a single parent. Right. Right.' I finally got the pages straightened out. 'Well, first of all I should say that being a single parent, it's ... well, it's a tremendous achievement and you know, I...er...I think that...' Sod it. I didn't realise how difficult it was going to be, trying to read my notes and talk to the audience at the same time. They were beginning to fidget already. I could see Brenda frowning, probably wishing she hadn't asked me to talk. That's the first thing we've agreed on, anyway. This was a night-mare. Maybe I could just say I'd got a sore throat, a sudden attack of laryngitis, and move straight on to the cheese and wine?

'It's…' I abandoned the notes and looked straight into the faces of the women in the audience. It was no good; I was never going to be able to inspire them like Millie Millie had. I might as well give up now! 'You'll have to forgive me,' I announced, suddenly finding my voice a bit stronger now that I'd decided to stop trying. 'I don't know much about women's empowerment. I suppose I do know quite a bit about being a single parent, but I'm not sure I'm the best person to talk to you about it.'

There was an uncomfortable shifting of bums in seats. What was this? A speaker who didn't know how to speak? Whatever next? Had Brenda Cook cocked up completely with this one?

'I think you wanted someone to speak to you about what a wonderful experience it is to bring up a child without the inconvenience of a man interfering in your lives and ruining everything.' There were a few nods here, and people began to relax and smile. I shook my head. Stupid bloody women in their paid-for designer jeans and expensive hairdos! What the fuck did they know about it? 'Well, sorry!' I told them brusquely. 'But it's not. It's not a wonderful experience. It's hard work, and it's lonely, and expensive, and … and it's scary. I never got used to it. I never stopped wishing I had someone to share it with me.'

There was a stunned silence. I'd done it now. I'd betrayed the Sisterhood. I'd better clear off before they started booing me. Pity – I'd been looking forward to the cheese and wine.

'Yes, but it doesn't have to be a man!' exclaimed a large lady in the front row.

'Nothing to stop you sharing the experience with a woman friend!' agreed someone further back.

'I've got a friend who's been fantastically supportive,' I told them, suddenly feeling homesick for Rachel and wishing she was here now. 'But it's not the same. I wanted… the real thing. I wanted my daughter's father to be there with us, watching her grow up, sharing the milestones—'

'Don't you think that's an idealised view of it?' interrupted the large lesbian in the front again. 'Most couples don't share milestones. They just argue and drift apart.'

'I know,' I said. I was beginning to feel sorry I'd started this. 'I know they do, but ... well, I'd even have liked to have the arguments. It's better than having nobody. Trust me. If you haven't done it yourself, believe me, you don't know what you're talking about. It's you that's got the idealised view of it. I love my daughter and I don't regret a single day of her life. But basically, being a single parent is not nice. It sucks.'

OK, that was it. I'd had enough. I'd seen Brenda's face and I reckoned I'd be getting a bus home.

'Sorry about the speech,' I added quickly, screwing up my notes and throwing them in a nearby wastepaper bin. 'I'm not really very good at this sort of thing.'

'Wait!' Brenda, flustered to the point of complete agitation, jumped from her seat and hurried to the front, hanging onto my arm to stop me leaving. 'Ladies, Maddy Goodchild!'

There was a half-hearted round of applause at this feeble attempt at polite protocol. I nodded, equally flustered, wanting only to get out of there.

'Thank you, ladies – the usual refreshments are now available at the back of the hall!'

'Stay for a glass of wine.' A quiet girl in a red skirt and white blouse a bit reminiscent of an air hostess was walking beside me towards the refreshment tables. 'It's the least we can do for you, after putting you through that awful ordeal.'

I looked at her and smiled.

'It wasn't that bad. I was just the wrong person. I should have said no. Sorry I ruined the evening.'

'You didn't. I didn't think so, anyway.'

'Nor did I,' agreed an older woman with blue hair. 'Made a change to listen to someone being honest, for once.'

'Yes, all that feminism can get a bit much,' joined in someone else.

229

I was beginning to feel better. So maybe I had a few supporters after all. Brenda was off on the other side of the room fluttering around Millicent M. Well, what the hell? It would be good to round off the evening with a quick drink – at least then it wouldn't have been a complete waste of time. I accepted a glass of red wine and knocked it straight down before I'd even cut myself a wedge of Australian Cheddar. Nothing for it but to follow it with another quick one to wet the whistle after eating the cheese. By now the three members of my new fan club (everyone else was ignoring me) were chatting nineteen-to-the-dozen about how important it was to keep your husband. In fact they were waxing so lyrical about love and marriage and fidelity and the importance of the family unit and how it was a wife's duty to keep a man happy and give him whatever he wanted whether it was kinky sex five times a night, steak and kidney pudding or unlimited nights out with the boys, that I was beginning to wonder how the hell these three had ever found their way into the Woolabong District Anti-Men Group in the first place. I gave up trying to talk to them and took refuge in another large glass of wine. By the time I'd downed the fourth, I was feeling a bit numb around the lips and guessed it was time to try to soak up some of the alcohol with some more cheese. But when I went back to the table the plates were being cleared, and I only just managed to get in quickly with another glass of wine before that was cleared away too. The hall was slowly beginning to empty. I sat on the table, swinging my legs, waiting for Brenda to finish talking to Mill Mill.

'Well, thank you again, and perhaps you'll come and talk to us another time? Maybe next year? Maybe I'll contact you when I've drawn up next year's programme?' she was saying.

'That'd be wonderful, Brenda, and thank you so much again for inviting me – I've really had a wonderful time. Goodbye, er...' Millicent held out her hand to me and frowned.

'Bye, Millie!' I slurred. I got down from the table, nearly falling on my face, and grabbed her hand to hold myself upright. 'Nice meeting you. Didn't like your speech, though. Load of rubbish.'

The look I got from Brenda as Millicent turned on her heel and stalked out of the hall was something I'd like to say I'd cherish for the rest of my life. But unfortunately my memory of it was slightly dimmed by what followed.

I don't remember much about the car journey back to Patrick and Brenda's house. I'm sure Brenda must have been giving me an earful, but I was probably asleep. The only thing I remember with absolute clarity was walking through the front door of the house and seeing Patrick coming out of the lounge to ask us how the evening had gone.

And being violently sick in the middle of the hall floor.

It's red wine. I should never drink it on an empty stomach.

Chapter 15

From the time I threw up in the hallway, my relationship with Brenda, such as it was, was doomed. I'd have been terribly mortified if only I hadn't been too pissed to feel anything. Brenda, furious in her disgust, snapped at me:

'I hope you're going to clear up,' before retreating to her bedroom and closing the door.

I couldn't blame her. It was probably the most disgusting thing I'd ever done – and that was saying something. I leant against the wall, swaying slightly, contemplating the mess on the wooden floor.

'I'll do it,' said Patrick quietly. 'You'd better sit down.'

'No! No, I'll ... I'll clean it up. Sorry ... so sorry...' I slurred, stumbling towards the kitchen to get some paper towels.

'Sit down.' His tone was surprisingly masterful now. 'You're too pissed. Don't worry. I'll do it.' He gave me a ghost of a smile. 'I've brought up a teenager. I'm not unused to clearing up sick.'

A teenage son's sick. Not the sick of someone old enough to know better, old enough to have learnt that getting slaughtered at the local Women's Group meeting and spewing your guts up in the home of your hostess is about as far from normal decent behaviour as you can get. I swayed into the lounge and fell full-length onto the sofa, where I lay listening to Patrick going from the hall to the kitchen, running the taps, filling a bowl, mopping the floor, and finally opening some windows to let the unpleasant smell waft away into the warm Queensland night.

'Sorry,' I muttered again as I opened my eyes to see him standing over me. 'I didn't mean ... I don't know how...'

'Forget it. These things happen.'

'Brenda hates me. I was rude to her special guest speaker.'

'Good for you,' he responded mildly.

'I'll go. I'll move into a hotel in the morning. I don't feel well enough at the minute.'

'Don't be silly. You're not going anywhere.'

'But Brenda...'

'An evening at Brenda's women's group is enough to make anyone throw up.' He sat on the end of the sofa next to me. 'Do you want any help getting to your room? Or... getting into bed?'

The tone of his voice made me *almost* sober up in an instant. Blinking open my eyes again in surprise, I caught him looking at me. And I caught the look on his face. My heart began to perform a war dance that was most uncomfortable considering the delicate state of my stomach. I wasn't imagining this. Patrick had put the kind of emphasis on the words *getting into bed* that could only be interpreted in one way. In case there was any doubt about it, the look in his eyes was confirmation enough. And all this, when he'd just finished clearing up the remains of my partially digested Australian Shiraz. Blimey.

'Come on,' he said as I gazed back up at him. I could feel myself going a bit cross-eyed trying to keep him in focus, but yes, he was definitely still the best thing I'd seen for a very long time. Wasted on bloody Brenda. What an unfair world! 'Come on; let's get you to your bedroom before you pass out.'

'Not going to pass out,' I protested feebly, but at that point he put both arms round me to pull me up to my feet, and to be honest I suddenly felt like I *was* going to pass out, not so much from the wine as from the sheer pleasure of the moment. 'That's lovely!' I slurred. I started to giggle as he

233

half carried me along the hallway to the guest bedroom. He deposited me on the bed, and for a moment he didn't let go of me. I watched his face. He smiled, then he frowned, then he smiled again and slowly laid me back against the pillows and straightened up.

'You're drunk,' he said a bit hoarsely, turning away. 'I don't want to ... I'd better go.'

The bedroom door had closed behind him before my befuddled brain had taken in what had happened. Or rather, what hadn't happened. Shit. He nearly kissed me.

I was up late the next morning.

'Your friend's on the phone,' said Brenda while I was eating my breakfast. Her voice was so stiff it might have been sprayed with starch. 'From England.'

'Rachel! Hold on – I'll call you back.' I took the phone out into the garden and lit a cigarette, ready for a good gossip. 'What time is it over there?'

'One o'clock in the morning.'

'I thought it must be. What's the matter? Can't you sleep?'

'Well, I tried to get you an hour ago and someone who sounds like she wants you dead told me you hadn't got up yet. I was worried she might have murdered you and hidden your body, so I thought I'd better try again.'

'She does want me dead.' I walked further away from the house, out of earshot and away from Brenda's disapproving glare while I lit up a fag. 'I messed up her Fascist Women's night, and insulted her guest speaker.'

'Why?'

'Basically because she was a prat. Oh, and I was drunk.'

'I suppose that wouldn't have helped.'

'And then I was ill. And her husband ... nearly kissed me,' I added in a whisper.

There was a silence.

'Are you still there?' I whispered into the phone. 'Can you hear me? I said...'

'I heard you.' Rachel's voice sounded almost as starched

234

as Brenda's had. How do people do that? I'll have to practise it. 'What did you do?'

'Do? Well, I kind of passed out, I suppose. Went to bed. Slept it off.'

'I meant, about the kiss. What did you do about the *nearly* kiss.'

'Nothing. It didn't happen. But I'd have liked it to,' I added on an impulse.

Silence again. I was just wondering whether there was something wrong with the line other than the normal delayed response you get with these trans-world phone conversations, where you end up asking a question again because you don't think the other person heard you, then no one's sure whose turn it is to speak and the whole thing becomes a jumble of mistiming, when she suddenly said, in that same prim schoolmistress starchy voice:

'So I presume you've got over Tom, now.'

'Tom?'

I didn't mean it to come out like that – as if it was the name of some foreign food on a menu in a restaurant I'd never eaten in before. I just didn't see the relevance. We were talking about Patrick, not Tom. Why did Rachel insist on changing the subject mid-conversation?

'Yes, Maddy – Tom. You remember? The one who asked you to marry him? The one you ran off to Australia to try to forget about? I presume it's worked, has it? Now you've found someone *else's* husband to make a play for?'

I nearly, nearly, cut the phone off on her. The only thing that stopped me was that I was too rigid with shock to find the button.

'I can't believe you just said that,' I told her, my voice shaking slightly. 'You *know* how upset I was about Tom, how confused I felt. But it's over. He knows that. I told him that. I'm not messing anyone around.'

'Only the couple you're staying with, by the sound of it.'

'Oh, Rachel, stop being so fucking *moralistic* about everything. Don't you ever feel like doing *anything* in your

235

life that isn't completely bloody noble and decent and respectable?'

'Yes. Yes, I do, Maddy. All the time, of course I bloody do – you're not unique! You're not the only person in the world who gets tempted to do these things.'

'But *you* don't do them,' I said contemptuously.

'I don't want to hurt other people.'

'Well, good for you, Saint Rachel. Thanks very much for calling.'

I didn't cut the phone off. I carried it, walking slowly back across the garden, holding it at arm's length and listening to her voice calling me over the oceans and over the continents: 'Madd! Maddy! Don't be like this! Maddy, talk to me! Madd – are you still there?' until I reached the house, where I put it gently down on its cradle, cutting her off in mid *'Maddy!'* so that I felt like I'd physically smothered her.

Then I went into my bedroom, lay on my bed and cried.

'Do you want a cup of tea?'

It was an hour or so later and Patrick was looking round the door anxiously, a steaming mug in his hand.

'Thanks.' I sat up on the bed and tried to wipe my face with a tissue. 'Sorry...'

'Do you still feel ill? Hung over?' He came over and put the mug on the bedside table. 'Want some tablets?'

'Yeah. A whole bottle, please.'

He looked at me in concern.

'Is it ... man trouble? Or shall I mind my own business?'

'No. No, it's not man trouble. I've just fallen out with my best friend.'

He sat down on the bed and looked at me sympathetically.

'Best friends do that, though, don't they? Fall out, and make up again, all the time?'

'No. No, we never normally fall out. And I don't think we'll make it up.'

He didn't try to argue. He just picked up one of my hands and studied it as if it was a fascinating work of art.

236

'What have you fallen out about?'

'My whole lifestyle and personality. She disapproves of me.'

'So how come you were friends in the first place? Has she only just found out what you're like?'

'No. She's always disapproved of me. She's a saint. And I'm ... not.'

'You're not?' He looked up from scrutinising my hand and met my eyes.

'No.' Especially not when you look at me like that. 'Definitely not.'

He leant over, put one hand behind the back of my head, pulled me towards him and kissed me, very gently, on the mouth. He tasted of tea, and smelt faintly of soap. I closed my eyes. This was what I'd been fantasising about, wasn't it? And amazingly, without me seeming to have done anything to prompt it or even deserve it, here it was, happening. I knew I shouldn't be letting it; but I felt, kind of resentfully, that I was doing it to spite Rachel. She'd assumed I was messing around with Patrick when I wasn't. All I'd done was admit I'd *like* this to happen; but if everyone insisted on thinking the worst of me, then maybe I might as well...

'Patrick!' screeched Brenda from the kitchen. 'Where are you? Are you going to help me unpack this shopping? Look at the mess in this kitchen!'

'Coming, Bren!' He jumped up from the bed as if he'd been shot.

'Sorry,' he whispered to me.

'Don't be.' I smiled.

But although the kiss had been lovely, it hadn't made me feel good. Bugger Rachel. She'd put the mockers on it.

So now that I'd abused her hospitality in two of the worst ways possible (which begs the question – which is the worst of the two evils? Vomiting on the floor or snogging the husband?) – I tried to talk to Brenda about moving into a

237

hotel. But she was having none of it. I suppose she thought it would look bad. Her neighbours and her friends at the Women's Group would think she was being unchristian. It would never do. Better to treat me as a charity case – a fallen woman who needed her help, however difficult it was for her – and let them all think she was a saint to put up with me. My life suddenly seemed to be shit-full of saints.

For a few more days, everything ticked over slowly and sadly. Sophie phoned and told me how beautiful New Zealand was, how she and Ryan had hired a car and were touring the mountain and glacier region of the South Island, how much she was missing me and how she hoped I was having fun with Ryan's lovely parents. Patrick and I skirted around each other, exchanging knowing looks, touching hands briefly when the occasion permitted, not daring to let the looks or the touches linger. At night I took out my frustrations on Kangy the Kangaroo, telling him how ridiculous it was that Patrick should be asleep in the bedroom next to me, lying next to that sour, miserable old crab when he could be having fantastic sex with me. Kangy maintained a dignified silence so I threw him across the room.

The truth was that I wasn't enjoying this. This wasn't what I came to Australia for. There was a whole vast continent here to explore, and what was I doing? Stuck in a nice suburban house lusting after another married guy in an unhappy marriage. I'd never admit it to her, but what I hated most was that Rachel was probably right.

Towards the end of that same week, I was sunbathing moodily on my own at the side of Brenda and Patrick's swimming pool. I had a cheap novel in one hand and a can of Foster's in the other and was trying to remind myself that whatever else, I was still on holiday, when I looked up and found Patrick sitting beside me on the edge of the pool. He was watching me while dangling his feet in the water and kicking them gently, sending ripples across the pool. He was wearing swimming shorts and a smile – nothing else.

238

'Didn't see you there,' I said with an involuntary leap of my heart.

'I didn't want to disturb you. You looked like you were engrossed. Good book?'

'Not really. Well, OK. You know – holiday reading.' I hadn't got beyond the stage of being flustered whenever I spoke to him, and the shorts weren't helping.

'Want a swim?'

'No. You go ahead. I'm … not very good. I can only just about manage a width or two.'

'That's not what I heard.' He was grinning now. 'Ryan told me you did a bit of snorkelling at the Barrier Reef!'

I blushed.

'That was the most embarrassing thing of my entire life. I was showing off. It served me right. I've learnt my lesson now – I won't even go out of my depth unless I've got something to hold onto in future, trust me.'

And you'd be just the thing to hold onto.

He looked back at me as if he knew exactly what I was thinking, making me blush even deeper.

'But you must have been fairly confident, to go so far off on your own in the first place.'

'Fairly stupid, you mean. Although to be fair, I didn't really get into difficulties. The lifeguards just brought me back because I was waving…'

He laughed.

'There you go. You probably would have been OK, but they can't take a chance. You'd probably be a good swimmer if you had a few lessons.'

'Oh. Touting for business, are you?' I responded with a smile. Patrick had been a swimming instructor for several years, apparently since he'd retired from his business ventures in Brisbane's city centre having made enough money for Brenda to be kept in the style she expected.

'Why not? It would give you something to do while you're here. Maybe a bit more fun than reading crap novels?' He picked up my abandoned paperback copy of *A*

239

Love Worth Waiting For, turned it over and handed it back to me. 'Unless you're desperate to find out what it was that she was waiting for?'

'I think I know, thanks,' I said, returning his smile and trying to ignore the shiver down my spine.

'Come on, then.' He ducked his head and rolled smoothly into the pool, gliding underwater and resurfacing with hardly a ripple on the opposite side. 'Let's see what you can do!'

The odd thing was that despite the shorts, and the near-nakedness, and the amount of closeness and touching involved in Patrick perfecting my breaststroke and my front crawl, I felt more comfortable with him in the swimming pool than anywhere else. It was as if, when we got into the water every day for my lesson, we became two different people – teacher and pupil, rather than a man and a woman who both knew that given half a chance, they'd shag as soon as look at each other. I guessed he was a true professional who probably spent half of his working hours watching nubile young women in swimming costumes and bikinis and had had to learn coping mechanisms to stop himself from getting excited by it. Much like a gynaecologist I suppose, but without the white coat.

We got into the habit of having a lesson early every morning, before it got too hot. Then, most days, unless he had an afternoon lesson at the local pool, Patrick drove me into the city centre and showed me all the sights. Every day he asked Brenda to come with us; every day she refused, with a sniff and a toss of her head. She was barely talking to me.

'I really ought to leave,' I told Patrick one day on our way into the city. Brenda had been particularly cold towards us both as we were leaving and I felt guilty about the fact that he had still shrugged, picked up his car keys and beckoned me towards his car. 'I shouldn't be coming between you and Brenda. It isn't fair.'

240

'No. It's her own fault. She could come with us if only she wasn't so stubborn. She's always the same.' I could well believe that. 'She wants me to be as bloody miserable as she is – but it's all of her own making.' He glanced at me and added softly, 'It's not as if we're doing anything wrong.'

'No.'

We weren't. Since that first kiss, we'd had many opportunities, well away from Brenda's watchful eye, to become more intimate. Sometimes when we crossed a busy road he'd reach out and hold my hand, and maybe we'd walk along a little way like that, his thumb stroking mine; or we'd link arms together as if we were just good friends. I wanted more. What was stopping me? My long-neglected set of moral values? Or was it just Rachel's criticism ringing in my ears?

'Not that I don't want to,' he added, turning to look at me again, leaving the words hanging in the air, watching, waiting...

'I know,' I said, looking away from him out of the car window. 'Me too.'

There was plenty to see and do in Brisbane, and somehow Patrick managed to keep finding more. Anything to get him out of the house and away from Brenda, I suspected – and who was I to object? We cruised up and down the river on the City Cat; we lazed away hours sitting at waterfront restaurants, strolling around the Botanical Gardens and South Bank Park. We climbed the clock tower at City Hall for a view over the city and wandered through the shops and bars in Chinatown.

'I think I know Brisbane off by heart now,' I told him on the way home towards the end of my third week.

'Are you getting bored?' he asked quickly.

'No!' My response was even quicker. 'Of course not.'

'I could take you somewhere different tomorrow. A day trip. To the Sunshine Coast or down to Surfers' Paradise. You'd love it.'

'To practise my swimming?'

He laughed.

'The beaches are great, but they're much too dangerous unless you're a really strong swimmer. Tourists get drowned at the Gold Coast beaches on a regular basis.'

I took a sharp intake of breath.

'Drowned? Aren't there enough lifeguards there, then?'

'People take risks. People like you, with all due respect, Maddy – you're the worst. If you can swim OK, you think you're safe in the sea, but you're not. If you're really keen, what you need to do next is to get some practice in a proper size pool. Your strokes are coming on really well but you won't build up your stamina by swimming up and down a small pool like our one at home.'

'So can you take me to one?'

'Of course I can! You can come with me tomorrow to the pool where I teach my classes. I'll get you swimming some lengths, and if you're really good I'll give you your hundred-metre badge!' he teased.

I didn't particularly want to be *really good*. I'd never been any good at being good. Every time I looked at Patrick, I wanted to be really, really, naughty. But that didn't seem to be on the agenda so, for the time being at least, swimming would tire me out and take my mind off things. And I'd just have to dream about him giving me a bit more than a hundred-metre badge.

'What do you think of Ryan's dad?' asked Sophie on the phone from New Zealand.

I took the phone into my bedroom and shut the door, giving myself a couple of minutes to calm down and think about my response.

'Patrick?' I tried to make my voice sound normal, like I was just talking about any old Patrick. A Patrick who didn't make me feel like snogging him every time I looked at him. 'Yeh, he's a really nice guy, isn't he. I can tell who Ryan takes after.'

'And what about Brenda? How do you get on with her?'

I had to be careful here. It wouldn't be a good idea to tell her that Ryan's mum was the ultimate bitch from hell, that I would have liked to strangle her in her bed one night, tie up her body and dump it in the Brisbane River, or that this would give me even more pleasure because I'd then be free to have rampant sex with her husband (sorry, widower) straight after the funeral.

'She's all right,' I said, trying not to smile at the fantasies I was creating for myself, 'but I prefer Patrick.'

'God, I'm glad you said that!' said Sophie in a whisper. 'I couldn't get on with Brenda, either. Isn't she a cow? But she's Ryan's mum and, you know, he loves her, so I had to make an effort and be polite.'

'You should have warned me about her,' I told Sophie. Well, it *was* a bit unfair, wasn't it, sending me to stay with these people, without giving me any bloody inkling that she was a psychopathic witch and he was a sex god.

'Sorry! But it was kind of difficult, and anyway, I didn't know if you might have got on better with her than I did. Have you met any of their friends yet?'

Friends, friends? What did their friends have to do with it? Probably didn't have any left. Brenda would have scared them all off

'No, but she did make me go to her bloody women's group and talk about being a single mother. It was horrendous! I made a complete arse of myself.'

'Why, what did you do?' asked Sophie, laughing.

'Told them the truth, and they didn't like it. They wanted to hear a load of crap about feminist empowerment. They hated me. So I got pissed.'

'Trust you!'

'Yeah. Then I threw up on Brenda's floor.'

'Oh, *Mum*.'

'Well, I'm sorry, but she bloody deserved it. I wish I'd done it on purpose. In fact I wish I'd puked right in her *lap*.'

There was a silence.

'You *really* don't like her, do you,' said Sophie eventually. Whoops. Did I make it that obvious?

'Well, sorry. I know she's Ryan's mum and everything...'

'It's OK. I won't tell him.' I could hear her smiling. I suddenly missed her, badly. My little girl, my baby, all those miles away across the...whatever sea it was. I wanted her here, now, so I could cuddle her, and be cuddled, and feel better. Not that I felt bad. Or did I? 'Are you all right?' she added, as if I'd spoken aloud.

'I suppose so. Just missing you.' I swallowed back the lump in my throat. 'And Rachel.' The lump swelled up again, bigger, nastier. 'I've had a row with Rachel, and she won't ever speak to me again.'

'Don't be silly. Of course she will. You two are like sisters. Phone her and make it up.'

'No. She hates me.' I was crying now. Shit. How did that happen? I grabbed a tissue, blew my nose, noisily, and fumbled around for my cigarettes. Mustn't upset Sophie and spoil her lovely time in New Zealand. Next thing I knew, she'd be rushing back to England, homesick, like Amy, and then how would I feel?

'What was it about?' asked Sophie, patiently, like a parent talking to a silly child. 'The row, what started it all off?'

Well now. I couldn't exactly tell my daughter I'd been arguing in support of my right to snog Ryan's father, could I?

'I don't know,' I said miserably. 'I just don't think she likes me any more.'

'Mum, honestly! I think you're just feeling a bit lonely and depressed. Aren't you having a good time in Brisbane?'

'Yes! Absolutely! It's great!' I said, tears pouring down my face.

'Haven't Brenda and Patrick been taking you out and about, you know – sightseeing, and meeting all their friends?'

'Friends?' What was all this about friends all of a sudden? Patrick and Brenda didn't even seem to be friends with each other, never mind anyone else, as far as I could see. 'I

244

haven't met any *friends*, no, but Patrick's been taking me into Brisbane.'

I wiped my eyes and sniffed. Even the thought of the trips into the city with Patrick was making me feel depressed. Might be different if we were at least having it off together.

'Maybe you ought to think about going back to England, if you're not enjoying yourself.'

'I am. Really!' I tried desperately to change the subject. 'And I'm having swimming lessons.'

'Oh! I thought you could swim already. Is Patrick teaching you?'

'Yes. I was useless, before. And now I can do nearly four lengths without stopping. Front crawl! I'm getting my hundred-metre badge next week!' I added for a joke.

'Well done, Mum! That's excellent,' said Sophie in her new, parent-of-the-difficult-child voice. 'What made you decide to take swimming lessons?'

'I think it was the snorkelling. I never thought I really liked swimming until I did that snorkelling. And then...'

'What?'

I hesitated. I hadn't told anyone this yet. I hadn't even mentioned it to Patrick.

'Well, I know it probably sounds a bit silly. But ever since that ... really bad episode at the Great Barrier Reef...'

'Yes?'

'I rather fancy becoming a lifeguard.'

Armed with the courage I'd gained from the fact that Sophie hadn't burst out laughing, I mentioned it to Patrick the next day at the pool. To my surprise, he didn't burst out laughing either.

'That's a great idea,' he said, looking at me with the sort of admiration I'd have preferred to see in his eyes when I *wasn't* sitting on the edge of a swimming pool with goggles on and my hair dripping down my neck.

'You don't think ... I'm being a bit silly? A bit too

245

ambitious? I've only just done my hundred metres, after all.'
Feeble attempt at a joke again. But he didn't laugh.

'No, it's not silly at all. If you've got enough determination I don't see why you shouldn't do it. A couple of weeks
ago you could barely swim a length, and now look at you!'

'It's just that I've always kind of liked being involved
with swimming.' Maybe best not to mention exactly *how*
involved I used to be when I was a teenager. 'But I couldn't
swim very well myself. Then,' I shrugged, a bit embarrassed,
'I got the idea of life-saving, after I got rescued in the Great
Barrier Reef because I was being a prat.'

'Good for you,' he said, with only a slight smile at the
corners of his mouth. 'We can never have too many qualified
life-savers.'

'Do you know what I'd have to do? Would it be very difficult?'

'You'll have a lot of work ahead of you. I think the fitness
test for the Bronze Medallion involves a four-hundred-metre
swim, for a start. And it's timed.'

Shit. Oh, well, better forget that, then.

'But I'm sure I could get you up to strength,' he added,
suddenly looking me straight in the eyes, 'as long as you're
staying here for long enough.'

Aha. The thousand-Australian-dollar question.

'That depends on Brenda, I think.'

And you. Especially you. Whether you want me or not.
Whether you're going to take the plunge, and I'm not talking
about swimming pools now. Whether you'll decide to say
bollocks to Brenda, and have a bit of fun in your life. Or
maybe I should say – whether I'm going to forget my new-
found moral values and start acting out my fantasies.

'Brenda will be very happy for you to stay. For as long as
you want to.'

He said this with no expression in his voice. We both
knew it was true that she'd never throw me out, but that
she'd also never make me feel comfortable or welcome. Not
after the vomiting in the hall.

'I don't know...' I began doubtfully. 'Perhaps it'd be better if I went back to England and took lessons there.'

Say No. Say Don't Go! Say Stay Here With Me, At Least Until We've Had Sex Together!

Nothing. He stared impassively across the pool as if it was far more interesting to contemplate the diving boards than it was to persuade me not to leave.

'I know what I'll do,' he announced, so suddenly, it made me jump so that I almost slid off the edge of the pool into the water. 'I'll get Brenda to invite some of our friends over this weekend. That'll buck her up. She always enjoys having half the neighbourhood over for a barbie. Gives her a chance to show off.'

Well, bloody good for good old Brenda, I thought resentfully. Why should I give a fourpenny fuck whether she bucks up or not?

'She'll show you off to all our friends as our English house guest. Then she'll want you to stay, because they'll all want to invite you to their barbies too. It's like that with her crowd,' he went on with an air of resignation. 'Kind of competitive.'

So now I'm the first prize in the local hostessing contest. Nice.

'But the main thing is, I'll invite a couple of *my* mates round too,' added Patrick with a grin, finally turning to me. 'And you'll need to talk to them.'

'Will I? Why?'

'They're guys from my swimming club. A couple of them are lifeguards. And one guy is the top life-saving instructor in the area. He put me through the course myself, a long time ago – trust me, he's the best. You'll like him.'

You know how some conversations stay with you forever? At the time, they don't seem significant, but years later, when you look back, you realise they marked the start of something really important: a turning point, or a crossroads in your life?

At the time, the only thing of much significance to me about that chat with Patrick at the side of Woolabong Public Swimming Pool was the fact that he'd just praised me for my hundred-metre crawl and I was hoping to impress him further, in or out of the water, at the soonest possible opportunity. Which obviously says far more about me than it does about Patrick.

Brenda bought the idea of the barbecue with uncharacteristic enthusiasm. After a frenzy of phone calls to just about every family in the neighbourhood, she set to with a vengeance, creating salads, coleslaws, flans, mousses and pavlovas. The fridge groaned and buckled under the weight of her potato salads and dips. The wine and beer accumulated in boxloads in the garage. And finally, Saturday afternoon arrived, as bright and warm as any good Queensland Saturday should be, and I was ensconced in a place of honour, on the patio, beside the buffet, forbidden to lift a finger lest any of Brenda's neighbours should think she was a less than perfect hostess. Suited me fine. I was just getting stuck into the white wine, nodding at Sylvia This, and Shirley That, and Sandra The Other, and wondering how come nasty Brenda had managed to acquire so many apparently fairly normal friends, when Patrick appeared at my side.

'Maddy,' he said, 'I'd like you to meet a couple of my mates from the swimming club. Pete's a lifeguard up at Bribie Island. He's just suggested we might go there for a bit of swimming later in the week if you like? There's a safe beach, away from the surf, where you could get some good practice in. Would you like that? And Joe – Joe's the guy I told you about – he teaches the life saving course at Woolabong pool. I thought perhaps we could ... Maddy?' He faltered and stared at me. I must have looked as if I'd seen a ghost.

It was Joe.

My Joe.

Ten thousand miles from home, nearly twenty years since the disaster of my marriage, I'd run away from my life and met it head-on coming back at me.

There in an Australian suburban garden at a barbecue for the boring middle-class neighbours of a woman I couldn't stand and a man I'd been fantasising about getting into bed, I'd been reintroduced, by a billion to one chance, to the man I once married.

'Fucking hell,' I said, and spilt a whole glass of wine straight into my lap.

Chapter 16

The Chance Meeting at the barbecue (which, of course, wasn't a chance meeting at all) practically caused a riot. Everyone except me was screaming their heads off. I was in a state of shock, lying in my chair with my mouth open *à la* goldfish, covered in spilt wine, staring at Joe and gasping for breath in a most attractive fashion.

'Is she all right?' someone was yelling close to my ear.

'Has she had some sort of attack?' Brenda was squealing. 'Should we get her to the hospital?'

'Is she asthmatic?' shouted someone else, shoving the others out of the way and staring at me very closely. 'It looks like an asthma attack to me. Quick! She's having trouble breathing!'

'What do we do?' screamed a woman who sounded in a worse state than me. 'Is she going to die?'

'Get her a glass of water!'

'Get a brown paper bag and make her breathe into it!'

'Put her on the ground! Put her in the recovery position!'

'Loosen her clothing!'

'Fuck off!' I exclaimed, coming to with a start as someone with greasy kebab hands and beery breath began to fumble with my buttons. 'I'm all right! I'm not dying! I'm just...' I looked up at Joe again and blinked quickly, convinced I must be dreaming. But this was no dream. It was Joe all right; an older Joe – heavier, sturdier, tanned and lined from the Australian climate and the passing of time but still with the same springy thick dark hair, tinged with grey now, and the same quick smile that creased up his face and made his brown eyes dance with lights. 'I'm just shocked,' I finished quietly.

'You two know each other?' Patrick sat down beside me, looking from me to Joe and back again. 'You've met before?'

'You could say that,' said Joe. He smiled at me, and my head began to swim again. This wasn't true. It wasn't happening. It just wasn't possible. People didn't get divorced and spend their whole lives apart, and then suddenly meet up by chance at a barbecue in Australia. 'We were married once,' he announced as if there was nothing remarkable about it. 'A long time ago.'

At this, there was another round of squeals and screaming.

'Married! You two were *married*!'

'Oh my God! How *amazing*!'

'Bloody hell! Married! They were married, back in England!'

'How *romantic*!'

'Champagne all round, everybody! Look at this! These two used to be married! Come on, this calls for a celebration – top up your glasses – here's to Maddy and Joe – discovering each other again after all these years!'

'Maddy and Joe! Here's to Maddy and Joe!' ran the echo around the garden.

'Cheers!'

'Good luck!'

'All the best!'

They were drinking our health as if we were the bride and groom. Could this get any more bizarre? Someone thrust a glass of champagne into my hand and I tipped it straight down my throat, guzzling it in huge gulps that nearly choked me.

'Sorry for the shock,' said Joe as I put down the glass and looked back up at him.

'You knew? You knew I was here, didn't you. How? I

glanced at Patrick. 'You organised this! How did you know?'

'Hold on, hold on!' Patrick shook his head, looking as dazed with surprise as I was. 'I didn't have a clue about any of this. It's all news to me!'

'I didn't tell him,' said Joe. 'This was nothing to do with Patrick or Brenda. I didn't tell anyone. I didn't want you to find out ... before I had the chance to meet up with you. I was too afraid you might run away.'

Run away? Me? Run off abroad to avoid emotional scenes with a man? Did that sound like my style?

Yes, quite.

'I probably would have done,' I admitted, looking down at my feet.

I had to look down at my feet to avoid continuing to stare at him with my eyes popping out of my head. I couldn't take this in. I couldn't get my head round it. Standing there in front of me was the man who'd walked out of my life nearly twenty years ago, not even hanging around to see the divorce go through, not even staying in touch to see how his daughter grew up, not even...

Daughter.

Sophie.

Sophie set this up. Sophie and Ryan! I slapped my hand against my forehead so sharply I nearly knocked myself out. Of course! It was obvious. But how? I rubbed the sore place on my forehead and frowned at the wine stains on my trousers, trying to work it out.

'Are you all right?' asked Joe. Patrick, muttering something about leaving us to it, got up and went off to serve some of his guests with more champagne and steak. Joe immediately dropped into the chair beside me. 'I know it must be a shock, but—'

'This was Sophie's doing, wasn't it? That's what all this was about. That's why she was so keen for me to stay with Patrick and Brenda. That's why she keeps on asking whether I've met any of their friends.' I turned to look at him again,

252

shaking my head with amazement. This was unbelievable, absolutely unbelievable.

'She was determined for us to meet up. At first I told her no, it wouldn't work, it was a bad idea. I didn't think she'd ever get you to agree to it. But you know Sophie!'

He laughed, and a shiver of annoyance ran through me. Know Sophie? Of course I bloody well know Sophie! I'm the one who's brought her up for the past twenty years! I'm the parent who *didn't* fuck off to Australia and somehow forget to send her twenty birthday cards, twenty Christmas cards, twenty years' worth of letters or phone calls or any sort of sign that he was interested in her! I'm the one who listened to her reading her first *Peter and Jane* book, who watched her ride her first bike, sing in her school concert, cry over her first boyfriend...

'Yes. I know Sophie,' I said between my teeth.

'Sorry. Crass thing to say.'

'Yes.'

He frowned to himself. He shifted uneasily in his chair. One hand strayed slowly up to his head; he grasped a clump of hair and began to twist it between his fingers. My heart jumped.

'You still do that!'

'What?'

'Twiddle your hair when you're stressed. I used to say you'd pull it all out and you'd end up bald by the time you were—'

'Forty,' he finished for me. 'By the time I was forty. I remember.'

He smiled and, finally, I smiled back at him.

'I admit it, this was Sophie's idea,' he said with a shrug. 'She said she'd try and get you to stay here, with Patrick and Brenda, and then just leave it to them to arrange one of their famous barbecues. Make it look like an accident. I've been crapping myself with nerves ever since Patrick phoned me about today.'

'You really thought I'd believe it was an accident?'

253

'Probably not. I guess it was a stupid idea. I just went along with it to please Sophie, that's all.'

'So how did you meet up with Sophie?'

That couldn't have been an accident either. I wasn't dumb enough to believe they'd just bumped into each other. Just walking down a road in Brisbane one day and oh, God, look at that – she must be my daughter! He must be my dad! The likeness is incredible!

No, things like that just don't happen. But other things do. Daughters find out their fathers are living in Australia and try to track them down. I couldn't blame her. I just wished she'd told me she was thinking of doing it. Maybe she didn't want to say anything about it in case it all came to nothing.

'When did she start trying to trace you?' I persisted. 'As soon as she arrived in Australia?'

'No.' He was looking uneasy again.

'Not till she got to Brisbane? She knew you were in Brisbane?'

'No.' The hair was being twiddled again. He'd pull it all out if he wasn't careful. 'Maddy, it wasn't quite like that. I thought she'd told you. I thought she must have told you she'd started trying to find me.'

'No. No, she didn't. I suppose, when she went off travelling, she had it in the back of her mind but she probably didn't want to get her hopes up because it was quite unlikely, wasn't it, that she'd actually—'

'No. Listen. She already knew exactly where I was.'

She already knew? *Already knew?*

The words hit me in the chest like a stab wound. I recoiled away from him, holding myself rigid against the back of the chair, waiting for the next blow.

'How? What do you mean? How did she know?'

'Sophie started trying to trace me a long time ago, Maddy. I know what you think. I wasn't a father to her at all. She didn't deserve that. I should have done more than just send you money. I should have kept in touch with her, shared all the milestones of her life – yeah, done all the right things. I

254

left it too late. By the time I decided I wanted to make amends, you'd moved. And anyway, I didn't really think I had any right by then to suddenly turn up and expect her to accept me. But I wasn't reckoning on Sophie.'

He smiled again; the secret smile that said he knew her, he knew my daughter – the daughter he'd rejected, the daughter I'd loved and cherished and protected when nobody else would. I wanted to shout at him: *Stop smiling about her! She's mine! You don't know her! You can't have her!* I wanted to smack him hard and wipe that smug smile off his face. I had to sit on my hands to stop myself.

'She'd been trying to get in touch with me since she was about fifteen or sixteen,' he went on. 'And she finally succeeded just before her eighteenth birthday. We've been e-mailing each other for about two years now. You've done a good job, Madd. She's a lovely girl.'

I'd sat on my hands for long enough. I stood up and hit him.

For the second time that afternoon there was pandemonium in the garden. Joe, ducking away from me in surprise, overbalanced his chair and tipped backwards onto the grass. A livid red mark was already visible across one cheek and a trickle of blood ran from his top lip where I must have caught him with my ring. As the chair tipped, he clutched at the table next to him to try to stop himself falling, and a bowl of salad that was awkwardly balanced on the edge of the table toppled over, landing beside him on the lawn, lettuce leaves and slices of cucumber fluttering in the breeze to settle like butterflies around his outstretched arms.

'What's going on!' shrieked Brenda, running as fast as her silly high-heeled sandals would allow her, from the patio where she'd been serving fresh fruit salad. She still had the glass ladle in her hand, waving it above her head like a gladiator with a sword. 'Joe! You've fallen! You're hurt! You're bleeding!' Each of these observations was accompanied by a

255

gesture with the ladle that almost amounted to a wringing of her hands.

'I'm OK,' he said, sitting up and wiping the blood from his lip with the back of his hand. He picked a piece of lettuce out of his hair, flicked a cherry tomato off his leg and got to his feet, touching the red area on his cheek delicately and giving me a look. People were nudging each other, raising their eyebrows in our direction and muttering about a fight, but apart from Brenda they'd kept their distance. Probably frightened I'd start laying into them too.

'Come into the kitchen!' commanded Brenda. 'Let me bathe it for you. It looks nasty.' Turning her back on me, she tried to take Joe's arm to lead him away but he shook her off. 'It's all right, Brenda – I'm OK,' he repeated. 'Sorry about the salad.'

She picked the salad bowl up from the grass and tried to scoop up the remains of the lettuce and tomatoes.

'Leave it,' I advised her stonily. 'It might take root and grow a coleslaw plant.'

Joe chuckled. Brenda and I both stared at him. He covered his mouth with his hand and looked down at the ground but I could still see the creases around his eyes, and his shoulders were beginning to shake. I'd just clobbered him – and he was laughing? Brenda, shaking her head in bewilderment, gathered up her salad bowl and her scraps of salad and headed back to the house.

'What's funny?' I hissed at Joe.

'You are,' he said, looking up at me and smiling quite openly now. 'You always were a force to be reckoned with. I'm glad you haven't got old and soft and boring. It would have been such a disappointment.'

I was still too angry to accept compliments about my bad temper.

'Sophie is my daughter,' I told him, spitting the words out at his face. 'You had no business getting in touch with her without telling me.'

'But it was Sophie who—'

256

'Two years! Two fucking years, writing to her behind my back, sneaking a pretend relationship, letting her think you were still her father. . .'

'I am still her father, Maddy. That's not something that changes, whatever else happened back then.'

'That's crap! That's bollocks! How can you suddenly start writing to her when she's a teenager, and meet up with her now she's twenty years old, and say you've always been her father!'

'I know. I know how it looks, how you must feel. . .'

'Don't kid yourself! You'll never know how I feel!'

'No. OK. I'm sorry.' He was silent for a moment, just watching me. My hand was still itching to deliver another slap. The first one hadn't got it all out of me – the fury and resentment at the sheer cheek of him. How dare he! How dare he try to seduce my daughter away from me! I blinked back the beginnings of tears, angrily, not wanting him to notice, but it was too late. Without comment, he got a hanky out of his pocket and offered it to me. I shook my head and wiped my eyes with my hand instead.

'I honestly thought Sophie had told you,' he said quietly.

'Well, you thought wrong.'

'Then I'm sorry. I'm sorry you feel hurt. She was just curious, that's all. Don't blame her for that.'

'I don't. I blame you.'

'And I was curious too.'

'About your daughter? To see how she'd turned out – whether I'd made a good job of bringing her up on my own?' I snapped.

'Yes, but not just that. I was curious about you as well. It's been a long time, Maddy – we were just kids back then. I've often wondered, since – how you were, what you were doing . . . what you were like now.'

'Well, now you know! So you can stop wondering, can't you!'

I stalked off to get myself another drink. My heart was still pounding with shock and anger and my legs were

257

shaking so much I had to steady myself against tables and chairs as I walked, but I was determined not to look back. I was hoping he'd be gone by the time I turned round. I poured myself a very large gin with just a splash of tonic, and took several large mouthfuls before I finally glanced back down the garden. Joe was still standing in the same spot, staring at the ground. But before I had a chance to look away, he raised his eyes and instantly met mine. And to my extreme annoyance he smiled again.

'Why didn't you tell me? I can't believe you didn't tell me!'

The phone line crackled and whistled. Christ almighty, it wasn't that far from New Zealand to Australia, was it? Why the hell couldn't they manage a decent bloody phone connection?

'Don't cry, Mum. Please don't cry. I can't bear it!' said Sophie, sounding like she was crying herself.

'I'm not crying. Don't you cry!'

Look what you've done. Get a man involved, any man – husband, father, divorce lawyer, anything – and we all end up crying.

'I'm sorry, Mum. I knew you'd be upset...'

'Then why did you do it?'

'I just wanted to find out. Where he was, who he was, what he was like. I was curious. Can't you understand that?'

Curious. That's what he said, too. Curiosity killed the frigging cat.

'All that time. Two, three years – writing to each other! Keeping secrets from me! From me, Sophie!' I wailed, feeling my hurt like an open wound.

'But Mum!' She was crying properly now, sobbing in big noisy gulps. I'd made her cry. My heart felt like it was going to break. I held my head in my hands, the phone tucked into my neck, listening to her crying, rocking myself as if I was rocking her in my arms. 'Mum, I wanted to tell you but I didn't want to hurt you! I didn't want you to think I was being disloyal.'

258

'You should have told me. I'd have understood.'

But of course I wouldn't.

I'd have sulked and cried and asked her not to do it – not to try to find him, not to write to him, not to go to him. I'd have been too afraid of the consequences. Too afraid of her loving him more than me. Too afraid of her finding out what I was really like.

'What has he told you?' I asked her now, my breath so tight in my throat I could hardly get the words out. 'What has he said about ... the reasons why we split up?'

'Why you split up?' she repeated, her voice registering surprise at the turn in the conversation. 'Well, the same as you've always told me, of course – you both being too young, too much responsibility too soon, both missing out on being single...'

Relief washed over me in a hot flood, making me feel weak.

'Both playing around with other people, I suppose!' she added teasingly.

'What!'

'Don't freak out, Mum.' She sniffed and gave a little laugh. 'Dad hasn't told me any deep dark secrets from your past. But it's pretty obvious neither of you were ready to settle down. I know I wouldn't have been, at seventeen! I'm still not.'

'I suppose you want to go and live with him in Australia, now,' I said all in a rush. It came out as a kind of demented squeak. Sophie laughed again.

'Mum, honestly – what are you like? Is that what you're so worried about? Don't be silly; I've only just met Dad. I still hardly know him. I'm not likely to turn my whole life around now, just to be with him. I'm going on with my travels, like I've always planned.'

Some mother. I'd been so obsessed with my own hurt and outrage I hadn't even asked her.

'Whereabouts are you now, anyway? What are you up to?'

'We're in Queenstown. I did a bungee jump yesterday,' she said in a mournful voice as if it was the most boring piece of news she could think of telling me. 'The second highest bungee jump in the world.'

'WHAT? You did what?' I'd been sitting on my bed, and at this point I fell backwards against the pillow like I'd been felled, almost dropping the phone.

'I said, I did a bungee jump.'

'Yes, I know – I heard you!' I retorted, ridiculously. 'For God's sake! What were you thinking of? Why?'

'It's what everyone does out here. It's the highlight – the most exciting thing...'

'Did Ryan do it with you?'

'No.' She paused. 'He wanted to, but he was too scared.'

'Why weren't you too scared? Why weren't you terrified?' I shuddered, trying – and failing – to imagine how it would feel to stand on the edge of a high cliff and then jump off into nothingness and free-fall the length of the bungee rope. I felt sick just thinking about Sophie doing it. My own flesh and blood! I didn't spend fifteen hours in labour, giving birth to her in a mass of contortions and screamings, only to have her throw that precious body I went through hell to produce off the edge of a cliff with such reckless abandon.

'Thank God I didn't know about it before you did it. I'd have got on a plane out there and stopped you!'

'I won't tell you beforehand when I'm going to do the parachute jump, then.'

'The what? You are not going to do a parachute jump! Sophie! Promise me you're not going to ... it's dangerous...'

'It isn't. It's safe, Mum. It's just – exhilarating, and ... fun. I'll be fine. It's not supposed to be anywhere near as scary as the bungee.'

'I want you back,' I sniffed miserably. 'I don't care if you think I'm selfish. I don't want you doing all these crazy dangerous things in strange dangerous places. And I don't want you having secret meetings with your father.'

260

'I'm not. Mum, please don't be like this. I'm not doing anything dangerous, and I'm not meeting Dad any more. When I've finished my travelling I'm coming home to England – to you. Meeting up with Dad was only ever going to be a part of it. We might not have even got on together.'

'But you did? You did get on?'

'Yes. That's why I wanted you to meet him again too. Sorry about the plotting and the shock tactics, but I knew you'd refuse if I asked you and I just thought it would be such a waste of an opportunity, while you were over in Australia. You might never have got another chance.'

'Chance at what? Making up? Getting back together? Dream on, Sophie – I'm sorry, but. . .'

'No. I'm not that stupid – I wasn't trying to be some sort of *Sleepless in Seattle*, whatever you might think. I just thought it could be healing for you both.'

'So much for healing. We argued, and I hit him.'

'You hit him?'

'Nothing serious. He fell off his chair and got salad all over him.'

'So it wasn't very successful. Sorry, Mum. I suppose it was a stupid idea.'

She sounded so upset. I couldn't let her be upset, could I? It wasn't her fault I was a man-beater.

'No, it wasn't a stupid idea,' I soothed her gently. 'I know you meant well. I just didn't cope very well with the shock.'

'So maybe you could try again before you leave Brisbane? Just, you know, so you don't leave with a sour taste. I don't want to feel like I've ruined your trip with my stupid meddling. Just perhaps meet him for a quick drink or something, and make your peace?'

I shook my head silently. No way. It just wasn't going to happen.

'Mum? Please? Just to make me happy?'

To make her happy?

Bugger.

'Please?'

'OK, maybe. I'll see.'

Maybe.

And maybe not.

I didn't go swimming with Patrick that week. I mooched around the house, sat in the shade on the patio with my boring paperback (still trying to guess what the heroine was waiting for), and spent hours composing conversations, inside my head, that I was never going to have with Joe.

'Your muscles will go flabby,' said Patrick with a sad smile as he came back from the pool one afternoon. 'And you'll lose your fitness – especially eating those.'

I'd been scoffing my way through a family-sized box of chocolates.

'I know.' I smiled back. 'So much for your star pupil, eh? No will-power.'

He sat down next to me and picked up the chocolate box, studying it as if the list of contents was terribly fascinating.

'I'm not big on psychology. But I don't think overindulging in comfort food is anything to do with lack of will-power. I think it's probably more to do with anxiety.'

'Oh really, Mr Non-Psychologist, is that so?'

'I reckon so. Anxiety, or depression. Or worries about ex-husbands turning up in your life and wanting to punch them.'

I laughed. 'You seem to have a better grasp of psychology than give yourself credit for.'

'What are you going to do? Are you going to see him again? Or do you want me to tell him you've left the country?'

'I suppose you've seen him at the pool?'

'Saw him today, as a matter of fact, and he was asking after you.' Patrick looked at me sideways and grinned. 'He had an enormous shiner on his left cheek, and a swollen lip. Apparently the teenagers in his class last night were giving him hell about it, asking if "some woman" had clobbered him for trying it on with her. I think he told them he'd fallen off his bike.'

I smiled and unwrapped another chocolate.

'I don't know what to do, Patrick,' I admitted. 'Sophie wants me to see him again before I go home – to kind of clear the air I suppose. I'm not sure I want to; I still feel like I'm in shock from actually coming face to face with him.'

'I can imagine. I'm sure Sophie had the best of intentions, but I think it was a crazy plan; she should have told you about Joe. She should have told us, too, come to that! Christ, I'm in a state of shock myself. I never knew old Joe had a kid at all, never mind the fact that she was hanging around with my son and stayed here at the house.'

'How did that come about? Sophie said she met Ryan in Sydney.'

'Yeah, she did, while he was living down there. They told Brenda and me they'd just met by chance, at a hostel, but apparently Joe set it all up. When he knew Sophie and her friend were coming over from England, he sent her a list of contacts – friends and acquaintances of his in every city they were visiting. Joe's known Ryan since he was a little kid – taught him diving and life-saving as a matter of fact – so of course Ryan's name was one of the contacts for Sydney. I don't suppose it occurred to him that he and Sophie would become such good friends, or that they'd come back to Brisbane together, but Sophie was obviously determined not to let on that he was her dad.'

'I don't understand it. It's just so unlike her to keep secrets.'

'All part of the plan, don't you think?' He looked up from the chocolate rapidly melting in my hand, and met my eyes with a ghost of a smile. 'It's up to you whether you see Joe again, Maddy. But I do think it's pretty naïve to imagine Sophie hasn't got ulterior motives here – whatever she might say. There's too much cunning and subterfuge gone into the whole thing to be just an innocent little suggestion about the two of you meeting up for a nice cup of tea and a catch-up about the past twenty years.'

'What do you mean?'

'Sophie's no different from every other child of a broken marriage. Deep down, whether she admits it or not, I bet she wants you and Joe back together.'

Huh! Like that's going to happen. No way! I leant a little closer to Patrick and tucked my arm through his. If I was getting together with anyone this side of the equator, it sure as hell wasn't going to be Joe.

Chapter 17

He phoned me a couple of days later.

'How are you today? Still in a fighting mood or has Brenda run out of salad to throw around?'

'I should probably say sorry. How is your face?'

'A nice colour of purple. I've taken some stick about it from the kids at the pool.'

'So I hear. Apparently you fell off your bike, then, did you?'

'Silly thing to tell them, really. I haven't got a bike.'

He waited, probably expecting me to laugh. I couldn't. I was sorry about hitting him, sorry about his purple face and not having a bike and all that, but no, I wasn't going to let him be chummy and nice and think I was going to be friends with him.

He cleared his throat and then said all in a rush:

'I was phoning to see if you wanted to give it another go. I mean talking to each other. Just meeting and talking, you know, without a fight. Not marriage.'

Like I said, forget the jokes, sunshine.

'Maybe not a good idea, then?' he added when I didn't respond.

I hesitated. 'Well, to be perfectly honest I'd rather not. I don't see the point, and I'm not sure if we can, anyway – talk without fighting.'

'I know. I'm only suggesting it because Sophie wanted me to.'

OK, call me unreasonable. Call me completely illogi-
cal. I didn't want to meet him, but I was kind of miffed
that he hadn't suggested it because he wanted to. He
should have wanted to take me out to dinner, treat me to
an enormous meal with wine and pudding and everything,
and bought me flowers and lavished loads of apologies on
me for the way he'd been carrying on this ... this clan-
destine fatherhood with my daughter for the past two and
a half years.

'Sophie seems to think it would be good for us to sort
things out between us,' he went on, 'before you go back to
England.'

'She said that to me, too. Stuff about healing. Healing!' I
said with a snort. 'Huh! You have to be ill, don't you, to need
healing?'

'Or hurt, I guess,' he said quietly.

Hurt? Yes, well; he was the one with the shiner on his
cheek. And I sure as hell wasn't going to be kissing it better.

'So what do we do?' he persisted. 'Shall we put a brave
face on it, for her sake?'

Put a brave face on it? Fuck you!

'If it's going to be that much of an ordeal to take me out to
dinner...!' I snapped.

'Dinner? Who said anything about dinner? I was thinking
more in terms of a bench in the park with a packet of chips
and a can of Coke.'

'You what?'

Too late, I heard him laughing.

'Fuck you,' I said out loud. 'You think this is a joke?'

'No. But if we're doing this for Sophie's sake, maybe we
should try not to fight the whole time we're in the restaurant?
And yes, I have booked a restaurant.'

'Bit presumptuous of you, wasn't it? I might not have
wanted to...'

'If you don't turn up, Maddy, I'll just eat twice as much on
my own. Mario's in Queen Street – tomorrow night at eight
o'clock. OK?'

How did he do that? I had a very uncomfortable feeling about not having been given any option.

And all this time, I didn't hear a word from Rachel.

I know what it looks like, but it wasn't me that was being difficult – honestly. I'd tried to call her. OK, not straight away; but you don't, do you? Trust me, when you've practically been called a slut by your best friend, and you've hung up on her, and pretty well accepted that your friendship is over, kaput, finished for good, you don't do anything about it straight away, other than feeling sorry for yourself and having a blub from time to time. But after a while I recovered a bit and, well, I suppose I started to admit to myself that Rachel might have been a sanctimonious, self-righteous, smug, arrogant, annoying, irritating cow, but she might also have been right. Not about everything, of course – not about the gym and the slimline tonic and the lettuce, for instance, but just possibly about me and married men, she might have had a point. Not that I'd ever tried to pretend I was any kind of angel, had I? I mean, if she didn't like my way of life, if she was offended by my total lack of moral fibre, she'd had plenty of time to piss off out of it before, rather than waiting until I was on the other side of the world and feeling vulnerable, and unable to defend myself, and . . . well, and missing her . . . to launch her attack on me over the phone. It was so hurtful!

But yes, I know, I know. I hold my hands up. I was guilty as charged. I'd had an affair with Tom while he was married, and didn't give a toss about Linda. The Rules of the Sisterhood are quite unequivocal about this. I was supposed to care about the feelings of the unknown wife, and imagine how I'd feel if I was her, and conclude that it was far more important not to hurt another woman than to have it off with her husband. Well, bollocks to that, I say. Linda wasn't my responsibility, she was Tom's. My conscience was clear. Or maybe I just didn't have a conscience? Should I be worried about this? Because there was no denying I'd have loved to do exactly the same thing now with Patrick, given half a chance – if Brenda would only look the other way, or lock herself in the garage for a couple of hours, or go off and join a commune in India or something – anything. So, you see, Rachel was quite right about me. Once a slut, always a slut, I suppose.

She never answered my calls, but I left messages on her voicemail. At first I just said stuff like Give Me A Call or We Need To Talk. Then, I began to get all emotional and started begging. *Please*, Rachel, please call me back. I'm sorry I hung up on you. Please talk to me. Eventually I sent an e-mail. I feel a bit embarrassed about the e-mail. It would be fair to say I poured my heart out in it. Very roughly, it told her how she was right and I was wrong, she was good and I was bad, she was a great friend and I'd never appreciated her, whereas I was a piece of shit who didn't deserve to cling to the sole of her shoe. All that kind of stuff. When she didn't even reply to that, I sent one more, even more cringe-worthy, saying in one long, tortured sentence how I presumed from her silence that she was never going to for-give me and although I could understand her hating me, I would always remember our friendship, blah blah blah. And that was that.

'She must have hated me for a long time, really,' I said thoughtfully to Patrick when I told him all about it. 'She must have just pretended to like me all this time.'

'Don't be ridiculous!' he laughed gently. 'Why would she do that? You said yourself, you've been friends for years.'

'But if she was really my friend, if she really liked me, she wouldn't have gone off me so completely, over one little argument, would she. It must have been brewing for a long time, and the argument over the phone just gave her the excuse she needed to cut me out of her life – ' I wiped away a tear – 'for ever.'

'Come on, I think you're being just a little bit melodra-matic. She's angry with you for hanging up on her, and she's punishing you. That's all. Leave it be, and she'll be OK with you by the time you go home.'

'But I need her now! I need her to talk to!' I wailed.

It wasn't fair. I had all this trauma going on in my life – Joe turning up, haunting me like the ghost of my wicked past, and Sophie keeping secrets from me and playing at Daddies and Daughters behind my back – and Rachel had deserted me just when I needed a sympathetic friend more than ever before.

'I need a friend,' I added with a self-pitying sniff, and blew my nose loudly and not very nicely.

'You've got me,' said Patrick quietly.

He put his arm round me and drew me in closer to him. The feel of him was good and strong and soothing. I laid my cheek against his chest, closed my eyes and breathed in the comforting male essence of him with a kind of shuddering sigh; and when I opened my eyes he'd lowered his face to mine and began to brush my lips with his, very gently. It was exquisitely arousing. For a few minutes I just lay still, savouring the feeling.

Then I grabbed him round the back of the neck and snogged him until we were both gasping for breath.

'Patrick! Patrick, where the hell are you? I've been calling you for ten minutes. I need you to take the bins round to the front of the house and fix that door in the kitchen where the hinge keeps squeaking, and also, I keep telling you … Patrick? Patrick!'

'Fuck!' Patrick jumped up as if he'd been shot and zipped up his trousers. We'd progressed from the bench at the side of the swimming pool to the little changing room built onto the back of the garage, and we'd also progressed from kissing to getting inside each other's clothes. The rate of progress, now we'd finally crossed the line we'd previously drawn, preventing anything more intimate than holding hands, had been quite spectacular and I was having trouble stopping now, Brenda or no Brenda.

269

'Mmm,' was just about all I could manage to say at that point. I grabbed his hand and tried to put it back where it had been.

'For God's sake, Maddy! Brenda's outside! For fuck's sake, pull your top down! Pull your...' He glanced at me quickly and swallowed hard. 'Pull your knickers up!'

'Oh, oh...'

'Now! Quickly!' He tried desperately to straighten me up himself, but I wasn't being particularly cooperative. He looked around wildly as Brenda's voice became even closer, even more loud and demanding. 'OK – get in the shower.'

'Ooh!' I giggled as he half lifted, half pushed me into the shower cubicle. But there was nothing kinky in his mind. With a final warning 'Ssh!' he shut the cubicle door abruptly in my face and ran out of the changing room to face the music – just in the nick of time.

'What have you been doing in there – I've been calling you for ever!'

I shivered as the reality of Brenda's screeching anger hit my dwindling sexual excitement head-on and reduced it to a limp tremble.

'Sorry, dear,' came Patrick's perfectly smooth reply. How did he do that? He didn't sound in the least perturbed. 'I was just getting rid of a spider in the changing room. One of those big black buggers you don't like? I think it's gone now.'

Clever, or what? I had to admire him. He knew Brenda wasn't about to come and check out that story. She started off again about the bins and the kitchen door, and he carried on making apologetic and conciliatory noises as they walked away back towards the house. Their voices grew fainter and disappeared. I sat down on the seat in the shower cubicle for a few minutes, waiting for my breathing to return to normal. I tried to feel sorry about it. I was doing what Rachel had accused me of: playing around with another married man. And at a swimming pool again! What was it with me and the smell of chlorine? I was a tart, a trollop, a harlot, a bloody

Jezebel. I had no respect for Patrick's wife, or the fact that I was staying in her house. I should have felt guilt, and remorse, and shame – deep, deep shame.

But I didn't. All I felt was frustration. Another couple of minutes and I'd have been fucking him.

I still hadn't got used to the Queensland evenings, or perhaps I should say the lack of them. Dark at half past six, day after day, week after week, like it or not, regardless of the weather or the time of year. Instant nightfall, with no warning and no time to go round the house pulling the curtains and putting on the lights – all the little evening rituals we associate with early afternoon darkness in the winter in England – and no sitting outside in blazing daylight until ten o'clock at night like we do on fine days in June. By the time I left the house to meet Joe at the restaurant the next evening, it already felt like the middle of the night. I hadn't been into the city centre on my own before and I wasn't too sure of the way.

'I'll drive you,' said Patrick, seeing me hesitate by the door. He picked up his car keys and shepherded me outside before Brenda could comment.

'Thanks.' I watched his profile as he concentrated on the road. 'Sorry about ... how it ended up, yesterday.'

'Don't worry. Brenda didn't suspect anything.'

Oh, that's OK, then! Unfortunately I wasn't really worried about Brenda. I was only sorry we didn't get to finish what we'd started.

'Maybe another time...'

'Maybe,' he said, flashing me a quick smile. 'Though it's difficult, isn't it.'

Oh, OK, fine. I turned away to look out of the window and seethed to myself silently. So this was how it was, then. He was obviously too scared shitless at the thought of being found out by Brenda to risk trying it again. So where did that leave me? Feeling used, and teased, and sidelined, that's where. Well, suit yourself, Mr Patrick No-Balls Cook. Get what you can from your prune-faced, slack-arsed, bleating

271

wife, or do it on your own with a porno magazine and the memory of my tits in your hands, and grow old and hopeless and desperate wondering for ever what it would have been like to do it together just once. Or preferably twice. See if I care!

'I'll get out here,' I snapped suddenly.

Was I being unreasonable? Sulking because he didn't want to jump me as soon as we were both alone in the car together? Maybe. Or maybe just smarting from the fact that he was trying salvage a modicum of decency whereas I seemed to be incapable of it.

'We're not there yet ... we're nowhere near the place.'

'That's OK. I'll walk from here. I could do with some air.'

'Don't be like this ... I didn't mean ... I said maybe...'

'Yes, I know. And maybe not,' I retorted fiercely. 'I'll get out here, please. Thank you.'

He pulled up outside an office block.

'Turn right at the top of this road,' he said, pointing ahead of us. 'Then second left and you'll come out almost opposite Mario's. Are you sure you want to walk?'

'Positive. Thanks.'

I watched him drive away, going safely back to Brenda to be nagged into submission about this or that mindless matter of domesticity, shook my head sadly to myself and began to walk.

It wasn't far, and I was still a little bit early when I arrived at the restaurant. Joe was waiting for me at the bar, studying a menu.

'Hi. You got here OK.' It wasn't a question. He didn't wait for an answer. 'Here,' he handed me a menu, 'take a pew and see what you fancy to eat. I'll get you a drink. Beer? Lemonade? Packet of chips?'

Surprisingly, and without meaning to, I laughed. He grinned, looking surprised himself, as if he'd given up all hope of ever seeing me do so.

'Vodka and tonic, please.'

He raised one eyebrow but beckoned the bartender and bought the drink without any comment.

'Mind if I smoke?' I asked him, lighting one up before he'd had a chance to answer. I took a long drag and closed my eyes briefly as I exhaled. I imagined myself breathing out all my frustration and disappointment about Patrick. When I looked back at Joe he was watching me thoughtfully.

'You look like you needed that.'

'Well, you know what it's like.' I flicked ash into the ashtray on the edge of the bar. 'Poisoning me inside and out, but I can't do without it.'

'Patrick said you were a keen swimmer?'

The question hung in the air between us. I knew what he was getting at but I wasn't up for a discussion about my potential fitness and its dependence on giving up my filthy habit. Instead I nodded briefly and changed the subject.

'Your face doesn't look as bad as I thought.'

'Sorry to disappoint you. It's gone down a bit.'

The bruise had that yellowish tinge they develop when they start to fade. I looked at it with interest, slightly fascinated by the idea that I'd delivered the blow that caused this damage. I never knew I had it in me. Wonder what I could do if I was really mad?

'I'll try not to annoy you any more,' he said, running his fingers ruefully over his cheek.

'Good.' I put the menu down on the bar. 'I'll have the ravioli to start. And then the pan-fried veal.'

He raised an eyebrow again and I just, barely, resisted the urge to snap, 'What now?'

'It makes a pleasant change,' he commented, sitting back after giving the waiter our orders, 'to eat out with someone who isn't counting calories, refusing fats or trying some cranky diet where you eat green food on some days and red foods on others, and no carbohydrates if there's an "R" in the month.'

In other words, I'm a complete glutton who stuffs her face with anything that comes her way, regardless of composition or colour.

'I meant that as a compliment, by the way,' he added suddenly with a grin. 'I hate going out with people who're frightened to enjoy their food.'

I pondered this for a while. Who exactly did Joe normally go out with? Who were these anorexic waifs with food phobias who bored him shitless with their slimming theories?

'Suzie, my ex, was a nightmare,' he added as if I'd spoken aloud, 'and so were all her friends. One diet after another. They'd have all been better off getting off their lazy arses and doing some exercise instead of half starving themselves.'

'You've been married? Since me, I mean?'

Not that I care. I couldn't give a shit if you've married every woman in Australia, to be quite honest, if you'd just leave my daughter alone and stay out of her life...

'No. Not married.' He gave me a very direct look. 'I decided a long time ago never to go down that road again.'

'I put you off for life, I suppose,' I said, taking a swig of my drink. Must have been a small measure; nearly all gone already.

'Let's just say it was a mistake, shall we? A mistake I wasn't anxious to repeat. So Suzie and I didn't bother – we just lived together. And split up fairly amicably a couple of years ago. How about you?'

'Me? Oh, I haven't bothered to repeat it either.' I put down my glass and glanced at his. Still almost full. Damn.

'Want another?'

'Not till you're ready.' Don't want you thinking I'm an alcoholic as well as a pig.

'It's OK. I'm driving. Anyway,' he motioned at the waiter, who was trying discreetly to beckon us in his direction, 'Looks like our table's ready, so I'll get some drinks sent over.'

'OK – thanks. No hurry.'

This was very, very weird. I used to sleep with this man. I was pregnant by him, gave birth to his child. I took his name,

274

wore his ring, promised to love him for ever. How weird, how peculiar, to be with him now, making polite conversation like two complete strangers. As the waiter settled us at our table I felt a sudden flash of exasperation. What was I playing at? Why should I care what he thought of me? Why shouldn't I just be myself, warts and all?

'Actually,' I said suddenly, leaning across the table and grabbing the drink from the waiter, 'I was desperate for this.'

Joe shrugged.

'And I'm desperate for another fag, too, to be quite honest,' I added.

He shrugged again, and smiled at me. The smile infuriated me. It was a kind of tolerant smile. OK, I understand that you have your disgusting little habits. I realise you can't help it. I'll try not to disapprove too much.

I polished off my drink and eyed the wine speculatively.

'In fact, that's more or less how I spend most of my time, really – drinking, eating and smoking. Oh, apart from shagging married men, of course. Nearly forgot that one!' I gave a very false, very silly laugh and began to tuck into my ravioli.

He watched me.

'Aren't you going to eat your prawns?' I prompted him.

Without answering, he poured me a glass of wine, and then picked up his fork and took a mouthful of his starter.

'You can have one little drink even if you're driving,' I told him.

'I know. I will, in a minute. But I thought you were desperate.'

So what if I am? I gulped at the wine and attacked the ravioli with increasing ferocity. Let him think what he bloody well likes! He already knows I'm not a very nice person, after all. . .

'So: you're not married, you're not attached – you just like married men?' he said calmly, pushing his plate aside half-finished.

'Well, I was "attached" for a while . . . before I came on

275

this trip. Kind-of attached,' I admitted, thinking of Tom with a momentary pang. Very momentary. Another swig of wine put paid to the moment.

'But you've finished the relationship?'

'He finished it, really. By asking his wife for a divorce and threatening to marry me.' I gave the false little laugh again.

Not that it's any of your business, of course.

'So...' He poured himself his permitted small glass of wine, and watched me over the rim as the waiter cleared away our starter plates. 'So, this penchant of yours for married men...'

I smiled back at him: a challenging smile. Yes – so what? What are you going to make of it?

'Does it extend to Patrick Cook, by any chance?'

I almost choked on my wine.

'What makes you ask that?' I managed eventually, after a couple more swigs to calm me down.

He laughed. 'Patrick! Good old Patrick!' He leant back in his chair and laughed some more.

This was extremely irritating. What about good old fucking Patrick? What was so funny, then?

'I expect you'd like to have if off with good old Patrick,' said Joe, giving me an appraising look as if he could see the passion for good old Patrick steaming out of my ears. 'Most women seem to fancy him rotten.'

'He's a nice guy,' I said defensively. Where was the waiter with my bloody veal? Where was an opportunity to change the subject? And why was I being so defensive about it anyway? 'But I'm sure he's completely devoted to his wife and isn't interested in anybody else...'

'Is that what he told you?' laughed Joe.

'No!' I retorted, smarting. 'No, it's just what I assumed. What the hell is all this about? What are you getting at with all these nasty, smarmy insinuations? What's the matter – not enough going on in your own love life, got to have a dig at Patrick's?'

Joe stopped laughing. At the same moment, the waiter

276

arrived with our main courses, and took about an hour to arrange the plates in an attractive fashion on the table, and put the little dish of vegetables nicely in the middle, and make sure our knives and forks were squarely stationed against our table mats, and our wine glasses were topped up, and everything in our lives was generally hunky-dory, before wishing us all the very best of luck for the future in pretend Italian and backing obsequiously away.

'I'm sorry,' Joe said calmly as soon as we were on our own again. 'This isn't what we were supposed to be talking about tonight. This was meant to be about Sophie.'

'It's too late for that now,' I snapped. 'You'd better finish what you've started.'

He took a mouthful of his fish. I waited.

'You want to know about Patrick?' he said eventually, wiping his mouth.

'I want to know what you're implying about him, yes.'

'Well.' He considered for a moment, as if trying to find the right words. 'Well, look, Maddy – don't take offence at this. I haven't seen you for bloody ages, obviously, but I'd say you're still a very attractive woman.'

Thanks for nothing.

'And I reckon Patrick probably does fancy you. Honestly – anybody would.'

'What are you getting at?'

'But you won't get anywhere with him. Trust me. You won't. I know him really well, and—'

'He's too worried about Brenda.'

'Brenda!' He snorted and put down his fork. 'Poor old Brenda. She knows all about Patrick and his other women. If you can call them women.' He regarded me quite seriously. Suddenly, I knew he wasn't bullshitting me. For whatever reason, he was telling me the truth. And I knew I wasn't going to like it. 'Maddy, if Patrick's used Brenda as an excuse for not having an affair with you, he's probably just trying to let you down gently. The fact of the matter is that you're not really his type.'

277

Not his type? How the hell would you know? I think I am so his type – I sure as hell was his type yesterday afternoon in the swimming pool changing rooms when we were just about on the point of...

'Not that he'd say no to a quick one with you, if you gave him the chance. I bet he'd be up for it – he's a randy old sod, at the end of the day, but...'

'But what?' I asked faintly, putting down my cutlery and giving up on the veal completely.

'But you're too old for him. Maddy, Patrick's into young girls. Teenagers. The girls from his swimming classes. Sixteen, seventeen – rarely anything over twenty. He never has any trouble – they flock to him. He just has to look at them and they're peeling off their bikinis. He's a bastard! Sooner or later someone's father's going to get him locked up. He's well known for it.'

'I don't believe you!' I said, staring at the tablecloth. But I did, of course.

'Sorry. Sorry if I've dashed your hopes, there. But I thought I'd better warn you. This particular married man might not be one for your collection.'

Collection? What are we talking about here? I've made myself sound like a nymphomaniac. The collection consists of precisely one!

'In fact,' continued Joe with every sign of satisfaction, 'I'd say that where Patrick's concerned, Madd, you're completely out of the running. Obsolete! Prehistoric! Over the hill!'

Would you have blamed me if I hit him again?

Chapter 18

'I'm moving on,' I told Patrick the next morning at breakfast. My case was already packed. 'Thank you very much... and Brenda. Thank you both very much for having me.'

I faltered over the phrase *having me*. So nearly true. So humiliating, now, to think how he would have hated himself for it afterwards. How he would have looked at my old, haggard, wrinkled body in the cold light of post-coital day and asked himself how he could have stooped so low.

'Why now?' asked Patrick immediately, looking at me in alarm. 'Why so suddenly? Stay till the end of the week! Stay at least until—'

'No!' I couldn't bear it. I couldn't bear another day, another hour even, of having him looking at me like that, pretending to care, pretending to *like* me, knowing all the time that he was comparing me with sixteen-year-old nymphets with pert little tits and smooth, firm, pierced little bellies. 'No. I'm going today. I want to see Sydney, and Melbourne, at least, before I go back. If I don't get going, I'll never make it – how embarrassing to go home and say I've been over here all this time and never got outside of Queensland!'

He caught up with me a little later. I was having a last look at the swimming pool.

'I hope this is not ... anything to do with me?' he asked me anxiously, in a whisper. 'Anything to do with *us*?'

I didn't want to feel any more humiliated than I already

279

did; but even more than that, I didn't want him to *flatter* himself that anything about him mattered to me.

'Of course not!' I sang cheerfully. 'I just want to get on with my travels, that's all.'

'Fair enough,' he said sadly. He stared down at the pool. 'Just promise me you'll keep up the swimming, though?'

Swimming? Bloody swimming? Who gives a . . .?

'Because I haven't said this to you, but I think you could actually be very, very good.'

I stared at him. 'Really?' Was he joking? Just trying to make me feel better? Make me stay?

'Really. Considering you've only been training such a short time, you've done amazingly well. You've got fantastic stamina. Keep it up, yeah?'

'Yeah.' It felt strange, being complimented, being told I was good at something. I was having trouble not smiling. But I wasn't going to let *him* see that. 'OK. Yeah, OK, I'll keep it up. I will.'

Might as well leave here with *some* sort of pride intact.

'Mum?' Sophie's voice sounded sharp with concern. 'I phoned Brenda and Patrick's place, and they said you'd left. You didn't say you were going.'

'Well, I knew you'd try my mobile if you wanted me. Don't panic, Soph – I just decided it was time to move on. You know, pastures new, see the world, and all that.'

'So where are you now? The Gold Coast? Sydney?'

'I'm . . . yes, I'm heading in that direction.'

I was actually in a little hotel five minutes' drive away from Brenda and Patrick, but I didn't see the need to tell her that. So much for seeing the world.

'I was phoning to ask how it went the other night,' she said.

'The other night?' I cast back my mind. What was I doing the other night?

'With Dad. You did meet Dad, didn't you?'

'Oh, yes. Yes, it was OK.'

280

Well, I wouldn't exactly call it an unmitigated success. After Joe told me about Patrick's predilection for girls younger than my daughter, the evening kind of went downhill. I drank too much wine (which isn't like me at all) and started complaining very loudly and vociferously about men in general and Australian ones in particular. When Joe quietly suggested that perhaps what Patrick was doing wasn't an awful lot worse, or more selfish, than my professed tendency to play around with married men, I swore at him and called myself a taxi. Thinking about it now, I actually felt quite guilty – if only because I didn't even offer to pay my share of the bill.

'So how did you leave things? Did you make up with him? Are you OK with each other now? Are you going to keep in touch?'

'Which question do you want me to answer? I think 'no' probably covers them all.'

'Oh.' She sounded disappointed. 'Oh well, I suppose at least you gave it a go.'

'Sophie, there was never going to be any great reconciliation.'

'I know. It just would've been nice if you could have... well, *tried*.'

Tried? I *tried*, didn't I?

'Well, I'm sorry, love. Some things just aren't meant to be.'

She told me at some length about their travels in New Zealand. She and Ryan were leaving Auckland in a couple of days' time to fly out to Santiago. I felt vaguely unsettled and bereft thinking about this. While she was in New Zealand I could tell myself she was only just across a little bit of sea from me. Distance was irrelevant; it was the next country along, after all. Chile was the other side of the world, whether I was here in Australia or back home in England.

'You sound really excited about South America,' I said, trying to keep the resentment out of my voice.

'It's Peru I'm looking forward to most, Mum – the Inca

Trail. It's what everybody goes there for. It's supposed to be a fantastic experience. We've met a few people here who did it last year and they were telling us…'

I listened, happy that she was excited, happy that she had these wonderful opportunities, happy about the adventures ahead of her. But still wishing, selfishly, underneath it all, that I could make her come straight home with me.

I wasn't expecting to hear from Joe again. How did he get my mobile number?

'Asked Patrick for it. Where are you? He said you were heading for Sydney?'

'Kind of.'

'So how far have you got?'

'The Redman Hotel in Wickham Street.'

He laughed. 'Can't find your way out of Brisbane?'

'I'm working on it. Preparing myself for the journey.'

What exactly *was* I doing? I couldn't seem to motivate myself. I hadn't even bought a ticket, never mind gone anywhere yet.

'Want some help?'

'What sort of help?' I asked suspiciously.

'Maps, guidebooks, bus routes, some advice about the best places to stay. It's not easy planning a trip on your own, especially when you don't know the country.'

Steady, steady. Next thing I knew, he'd be inviting himself round to my hotel room to plan routes and stuff with me. That'd be far too close for comfort.

'No ulterior motives,' he added quickly.

Glad *you* said that.

'So what are you suggesting?' And why? Considering I got pissed and stormed out of the restaurant the other night, why are you bothering?

'Have you been to Mount Coot-tha?'

'Where?'

'Thought as much. Didn't Patrick show you anything?'

'Yes! We went into the city every day.'

282

'But you've missed some of the best spots out-of-town. I haven't got any lessons this evening. I'll pick you up in an hour's time, OK?'

'But...'

'I'll bring the maps and stuff with me. We'll have a coffee at the top of Mount Coot-tha and I'll help you plan your route.'

'Well...'

'See you about half past six, then.'

It'd been a long time since I'd had anyone try to organise my life. In a strange kind of way I didn't find it too unpleasant.

It was dark by the time we arrived at Mount Coot-tha. Joe parked the car at the lookout point and threaded his way through the crowds, beckoning me to follow him.

'This is a popular spot in the evening,' he said as we reached the railing at the edge of the lookout.

'I can see why.' The lights of Brisbane were laid out beneath us like a set of glittering fairy jewellery. 'It's beautiful,' I added.

He turned to look at me, smiling with surprise.

'That's the first time I've heard you say something positive.'

'It's the first time I've seen it,' I protested.

'No. I mean about anything.'

Am I *that* bloody miserable? What: am I a moaning, fault-finding, complaining old cow? Does *everybody* think that about me? When I turn up in the pub at home, just for instance, does everyone try to hide behind their beer glasses, muttering to each other: *There's that moany old grouch Maddy Goodchild. Pretend you haven't seen her.* Does Sophie say things to Amy behind my back about me being a misery? Is that why Rachel's had enough of me? Well, is it?

*

283

'What's the matter?'

We'd found a table outside the café and he'd bought me a cup of hot chocolate and a blueberry muffin without even asking me what I wanted. I started to make a caustic, snappy comment about making up my mind for me, but then I stopped mid-grouch and stirred my hot chocolate in complete silence.

'Is it something I've said?' Joe persisted.

'Well, maybe you're right. Maybe I'm a moany, miserable, whingeing old cow and everybody hates me. But I didn't realise it.'

'Oh! Is *that* all!' he laughed.

Is that all? Just destroy every shred of my self-confidence, and then laugh it off, why don't you!

'I didn't mean it like that,' he added.

'That's too easy to say. What *did* you mean it like, then? Only it's quite a hurtful thing, you know, for someone to say you're a moaner, when you've only just met them. . .'

'Only just met?'

'Well, you know. This time around. This decade.'

He took a bite of his cake and studied me thoughtfully as he chewed.

'I didn't say you're a moaner. It was just a surprise to hear you saying the view was beautiful. I don't think you often say things like that. I think you've got too used to. . . sarcasm. Taking the piss.' He took another bite, and then added: 'But then, what do I know? Like you say, I've only just met you again. Tell me to fuck off.'

'Just to prove your point? Or so you can say I'm a foul-mouthed bad-tempered bitch as well as being a sarcastic piss-taker?'

'OK, sorry I spoke. Anything you want to say about *me* to get even?'

'What, apart from the fact that you're trying to steal my daughter?'

Whoops. That just kind of slipped out. And the evening had started off so well.

*

We finished our drinks in an uneasy silence.

'I've brought the maps and guidebooks with me,' he said at length. 'Do you want me to show you, or would you prefer me to take them away and throw myself in the Brisbane River?'

'Up to you.' I shrugged.

He unfolded the first map and showed me the route the long-distance bus would take from Brisbane down to Sydney and then on to Melbourne.

'Why would I want to get a bus?' I asked without much enthusiasm. 'I've got enough money to fly.'

'And what would you see, from the plane?' he retorted. 'How much Australian life are you going to experience from up above the clouds? It's your shout entirely, but if this is a once-only trip, and you'll never cross this way again, why miss out on the scenery in between?'

'I s'pose so,' I admitted grudgingly. 'But a *bus*?'

'Air-conditioned, all facilities...'

'OK, OK – what, have you got shares in the company?'

'Wish I had!' He smiled ruefully. 'Backpackers have made them rich during the last few years, trust me.'

The bus it was, then – never let it be said that I didn't support the Australian economy.

'I'll leave these with you,' Joe offered, handing me a map of Sydney and a directory of hotels. 'You can post them back to me when you get home.'

I listened to him describing the places I ought to go to, the sights I ought to see, the areas I should avoid, and I concentrated hard on not saying anything that could be deemed to be sarcastic or taking the piss. And I thought: *So I'm really going, now, am I?*

There may be a lot worse things in life than sitting on a crowded long distance bus full of noisy students with their smelly rucksacks and smelly feet; but to be quite honest I can't think of many. I leant back in my seat, closed my eyes and tried to shut everything out. I could only do it by pretending I was somewhere else. OK, I wasn't really on a bus full of twenty-year-old travellers. I was on a cruise liner on the Mediterranean, resting on deck before getting ready for a five-course banquet at the captain's table. I was going to be drinking champagne, eating those funny little bits of fish off silver platters passed round by waiters with white gloves on, and dancing the night away in the company of lots of good-looking men in dinner jackets. This was the life!

I opened my eyes with a sudden start. I was right! That *was* the life! That was the life I *ought* to be living! I wasn't a poor student, touring Australia on a shoestring, living rough, hoping for some work in a pub, or picking fruit, so that I could buy another bus ticket to the next city on the map. I was thirty-seven years old, and I was used to eating in restaurants, and travelling by car, and sleeping in a proper bed in my own room. For Christ's sake – I was a lottery winner!

The girl sitting next to me shifted in her seat, digging me with her elbow as she leant over the seat back to say something to the couple of lads sitting behind her.

'Mind that lady, Nicky!' warned one of the boys.

They'd all got on the bus at Surfers' Paradise. The bus had left Brisbane at half past eight in the evening, and by the time they got on it was quite late at night and the bus was full. Up till then I'd enjoyed spreading myself out across the whole seat, but I was lucky really – she was only a skinny waif of a girl. I could have been squashed into the corner by one of the big hunks she was talking to.

'Sorry!' she said politely enough, in a very English accent, and then added, apparently deciding to be even more polite, probably on account of the fact that I reminded her of her mum, 'Are you travelling far?'

'Sydney,' I said, wishing I wasn't.

'Me too. It's so exciting, isn't it? Can't wait to see the Bridge and everything!'

She was almost childlike in her enthusiasm. I felt older than ever.

'Are you travelling on your own?' I asked her, thinking of Sophie, wondering if this girl's poor mum was worried about her.

'Yeah, but like, you don't end up on your own for long. All this lot,' she gestured vaguely at half the bus, 'we were all staying at the same hostel in Surfers' Paradise. We've had a laugh so we're going on together for now.' She gave me a curious look. 'What about you?'

'Yes, I'm on my own,' I said. No crowd of hostel-mates tagging along with me. No one to have a laugh with. No Sophie. No Rachel. I blinked back a sudden spurt of self-pity.

'Going to visit someone?' Nicky asked hopefully. Probably didn't like the thought of sitting next to some freak with no life, for the whole of an eighteen-hour bus ride.

'No,' I said, being a freak with no life. 'No, I'm just... touring.'

'Well, good on yer!' she said, surprisingly, showing off the Aussie vernacular she'd picked up. 'Never too late, is it!'

I smiled. *Never too late*. She probably thought I was at least sixty.

'I had a win on the lottery, you see,' I added, suddenly wanting to tell someone. 'Only a small win. But my daughter's travelling, like you, so I thought...'

'You thought if she could do it, so could you!' exclaimed Nicky triumphantly.

'Something like that,' I agreed.

That, and a desire to run away from someone who wanted to marry me. Run away from life. But she'd be even more worried about sitting next to me if I tried to tell her all this stuff. She turned back to the guys in the seat behind and they started laughing at some in-humour about one of their friends who'd got very pissed on their last night in Surfers' Paradise and ended up passing out in the street. I closed my eyes again and worried briefly about Sophie, before realising with a pang that she probably had far more reason to worry about me getting pissed and passing out than I did about her.

287

I dozed off to sleep and dreamt I was on the *Titanic* and Leonardo Di Caprio was trying to get me to jump overboard.

'Are you getting off?'

Getting off? Where was the lifeboat? I wasn't getting off without seeing the lifeboat!

'We stop here for breakfast. Don't you want to get off for a bit?'

Breakfast? I struggled through the stupor of my sleep. Was it morning already? I'd expected to be awake all night, what with the chat and the laughter and the people clambering over their rucksacks to get to the toilet, but I must have slept through it all. Nicky and her friends were watching me with some concern.

'Are you OK?' she said. 'You were completely out of it, there.'

I realised with a shock that they thought I'd tripped out.

'Yeah, don't worry, I'm fine, thanks.' I smiled. 'Just slept a bit heavily.'

I got up, stretched, and followed them off the bus. It was early morning and we had half an hour to stretch our legs at a service station somewhere between a town beginning with B and a town beginning with K, neither of which I'd heard of. I bought myself a coffee and lit a fag, and found myself smoking it alongside Fat Frank, the only guy on the bus who was travelling alone. Judging by the smell of his sweaty shirt and sweaty armpits, his personal hygiene could have gone a long way towards explaining the reason for this, but he seemed to think that both of us being alone and both of us being smokers, we were a match made in heaven.

'Needed this, eh?' He gestured with his cigarette. 'Fucking needed this.'

'Yes. Wish I could give up.'

Where did that come from? Since when did I wish I could give up? He looked back at me through a cloud of his own smoke and shook his head sadly as if he was disappointed in me.

'I live for it, me. 'S what I get up for. Nothing like the first fucking ciggie of the day.'

'Know what you mean.'

I stubbed it out half-smoked, and got back on the bus. Even the cigarette smoke hadn't masked the smell of him. From that day on, every time I lit up a fag I thought I could smell the nauseating BO of Fat Frank from the bus. If I could find him again one day, I'd have to thank him. He was, eventually, instrumental in helping me give up.

We arrived at Sydney just after lunchtime. By now I was fidgety, tired, bored, agitated and cross. Why the hell had I let Joe talk me into this? I could have been here hours ago, bright and fresh from a nice short flight. The only Australian culture I'd absorbed during these eighteen hours of purgatory had been the courting rituals of the Lesser Spotted Aussie Male when confronted with anything, of any nationality, looking remotely female – which, given the unisex plumage of shorts, T-shirts and boots, wasn't always immediately obvious. I spent longer than necessary in the Ladies at Sydney Central Station, waiting until the last of my travelling companions from the bus had gone off in search of their hostels. Then I went to buy myself a cup of tea, got my phone out and rang the first hotel on Joe's list. The Winchester. He'd marked it with an asterisk and I remembered him recommending it particularly, but I'd have gone for it anyway because it was the first one. I was in no mood for working my way down lists.

One booking and one short taxi ride later, I found myself staring up at the marble and glass frontage of one of the poshest hotels I'd ever been near, never mind stayed in. Having punished me by sending me on the long distance bus, Joe had obviously decided it would be a good laugh to see how much money I was really made of. Well, sod it – all the time I'd stayed at Patrick and Brenda's I'd hardly made a dent in my lottery winnings; it would have offended Brenda's pride too much to take any money from me. So why shouldn't I splash out a little now? I probably wouldn't be staying for long.

A doorman in traditional grey garb pushed the revolving doors for me with a flourish before I could even touch them.

'Thanks,' I muttered uneasily. I put my bags down on the vast tiled floor of the reception area, where real trees grew out of enclosures of polished grey pebbles and real birds twittered and preened colourfully among their highest branches where they did a dappling job on the sunlight coming through the sloping glass roof. Soft music was being played by a lady in an evening dress seated at a piano in the far corner, accompanied by the tinkling sound of water trickling from a green-lit waterfall into a kidney-shaped indoor pool (complete with carp). For a minute I thought I'd stepped through the wrong door and ended up in heaven, but then I remembered I'd have failed the admission procedure even if I'd acquired the necessary state of decease without being aware of it. My bags were promptly whisked away from me onto a trolley and I was directed towards the reception desk with silent, beaming gestures by a guy in a short blue jacket who, if he bowed any nearer the floor, could have achieved a gold medal in contortions at the next Olympics.

'You have a reservation, madam?' asked the receptionist in tones of hushed awe as if I were a visiting dignitary from a very powerful neighbouring country.

'Yes. I just phoned from the ... er ... from the station. Madeleine Goodchild.'

She consulted the book on her desk very briefly, and then looked back at me with raised eyebrows. Here it comes. I'm obviously in the wrong joint. Should have been the little poky place next door, I knew it.

'Miss Goodchild!' she exclaimed and, to my embarrassment, reached across the desk and shook my hand. 'I'm delighted to meet you. If you'll just bear with me for two minutes, I'll page Mr Curtis to come and meet you.'

Mr Curtis? Who the raging fuck was he? Was I supposed to know him? Had she mistaken me for someone attending a business convention, somebody perhaps who was late for a meeting or – God forbid – a lecture with Mr Curtis's company?

'Excuse me,' I began timidly. 'I'm sorry, but I—'

Before I could get any further, there was a 'ding' of the lift arriving, and a 'Good afternoon!' rang out across the reception area as a very tall, very upright man with very little hair marched purposefully towards me, took my hand in his with an unnervingly hard, dry handshake and repeated: 'Delighted to meet you, Miss Goodchild – or – may I? – Madeleine. Henry Curtis.'

'Maddy,' I said faintly. 'How do you do, Henry.'

So maybe I was a visiting dignitary from a very powerful neighbouring country. How should I know?

'If you'll permit me, Maddy, shall I show you to your room? And perhaps en route', he laughed modestly at the cleverness of his French accent, 'I could point out one or two of the rather exceptional features of the hotel?'

An inspector. That was it. They'd got me confused with an inspector from the hotel star gradings people. Or from one of those books – *Australia for Travellers* or *Where To Stay Down Under* – that give you a good write-up if you have nice lined curtains in the room, fruit on the breakfast table and top-ups of coffee without being asked.

'OK – why not?' I agreed, thinking it less awkward at this stage to make a few appropriate comments about the dining facilities than to admit to being an impostor. I followed Henry Curtis into the lift (carpeted, with watercolours of Sydney Harbour on the walls and soft music coming out of the ceiling), and smiled at him awkwardly as we were whisked smoothly upwards ... no, hang on. We were going downwards! He saw the surprise on my face and laughed his already-irritating little silent laugh.

'I thought you'd like to see the Health Club Spa, madam. I mean, Maddy,' he said, in a tone that implied he knew I was going to be overwhelmed with gratitude. Health Club Spa? I was wrong about being in heaven. This was beginning to sound more like the other place.

'Great,' I said with badly concealed sarcasm. 'Thanks.'

We stepped out of the lift again, and the mixed fragrances of chlorine, perfumed oils and body lotion hit my sinuses like a snort of cocaine, making me sneeze violently.

'This way,' said Henry, leading me through a luxuriously furnished changing area without appearing to notice as I sniffed, rubbed my nose and rummaged around in my pockets for a tissue, 'is our newly refurbished Fitness Centre. Open daily from eight till six, staffed by our team of fully qualified *Fitness Trainers*', (he stressed these last two words to underline their apparent importance). I looked with a sinking heart at the objects of loathing from my previous life in England: the treadmill, the bikes, the step machine, the Chinese torture device. I looked with equal dislike at the fitness trainers with their little fit bums in their short little white shorts and their bulging biceps displayed by their tight-fitting cutaway vest tops. I turned to Henry Curtis to ask him why the fucking bollocks he was bringing me down here to show me the most depressing sights I could imagine, when I was supposed to be on my holidays, but he'd already marched on ahead of me, leading me through another area of white sofas, mirrors and hairdryers where women with heavy suntans were sitting wrapped in several large white towels each, studying their toenails and fingernails. I hurried past them, half expecting them to rise slowly from their sofas and come after me ... down some steps, through another door, and –

'There!' exclaimed Henry, throwing out his arm in a gesture of immense pride. 'The pool!'

It wasn't huge, but it was certainly a lot bigger than your average hotel pool. At one end, a kidney-shaped area to match the fishpond on the ground floor was designed for families, with wide steps and shallow blue water and a little island within paddling reach of the kids, where a statue of a shocked-looking fish gushed water from his mouth back into the pool. The other side was a properly marked-out lap pool, clean and clear and inviting in its empty stillness.

'I knew you'd be impressed,' said Henry smugly, watching my face.

'Doesn't anyone use it?' I asked.

'Oh, yes. But it doesn't get too crowded, of course, because of the Aquatic Centre.'

'The what?'

'The Olympic pool. You didn't realise? It's just opposite the hotel. This is where the swimmers stayed in the 2000 Olympics, Maddy. I thought you realised that's why Joe Appleby suggested you stayed here.'

I should have known. It was obvious really, wasn't it? A friend of Joe's. Someone off his list of acquaintances – the same list that he gave to Sophie, no doubt, when she was visiting Sydney. And I suppose he knew people at the Aquatic Centre, too. All I needed was my own personal swimming trainer and I'd have no excuse whatsoever.

'It's very nice.' I smiled to Henry, who was practically jumping from one foot to another waiting for me to say something. 'In fact, it's so nice, I think if you'll just show me to my room, I'll find my swimming costume straight away and come down here for a swim. Just what I need after my journey.'

Rubbing his hands together with pleasure, Henry led me back to the lift and took me up to Room 404, which was probably about the size of my house back in England, with almost as much furniture and certainly more in the way of bathroom facilities, where he finally took his leave of me with much hand-shaking and obsequious nodding and murmurings about hoping everything was to my satisfaction.

Ten minutes later I was starting fifty lengths of the beautiful, completely empty swimming pool and wondering what the hell this was all about.

Chapter 19

Trust me, there's a lot to be said for living in the lap of luxury. I wouldn't ever have said I was materialistic or spoilt, but I think I could eventually, given time, get used to having someone pandering to my every need and treating me like royalty.

I spent my first week or so in Sydney just *luxuriating*. I ordered breakfast in my room. I sent my washing to be laundered. I called cabs to take me to the shops and spent more money on clothes in one week than I normally spent in a year, telling myself that I couldn't stay in one of the smartest hotels in Sydney looking like a backpacker who'd just crawled out of the Bush. I ate four extravagant courses every night in the hotel restaurant, served by charming, discreet waiters who made me feel as though it was the most natural and desirable thing in the world to be dining alone in such sumptuous circumstances rather than feeling like a social pariah with no mates. I had my hair cut and coloured in the hotel salon. I had my nails done, my skin toned, moisturised, scrubbed and pummelled. I soaked in the hot tub and sweated in the sauna. And I swam. Three or four times a day, increasing my distance and my speed barely perceptibly day by day, feeling my muscles become taut and strong again, enjoying the power of my body moving through the water, thinking about nothing in particular as I turned, and swam, and turned again, and swam, and worked up an appetite for my next meal, and became fit.

Sophie e-mailed me from Chile towards the end of the first week, lyrical with excitement about the sights they'd been seeing in a little place called San Pedro, where the altitude was nearly three thousand metres, the houses were made of mud, the surrounding deserts were sparkling white and the sunsets purple, red and gold.

'How are you enjoying Sydney? Have you seen the Opera House yet? Or the Bridge?' she finished.

I sighed and stared out of the window of my hotel room. I supposed it was time I got off my arse and ventured out to see the sights. Why did I feel so reluctant? Could it be that this place had become a comfortable oasis in the desert of my otherwise arid life? It was fine to take a little break from reality, wasn't it? Plenty of time for sightseeing once I'd had a little breather...

It was early November and very hot in the city streets outside my air-conditioned cocoon. Inside, day passed after peaceful, calm, ordered day. Get up, swim, eat, rest, relax, swim again, eat again, go to bed. I was lulled and anaesthetised by the sameness, the evenness, the pleasantness of it. Every night I fell asleep thinking: Maybe tomorrow I'll go out and do something different. Every morning I thought: Nah, can't be arsed.

It's easy to work things out when you look back. Any fool can see I was having some kind of a crisis, there. I wouldn't go so far as to say it was like my spell of depression after Sophie was born. Apart from anything else, I wasn't having sex with young lads at the swimming pool this time. In fact, I wasn't even thinking about sex at all. I think the experience with Patrick had finished me off. It wasn't so much that I was sick of sex, or sick of men, or even sick of life. I think I was ... sick of myself. I wanted to be someone else for a while. I wanted to lie low, and be left alone, and be quiet, and well behaved. Surprised? Not half as much as I was, when I finally realised what I was doing.

Two weeks into my stay at the Winchester, I emerged

295

from having a swim and a hot shower in the Health Club Spa and was on my way back to my room for a rest before dinner when the receptionist beckoned me and told me, in the hushed tones of respect I'd become so used to that I'd finally stopped looking over my shoulder to see who she might be talking to, that Mr Joseph Appleby was waiting for me in the Green Lounge.

'What are you doing here?'

'Nice to see you, too, Maddy.' He got to his feet and looked me up and down. 'You're looking great. I like the new look.'

'Thank you.' I touched my damp hair awkwardly. 'I thought it'd be easier very short, for swimming.'

'You like the pool?'

'Yes, it's very...' I stopped. This was farcical. Why had he turned up here? What made him think I wanted to talk to him about my haircut, or the swimming pool? What made him think I even wanted to see him? 'Why are you here?' I repeated stonily.

'I'm on business, if that's OK with you.'

'Oh.' I frowned. I wanted to ask what kind. Why did a swimming instructor need to travel halfway across the continent on business? Was he perhaps visiting the Aquatic Centre over the road? Was he training some new Olympic hopeful? I didn't want him to think I was interested, so I merely shrugged and asked, as if we were polite strangers meeting in a bar, how long he was staying.

'A few days, probably. Perhaps a week.'

Maybe time I moved on, then.

'Have you been to the Opera House yet?'

If one more person asked me if I'd seen the Opera House or the Bridge, I'd probably throw myself off it.

'Or the Harbour Bridge?'

'No, but I'm thinking of throwing myself off it.'

He laughed. 'Want me to come with you? I could hold your shoes while you jump.'

I glared at him. What was going on here? What did he think he was doing, turning up here looking for me, irritatingly guessing correctly, I supposed, that I'd have chosen the first hotel on his list, intruding into my peaceful self-enforced isolation with his comments about my hair and his quips and his jokes and his maleness. I didn't want him around. I thought we'd established that in Brisbane. I thought, in fact, that we'd established it twenty-odd years ago. What does it take to get rid of a person?

'Piss off,' I told him morosely.

'OK, I will. After dinner.'

'What?'

'I've booked us a table in the restaurant. Eight o'clock. Does that give you enough time to dry your hair?'

I wanted to say 'How dare you!' in an outraged voice but I felt too ridiculous. 'I don't want—' I began, but stopped, floundering awkwardly and crossly for the right words. What didn't I want? Company? I hadn't had any for two weeks. The sound of my own voice was beginning to startle me. Or was it just his company I hated the thought of? 'What makes you think I want to have dinner with you?' I managed to come out with eventually, sounding uncomfortably too much like a moody teenager sulking in her bedroom.

'I didn't even think about it, to be honest,' he responded perfectly calmly. 'It was just what I wanted, so I booked it.' He glanced at my outraged expression and laughed out loud. 'You know what we men are like, Maddy. Selfish to the core! I'll be at the table in the window, in the far corner, at eight o'clock. If you don't want to join me, it's no skin off my nose.'

I began to walk out of the lounge, my shoulders stiff with offence, my mind rigid with determination that not only would I not join him for dinner, I would be getting the hell out of this place as soon as my bags were packed.

'I'll just see you for breakfast tomorrow instead,' he added.

I looked back at him as I left the room. He laughed again and gave me a little wave.

'You're very sure of yourself,' I told him after we'd ordered our starters.

'Not at all. I thought you were going to hit me again, if you want to know. The bruises have only just faded from the first time.'

I ignored this and fiddled with my fork on the table.

'I'm only eating with you because I'm a bit bored with my own company.'

'Fair enough. I kind of figured two weeks would probably do it.'

I stared at him, annoyance mingled with a kind of fascination at my own inability to walk away from this situation. Why hadn't I packed my bags, as I'd promised myself, as soon as I got back to my room after our meeting this afternoon? Why, instead, had I spent longer than normal doing my hair and make-up and putting on one of the new dresses I'd bought in one of the most expensive shops in Sydney? It was just to show him, wasn't it; just to let him see that I didn't need him turning up like a character from an out-of-print novel, interfering in my life, booking tables for dinner and offering to hold my shoes while I committed suicide. I'd moved on, thank you very much, moved on to bigger and better things, to hotels where I was treated with deference as if I was someone rich and important, to dress shops where the assistants stood simpering in admiration as I preened in their most expensive outfits and ordered two at a time to be delivered to my room in a taxi.

'You look very nice tonight,' he said, breaking into my thoughts as the waiter deposited our first course and backed away reverently. 'New dress?'

'Yes.'

I waited for him to ask me where I'd bought it. I wanted to see his eyebrows raised in recognition of the class of person he was dining with.

298

'Probably about time you had something half-decent to wear,' he said instead.

'Well, if I was going to spend the rest of my time in Australia bumming around on those awful buses you recommended,' I retorted, stung, 'I'd only need shorts and a rucksack.'

'Mm. Nice!' he smiled. 'You can wear your shorts tomorrow when we go sightseeing.'

'Who said anything about that?'

'Unless you'd prefer to come over to the Aquatic Centre with me? I presume you've made good use of the hotel pool for the past two weeks? Got yourself into shape again? Worked off some of the flab?'

'Flab! Let me tell you, I've been swimming about five miles a day, every day. There isn't an inch of flab...'

'Excellent. So are you up for it, then?'

'Up for what?'

'Moving on to the Olympic pool. Doing a bit of real training.'

'With you, I suppose?' I sneered.

''S up to you,' he shrugged, taking a sip of his wine. 'I've only got the morning free; like I said, I'm here on business.' He stopped, and glanced at my untouched glass of wine. 'Aren't you drinking?'

I looked at the glass myself, with a shock of realisation.

'No. I don't seem to be, do I.'

'Or smoking?'

'Not so much. It's making me feel a bit sick.'

I told him about Fat Frank on the bus and his BO, and by the time we'd finished laughing about it, our plates had been taken away and our main courses delivered, and I told him a bit about what Sophie and Ryan were doing in Chile, and finally, only because he was listening and not interrupting and it was good, after two weeks on my own, to talk to someone again – anyone, even an ex-husband with an annoying habit of turning up repeatedly when I thought I'd seen the last of him – I told him about Rachel, and the way

299

we'd argued, and how she'd refused to answer my phone calls and my e-mails and had cut me out of her life completely. Through all this, he listened carefully, eating his dinner and nodding occasionally, looking at me so intently that I was almost fooled into believing he was interested and concerned.

Almost.

But don't worry. I hadn't forgotten that he'd offered to hold my shoes while I jumped.

He stayed at the Winchester for another week, during which time we duly visited the Opera House and the Sydney Harbour Bridge (without jumping off it), and had coffee in a very nice restaurant overlooking the view of the harbour. It was here that we finally had The Talk. The talk I'd been dreading, of course, ever since we came face to face at Brenda's garden barbecue. I'd been carefully avoiding it, steering the conversation skilfully away every time it looked like nudging towards anything about the break-up of our marriage. I mean, why would I want to talk about that? It was dead, gone, buried, history. Nothing to be gained from digging it up and starting a post-mortem on it after all these years. The stink of its horrible old bones would be unbearable.

But it sneaked into the conversation unexpectedly by the back door, while I was lulled into the false security of a discussion about my travels in Europe. Joe was encouraging me in the telling of all my funny stories – some true, some a tiny bit embellished. He laughed about Rachel in France, with her sudden new interest in food and men. He laughed about the speed cops in Belgium. He even laughed about Tom turning up in Lille and threatening to divorce his wife.

'And then there was the whole thing with the drugs, in Amsterdam!' I said, gaily, conscious that I was showing off, enjoying the fact that I had his attention.

'Yeah?' He smiled.

'Yeah. Well, Rachel wasn't really up for it, but you know me – anything immoral, illegal or unhealthy and I'm your girl—'

'Why do you always do that?' he interrupted.

'Always do what?'

'Put on this act – the whole Bad Girl thing. Look how terrible I am. Look how bad, how immoral, how corrupt...' He paused and gave me a very direct look. 'You're not really like that.'

'Oh no?' I raised my eyebrows at him meaningfully. 'You of all people should know different.'

That was exactly what I didn't mean to say. I so didn't want to start that conversation.

'I don't think it's very useful going back over old ground.'

See? He didn't want to discuss it either. So how come we were?

'We weren't much more than children back then, Maddy. Neither of us behaved exactly honourably, did we, but we should have put it all behind us long ago.'

'Yeah. Well, yes, obviously, I have put it behind me, but—'

'I don't think so.'

And what the fuck do you know about it? Excuse me, but you've only just waltzed back into my life, so I don't really think you're qualified to make such sweeping statements about my psychological profile.

'I think, if you don't mind me saying so,' he went on without pausing for long enough to let me mind him saying so, 'I think you've been punishing yourself for years with this Bad Girl label around your neck.'

Punishing myself? Wasn't that what Rachel said about me too? What was this – a conspiracy?

'You think you're something special, something different, because you wrecked a marriage that was never going to work anyway, but—'

'What do you mean, never going to work?! It would have ... if it wasn't for me.'

301

'Of course it wouldn't. We should never have got married. We both knew that really. It was only because of Sophie, wasn't it.'

'Yeah, but if I hadn't been such a cheap little tramp, messing around like that.'

'If it hadn't been you, it would have been me.'

CLANG. CRASH. WHOOSH. FLASH.

OK, there wasn't actually a clashing of symbols. There wasn't actually a bright flash lighting up the sky or stars shooting across the horizon. It just felt like it. *It would have been me.*

'It would have been you?' I whispered.

'Of course. Eventually.' He grinned at me across the table. His hands hovered over his empty coffee cup and for a minute, just one ridiculous minute, I thought he was going to grab hold of my hands and hold them; but instead, he leant back in his chair and put his hands in his pockets as if they needed restraining. 'Do you think, at eighteen, nineteen, I would have put up with that for long? Living in one room at your mum's, coming home every night to a moody wife and a screaming baby...'

'But you never said! I thought it was just me!'

'It was hell on fucking earth. The only reason I sent you out at night was to get some time to myself. I was sick of the sight of you.'

'What!'

'It never crossed my mind for a minute that other boys were still going to find you attractive. I was so full of my own bloody disappointment with life.'

'But you always seemed so ... so good. So patient, so ... so ...'

'Boring? Smug?' He shook his head, still smiling. 'We can all put on acts, Maddy. Mine was the Trapped Husband. I awarded myself a gold medal for what I saw as my self-sacrifice: marrying someone I didn't really love, just because of the baby.'

'Didn't really love?'

He met my eyes, and for a full minute we stared at each other across that table, in that restaurant with its famous view of the sparkling waters of Sydney Harbour, its noble bridge set against the cobalt-blue sky of an Australian summer, and, for the first time since I was nineteen, I recognised the truth.

'You weren't a Bad Girl, Maddy,' he told me very softly. 'You were just a Girl, too young to be a wife and a mother. And don't ever think I was a Good Boy. I used your infidelity as an excuse to do a runner. It wasn't anything to be proud of.' He stopped, swallowed, drummed his fingers on the table for a few minutes and then added, 'It took me quite a few months of expensive therapy to get my head around all this. So please don't tell me it's shit. I really needed the money at the time.'

'Maybe I should have had the therapy too,' I said, my voice wobbling just a bit.

'Probably.'

'I always wished I could have said sorry to you. I thought it would have made me feel better. Less like the Wicked Witch.'

'Me too. For running away. Especially for abandoning Sophie.'

'Well, then. Sorry, I suppose.'

'Yeah, I guess so. Sorry too.'

It felt a bit yucky at that point, so I added very quickly:

'Let's go and have a walk over that bridge, then. Now I don't have to throw myself off?'

'Unless I push you,' he added with a smile.

And, because we were both embarrassed by what had been said, and didn't want to think any more about it until we were on our own, when we could go over it in our minds and dissect it properly, and weigh every word, and decide whether or not we had been completely honest and whether or not the whole conversation had made any difference, made any impact, we retreated into jokes, and digs, and insults, for the rest of the morning. Much safer than all that

303

scary stuff about long overdue apologies. Although I must admit, I did feel better for it.

Every day that week we visited the Olympic pool over the road, where Joe started me on an intensive life-saving course.

'You'll have to register for a proper course when you get home. This is just an introduction,' he said, watching me get my breath back after the fastest timed swim I'd done so far. 'But you'll have no problem completing it.'

'You don't think so?' I gasped.

'Absolutely not. As long as you don't let your fitness go again.'

'Well, thank you,' I said sarcastically. 'If I do, I'll just book myself into a posh hotel with an empty pool again for two weeks, shall I?'

'Why not? As long as your lottery money hasn't run out.'

Shit. Money. I forgot about money.

I suppose if you're a naturally very wealthy person – say a film star, or a famous sports personality, or some sort of princess or highness person, you never actually have to worry about reaching that point where it all runs out. You can just go on and on and on, buying ridiculously expensive dresses you're hardly ever going to wear, and staying in impossibly lavish hotels eating their oysters and their steaks and their strawberries off their silver dishes, and wrapping yourself in their six-inch-thick white fluffy towels – and never have to phone, holding your breath, for an automated bank balance that pours the cold water of consciousness over the enjoyment of your little luxuries.

'I can't believe I've been so bloody stupid,' I complained to Joe on his last evening. We'd been having dinner together every night, despite all my promises to myself. Well, it was just someone to talk to, wasn't it. And I wouldn't have to see him any more after tonight. 'I've been living in this ... this ridiculously expensive hotel, spending money like water, acting like ... like...'

'Like a lottery winner?'

'Yes, but look – it's not funny!' I snapped. 'I didn't win *huge* amounts of money. I was supposed to be doing this trip on some sort of a budget. I wanted to have a bit left, when I got home, for ... well, for curtains, and carpets, and stuff.'

'Boring!'

'I know.' I looked at him sharply. 'But instead, I haven't even got enough to go on to Melbourne!'

'That's no great loss. Nothing much to see there. Stay here for a bit longer. I can tell you where all the best beaches are.'

'You're not listening, are you!' I snapped. 'I've only just about got enough for the hotel bill. And it's your bloody fault, anyway.'

'How do you work that out?'

'You put this hotel on the top of the list, knowing perfectly well I'd come here, without warning me it was going to be so... so...'

'So nice?'

'Yes, of course it's nice. But now I've spent more than I should have done, and ... well, now it's all over.' I looked at him glumly. 'I'll have to go back.'

He looked at me in silence for a moment, his head on one side as if considering this.

'Well, there you go,' he said eventually. 'All good things come to an end. You'll be home for Christmas, then.'

I don't know what I wanted him to say – something reassuring, something to cheer me up, or just something sarcastic along the lines of having to pull myself together and get on with life the same as everyone else. But – home for Christmas? Fucking Christmas? Christmas with no family and no friends – when Sophie was in some godforsaken place full of mud huts in a desert in South America, and I'd dumped Tom without a backward glance, and Rachel was refusing to talk to me? Christmas with no money left for presents, even if I had anyone to buy them for? Christmas

305

with no job, no cheery merry work colleagues to go out to the pub with? Christmas in cold, dark, damp, dismal England in the same old house with its horrible wallpaper and worn-out carpets? What was there to look forward to about that? And the awful thing was, I felt so utterly miserable at the thought of being home for Christmas that I couldn't even answer him. I couldn't summon up the energy to deliver the stinging riposte I'd have liked to sling back at him. I couldn't, actually, even open my mouth to say a single word. But it might have had something to do with the bloody great lump in my throat.

I put down my knife and fork, swallowed a few times, took a few sips of my water (yes, water), and fought back the urge to walk away and go and shut myself in my room. I didn't want to give him the pleasure of remembering me, on the last night we were together, as a sulky spoilt brat who'd spent all her money on silly extravagances and then cried when she had to go home. Trying to maintain my dignity, I picked up the cutlery again, cut myself another mouthful of fish, and began, painfully, to chew it. When I looked up he was watching me.

'Things will work out,' he said very gently.

No idea what the fuck he was talking about.

In the middle of the night, I tried again to phone Rachel. I hadn't even stopped to work out the time difference, but while I listened to the ringing tone, listened and listened and imagined it ringing away in her kitchen with nobody answering it, I thought: If it's night time here, it must be daytime there. I knew it wasn't really quite that simple. And I knew that if it was daytime, anyway, Rachel would be at work. But, as far as I was concerned, that phone ringing and ringing and ringing on the other side of the world with nobody answering it just said it all. I had nobody in England who cared about me. How could I face going back?

*

Joe was leaving for Brisbane early the next morning. I purposely stayed in bed until I knew he'd have gone, then I presented myself at reception and asked for my bill in what I hoped to be the confident tone of voice of someone who had no worries whatsoever about paying it. There was a young girl on duty. She tapped a few keys on her computer, stared at the screen for a moment, glanced up at me, tapped a couple more keys, and finally, with a beaming smile and in a very polite voice, asked me if I'd mind waiting for a moment while she just checked something with her manager. I went and sat next to the carp pond, watching her as she made her call. She looked over at me, nodding as she spoke, and I looked away quickly, pretending to find the fish overwhelmingly fascinating. My heart was going nineteen to the dozen. Had I spent even more than I thought I had in the restaurant? Maybe I should have only had two courses every night. Why did I have to be such a pig? Or perhaps my room was even more expensive than it said in the tariff? Were there other charges I didn't know about? Perhaps there was a hidden fee for the use of the swimming pool. Was I going to have to offer to wash up for the next six weeks in order to pay my bill? Come to think of it, at least I wouldn't have to go home yet...

'Miss Goodchild?'

I got up and strolled back to the reception desk, not wanting to look too worried.

'Sorry to keep you waiting, madam.' She pushed some paperwork across the desk towards me. 'If you could just sign here? And here? Thank you, madam. There's nothing to pay.'

'Nothing?' I stopped mid-signature, holding the pen in the air as if it was a magic wand I was about to wave. 'Nothing to pay?' I repeated stupidly. 'But I ... Surely I ...'

Not that I was about to argue. But they must obviously have made a very serious mistake here, or else the manager was suffering from some kind of mental health problem.

'Courtesy of Mr Appleby, madam. Everything taken care of.'

'What?' I dropped the pen. 'Oh, no, really – I don't think that's possible. I think it might be a ... well, I think he might be having a laugh. I don't think he really meant...'

'Yes, seriously, madam. It's certainly not a joke. If you'd just like to sign.'

'No, come on, honestly.' I pushed the papers back towards her. 'I don't actually think this is on. I mean, I don't think you can possibly understand. He's my ex-husband. There's no way I can accept.'

'He was absolutely insistent, madam. Your stay here was always intended to be completely free of charge.'

'Free of charge? How can it be free of charge? He can't just say ...'

'He gave his orders, actually, madam.' She smiled at me charmingly. 'It's his privilege!'

Privilege? I stared at her, completely bemused. I still had the pen waving in mid-air, forgotten. How could it be a privilege?

'It is his hotel, after all.'

His hotel. His own fucking, bloody bollocking hotel. The pretty little receptionist was still smiling at me, waiting for my signature on her stupid papers.

'You did realise Mr Appleby owns this hotel?' she said sweetly.

Realise? Of course I didn't realise, you silly, grinning little person. If I'd realised, I'd never have come here. I'd never have set foot inside the poxy revolving doors. I'd never have eaten like a pig in his restaurant every night, or swum in his swimming pool, or slept in his – in his (I shuddered) bedroom!

'Of course I knew that,' I lied. 'But I still want to pay. I insist on paying!'

Her smile faded abruptly.

'Oh, but I'm afraid, madam, we don't have a facility for

308

that. You see, there's no bill, so there's really nothing to pay. Mr Appleby quite clearly left instructions . . .'

'Yes, you've already explained about Mr Appleby's instructions,' I said.

What was the point? She'd never understand, never in a million years, unless she lived long enough and unhappily enough to have been married, to have cocked it all up, to run into her ex-husband again on the other side of the world and the other side of her life, and to be patronised and insulted by him throwing a hotel at her.

'I hope it never happens to you,' I muttered as I signed the paper to check out.

'I'm sorry, madam?' she responded, looking worried.

'Probably best to stay single.'

She laughed, looking relieved that I now appeared to be joking rather than being a raging nutcase who wanted to pay for a free hotel room.

'And I'm not joking,' I added as I picked up my bags and headed for the revolving doors for the last time. Two men in uniforms dived towards me simultaneously to help me with my bags. 'Piss off,' I said mildly. 'I like carrying them.'

I gave him time to get back to Brisbane and then I phoned him every half-hour until he answered.

'I'm paying that bill,' I said as soon as I heard his voice.

'There is no bill. Don't take offence, Maddy. I just—'

'Too late. The offence has been taken. I want to pay. I'm not that bloody hard up.'

'No, but as you pointed out, it was my fault for recommending the Winchester; you'd never have stayed somewhere so expensive otherwise. So I'm just making amends. Now, maybe, you'll have enough money left to stay a bit longer, or go on somewhere else.'

'No! You don't get it, do you? It was my idea to come on this trip, with my money. If I'd wanted to be . . . well, to be financed by a man, I could have stayed with Tom and bloody married him and bloody moved to bloody Scotland.'

He laughed.

'Don't laugh!' I snapped. 'It was quite nice in Edinburgh. I could get used to it.'

'It'd be too cold for you! Please, Maddy, let's stop arguing.'

This took me so much by surprise that I couldn't think what to say for a minute.

'Well, you should have told me you owned the bloody hotel. How come you own a hotel, anyway? Do you make that much money from your swimming lessons?'

'No. I inherited it, actually, years ago when my dad died.'

'Oh. Sorry. I didn't know, obviously. . .'

'No. You never met my dad, did you? He and my mum split up when I was only young, and he came to live out here in Sydney. He'd always been in the catering business and he did well for himself – started his own company and made a lot of money, and—'

'So you were copying your dad? Coming out to Australia when we split up?'

'I came here to be with him, yes. I worked with him in the business for a while, but I kind of wanted to do something of my own, so I took the swimming and life-saving instructors' courses, and after Dad died I moved up to Brisbane. I'm happy doing what I'm doing. I employ a manager at the hotel. I just turn up when anything needs my attention.'

I thought about this for a minute. It must have been hard for Joe, losing his father after coming across the world to be reunited with him. But it didn't excuse the way he'd tricked me!

'You should at least have been honest with me. How do you think it made me feel when the receptionist told me? All that time. . . eating in the restaurant with you, and every-thing. I felt an absolute idiot.'

'Sorry. I thought it'd be better like that. Just two lonely people, stranded by circumstances in the same hotel, lost souls drifting together. . .'

'Don't you ever stop taking the piss?'

'Occasionally,' he responded seriously 'Usually when I'm totally bored with the conversation.'

'Is that supposed to make me feel better?'

'I hope so.'

For a minute neither of us seemed to know what to say. And then, finally, with a great effort, I said:

'I suppose I have to say thank you, then.'

'No problem. My pleasure. Are you flying straight back to London now?'

'I guess so. I have to go back sooner or later, and look for a job, and buy some new curtains, and . . . all that stuff.'

'Real life.'

'Yeah. It's a bummer, isn't it.'

'I'm glad we had a chance to talk, Maddy.'

'Me too,' I said, still squirming with reluctance and embarrassment.

'I'll be keeping in touch with Sophie – you know? Are you OK with that?'

'I suppose so,' I said, even more grudgingly.

'No hard feelings, then?'

No hard feelings. So what was this hard lump in my chest all about? I think, as far as relationships with ex-spouses from many years ago are concerned, this was perhaps just one question too many.

'Bye, Joe,' I said. And ever so quietly, ever so gently, I just laid down the phone.

And got straight on with organising my flight home.

Chapter 20

I spent the last few days of my time in Australia in a little guest house in the outer suburbs of Sydney. It was important to me, somehow, to spend as little money as possible now – despite (or maybe because of) the fact that those luxurious weeks I'd spent at the Winchester had turned out to be courtesy of Joe. I didn't do much during that last week. I went out for walks on my own. I ate plain, cheap, meals in a nearby restaurant, without alcohol. I read my book. And I e-mailed Sophie.

It was on one of those occasions, logging onto the computer for my allotted ten minutes in the local internet café, that I found Rachel's message in my in-box. By now it'd been so long since I'd heard from her that seeing her name actually made the hairs stand up on the back of my neck. I clicked quickly to open the message.

Hello Maddy.

I hope you get this message before you leave. I've heard on the grapevine that you'll be arriving home on 5th December. This is just to let you know I'll be there to meet you at Heathrow.

See you then.

Rach

I stared at the message for so long, the words began to blur on the screen and I had to rub my eyes several times to be

sure I wasn't inventing them. 'I'll be there to meet you'??
'See you then'??? What, with no mention of the fact that
she'd been studiously ignoring me for about two months?
What the hell...? I clicked on 'Reply' and typed, quickly and
furiously:

*What grapevine? Who told you I was coming home? Who
said I wanted you to come and meet me?*

Then I thought better of it and deleted it. What was the
point? I'd wanted to make up with her, hadn't I? I'd sent all
those creepy begging messages, pleading with her to forgive
me and be my friend again; so it really didn't make a lot of
sense, now she'd finally made the first move, to reject her
out of hand just because she'd left it so late. Too late? Or was
it never too late? Maybe I needed to swallow my pride and
just be happy about it.

Dear Rachel
  *Nice to hear from you. I suppose Sophie has told you
I'm coming home. That would be very nice to see you at
Heathrow if you're sure it isn't putting you out. I'm afraid
my flight is due in at the unearthly hour of 5.50 am, British
time. I realise you have to go to work that day, so if this is
difficult, don't worry; I'll get a cab.*
  Maddy

I read and reread this message until my time on the computer
was up, forcing me to press 'Send' in a hurry at the last
minute, immediately regretting the strange formal tone I'd
adopted, as if I was writing to a distant relative or a business
colleague.

Stupid, stupid, stupid. She'd probably take one look at
that message and change her mind about bothering to come
to Heathrow. I should have made it more personal. I should
have asked how she was, how she'd been, what she'd been
up to. I should have taken the bull by the horns and asked if

she'd forgiven me now. Or demanded to know why she'd taken so long over it. Anything, anything rather than that pathetically proper, standoffish little message that smacked of offence being taken, and the hand of friendship being pushed away. Well, there you go. She'd made an approach, and I'd blown it. *C'est la vie*. One more thing I'd cocked up. I went back to my guest house, lay on my bed and buried myself in my book again. Suddenly, I'd had enough of Australia. I'd had enough of the heat, and the humidity, and even the casual friendliness of the people and their ever-questioning accent. I wanted to go home.

Three days later, I wondered why I'd ever complained about the heat.

Heathrow Airport at six o'clock on a December morning, when you've just spent three months in the lead-up to the Australian summer, is not something to be experienced with a heady rush of joy. I shivered so hard, my knees were knocking together and I had to clench my jaws to stop my teeth chattering. The wait for our baggage seemed interminable. I wanted a pee, and for the first time in weeks I wanted a cigarette, but I didn't want to walk away from the luggage carousel in case I missed my bags and had to wait for them to go round again.

'This is the pits, isn't it,' complained a very heavily tanned woman with very bright blonde hair who looked about sixty. 'Every time I go out to Oz to stay with my sister, I say, That's it – I'm going to move out there. I don't know why I don't do it.' She sighed and scanned the carousel hopelessly for any sign of our baggage. 'It's not as if there's anything here for me. Bloody cold, bloody dirty, bloody delays everywhere. Where's our bleeding luggage?'

'I don't know. I think...'

'Everywhere you look, muggings and rape. No one's safe. You could be murdered in your own bleeding bed. And as for the NHS...'

I made an excuse and moved away, round to the other side

of the carousel, where at last I identified the first few suit-cases from our flight appearing from the tunnel. With a lifting of my spirits I saw my own bags coming through fairly quickly. Once I'd got them on the trolley and managed to stop off at the toilets on the way through to customs, I was beginning to feel better, despite the warnings of the prophet of doom at the carousel. I didn't think I was likely to get mugged, raped or murdered. I didn't think things looked any dirtier or more dangerous than before I went away. It might be cold, but I'd probably get used to it again. I was home. Surprisingly, I was *glad* to be.

'Maddy! Over here!'

Not only hadn't I seen Rachel for over three months – for two months I hadn't even heard her voice. She was lucky I recognised her. Actually, judging by the surprise she was trying to hide as she looked me up and down, I seemed to be lucky she recognised *me*.

We hugged, briefly and without holding each other too closely – almost as if we had a sheet of very fragile glass in between us.

'Glad to be back?' she asked me brightly. The brightness was false, like glittery Christmas tinsel.

'Yes – yes, I am, apart from the cold!'

We pushed the luggage trolley together, one each side, our hands twitching slightly as they touched. I was aware that she was watching me, looking at me sideways with a slight frown, like there was something she wasn't quite sure about. Something she didn't quite understand.

'You've lost weight,' she said eventually.

She didn't make it sound like a compliment.

'Not really. Maybe just *toned up* a bit. You know, like you always said I should.'

'But you haven't been to the gym, have you, surely! You must have been doing some exercise...'

'Yes, a bit. Not the gym. Swimming. Australia's got a great climate for swimming.'

'Good. Good for you.'

I wasn't sure if she was being sarcastic. For years, I'd got so used to Rachel being the healthy one, the sensible one, the *good* one, that it was kind of strange to admit to her that I'd improved myself a little. I felt a bit like a delinquent child who'd been caught out doing something exceptionally noble and charitable. It was kind of embarrassing.

'Don't worry,' I said, awkwardly, manoeuvring the trolley onto the escalator. 'I still drink and swear, and I still don't eat fucking broccoli.'

'Well, that's a relief,' she said with a faint smile.

'So if you want a night at the pub, I'm still your man.'

'OK. Only I still drink slimline tonic. And I still don't eat salted peanuts.'

'That's a relief,' I echoed, and we both managed a laugh as we went out of the terminal building into the sharp cold of the December morning.

But I had an uncomfortable feeling that we were fooling ourselves if we tried to pretend that nothing had changed, because obviously something had. Good friends don't cut each other dead for two months and then just get together, hug like they're holding cut-glass ornaments in their arms, laugh nervously together as if they're meeting for the first time – and never bother to find out what the fuck it was all about.

'What the fuck was it all about, then?' I asked loudly and deliberately as I settled myself in the passenger seat of her car and she started the ignition.

'Sorry?'

'Don't let's pretend, Rachel. There's been something very wrong between us. Probably my fault – I realise that. If everything's OK again now, that's great. But I think we need to clear the air, don't we?'

Slowly, and in silence, she pulled out of the airport car park and turned onto the approach road to the motorway.

'I'd rather just leave it for now, if you don't mind,' she said eventually.

'For now? What, till later? Till tomorrow? When, then? When are we going to discuss it?'

'I don't know. Maddy, I'm sorry about how it's been. OK? Can we just leave it at that?'

She looked uncomfortable and miserable. Oh, what the hell? I was curious: curious about why she'd been so angry with me, why she'd stayed angry for so long, and why she'd suddenly decided now to be sorry. But maybe my curiosity wasn't worth making her squirm. I'd probably find out eventually.

'OK,' I said more gently. 'I'm sorry about it too – but at least we're friends again now, yeah?'

She smiled back at me gratefully. I thought she still looked a bit uneasy. But maybe it was just the traffic.

The next day was a Saturday. I'd tried, and failed, to have a lie-in. I'd done nothing all the previous day, after Rachel dropped me home, but I still went to bed at ten o'clock feeling knackered, and now I was awake early, tossing and turning in the strangeness of my own bed. The central heating was on full blast and I wasn't used to the noise it made. Eventually I got up and made myself a mug of coffee, and suddenly there was Rachel at the door.

'Did I get you up?'

'No. Been awake since about half past six.'

'Jet lag?' She walked past me into the kitchen and helped herself to a coffee.

'I don't know. Can't ever remember whether you're supposed to get jet lagged on the way out or on the way back. It does my head in trying to work it out.'

'Well, whatever. It obviously must mess up your body clock.'

'I suppose.'

I watched her moving about my kitchen with the easy carelessness of an old friend, going to the fridge, pouring milk into her coffee, putting the spoon in the sink, perching herself on a stool to drink it ... and I stared at her and thought: This is so fucking weird. It was as if nothing had happened. As if I'd never even been gone, never mind the fact that we'd fallen out.

'Are you cold?' she asked.

Despite the central heating, I was wearing my thick fluffy pink dressing gown on top of my pyjamas but I couldn't seem to warm up. I was holding my mug of coffee between my hands, trying to get some feeling into my numb fingers.

'It's not exactly like Sydney here, you know.'

'Have a hot shower and get dressed, then, Madd. I'll wait for you.'

Well, that's good of you considering I didn't even invite you in.

'And have some breakfast,' she added. 'No wonder you feel the cold so badly, slopping around in your dressing gown and slippers and living on coffee and cigarettes.'

'I've given up, actually.' I pulled up the other stool and sat down next to her. 'But then, you always have disapproved of everything I do.'

At this, she looked a bit uncomfortable and made a great thing of wiping an imaginary drip of coffee off her jumper. Obviously not ready to talk about it yet, then.

'I'll make some toast,' I said. 'Want some?'

'OK, then. Thanks.'

Blimey. I raised my eyebrows to myself as I put the bread in the toaster. What happened to the strict diet of fruit and muesli?

'Pity we haven't got any croissants,' I said with a smile, suddenly remembering. 'You enjoyed them, didn't you, when we were away in Europe.'

'Yes, I did. I know I did. I enjoyed a lot of things then, that I don't normally do.'

'Yeah!' I laughed, and then paused and added quietly, 'We had a great time, didn't we, Rach? With the guys in Carnac? And then Paris, and ... oh, what about the speed cops in Belgium! And Amsterdam – that was brilliant...'

The toast popped out and she buttered hers very sparingly,

318

just a couple of calories' worth. 'Yeah. We did have a good time. But like I said then, we were living outside of our normal lives. It was an adventure. It wasn't real.'

'What *is* real, though?' I mused. 'Living through another dark, cold English winter, getting up early every day, going to work, earning a crust, coming home, going to bed?'

'We all have to live somewhere,' she retorted crisply. 'We all have to earn a living. Yes, it's reality.'

'Well, right now I don't think I like it,' I told her petulantly, biting deeply into my hot buttered toast.

'Give yourself time,' she said a bit more gently. 'You've only just got back, haven't you. It'll take a while. What are you going to do... with yourself?'

'Look for a job, I suppose. Maybe Deanna from Jobs 4 U will give me another chance at the matrimonial and family law place.'

'I doubt it,' she laughed.

'Me too. But meanwhile ... I've got other things to sort out.'

'Yeah?'

'I need to enrol at the pool. In a class.'

I felt, ridiculously, embarrassed telling her this. She looked at me questioningly.

'Pool? Class?' she repeated as if they were particularly difficult words in Spanish or German.

'Yes. I'm learning life-saving. I need to get on a course, to get qualified.'

'Life-saving?' Rachel's face was a picture. 'Bloody hell! That's a tough challenge – good for you! I'm really pleased for you, Madd – no, I mean it – really pleased. Did you start this out ... there?'

'Of course. Yes, I had swimming lessons in Australia, and he said...' I tailed off. 'My teacher said I should have no problem with the course, so there you go. Maybe I won't need to go to Jobs 4 U at all. Maybe I can just get a job as a lifeguard!'

'Excellent!'

319

She was so busy being impressed, she hadn't noticed me hesitating over the bit about my teacher. I'd thought about it, but it was no good; I couldn't tell her. Maybe I would one day. Maybe when we were back to being proper friends again, without this weirdness between us, maybe then I'd tell her all about Joe. But not yet. I wanted to keep it to myself for a while.

It was sleeting lightly, stinging my face as I crossed and recrossed the High Street, staring in the brightly lit shop windows, my hands thrust deep into my coat pockets and my hat pulled down well over my ears. I'd been home for nearly two weeks, it was only a week till Christmas and I still hadn't bought any presents. I stared at a display of children's games and books in the window of WH Smith. That game there looked good; it was based on a TV quiz show. Or what about the latest Harry Potter book? Then there was Boots next door, with all their festive, glittery displays of fancy body lotions, bath foams and bubble baths on one side, and electrical goods on the other side. Curlers, straighteners, massagers, driers, shavers and pluckers – everything you needed to be beautiful. Perhaps. I went inside and chose a pair of hair straighteners, queued up to pay, and watched the girl as she put my purchase into a carrier bag.

'Nice present for somebody!' She beamed happily as she took my money. 'Hope they like it.'

'Yes.'

They'd better. It was for me.

Well, I'd been kidding myself, hadn't I. Looking around the shops, pretending I had a list to consult, a frantic mission to buy at least all the uncles' and aunties' presents today, and the children's stocking fillers – a sense, like everyone else, of the urgency of the approaching holiday, the excitement and stress of needing to buy everything in time, have everything ready, everything wrapped and hidden away … when actually I didn't have anything to buy. Or anyone to buy for.

I could buy something for Sophie. But we'd talked about it in our last few e-mails, and she'd told me not to bother. She hadn't got an address to send anything to. She didn't even know where she'd be on Christmas Day.

'We'll make up for it next year,' she told me, and then, because she'd guessed how I'd feel about this, she added, 'Why don't you buy a little something for Amy, instead? I'd like that – tell her it's from me as well.'

But I didn't want to buy a little something for Amy. I didn't want to buy things for Rachel's daughter – I wanted to buy things for mine! At least Rachel had her daughter with her for Christmas.

I supposed I could buy something for Rachel. Some cottage cheese, or low-fat yoghurt, or a new pair of those Lycra cycling shorts she wore to the gym. Or I could be a complete bitch and buy her some really rich, really sickly but disgustingly irresistible chocolates. The kind I liked. Except that she'd probably manage to resist them anyway. But Rachel was being very odd about Christmas. I'd invited her and Amy and Simon over to my place and what had I got in response?

'I'm not sure whether we'll be around.'

'Oh. OK, then. Boxing Day, perhaps?'

She'd looked strangely shifty now.

'I'm ... er ... not sure, Madd. I don't know. I think ... we might be away for the whole of Christmas, actually. I think maybe it might be better if we just ... kind of leave it, this year. Maybe we'll get together over New Year instead. Do you mind?'

Mind? Of course I bloody minded. It wasn't as if I could say that two or three less for Christmas dinner wasn't going to make much difference. It meant the difference between making an effort, trying to cook a proper dinner, or having beans on toast with a sprig of holly on top. I cancelled the order for the turkey, ate the Sainsbury's Christmas pudding and the six puff pastry mince pies a week before Christmas on purpose, and walked around the shops on my own, sulking, pretending to have people to buy for.

I'd spent ten minutes in Marks & Spencer, looking at the underwear, thinking about buying myself some new knickers and wrapping them up together with the hair straighteners so that I could unwrap them again on Christmas Day, when I suddenly became aware that my mobile phone was playing its merry little tune to itself in the depths of my handbag.

'Hello!' I shouted, trying to raise my voice above the tasteful background rendition of 'The Holly and the Ivy' being piped through the store.

'Hi! How are you?'

No mistaking the Aussie inflection. No mistaking his voice anyway.

'Joe. Hi. I ... didn't expect to hear from you.'

Ever again? Is that what I was saying? Or just right now, at this minute, as I was rifling through the rack of lacy red knickers (high leg, cotton gusset), looking for a size twelve?

'Just wondered if you got home OK? Had a good journey?'

'Oh! Yes, it was fine. Thank you. Fine.'

'And are you OK? Is it good to be home?'

What do you think? It's shit. It's cold, and it's dark, and instead of a clear blue sky and a view of a clear blue sea, I'm looking out at grey clouds and grey streets and grey people's faces. And I'm lonely.

'Yes. It's good. Rachel and I are talking again.'

'That's great.'

There was a pause. I didn't know what else to say. Why was he phoning?

'I'm out shopping at the moment,' I said pointlessly, staring at the row of knickers in front of me.

'Well. I won't keep you, then. I just wondered if you'd let me have your address?'

'My address?'

'To send you a Christmas card. Bugger. It won't be much of a surprise now. But I thought it was the least I could do.'

'Oh. OK, thank you. That'd be nice.' I read out my address. 'So I'll look forward to receiving that, then.' I was aware of sounding like a very polite secretary ordering an official publication over the phone. 'Are you doing anything nice for Christmas?' I added, trying to sound as if I cared one way or the other.

'Not sure yet. Probably going to see a few people, yes.'

Well, bloody good for you. Looks like everyone I know, even those on the other side of the world, will be having a lot more fun than me.

I bought two pairs of the knickers, and a bra to match. I'd wear them on Christmas Day and pretend to myself that someone other than me was going to see them.

I could have gone straight home that afternoon. I could have loaded up the car with my hair straighteners, my bag of underwear and my two sheets of Christmas wrapping paper, driven home and made myself my usual burnt offering for tea. Or I could have gone to the pool. I might, quite easily, have decided to go and do an hour or so of fast laps to shake myself out of my self-pitying mood and keep up my fitness, ready for the start of the course of lessons I'd booked for the New Year. Or I could have gone round to Rachel's, to have a cup of tea and hear about her last day of term and have a chat in our new kind of stilted way that avoided anything too personal or too close to the bone. I might have done any of those things, but instead I did something completely different and quite out of character. I went to the pictures. On my own, with a bag of sweets and a can of Coke, I went and sat in a row near the back and watched the famous Harry Potter film, and when it was finished and we all poured out into the freezing, dark, sleeting evening, I went into McDonald's and had a Big Mac with fries and a banana milk shake, and a choc nut sundae, and then sat for a while with a coffee, looking out at the street, at all the silver and red Christmas lights on the shop fronts blinking through the sleet, and all the people rushing by in their big coats and

323

scarves and boots, laughing together in their couples and their groups, off to their parties or their pubs or their nice dinners in nice restaurants, and I thought: This time next year, things are going to be different. I didn't bother to think how. It was just enough to make my mind up that they were going to be different.

Then I drove home.

And he was waiting outside my door.

'But you're in Australia!' probably wasn't the most intelligent thing I'd ever said in my life.

'I hope not! It's not usually this bloody cold!'

We stared at each other.

'Any chance you're going to ask me in?' he said eventually. 'Only I've been waiting for a couple of hours and my feet have gone completely numb.'

'Oh my God! I'm so sorry!' Flustered, I searched for my door key, dropped my carrier bag, and watched with horror as it fell open and disgorged its load of red underwear onto the damp pavement.

'Nice!' he commented with a grin as I picked it up and shoved it roughly back into the bag. 'Christmas present?'

'Yes. For a ... for a person. Another person. Not me,' I stammered, blushing a brighter scarlet than the knickers. 'Come in. Sorry it's ... small. And messy. And anyway – what are you doing here?'

'I'm over on business. Looking at a hotel in London.' He looked around the living room. 'It's not messy. Do you mind if I take my shoes off and warm my feet up?'

'Course not. I'll make you some hot tea. You must be absolutely frozen.' But instead of going to the kitchen I stood, rooted to the spot, watching him sitting on my sofa, taking off his shoes, rubbing his feet and holding them up to my radiator. I realised I was shaking my head in disbelief. He looked up at me.

'What's up?'

What's up! What, apart from this being the most peculiar

324

thing that's ever happened to me? My ex-husband, who's supposed to be in Australia, suddenly turning up on my doorstep, waiting for me in the cold for two hours until his feet go numb? I think I could be forgiven for looking ever so slightly gobsmacked, don't you?

'I thought you were phoning me from Australia,' I said faintly.

'I know. I didn't want to tell you I was coming.'

'Why? I'd have come straight home. I wouldn't have gone to... Harry Potter. Or had a Big Mac.'

'Harry Potter? Big Mac?' he repeated, equally faintly.

'Why didn't you say?'

He looked back at his feet.

'In case you didn't want me to come.'

Sometimes there isn't any more you can say. I went and made the tea.

'So you didn't know he was coming?' Rachel was giving me a look that implied disbelief. 'He just turned up?'

'Exactly. All I had was this phone call, like I said, just as I was...'

'... knicker shopping. I heard you. And you thought he was still in Australia.'

'Rachel, I know it sounds a bit unlikely, when you put it like that, but...'

'Well, yes, I have to admit it does, considering that I knew he was coming.'

'What?'

So it wasn't Sophie, apparently, who'd told Rachel the date I was flying back into Heathrow – although it was Sophie, of course, who'd given Joe Rachel's e-mail address.

'I was a bit taken aback, to be honest. I mean – out of the blue, I get this e-mail from this guy who claims to be your ex-husband, and he says he's living in Australia and you've been spending time together out there. I wouldn't mind so much if I'd known about it.'

'But I didn't know myself.'

She was silent, watching me above the rim of her wine glass. For this conversation, even Rachel had agreed that we both needed alcohol.

'So it wasn't planned?'

'Meeting him in Australia? Of course not! Is that what you think? That I knew he was in Brisbane? That I'd planned all along to meet up with him? Are you joking? Do you think I could have kept that quiet from you? Why would I want to?'

'I don't know.' She shook her head. 'I thought we knew each other, but after you went to Australia, after we had that row on the phone...'

'Rach, I had absolutely no idea where he was in the world. It was all down to Sophie. She tracked him down and—'

'Yeah. He told me in the e-mail.'

And apparently told her a few other things, too. Like how he was worried about me coming back to England, with no family and no friends, and no one to meet me at the airport. Like how upset I was that we weren't on speaking terms and how he thought life was too short to bear a grudge with a friend. Like how he'd heard so much about her and looked forward to meeting her when he came over for Christmas.

'I'll be honest.' She shrugged. 'I was furious when I got his e-mail. I thought – Who the fuck does he think he is?'

'I can understand that,' I admitted. 'He had a cheek.'

'But gradually, it got to me. Even though I'd deleted it. Even though I refused to answer it, and tried to forget about it – it got to me, and I couldn't go on ignoring it. That's why I e-mailed you and met you at Heathrow.'

'He's an interfering bastard,' I said mildly. But I was smiling despite myself.

'And that's why I wasn't too worried about not spending Christmas with you,' she added, fiddling with her hair, looking down into her drink. 'Because I thought you knew he was coming.'

'But I'm not ... you seem to have got the wrong idea. We're not...together.' I felt myself trembling with shock at the thought of it.

326

'Aren't you? Oh, shit. Oh, well, I have got the wrong idea, haven't I. So what's he doing for Christmas, then?'

'Spending it at this hotel in London. The one he's negotiating to buy.'

'I see.' She nodded wisely.

'What?'

'Nothing.'

'And anyway!' I exclaimed, wanting to change the subject, 'Never mind about all that. What, exactly, are you up to this Christmas? You never normally go away.'

'No,' she agreed vaguely. 'I don't, do I? So I . . . thought it might make a change, this year. You know. Time to move on, and all that.'

She giggled nervously, and I stared at her.

'Is there a man involved in all this?'

'A man?' she retorted as if she'd never heard of them. 'Why does there have to be a man?'

But I'd seen the look flash briefly across her face, and I knew I'd hit the nail on the head. So that was what it was all about. A new man. Well, fuck me. Maybe all the sex on holiday had started something with her, after all.

Sophie and Ryan were in Bolivia for Christmas and, judging from their e-mails, I was lucky to be in the comparative warmth and safety of an English winter.

This is the highest city in the world, she wrote from somewhere called Potosi. *And most of the people in our hostel are suffering from altitude sickness as well as being freezing cold, especially at night. But there's loads to see here. The women wear hundreds of skirts on top of each other – they probably need to, to keep warm! – and have their hair in a long thick plait down their back, topped off by a bowler hat! It's very cheap to eat here, so don't worry – we'll get a great dinner on Christmas Day – probably llama steak!*

327

I looked at the frozen turkey burgers I'd decided to make do with for my Christmas dinner. Why wasn't I more adventurous? Did they even sell llama steak in Tesco, anyway? And would I know how to cook it, if they did?

It was Christmas Eve and I'd already opened the only present I'd had – a new swimming costume, from Rachel – and was thinking about settling down in front of the TV and starting on the chocolate biscuits and port I'd bought just to make the house look a bit more festive, when the doorbell rang.

'Better not be Jehovah's Witnesses, today of all days,' I muttered to myself.

But of course, it wasn't. It was carol singers. I could hear the carol as I walked towards the front door.

'"Silent night, holy night..."'

'"All is clear, all is bright,"' I joined in, humming to myself fairly cheerfully as I searched in my bag for my purse. Better give them a pound. Fifty pence always looked a bit mean.

'"Round yon virgin mother and child, Holy infant so tender and mild..."'

'"Sleep in heavenly peace!"' I sang out loud as I flung open the door. '"Sleep in..." Oh. Oh, shit.'

There was only one carol singer standing on the doorstep. He was wearing a Father Christmas silly hat and behind him was parked the biggest, most posy car I'd seen down our street since the girl next-door-but-one married that West Ham footballer.

'My sledge awaits, madame,' said Joe with a smile. 'Would you care to accompany me to my grotto?'

And that was how I came to spend Christmas 2003 in one of the more superior hotels in London's West End. With my ex-husband.

Chapter 21

19 June 2004: The Tarrant Hotel, London W1

I don't know half the people here. But then, I suppose I wouldn't – a lot of them must be friends of his – colleagues from his work. The men are all in suits, the women all dressed up to the nines in posh frocks and hats. Glad I bought this extravagant dress in Sydney, after all.

'You look lovely,' says Sophie, slipping her slim brown arm through mine. 'Honestly, Mum, you've lost so much weight – you look ten years younger than before I went away.'

'Go on with you,' I laugh, pleased nonetheless. 'Just got rid of a bit of the flab – with all the swimming.'

'It's fantastic. Honestly, I still can't believe I've come home to find I've got a fully qualified lifeguard for a mum! What will you do if I go away again – take up water-skiing? Or scuba diving?'

'You're not going away again – are you?'

'No! Don't panic!' She laughs and nudges Ryan, who's standing beside her, looking particularly beautiful in a sharply cut pale grey suit and yellow shirt. 'Mum's terrified we're going to piss off travelling again.'

'No way, Maddy! Give us a chance – we only got here a couple of weeks ago!'

'Anyway, Mum, we're skint. We both need to settle down and get ourselves jobs now.'

Settle down. I sigh contentedly. There's something

329

infinitely reassuring about those two words, all of a sudden, even though I know they won't actually be settling down together, as such, of course … But what can I say? Ryan's been true to his word – he and Sophie have stayed the best of friends, and he's hoping to stay in the UK for some time, if he can get work.

'The dress looks lovely on you,' I tell her. 'You look…'

But I have to stop there. My eyes are filling up and I'm in danger of embarrassing her. She notices, reaches over and gives me a quick kiss.

'It's good to be home,' she whispers.

All I can do is nod.

'Happy?'

Joe appears at my other side and helps himself to a vol-au-vent from the buffet table.

'Of course.'

'What're you crying for, then, you dope?' he says, throwing an arm round my shoulders affectionately.

'I'm not. It's just … well, you know. Sophie …'

He follows my gaze.

'She looks beautiful,' he agrees, his eyes lighting up. Then he looks back at me and adds, 'And so does her mum.' He swallows his last mouthful of pastry and tugs me by the arm. 'Come on, let's have a dance.'

'No! No, we're supposed to wait until the bride and groom have started.'

'They have. Look.'

They're wrapped in each other's arms, swaying slowly to the music: 'I Will Always Love You'. A few months ago I'd have puked at the disgusting sentimentality of it. Now, it's threatening to make me cry again. What's happening to me?

'Come on.' Joe pulls me onto the dance floor. 'Anything they can do, we can do better. Yeah?'

Well. I don't know about that. Slow dancing? Holding each other as close as this? I don't know if I'm quite ready for it. We've been seeing each other, you know; since Christmas – just as friends to start with, and now …

330

well maybe you could say we're kind-of going out together again. He's settled over here for the time being, overseeing the running of the new hotel until he's sure the manager's got everything back on track. The previous owner went bankrupt and staff morale was rock bottom but he's going to turn it around and make it as grand as the hotel in Sydney. He says you have to take things slowly and build up the business gradually. We've been taking things slowly ourselves, too. Ridiculously slowly, you could say. I don't think I've ever even imagined, before, the concept of seeing someone for six months without having sex with them.

Not that I don't want to.

Especially now, with him holding me as tight as this, breathing his warm breath on my neck, brushing his lips ever so gently against my cheek, extending his fingers behind my back so that they just, ever so slightly, touch my bum as I move against him somewhat more suggestively than is strictly necessary ... no, not that I don't want to, you understand.

Just that it's a bit complicated, isn't it. It's pushing our luck. First time around, we messed it up really badly. Second time around – can it really be any different? We're still the same two people, after all. This time we both want to be really, really sure this is what we want. Tonight, right now, I'm almost sure.

'Come on, you two – the slow number finished about five minutes ago!' laughs a familiar voice behind me. 'Are you going to give me a dance tonight, Maddy Goodchild? Or don't I get a look-in now I'm a married man again?'

Reluctantly, I turn away from Joe and we swap partners. Joe starts an energetic dance with the bride. I watch as she whirls around him, whooping with laughter, her dress swirling about her ankles, her hair flying.

'She looks absolutely stunning,' I murmur to her new husband.

'Yes,' he says simply, following her with his eyes.

331

'You know I'm very happy for you both, don't you.'

'I hope so,' he replies, turning back to me, looking into my eyes with sudden solemnity. 'I hope so, sweetheart.'

Of course, I'm not his sweetheart any more. I want to tell him that I never did like him calling me that anyway. But there's no point. He's happier with Rachel than he ever was with me. She'll be his sweetheart now – hopefully forever! I reach up and give him a kiss on the cheek.

'Congratulations, Tom.'

I found out about it on New Year's Eve. We'd arranged to meet at the pub near my house, the one where I'd danced on the table the night we celebrated winning the lottery. It seemed like a lifetime away. I'd had a wonderful Christmas – all the more so because of the contrast with the turkey burgers on a tray in front of the TV I'd been expecting. There'd been a party atmosphere at the hotel, with a five-course dinner, entertainment, a roaring log fire and a huge Christmas tree with thousands of tiny brilliant white sparkling lights, like diamonds. I felt like I was in a fairy-tale castle. And ... well, and the company had been good, too. I hadn't even begun to admit it to myself at that stage, but Joe and I were having a good time together.

So I was in a mellow mood when I arrived at the Dog and Duck on New Year's Eve – looking forward to catching up with Rachel and maybe, when she'd had a drink or two (surely even Rachel couldn't stay on slimline tonic all night on New Year's Eve?), she'd loosen up a little and tell me all about this new man in her life, the one she'd obviously spent Christmas with.

So come on, spill the goss! I'd say; and she'd giggle and look all coy and silly for a minute, and then she'd start to tell me all about it: how they met ... and what he looked like... and what he was like in bed.

I sat at the bar, and ordered my first drink. You know what it's like when you're on your own, waiting for some-one. No one else to talk to, so you tend to knock it back a bit quicker than you would do normally. Then you feel a bit daft sitting there nursing an empty glass so, obviously, you get yourself another drink, and you hold onto it for a while, looking around the pub, making sure everyone realises you're waiting for a friend and not just spending the evening on your own at the bar, like a Johnny No-Mates. But eventually of course you start drinking the next drink too, and before you know it you're empty again and having to get another one. Rachel was late. And the thing was, I wasn't quite so used to vodka now. I'd cut back quite a lot on my drinking, you see, since I'd been swimming more seriously. So it went to my head pretty quickly, and by the time I saw her, through the crowd in the pub now, coming in at the door, looking around for me, I was already swaying ever so slightly as I got to my feet and called out to her:

'Rach! Rachel, I'm over here! What time do you call this? Shall I get you a drink? What—?'

And then I stopped, mid-sentence, mid-sway, so that I would have fallen over if it hadn't been so crowded at the bar that the man next to me was holding me up without even realising it.

'What the fuck,' I demanded, loudly enough to get a row of heads turning all at once in my direction, and then back in the direction I was staring, like a row of spectators at a tennis match, 'What the fuck is he doing here?'

There was a bit of a hush. Probably everyone wanted to know the answer, I suppose. But they'd have had to strain their ears to catch it.

'Maddy,' said Rachel, her voice not much more than a whisper, and trembling as if she was going to cry. 'Maddy, please don't shout. Tom's with me.'

She'd started seeing him after we had the row on the phone. Apparently he used to phone her every now and then, to find out if she'd heard from me: how was I, what was I doing, and had I asked after him at all?

'He didn't like to phone you himself. Not after you made it so obvious you weren't pleased to hear from him.'

Maddy, the Bitch from Hell ex-mistress. Refuse to marry the guy, run away to the other side of the world and then make him too scared to phone you. Yeah, sounds like me.

So on this occasion, of course, when he called to ask after my state of health, I imagine he got a torrent of verbal about how I was the nastiest piece of work in the universe with the morals of an alley cat. Picture it if you will? Rachel, having had the phone slammed down on her by me, crying into the arms of my ex-lover about what a rubbish friend I was, while he, presumably, seized the opportunity to pour out his heart to her about what a lousy life I'd given him. And, apparently, seized the opportunity of a quick shag at the same time.

Not that I'm bitter.

No, really, I'm not!

Looking at them that New Year's Eve, standing together at the bar, watching me with genuine fear in their eyes, obviously seriously afraid I was going to run amok with a broken glass or scream and throw a tantrum, I realised two things. Firstly, I was relieved that Tom had found someone else and was off my back. Secondly, they were so well suited, it should have been obvious they were going to get together. It was, in fact, amazing they'd taken so long over it. Hadn't I always said it? Look at the pair of them! Both into fitness and health, and cooking properly. They could hold long conversations about low-fat diets. They could spend whole evenings together planning healthy alternative meals. A match made in gourmet heaven.

And do you know what else? I was glad I knew the reason for it all now – all those months of silence while I was in Australia. All that time I'd thought it was my fault – something I'd done to upset her, like being myself for instance. To think I'd thrown myself on her mercy, begging to be forgiven, promising to change! No wonder she didn't reply.

'I didn't think I'd ever be able to face you again,' she admitted miserably.

We'd taken our drinks to a corner of the pub where the raucous sounds of pre-midnight drunkenness were just a tiny tad softer. Tom, probably very sensibly, had lingered at the bar for a while, chatting to a couple of guys he used to know when we used to visit the pub together, leaving Rachel and me a bit of space.

'You felt guilty? You shouldn't have done. I'd finished with him.'

'Yes, but, come on. What kind of a friend does that? Has it off with her best mate's ex, while the whole thing's still... well, you know. Still raw.'

'I wasn't raw. He might have been, but I was just ... well, trying to shake him off, to be honest.' I glanced at her. 'Trying to get laid by other married men, in fact, as you so rightly said.'

She flinched visibly.

'You see? How do you think that made me feel? One minute I'm coming over all self-righteous with you on the phone, and the next minute I'm in bed with Tom!'

'Jesus! That quick?'

'Not literally. It wasn't funny, Maddy – I felt terrible. You can't imagine what I went through.'

She took a gulp of her drink. Bloody hell, it was a double rum and Coke and the glass was almost empty. She'd be on the floor in a minute.

'It wasn't deliberate, Madd. Tom and I ... we didn't set out to hurt you.'

'I know.'

'It's just...' She toyed miserably with her glass. 'Well, I think we were both feeling hurt and rejected by you.'

Oh, so it was my fault after all!

'And...you know how it is.'

'One thing leads to another?'

'Yes. And before we knew it...'

'You were screwing him.' I nodded with complete understanding.

'Don't put it like that!' she wailed. ' It wasn't like that! It was...it was because of...'

I waited. I was interested, genuinely interested, to know what it was because of. Because of me being such a bitch? Because of them both being hurt, both being lonely, both being fitness fanatics (nothing quite like a good shag to use up a few surplus calories)?

'Because of?' I prompted her.

'Because of how I felt about him,' she said in a whisper that was almost drowned out by the hoots of drunken laughter coming from a well-oiled group at the next table. I had to lean right over, so that our faces were almost touching, before I could hear her. 'Because,' she went on, looking up from her empty glass and finally meeting my eyes, so that I actually saw it there – saw it staring out at me from her eyes a split second before she even uttered the words: 'Because all the time you were together, Maddy, I was always, always, madly in love with him.'

So that was a turn-up for the books then, wasn't it?

All that huffing and shaking of the head, all that rampant condemnation – it was all a cover for the fact that she really wanted to be doing what I was doing.

There was I, feeling the heavy weight of her disapproval every time I mentioned Tom's name, every time I saw him; well, every time I moved, or breathed, to be fair – and all the time, Rachel wasn't really feeling superior at all. She was jealous. She wanted to be the bad girl for once.

'But it's all above board and honourable now,' I told her with a smile. 'He's not with his wife any more. You can go ahead without any guilt trips.'

'No guilt trips? Are you joking? It's been one continual guilt trip all the time we've been together. All I've thought about is how you were going to react – what you were going to say...'

'Well, you can stop worrying now. Bloody good luck to you.' I reached across the table again and gave her a hug, knocking both our empty glasses over. 'Let's get another drink! Tom! What's he doing gossiping over there? Tell him

336

to get us some bloody drinks. It's New Year's Eve! We shouldn't be sitting here in the corner like two boring old farts – we should be dancing and singing and getting pissed!'

I pulled her to her feet and tugged her towards the bar. Tom, seeing us coming, watched me warily as if he was expecting me to punch him.

'Get us some champagne, Tom, for God's sake,' I told him, clapping him on the back. 'We're celebrating!'

'Are we?' he asked, looking from me to Rachel with a bemused smile.

'What are we celebrating?' she asked me with a giggle as Tom called the barmaid and obediently ordered a bottle of champagne and three glasses.

'You and Tom getting married, of course!'

'Married! We're not ... I never said...'

'Maybe not yet. But you will. I just have a feeling about it. Trust me!'

So maybe I've found my vocation at last! I reckon I could get a job as a clairvoyant.

The bride and groom have left for their honeymoon in Marbella. The remnants of the supper buffet have been cleared away and it looks like it's last orders at the bar. I haven't drunk very much, considering it's the wedding day of my best friend and my ex-lover, and I feel surprisingly sober. Strange feeling. Maybe I'll get used to it eventually.

'We're off now, Mum,' says Sophie, clasping me in a bear hug. Ryan puts his arm round me and hugs me too.

'See you soon, Maddy,' he says. 'See you, Joe. Thanks again... for—'

'Don't mention it,' Joe cuts in quickly.

'What was that about?' I ask as we watch them leave together.

'Oh, nothing, really.' He catches my eye and he adds, defensively, 'Well, Sophie's my daughter, Maddy, and after everything... you know. I just wanted to help.'

'You paid the rent...? Ryan's too?'

337

'Don't get mad. I know you wanted her to come back and live with you at home, but...'

'She didn't want to. I know. She's got used to having her independence, and Ryan needed somewhere to stay.'

I understood completely. Amy had already planned to leave home and was looking for a couple of flatmates before Sophie arrived back from travelling. The pair of them spent most of last weekend closeted together in Sophie's bedroom, and judging by the tears and the hugs in evidence when they emerged, they'd talked through their falling out and were better friends than ever.

'It doesn't matter now,' was all Sophie said when I questioned her – and in the circumstances, I couldn't argue. It doesn't matter that Rachel and I had to cut short our travels in Europe to rush home for Amy when she was homesick. It doesn't matter any more – because of how things have turned out for us all since then. Until now, I just haven't understood how Sophie and Ryan could afford the deposit on a flat-share, and a month's rent, when they've only just got back, skint, from their travels.

'I told them both it was just a loan,' says Joe. 'They wouldn't have accepted otherwise. But I won't let them pay me back until they become millionaires. You're not mad at me?'

'Christ, am I that scary?'

'Well.' He smiles. 'I do remember a certain occasion when I got attacked and beaten up for trying to inveigle my way back into Sophie's life.'

'Just as long as you always remember what I'm like when I'm riled!' We laugh together easily.

'But you don't mind any more?' he persists. 'You don't object if I'm a sort of ... honorary member of the family?'

I have to admit I give this a minute's thought before I answer. Maybe even two minutes. But no longer.

'You are a member of the family.'

He turns to me, and well, guess what? I'm beginning to

think I am clairvoyant. Because I suddenly know exactly what he's going to say next.

'So can we make that official, one day?'

I'll have to give this one a bit more than two minutes' thought. In fact, I'm going to tell him to let me have a few weeks. Maybe even a couple of months. But it doesn't matter, does it? We've got all the time in the world. Neither of us is going anywhere. Not without each other, anyway. I've had enough of travelling alone.

In a lot of ways, I'm back at the start of my journey – and this time, I'm not in a hurry to get anywhere. What's the rush?

I kind of like it where I am.